A PLACE
NO PAIN

To Roger,

Thanks for all the help you give to my mother,

All the best,

Simon (Bridges)

BY

SIMON BRIDGES

ISBN-13: 978-1517719081
ISBN-10: 1517719089

CONTENTS

PART 1. DEATH 1

CHAPTER 1 1
CHAPTER 2 5
CHAPTER 3 19
CHAPTER 4 37
CHAPTER 5 50
CHAPTER 6 58
CHAPTER 7 69
CHAPTER 8 76
CHAPTER 9 85
CHAPTER 10 98
CHAPTER 11 107
CHAPTER 12 118
CHAPTER 13 142
CHAPTER 14 150
CHAPTER 15 175

PART 2. REBIRTH 182

CHAPTER 16 182
CHAPTER 17 194
CHAPTER 18 208
CHAPTER 19 220
CHAPTER 20 239
CHAPTER 21 261
CHAPTER 22 267
CHAPTER 23 286
CHAPTER 24 306
CHAPTER 25 323
CHAPTER 26 333

PART 3. PASSION 339

CHAPTER 27 339
CHAPTER 28 353

Epilogue 362

"And God shall wipe away all tears from their eyes; and there shall be no more death, neither sorrow, nor crying, neither shall there be any more pain: for the former things are passed away."

– Revelation Chapter 21, Verse 4.

PART 1

DEATH

CHAPTER 1

Forget about talking to yourself or hairs on the palms of your hands. Or the punch line – looking to see. The real measure of insanity is found incontrovertibly in the length of trouser. We're not talking about that strange fashion trend that saw elderly people tottering about looking like geriatric pirates. More that sort of jolly jack ashore, flying at half-mast sort of length. By this yardstick he must ergo be barking mad, he thought, as he looked down at the regulation issue pyjama bottoms whose legs terminated somewhere between the base of his calves and the ankle bones. His excuse could be that he hadn't chosen them but it was pretty flimsy. The fact that they had even been allowed to choose him was a sufficient indictment in itself.

Not that he could see the funny side of anything at four a.m. on an unseasonably cold March morning with the dust and grit from the hard linoleum floor sticking to the soles of his bare feet. The pyjama jacket was open and he fumbled listlessly with the buttons before abandoning the attempt and lifting his gaze to the three figures ahead. From where he stood at the doorway to a large communal lounge he made out the silhouettes of two of them lying curled under mountains of linen in makeshift beds of two armchairs pushed together. The other, directly opposite to him, he could make out as male from the light that filtered through the faded blinds fronting the tall windows. This one slumped uncovered in a chair in creased black trousers and a white shirt, the knot of a diagonally striped tie almost disappearing behind a bullish neck. The large feet that were crossed over the end of the footstool were clad in black boots in readiness for potential action but the tongues were loosened and the laces undone. Although his nesting arrangements were less elaborate than those of his colleagues it had evidently not affected the quality of his sleep and his chest rose and fell to the tempo of a porcine, nasal snore.

He approached slowly and stood over the man, deliberating on how to gain his attention. The proximity of his presence alone was clearly not going to penetrate his oblivion so he said quietly, "Excuse me, mate." He looked the sort of man you would address as 'mate'. He grunted and shifted position but remained asleep. The standing man, immobilised by indecision, prevaricated by scrutinising a badge clipped to the breast pocket of the shirt and the words and photograph on the embossed plastic told him that the unshaven, balding oaf slumbering beneath his distressed gaze was, or had been in a former existence, a grinning, fresh-faced young man by the name of Geoff Rankin, Healthcare Assistant. His fingers returned to the pyjama buttons and this time, with conscious effort, he found the corresponding holes to slip them into. He was reluctant to surrender the initiative but impelled by necessity he gripped Rankin's shoulder and shook him gently. He woke with a sharp jolt of the neck and his eyes reconnoitred the room before resting on the other with a look of malevolence.

Without feeling the need to sit up he said, "Yeah?" The grunt reinforced the visual impression and kept the other man on the defensive.

"I'm sorry to bother you but I can't sleep. I need a cigarette and a cup of coffee." Rankin stretched out an arm and bent it at the elbow to look at his wristwatch.

"What's your name?"

"Prior. Robert Prior." He looked up at the ceiling as he tried to recall the name from the handover of eight hours earlier but he couldn't; and he rarely needed to. That was why he liked working nights.

"Well no. You can't. The kitchen's locked at night and this is a no smoking hospital. Get back to bed and we'll sort you out later." Prior discerned what appeared to be a female head protruding slowly from the heap of bedding in one of the other chairs like a tortoise stretching out its neck. He turned back to Rankin, whose eyes had already closed again, and felt an urge to lift his foot and drive its heel into the complacent face. What was he – eight, ten years his junior? Did he measure his achievement by how many hours he could cheat from his NHS employers and the taxpayer by sleeping on the job? But he felt impotent. Disempowered by the strange relationship shift in mental health that sees the patient the servant, the nurse the master. Enfeebled by the depth and darkness of the hopelessness and misery of his condition. Rendered mute and subservient by the mind-paralysing drugs they had been coercing him into taking for three days. He moved tentatively towards the woman who had moved earlier but then shied away from the inevitable closing of ranks and more nourishment for the insidious persecutory emotions. The nurse was now snoring again, the face serious and concentrated in its mission to buy as much waking time as possible for his off-duty hours at the expense of Prior and the five sleeping men he passed on the way back to the bed by the window. The anger returned in a rush and with nowhere else to go, turned inwards on a brain that was limping and labouring like a holed vessel, its fragile structure no match for the rapacious power of the sea.

***

He lay 'til seven, enduring the interminable minutes elongated and then slowed by the evil pact between time and discomfort. The only saving grace of the medication was the fact that in the main it blocked out intelligent thought and therefore suspended reality. But feeling remained. Vague, ominous portents of a doomed battle ahead accompanied by an anxiety that made him feel physically sick. The sense of detachment from the rest of humanity – the once prized uniqueness of individuality now a source of terror in its invitation to judgement. He experienced a rising panic at the correlation between a non-existent support network built on the foundations of a callous subjugation of the needs of others in favour of his own and the power of the likes of Rankin to exploit this unfamiliar vulnerability. He was in no doubt that more – and worse – lay in wait.

A man in the bed by the door hawked theatrically and he heard the spit, followed by the dull thud of the phlegm hitting the floor and got up, propelled only by the craving for nicotine; the need to experience for the umpteenth time the catch of the smoke on his chest and the indefinable sensation of the drug entering the bloodstream and reaching the brain. He supposed it just bestowed an ordinary feeling of well-being that those who had never smoked experienced all the time. Right now on a mood scale of one to ten, with one being the worst, it might take him briefly to one and a quarter. Apart from that he couldn't think of a single reason to get out of bed.

Opening the door to his bedside cabinet, he took out what they used to call a sponge bag. Perhaps they still do. He hadn't a clue how it had got there but he parted the blue canvas and buried his nose in its plastic interior searching for an evocation of happier times in the stale aromas of soap and toothpaste, tainted, though not unpleasantly, with the musk of time. He sat on the bed and again sensation, rather than conscious memory, recalled a wholly different person striding heedlessly through the impressive locations that had layered the bag with the redolence that mocked his current circumstances as he walked to one of the bathrooms.

He could scarcely bring himself to look in the mirror as he picked up the disposable razor, and when he did his worst fears were confirmed. His mirth reflex had gone and the muscles had slumped in a normally fleshy face. His jowls hung like hammocks from either end of his jawbone and the grey-hued skin sagged below watery bloodshot eyes. He looked ten years older than his forty-two and what were considered his best features – the electric blue of the eyes and the thick luxuriance of the chestnut hair were a fading memory as he shied away from eye contact, even with himself, only catching a brief glimpse of the greasy, lifeless hair making his ears look bigger and stick out more as he turned away. Perhaps what was even more disturbing was the fact that he couldn't have cared less.

CHAPTER 2

He looked back and supplanted the acerbic scold of hindsight with the tease of the possession of an imaginary foresight. If he had known eight days ago where events were going to take him would he – could he – have just extracted the good and forestalled the bad? He had an uncomfortable suspicion that the beast that had germinated within him had a will of its own, unregulated by any conscious imperative. As he fought a debilitating exhaustion and forced himself through the ordeal of replacing nightwear with daywear his mind turned incongruously back to the question of foresight. If it had existed beyond the imagination he supposed that its appeal would be regulated by the fact that everyone would possess it, resulting in one person's use of it being hopelessly complicated by the machinations and manipulations of the other. This would lead to a maelstrom of conflicting aims and a hell worse than a life without it. And then if we all knew the future that very knowledge would inevitably cause us to change it in the scramble to exploit that knowledge, so we'd need another foresight for a clue to the alternative future and so on and so on and… He fell back onto the bed and lay with his hands covering his eyes, the thoughts piling up on top of each other obsessively and inconclusively, each one leading him further and further away from the haven of reason.

***

He had left the press conference at the imposing football stadium in a European city in a state of mild excitement. The English club team had narrowly failed to progress to the quarter-finals of the Champions League tournament but he felt invigorated by the Picasso brushstrokes painted on the grass by the Spanish boots and the customary high quality of the copy he had emailed to the sports editorial department in London. His flight was not until nine the next morning and he felt inclined to fill the hours between with some moves of his own.

Back at his hotel, showered and changed, he sat at a table in the streetside bar/restaurant, furtively eyeing the passing women. He sipped at his second glass of beer with the foam of the first still completing its journey to the bottom as a mild breeze fluttered the frill of the umbrella over his table and rustled gently through the bougainvillea and oleander trees that framed the elegant patio. The assiduous waiter took away his empty glass and replaced the ashtray in swift birdlike movements, his eyes poised between Prior's potential enquiry and a rapid assimilation of the stages of progress at the adjacent tables. He ran his fingers along a jawline sharpened by very little to eat that day and then leant back and turned to look unashamedly in the window behind him. It confirmed what he already knew in its reflection of a handsome, charismatic man in the prime of his life. He drained his glass and stubbed out his cigarette but before he could catch the waiter's eye three men approached his table and sat down at the empty chairs. They were younger than him. Two of them emanated spare athleticism, their torsos lean and compact under their tight designer shirts. Their eyes and teeth were almost fluorescent in their whiteness below their carefully gelled hair as greetings were exchanged with a leisurely bonhomie. The third man was less imposing. There was a suspicion of flabby undulation beneath his loose-fitting shirt and his haircut gave him a look of Dennis the Menace. The drinks he ordered were delivered with indecent haste and Prior, aware of the attention on his group, basked a little in the reflected glory. He was a mature man of the world, yes, but we're all human.

"What can I say boys?" he said, splaying his arms and cocking his head to one side. "Very unlucky. No shame in going out to the best team in the world."

The two athletes narrowed their eyes and smirked before turning their heads to survey their surroundings as the other man nodded animatedly in agreement and muttered, "Bloody travesty," and then shook his head in incomprehension at the injustice of life.

"And what entertainment have you got lined up for me tonight,

Jimmy?" said Prior, eyeing his younger colleague who glanced at the other two.

"Wayne and Darren are up for a session. They don't play again 'til Sunday. We're going to meet some of the other lads at La Scala and then on to a club. You comin' Bob?"

The speed of both his last sentence and release of eye contact suggested he would not be disappointed with a negative response but Prior feigned indecision and said with a world-weary sigh, "Well, I suppose someone's got to keep an eye on you reprobates." Jimmy and the other men got to their feet and drained their bottles of lager, prompting Prior with a little reminder of the age gap as he emptied his glass, and they set off.

The footballers walked a few strides ahead of the other two and in spite of ninety minutes of fevered exertion their easy glide took them effortlessly away from the journalists, who were laboured in comparison. Every twenty metres or so Jimmy had to break into something approaching a run to repair the gap but Prior let him go, his emotional and physical detachment from the others reaffirming his self-belief.

The bar was already busy although it was only 11:00 p.m. – early for this city – and Prior and Jimmy stood at the edge of the dance floor cradling the drinks the younger man had battled to procure. Robert Prior was the Chief Sports Writer on their national, non-redtop tabloid daily, Jimmy Bayliss a football reporter. Prior had a virtual carte-blanche to cover any sporting event of his choosing, such was his expertise and value to the paper, but Bayliss reported only football and had no ambitions beyond his current role. He was basically a football fanatic with a workable grasp of English who often pinched himself at his monstrous good fortune. He possessed a likeably self-deprecating manner that never crossed over into sycophancy and an uncomplicated masculinity that endeared him to the players. Apart only from an inability to hit a barn door at three paces, he was one of them. He had been a school friend of one of the players they were with tonight which explained the bestowal of their favour which then filtered down to his senior colleague with him as the common denominator. Bayliss couldn't say he disliked Prior but he never felt comfortable with him. He had a way of making him feel gauche and stupid and he never knew what mood he might find him in. Prior's age and journalistic reputation set him naturally apart from Jimmy and the players but he suspected, with a sense of bewilderment, that he would never have been 'one of the boys', even as a younger man. There was something self-contained and secretive about him and other than that he originally came from the North West of England and was divorced, he knew little about him.

The night around them took its customary course. The gradual deterioration in the quality of conversation and the disproportionate swell of laughter; the increased tactility; the escalating potential for misunderstanding. Prior however, felt different.

He experienced a clarity of mind and sense of impregnability which seemed to sharpen with each drink. He thought he noticed men glancing at him before turning away hurriedly as he returned their look. Most of them seemed to be English and possibly recognised him from the photograph at the top of his articles. The women though, seemed to allow their gaze to linger beyond the merely inquisitive and he discerned an intrigue in their eyes.

One girl in particular seemed to look longer and more often at him than the others. She must have been about twenty-five and was tall and full-figured with a Hispanic beauty. He went over to her and smiled.

"Hola. Beber?"

The girl looked down shyly and he felt a stirring at the sight of her long dark lashes and lightly freckled nose. She looked up and said in English, "Okay. White wine please."

He ordered the drinks and over-tipped the barman, and they managed to find a table where they sat looking at each other for a few moments, the mutual desire implicit in the relaxed eye contact and involuntary half-smiles.

"How did you know I was English?" She shrugged.

"I don't know – I just guessed." He shook his head.

"Oh dear – is it that obvious?"

They laughed and exchanged brief biographies and he learned that Catalina was a buyer for a prestigious city fashion store who had graduated three years earlier with a degree in economics, spending part of her gap year in London where she had honed her schoolgirl

English. Prior was enigmatic, suggesting a connection with tonight's big game without being specific and as the noise gradually rose to make conversation difficult they edged their way to the dance floor. They were both good dancers and found an immediate rapport as their hips and shoulders swayed in time to the rhythm with an understatement that contrasted with the jerking limbs and frenetic contortions of the people around them. When a slow romantic song came on and the first insinuation of a later consummation took place, their joined bodies were as synchronous as when they were apart. Prior broke the little moment of awkwardness at the end of the track by making a pony tail of her glossy black hair and gently tilting her head back, kissing her softly on the mouth. She reciprocated without any hint of restraint but the intimacy of the moment was interrupted by Bayliss and the other two who had been waiting for their chance to speak to him, and Prior's colleague looked at him with an air of mistrust, his restless eyes and smirk suggesting grudging admiration and stifled resentment, his proficiency on the dance floor another mystifying example of the chasm between them. It wasn't what British blokes do.

"We're going to a club Bob," he shouted above the noise of the loud rap music now playing.

"You'll be otherwise engaged I take it."

Catalina clung to Prior's arm and he noticed the footballers eyeing her proprietarily. He smiled and nodded.

"See you tomorrow. Be good." As Bayliss turned to go, the footballer called Darren took Catalina's arm and said something in her ear which she answered perfunctorily before turning sharply and propelling Prior back towards where they had been sitting. Their seats were taken and she stood waiting by a pillar as he went to get more drinks.

He returned and she said without his prompt, "He said for me to go with him." She shook her head and smiled wryly, appearing more amused than offended by his audacity.

The offence was for Prior to take and his look was vicariously intimidating as he said, "Do you know who he is?"

"Sure – you can't get away from football in this country whether you like to or not. He plays for England, yes?" She shrugged as if to impart her indifference. Prior nodded. He felt a surge of affection for this beautiful girl. He would make sure her loyalty was not misplaced.

They finished their drinks quickly and left, and the air outside was refreshing after the stuffiness of the bar. Her apartment was a ten-minute walk and they elected for that in preference to his hotel. For five minutes they dodged the late night revellers in denial of the dawn spilling out onto the narrow streets of kaleidoscope lights, before the labyrinth of clubs and bars gave way to wide avenues of shuttered shops and tall commercial buildings. She clung tightly to him as they moved, their steps quickening as the residual body heat diminished in the rapidly declining temperatures. When they reached the branch of a Santander bank she turned them left into a side road and her first floor apartment was in a large block a few metres down on the right.

As she put the key in the door she turned to Prior with her index finger resting vertically against her full pursed lips, her dark eyes wide and conspiratorial, increasing his already fervent desire. With the closing of the door and the soft glow from the table lamp came a powerful sense of relief and intimacy and they stood and embraced passionately. She broke away to delay the moment of fulfilment, busying herself with practical preparation for the night and day ahead as Prior sat on the sofa with a scotch and ice. She had made her home an oasis of escape amidst the concrete and traffic and commerce and Prior smiled ruefully to himself at the contrast with his own East London flat.

Catalina came and stood before him. She held out both hands and he took them and stood up and then followed her through to the bedroom, her fluttering kimono fanning her perfume to his nostrils and intimating the promise of what lay beneath. *It doesn't get much better than this*, he thought as he gently closed the bedroom door.

***

He stood at the window at 5:30 a.m. and looked down on the street below. He had only slept for three hours at most but he felt replenished and exhilarated. Isolated figures in dark clothes were visible, trudging reluctantly towards what could only be days of uninspiring menial toil. The better remunerated would still be in their beds restoring their brains for the cerebral challenges ahead. The power brokers, decision-makers, filthy rich would no doubt be pounding the streets, pumping iron, swimming their lengths to confirm to themselves and explain to the rest of us why they got to be where they are. The sun was just emerging above the horizon and he heard Catalina behind him turn over and moan softly. He drained his coffee and put out his cigarette and readied himself in the bathroom, using her toothbrush. He was tempted to shave using her toilet soap and leg razor but he rather liked the disreputable look his heavy day's growth gave him. It was now ten to six and his transport would be at his hotel by half past so he woke Catalina with a kiss and she stretched gracefully back to life in a way he found almost irresistible. She ordered him a taxi and they waited, his arm around her neck, she holding the outstretched hand in both of hers as they engaged in the hurried, disjointed conversation of impending separation. The taxi hooted loudly with scant disregard to the sensibilities of those not attuned to the concept of a twenty-four hour city and they clung together for the last time, feeling slightly self-conscious and a little sad.

***

Bayliss and Prior bought a copy of their own newspaper and that of their closest rival and they turned to them as they waited in the departure lounge. Prior, as the senior man, had first pick and he crowed at the flowing erudition of his own article in comparison with the stilted, limited style of his counterpart on the other paper which Bayliss flung listlessly onto the table after a cursory glance at it. He laughed aloud and spoke animatedly to his colleague who sat slumped in his seat with his chin on his chest and his feet on the low table in front of him, mocking the younger man's decrepit condition; gloating in satisfaction at his own energy and powers of recovery. At Heathrow Bayliss was relieved when Prior told him he wasn't going into the office today as he was going home to write a more considered and analytical piece on the game for Friday's edition, which he would email in.

When he left home the day before he had taken the longer but more straightforward route via the Dartford Crossing and the M25, but with the way he was feeling today the journey through the city centre held no terrors and he drove across London like Lester Piggott bringing his horse through a packed field from last place two furlongs out. The loud, fast music on his CD compilation increased his adrenaline and created an appropriate backdrop to his hazardous driving, and the powerful two-litre engine saloon devoured the smallest of spaces. He was alive to every opportunity for advancement and marvelled at his skill, ignoring the angry admonishment of other drivers whose caution he had nothing but contempt for. He approached the familiar streets close to his flat too excited to contemplate the rapid changes to the landscape that had taken place in the years he had been there. The small suburb had grown at an alarming rate with seemingly little thought going into an overall plan. Despite the density of the population and the almost constant hubbub the impression was of people in isolation with little heed or care for each other beyond the cursory communication necessary for receipt of whatever service was required. If he hadn't been so driven by this strange thrill he might have reflected that people weren't really like that, but had been given little choice but to accept the terrain fashioned by the political ideology of the eighties and first half of the nineties.

The flat he owned was on the first floor of a three-storey block of six built in the 1970s and it served his purpose. There were parking facilities and a communal garden and his fellow residents were unobtrusive. He could afford to move to something better now but was quite content for the time being to reap the relative rewards of habit and familiarity.

He had come down to London from the North West twelve years ago when promoted to his present position and the possibility of his wife and three children joining him diminished with each clash before dying on the vine of mutual acceptance. His fatalism convinced him that the job opportunity was the compassionate release of Providence from a relationship that couldn't ever quite complete its death throes without some kind of external intervention. He was consumed initially by the usual ambivalent feelings; revelling in the unaccustomed freedom, the challenge of the job, the new acquaintances, the excitement of the capital, his contentment tempered by the guilt and the sadness. He rather unrealistically tried to consciously close his mind to thoughts of his children, to block them out, but unsurprisingly found it impossible. So at first he kept fleeting contact, roaring up and down the M6 in a mood of quiet desperation when his work gave him a window of opportunity. As time moved on and his displaced roots began to recover and draw in different nutrients, his visits became less frequent, and after the decree absolute two years later they stopped altogether. Caroline had a new partner and the children seemed to like him. They were by then ten, nine, and seven and he hadn't seen them in the ten years hence.

He climbed the stairs, idly reflecting on how much living he had packed into the past twenty-four hours, before opening his front door and making a brief tour of the flat, flinching at the disarray of unwashed crockery, strewn clothing, unmade bed and littered floors. At the door to each room he spun away from the carnage on the heels of his shoes, shaking his head in admonition of the slob who had lived here. He immediately set about restoring order with a single-minded intensity, singing along loudly to another of his compilations. As he overlaid the music with his own husky bass voice he mistook the flattering camouflage of Bruce Springsteen's Dancing in the Dark for an indication of his own brilliance and told himself he could probably still make it as a singer. He was eighteen years the man's junior for goodness' sake. He carried the two black bags he had filled down to the communal refuse area and amidst the neat rows of coloured bins he stretched like a cat in the watery March sun, which was warm on his face despite the chill in the air. He rotated his hips and tensed his legs and outstretched arms and felt the illogically pleasant arthritic sensation in his neck as he drew up his shoulders and rocked his head slowly from side to side. As he returned to his flat taking the steps two at a time he felt as fit as a man half his age and twice as strong.

With his surroundings restored to order he sat in front of his laptop and wrote Friday's piece in less than an hour. He had agreed with his paper that he wouldn't be returning to the office until Monday morning; he would write a column for Saturday's edition tomorrow and cover an event on Saturday for publication on Monday. At this time of year the national obsession with football was building to a fevered climax and he was obligated to feed that insatiable appetite in preference to whatever else was going on. It was now mid-afternoon and the brief promise of spring had not materialised. The clouds had thickened and rain was falling. Prior's computer sat in front of his living room window at the back of his flat and he looked out across a small park. The wind was picking up and the upper branches of the tall chestnuts swayed as a mother negotiated a departure with a reluctant toddler. He watched as she strapped the wailing boy into his pushchair and half ran from the playground, one hand on the pushchair, the other trying to hold the hood of her anorak down. Prior felt the familiar stirring as her mackintosh rose above the backs of her bare knees and he thought again of Catalina. He wondered what she was doing now and whether she was thinking of him. As he mused, fatigue began to encroach and he reluctantly hauled himself away from the window and pottered about the flat like a child's toy whose clockwork was fading. It eventually clicked its last rotation and he collapsed on his bed, entering a deep sleep within minutes.

***

He came to without knowing where he was for a moment. The light was almost gone but there was enough to make out from the bedside clock that it was twenty to seven. He loved this time of year – the lengthening daylight and then the impending leap to British Summer Time and he sprang off the bed and stretched again, his mouth widening in a spontaneous smile. He began running a bath and as he waited for it to fill he checked his phone messages. There were two, and the first was the blokish cockney voice of his sports editor, Dave Partridge.

"Hi Bob, it's me. You didn't reply to my email so I'll leave a message as well. Excellent articles both. Need fifteen hundred words for Saturday and two thousand for Monday. You don't need to get back to me unless you've got anything. See you Monday – have a good one." As a footnote he added, "Bayliss tells me you've been very naughty – don't know what they see in you."

His heartbeat quickened as the second message came through after some crackles and pauses. "Hola babe, I'm missing you. I'm home about six so try me then. Hasta luego." He must have been in a deep sleep as he hadn't heard the phone.

After washing himself meticulously in the hot water he chose a favoured outfit with half a mind on venturing back out into the night to perpetuate his irresistibility with a further conquest, or even catching a flight to Spain and surprising her. He put on some more music and drank beer followed by lovingly prepared gin and tonics, assuaging his restlessness by dancing, turning up the volume when he went through to the bedroom to observe his gyrations in the full length mirror. Standing at the computer, unable to sit, he established that there were available seats on the 11:50 flight to Barcelona. It was still an option. In stretching across the console to close the curtains he pulled too hard and too vertically, and the flimsy plastic rail came away from the wall, causing him to lose balance and fall backwards onto the floor. As he lay on his back he convoluted his Northern vowels into those of East London and shouted aloud, "The world is your lobster my son," and looked up at the cracked and flaking ceiling, his chest wheezing and palpitating with laughter.

Catalina answered on the second ring. He was just this side of being able to retain some vestige of control over the enticing deceit of the alcohol and still play the part of sobriety.

"Hola darling. I got your message – I was out." He felt an obscure sense of mild guilt at sleeping during the day. He wanted to sound light and happy but felt an irritating constriction. Last night they had been incognito and floated by lust and alcohol, the encapsulated evening had sailed effortlessly towards the intimacy that was in itself a natural conclusion. He was unused to the paths and pitfalls of the longer game.

"It's okay. I just wanted to know you were home safely. Have you been in your work?"

"Er... yeah. I went in for a bit. So anyway, how's your day been – you must be tired?" Catalina laughed.

"Well you are to blame for that you naughty man." While they laughed he had an intrusive vision of the '60s comic Dick Emery and felt again the self-consciousness of yesterday. What was it? Where was it coming from? Divergence, he supposed. Gender, age, culture, nationality, experience, memory. Just for starters. All subjugated by that old devil called lust. He was no prude but there was a kind of poetic justice in paying for taking the nice bit at the end before earning it with the slog of the chase. He laughed off the brief intervention of the superego and remembered her smile as she continued, "No, it's been okay – just glad the day's over. I'll go to bed early tonight and be fine in the morning."

There was silence for a few moments. He hated talking on the phone. Periodic silence was alright in face-to-face conversation but the cardinal sin of telephone interaction. The ultimate disaster. He overcompensated and blurted out, "I miss you, Catalina. When can I see you?"

"I miss you too, Robert." There was another silence and he looked abstractedly at a yellowed curtain hook lying on the worn carpet.

"I could make next weekend. I promised to go to my parents' in Seville this Saturday." He felt a stab of disillusionment at her priorities before the insuperable optimism of tonight's mood germinated an idea to turn disappointment to advantage.

"Do you do internet banking?"

"Yes, why?"

"I'm going to transfer £1,000 to your account tonight. Book your flight for next Friday afternoon to return Sunday night. I'll meet you at the airport. Use the money left over to treat yourself." There was a pause while she took in the information. In a few seconds the complex synaptic brain processes took her from vague discomfort at his didactic assumption of control through to excitement at the prospect. In deference to the former emotion, she was hesitant.

"Wouldn't it be easier for you to come to me?" She couldn't think of a reason why it would be easier but stalling him gave her more thinking time.

"I need to cover a sporting event on the Saturday sweetheart. I don't think I can find an excuse to come back to Barcelona. Bull fighting's not very big over here. It's only for a couple of hours and you can come too or do some shopping or something. Besides, I want to show you some of the London you didn't see."

"Well yes, I am off next weekend. I could take also the Friday and Monday." He heard her voice becoming more assured as she wrested back the initiative. "I'll take an early flight on Friday and come home on Monday. It's a pity to come so far for only two nights; and don't send any money. It is 2011, you know."

It was Prior's turn to experience conflicting aggravation and exhilaration.

"Listen Catalina. I'm not old enough or ugly enough to be your sugar daddy. Let's put it this way – I'm not short of a bob or two. I want it to be my treat – you're my guest. If it makes you feel better you can return the compliment next time."

Despite his unthinking use of idiom she appeared to have understood and ended her reply with an attempt at her own as she said, "Well okay. Thank you. Oh Robert – I can't wait. How do you say – to take it up where we left it off?"

"So that's decided. We'll have a weekend to remember." He took her bank details and they talked some more, neither of them wanting to be the one to close the conversation.

Eventually it was Catalina who said, "Okay da mia, I must let you go to send the money off. Phone me at my parents' tomorrow night." Prior was slightly disconcerted. He had expected to be the first.

He took down the number and said, "Alright. Goodnight and sweet dreams."

"Of you, I hope. Hasta luego."

He put the phone back and pondered briefly on the mechanics of the conversation, contemptuous now of all that earlier guff about the expedience of the courting ritual. In a few moments he had passed a verdict of more than satisfactory and he punched the air and moved to the kitchen to get another drink, lighting a celebratory cigarette on the way.

Sitting at his computer, he transferred the money and began browsing the internet. Through the open, uncovered window he was distracted by a group of teenagers hanging around the swings, illuminated by the glare of the LED streetlights in the road between his flat and the playground. The boys were swigging from cans and talking in the London patois of Caribbean cockney, their recently broken voices alternating between hysterical laughter and what sounded like taunting of the girls who swung themselves towards and then away from them in amused contempt of their immaturity. Prior closed the window and duct-taped the recalcitrant rail and curtain against the wall to block out the unsettling air of caprice, and then entered the unfamiliar world of home furnishings.

The seeds that had been planted in Catalina's apartment and nurtured by the bleak perusal of his dowdy flat now took root. With a determined frenzy he trawled the websites of Harrods, Ikea, DFS, and many more of the like. Fuelled by caffeine, brandy, and nicotine he ordered, paid for, and arranged express delivery of goods to completely rejuvenate his surroundings. From Harrods he would be expecting a Canadian goose double duvet at £549 with four Hungarian goose down pillows at £229 each. His Versace Casa bed linen including bolsters and cushions, comforter, sheets and pillow cases totalled £2,500. He ordered top of the range furniture to replace in their entirety the dull functional items of twelve years ago. Working with a decisiveness bordering on the reckless he purchased a corner sofa and recliner, dining table and chairs, lamps, occasional tables, bookcases, cabinets, and his and hers wardrobes. He themed it in leather and glass which led him to reappraise his worn carpeting and appreciate the need for tiled flooring to provide an appropriate stage for the furniture. He hesitated on the question of the bed. It had been the only thing of real quality he had bought – a king size divan with a mattress that had become like a welcoming old friend in its comfort and familiarity. Discretion briefly prevailed as he imagined the perfect match between the old bed and the exotic new linen arriving to adorn it. He would keep it. Another advantage was that it was the one item that was awkward to get up the stairs. The damaged plaster and scraped banisters still bore testimony to the struggle to this day. Buoyed by this admirable restraint, his fancy took flight again and he clicked randomly and impulsively on 'finishing touches'. Candles with enticing scents of lemon verbena, passionflower, pink pepper and mint. Rugs in bold patterns and colours, bamboo room dividers and a large mural depicting a tropical sunset. New crockery and cutlery. Mature yuccas and oleanders in flower – a white and a pink.

The time had moved on to 2:00 a.m. on the Friday morning and his battery was at last running down. There was still enough in it for him to turn his attention to electrical goods and he finally got round to choosing the fifty inch plasma TV he had been meaning to buy for ages, and whilst on that site he couldn't resist the state of the art music system he didn't really need as a present to himself.

"Because I'm worth it," he said aloud in the pampered tones of a child of the contemporary West. He giggled to himself as he logged off and finally his complaining body dragged his reluctant mind to a brief sanctuary between sheets grown thin and grey with age and the desolation of solitude.

CHAPTER 3

He woke at 5:00 a.m. and lay for half an hour charting the leisurely onset of the dawn by the gradual lightening of the curtains.

"Curtains. I forgot curtains!" As further thoughts rushed in he knew there was no prospect of a return to sleep and he threw back the covers and went to the window to look out on a damp and misty morning. He got ready quickly, impatient with the tedious ritual, and sat in his living room with a coffee making out copious lists on different pieces of paper. On one he recalled instantly all his orders of last night and listed them with the cost alongside. Another contained jobs to do and a third imagined a proposed itinerary for the next two days. His target deadline for completion of the revamp of his 'apartment', as he was now thinking of it, was 6:00 p.m. on Saturday evening.

The time until 9:00 a.m. when he could start to progress his plans hung heavy. He railed audibly against the time it took a nation to rouse itself to activity. He paced the apartment impatiently, chain smoking and drinking endless cups of coffee and he walked to the supermarket two blocks from the front of his home and bought his paper and milk. As always, he turned first to his own article but today he didn't experience the usual flicker of pride at the flattering photograph of the thirty-year-old man freshly arrived in London with a weight off his mind and a load on his conscience. There were other distractions.

At two minutes past nine he began making his phone calls and by nine fifty he had made the necessary arrangements to confirm the orders and delivery times. The majority of the smaller items would be arriving this afternoon, plus the curtains he had added to the order, and the furniture the following day. He wrestled with the complicated logistics of the order in which things needed to happen with the precision of a military commander, his voice meandering from cajoling to pleading to hard-edged menace to achieve his goals. He could not make the dullards and half-wits see the wider picture. None of the above worked on the tradesmen until generous financial inducements ensured that the tiler, carpet fitter, and painter and decorator would be there at his appointed times.

The ten minutes he had to wait for a local charity dealing in furniture for the poor and disadvantaged to open seemed like an eternity. He knew they held the key to the success of the whole operation. At one minute past ten he dialled. The number rang endlessly but a slightly breathless voice answered just as he was about to replace the receiver.

"Good morning. Sisters of Mercy."

"Ah, good morning. I'm rather short of time so listen up. I'm clearing my apartment this morning and I want to donate everything to your good selves." He spoke in a loud staccato, emphasising each word and curbing with difficulty an urge to speak too quickly, feeling impatience with the tiresome necessity for language.

"It's good stuff – three-piece suite, dining set, tables, cabinets, wardrobe, nearly new hi-fi system, TV in excellent condition. Crockery, lamps. The list is endless but here's the catch. I need it removing within the hour."

He had formed a mental image of the person on the other end of the line from the introduction and pictured a woman of late middle age, plain and matronly.

"Well thank you Mr… I don't think you gave your name?"

"Prior. Robert Prior."

"Well thank you Mr. Prior. I'm sure we'd be most grateful to receive your donations but it is rather short notice. Our driver isn't here yet." Prior sighed in frustration and tried to disguise his irritation.

"I need a yes or a no. I've got decorators and carpet fitters arriving at any minute. If you don't want the stuff I'll try elsewhere."

The woman's voice maintained its equanimity. "Well I didn't say we don't want it. I said I can't say when we could collect until Wesley comes in. He has his own timetable and I don't know what he has booked in this morning. I'd like to be more helpful Mr. Prior, but you can see my position."

"What time does he start?" Prior glanced through from the hall to the kitchen wall where the clock showed 10:10, his discomfiture rising with each passing minute.

"No set time really. And then sometimes he'll go straight from home to his first collection." Prior lost his struggle to keep a lid on his vexation.

"Well what sort of an outfit are you? You roll in when you feel like it, no-one knows what anyone else is doing, you seem indifferent to the offer of at least a couple of grand's worth of stuff…"

The woman interrupted him, but again without a change in her voice. "We are a charitable 'outfit' Mr. Prior. We are all volunteers. We try in our small way to reduce waste and provide for want. Perhaps we're not run on strictly commercial lines but we do our best. By all means try elsewhere, although I don't know of anyone else like us in the vicinity. If you'd like me to phone you when Wesley comes in I'd be most happy to." He felt a twinge of guilt but couldn't allow any compassion to deflect him from his aim.

"Hasn't he got a mobile?"

"No. I'm afraid we're a bit behind the times." Prior passed on his number and address and ended the call, and went back and surveyed his sitting room with a momentary pang of nostalgia as he looked at the comfortable suite with its well-worn springs and threadbare arms, but before the sentiment had any opportunity to grow he upended the sofa and manhandled it out into the hall followed by the two chairs.

By late morning his hallway and second bedroom, which had metamorphosed over the years from unused playroom to dumping ground to study, were filled with his now obsolete furnishings, and his clothes and personal effects were piled haphazardly on his bed. The decorators had started on the living room – one stripping the nicotine-stained floral wallpaper while the other glossed the woodwork. Prior raised his voice above the loud music coming from their paint-splattered portable radio and spoke to the older man as he knelt by the skirting board.

"You interested in all this stuff?" The man stopped painting and rubbed his eyes with the back of the hand holding the brush.

"What, all that gear out there?" He sniffed through his red veined nose and pursed his lips. Prior nodded.

"Nah, governor. Got a mate though who might take it off your hands for a few quid."

After a call to a mobile and some minimal bargaining the deal was done with the mate agreeing to clear all the goods, including TV and music centre for the inducement of the £100 that Prior had mistakenly assumed would be coming in his direction. He didn't care as long as it was cleared today. Money was nothing when weighed against the promise of next weekend. What the hell good had it done him piling up in the bank all these years anyway? By 7:00 p.m. the room was finished and an ox of a man and his even larger teenage son had cleared the hall and study and loaded Prior's possessions into a transit van. The Harrods order had arrived before the removal men and was now stacked in the two bedrooms Other retailers came and went, Prior signing their delivery notes with an imperious flourish and a disdain for their attempts at small-talk that kept their stays mercifully brief, and the painters arranged to return at 7:00 a.m. to do the two bedrooms before the carpet fitters arrived.

He sat on the floor in the bare living room with a bottle of cold beer and gazed at the startling black and gold wallpaper on three walls. The other wall, painted white like the ceiling, was awaiting the sunset scene mural. He had emailed his copy to the paper with indecent haste and little interest, work being an irritating distraction from the main task at the moment, and he got out his inventories and itineraries and struck off what had been done, assimilating what remained for tomorrow:- Finish decorating throughout (the painters were bringing a third person with them), 9:00 a.m. tiler coming to lay marble tiles in lounge, kitchen and bathroom (hopefully the gloss would be dry), carpet fitter 11:00 a.m. to lay carpets in bedrooms and hall, furniture delivery any time after noon. As an afterthought he grudgingly added 'do article'. *Bugger it*, he thought. *I'll watch a Six Nations match on TV and scrawl off some rubbish*, but then remembered he didn't have a television set up.

The brief surge of anxiety caused him to jump to his feet and trigger a long bout of feverish activity culminating three hours later in all his new possessions being piled to the ceiling of the hallway with a small aisle left for the tradesmen to move freely and access the adjoining rooms. The two bedroom and sitting room carpets were rolled up and the floors beneath them brushed and mopped. His new flat screen digital TV was on in the kitchen, its high definition picture causing Prior to smile and nod his head in appreciation as he took another beer from the fridge. After a shower he made himself a gin and tonic and climbed onto a stool at his breakfast bar, drinking it quickly and then pouring some bourbon onto some rocks of ice. He had always been a capricious drinker with a catholic taste. Too late and a little too drunk, he remembered Catalina.

The call was answered in Spanish by a gruff, elderly male voice. A confusing discourse ensued with neither understanding the other's language and the older man eventually terminated the conversation by abruptly putting the phone down. Prior cursed and refilled his glass. He felt too alive to be bothered with the television and set about assembling the separates of his music system in the kitchen, finally exulting in the rich, enveloping sound before turning it off, reluctantly delaying his gratification. He recalled that he hadn't eaten but food held no attraction. He didn't want anything to dampen or dilute this feeling so he rummaged through the pile of clothes on the bed and found his North Face coat and headed for the car. Without heed to drink-driving or speed laws he was soon ensconced in a pub he liked just south of the river.

With an hour left to closing time he sat on a stool at the intersection of the end of the bar and the adjoining wall observing the ebb and flow of the scrum at the counter with a supercilious air, feeling again the same unassailability he had experienced in Barcelona. A few men caught his eye but despite the Dutch courage in their bloodstreams they quickly looked away from his intense stare. Shortly before the bell rang for last orders he drained his second large gin and tonic as a girl half his age stepped alongside him and smiled pleasantly. He smiled back and said above the din, "You shouldn't be having to do this love. Let me. What are you drinking?" The smile left her lips and he wondered if his endearment had fallen on a full barrel in the Russian roulette of gender politics. It was a habit he knew he should break even though it could be a useful vetting technique.

She answered in a strong south London accent, "Oh no, honestly. Thanks all the same but it's my round." He ignored her protest and shouted down the counter to the barman he knew who was pulling a pint, leaning back and concentrating on the moment at which to release the pressure.

He called back without looking at him, "When I've finished this one Bob," and the anxious jostlers alongside turned their heads sideways towards him and then ahead again, their discontent unvoiced. He turned back to the girl with his most charismatic smile and looked her briefly up and down, voraciously consuming the abundant curves emphasised by the tight black mini-dress. Her hair was blonde and cut short and he liked the way it contrasted with the dark eye shadow and heavy mascara. The barman moved along and asked Prior what he wanted.

"Same again for me and whatever my friend's having." She started to object again but he raised a hand and put a finger to his lips as Catalina had done.

"Oh well, okay then – if you insist. Two large vodkas and Coke and four bottles of Bud." The bartender turned away to get the drinks, ignoring the muttered dissension at the queue jumping and she continued, "You really shouldn't – I don't even know you." He put out his hand.

"Well you do now. Bobby."

He prompted her with an enquiring look and she said, "Emma. Pleased to meet you, Bobby." They retained the hand hold and she didn't resist the gentle pressure that pulled her towards his splayed knees. The increasingly desperate throng behind her immediately filled the space where she had been standing, leaving her no alternative but to stand between his thighs.

With their faces close he said, "You're very beautiful Emma, do you know that?" She looked away with a shy smile and then back at him, her pupils nearly eclipsing all of her brown irises. Prior paid for the drinks and asked for a tray as a female voice behind them called her name. It was her friend who had come to help carry the drinks.

With difficulty she extricated herself from Prior's web and shouted, "It's alright Donna, I've got a tray." As Prior eased himself from the stool and went to grab it she put her hand on his arm to stop him.

"No, Bobby – my boyfriend's there." He feigned indignation.

"Now she tells me. The round-heeled lush. And here's me finking fate had frown us togevver." She looked at him in slight bemusement and her eyes flashed.

"You're not taking the piss out of me are you?" He immediately regretted his facetiousness and moved quickly to repair bridges, suddenly becoming serious.

"As if I would, Emma. Just my stupid sense of humour. Can I have your mobile number?"

She looked anxiously over to where she was sitting and turned back and said in a whisper into his ear, "Have you got a pen?" It was possibly the most arousing thing anyone had ever said to him.

He drove home through the insistent rain singing loudly along with the CD, protected from the law by his own aura of invincibility, picking up a doner kebab on the way, parking outside on double yellows with the door open and music playing, and then eating it with one hand while the other steered the wheel. Beds were the only furniture he now possessed but he still contrived to fall asleep on the kitchen floor amidst the electrical paraphernalia with the fridge door open as he lay motionless between the pork pie and its intended brown sauce.

***

He had been up for two hours when the doorbell rang, recovering ground lost during his drunken revelry and restoring his flat to a state of preparedness. The caffeine and nicotine re-focussed his mind and he joked and bantered with the painters as they moved quickly and efficiently around the bedrooms, managing to finish before the carpet fitters arrived and moving on to kitchen and bathroom. They had completed their work by the time the tiler had laid the last marble square in the living room and gone onto the functional rooms. *It's all going like a well-oiled machine*, he gloated to himself as he sat on the virgin floor, absently watching thirty men kick and throw and wrestle for an oval heirloom on the TV he had brought in to allow the tiler access to the kitchen. His copy was sent by 5:30 p.m. and he had seen off the last of the tradesmen with a further thick wad of notes. He bounded back up the stairs two at a time and had just reached the landing when there was a ring at the door. He assumed somebody must have forgotten something but at the communal door stood a black man of late middle age. The elbow patches on the sleeves of the ragged tweed jacket owed more to genuine wear than the current fashion mode. The collar and cuffs on his cream viyella shirt were frayed and the waist of his baggy grey trousers hung over a belt fastened below the broken loops. He looked at Prior through bloodshot eyes and spoke in a deep West Indian accent.

"Mr. Prior? It's Wesley. I finally got to you, man. You got some stuff for us I believe?" It took Prior a moment to work out what the hell he was talking about and then he remembered his call to the Sisters of Mercy yesterday morning. It seemed months ago. He felt something between impatience and irritation. His triumphant return to his new palace had been delayed by a representative of this incompetent bunch who had no place in his brave new world. He didn't even try to disguise his feelings.

"Oh no – that's all well gone. I told the woman it needed shifting early on Friday. Now I'm sorry pal but I'm very busy." Wesley gave a shrug and sighed.

"Ah well. I thank you for your offer. Enjoy your evening." Prior momentarily remained on the doorstep as the man turned and walked back to a battered van across the drive. He noticed he walked with a slight limp. Between his shirt collar and pork pie hat, tight ringlets of grey hair could not conceal a rather antiquated hearing aid. Prior experienced a sudden shift of emotion. To his surprise his throat felt tight and his eyes moist and he felt in his pocket and drew out another wad of notes. Wesley was just pulling away as Prior called his name. He broke into a run and followed the van waving the money, but Wesley accelerated swiftly through the gears and drove off, oblivious to the guilt of the pursuing philanthropist.

Back in his flat he had pulled himself together and consigned Wesley to history. The basis of his new 'apartment' was established. It just needed assembling, arranging, embellishing. He moved mercurially from room to room pawing at the boxes, ripping some of them open and inspecting the contents suspiciously like a two-year-old at Christmas with the toys his impatient parents had bought for the older child they couldn't wait for him to be. Eventually some internal sorting system prioritised his needs and he came to rest in front of the computer screen. He discovered a vacancy at an exclusive hotel near Hyde Park and booked a suite for tonight at a cost of £2,000 before phoning a slightly perplexed Emma. She had no plans for tonight other than staying in and nursing her hangover through its final stages but his powers of persuasion and her curiosity got the better of her and she agreed to be picked up at nine by a taxi he would order. He logged off with a flourish and phoned Catalina, who answered herself this time.

"What happened Robert?" Her voice sounded listless. He couldn't tell if she was upset or didn't really care what happened. He tried to sound remorseful.

"I'm so sorry darling. I was called out on a job and didn't want to phone 'til I got home." He excused himself the white lie on the grounds that he couldn't tell her what he had really been doing. He wanted her to think he always kept his home as she was going to find it. "I was so preoccupied that I forgot the time difference. I think I spoke to your dad. I'm sorry to have disturbed him so late." There was a pause.

"Oh. He didn't say anything; but then he seldom does. Men seem to stop talking when they get to about sixty."

"Didn't you hear the phone?"

"Er… no. I went to bed early. I was very tired, and very sad not to hear from my Robert." Prior felt uncomfortable. She was in the wrong compartment. She was for next weekend, not now. As well as that, the endearments felt obligatory and contrived without the authenticity of real emotion. It was that back-to-front feeling again and he felt like a gauche schoolboy from a single-sex school taking his first tentative steps into the unknown. It was fine when he could enter a fantasy world of rose-tinted delusion and intoxicating self-love between the actual contacts. The reality was harder to deal with and left him feeling for the most part, rather silly, for want of a better word.

"Well you could have phoned me," he said, and cursed his impulsive tongue. He had no desire to back her into a corner or ask the unanswerable question.

"Oh Robert, I don't want to argue. Let's forget it. You are forgiven. You will just have to work extra hard to make it up to me. Anyway, my flights are booked." Prior felt a sense of relief that her commitment appeared to still be there. His options were still open. They talked of practical things and ended with his promise to phone tomorrow evening when she would be back in her own apartment.

***

He opened the window of his second-storey suite, lit a cigarette and looked across the road to the tube station and Hyde Park beyond. Fresh from the scented bath, the white towelling dressing gown he had bought on his way to the hotel soaked up the residue of moisture on his skin. Dusk had given way to nightfall and the excitement of the early Saturday evening was evident in the exuberant voices and behaviour of the people mounting the steps of the station and spilling out onto the broad, elegant road flanking the south of the park. He sipped at the glass of Tattinger from the bottle provided by his twenty-four hour butler and checked the time. He had nearly an hour. He flicked his cigarette end out into the evening air and watched it come to rest by a bowler-hatted concierge on the pavement below and then shut the window and turned back into the Georgian-themed room to finish getting ready. The mid-grey wool trousers from his best suit were laid out on the bed with the blue and white striped cotton shirt, the suit jacket hanging from the back of the door. He threw off the gown and splashed himself liberally with cologne, pulling on a pair of black boxer shorts before going again to the bathroom to remove the hair from his nostrils with a pair of tweezers. The pain was strangely cathartic and he gargled with mouthwash, spat it out and looked with satisfaction at the smiling face in the mirror, the light from the fluorescent strip over the basin glinting on his slightly crooked white teeth.

He hardly recognised her when she entered the foyer. The hair was now an aubergine colour and her lilac skirt barely covered her behind. With the fishnet tights and low cut black lace blouse, he could barely conceal his delight. She was obviously dressed for action. As she tottered unsteadily towards him on six inch heels with a matching red handbag and plastic mac over her arm he stood up, insensible to the incongruity of the two of them in a place like this and the looks of the staff and the other guests. She smiled prettily as she reached him and he held her by the arms, his lips lingering on hers in an over-long greeting. He relinquished his hold reluctantly, sensing a discomfort, and stepped back to look at her again.

"Wow, you look gorgeous." Her look suggested that she knew, and he slipped his hand in hers and led her through to the cocktail bar where he sat as close as he could with a possessive arm around her, smirking defiantly at anyone whose eye he could catch. A waiter brought them cocktails which he put on the room bill and they both started to speak at once and smiled, Prior assertively deferring to her.

"Ladies first."

"I was just going to say what are we doing tonight?"

He hesitated. He hadn't put much thought into the timetable between now and the final goal. Resisting the trite, knee-jerk innuendo the question invited he said, "Have you eaten?" He was reminded that that he'd had nothing since revisiting the aborted pork pie at midday, over nine hours ago. She had. "Pity. The hotel's got a Michelin-starred restaurant. Anyway – let's spend a little time here getting to know each other and then we could find a club if you like. So what do you do?"

She told him she was a hairdresser and with some half-hearted prompting from Prior went on to tell him about herself – her hopes of one day having her own salon, of moving out of the parental home and her desire to see the world. The conversation put him in mind of the thankfully defunct beauty contests and the interrogation of the contestants by some arch smoothie in a dinner jacket. He listened with barely disguised boredom, impatient with the preliminary compromises necessary to further his aim. He was vague about himself, as he had been with Catalina, giving away enough to inspire her admiration without being too specific about his identity. Not that her inapt questions and responses gave him much cause to worry about being tracked down by an outraged father or a vengeful boyfriend.

When he came back from the lavatory she was deep in texting. To his annoyance she didn't look up to acknowledge his return but carried on, her eyes glued to the diminutive phone, the fingers poking at the buttons. Prior's irritation was further increased as she held up one hand to cut short his sentence.

"Just a minute, nearly finished."

"Who's it to?" he said peevishly, his voice flat and resentful.

"Mm?" She smiled, but at the phone, not him. Before he could respond she pressed again with a final flourish and turned to him.

"Sorry about that, Bobby. Just telling Donna and Lisa where I am and that I'm with a famous journalist. They'll be like, green with envy?" She turned the statement into a question in the modern parlance with an annoying inflection on the last three words. "Anyway, I'm all yours now."

He took her invitation literally and his hand went to the inside of her thigh as he moved his head to seek out lips that turned away at the last moment so that he planted a kiss on her cheek. He was rapidly tiring of this. He realised that their relationship was subject to the law of diminishing returns and the sooner he acted the better. He put his mouth close to her ear and whispered, "Let's go to my suite and freshen up before we go to the club." He saw the apprehension in her face.

"Er… I'm okay to go now actually." She tried to introduce a lightness. "I'm fresh enough."

He couldn't cover his displeasure but quickly replaced a frown with a bright look and said enthusiastically in the manner of someone recommending a play or a film, "Oh Emma, you should see the suite at least – it's out of this world." She wrestled with her ambivalent feelings. Her curiosity and the Brownie points provided by the pictures she could take on her phone weighed against her heightening unease with the disturbed look in his eyes and the intense transparency of his purpose.

"Well maybe another time."

"What, like after the club?"

"Well it's a bit soon really." She bit her lower lip and glanced across at the barman who was discretely drying a glass. She suddenly looked very young. It should have deterred him but it had the opposite effect.

"So you think I stay in a place like this all the time. That I'll just come up with another two grand when you think you're ready. What the hell did you think tonight was all about? A teenage date and walk you home to Mummy and Daddy?" His rampantly libidinous impulse made a final play at redemption but his attempt at conciliation only sounded wheedling. "I'm sorry to raise my voice honey but I'm disappointed because I like you so much. You can understand can't you?"

She put her hands on her bag which sat on the table in front of her.

"I think I want to go home now. I'm sorry too if you got the wrong idea. To be honest I was mad at my boyfriend and you seemed nice and funny and good looking in an older sort of way. I just thought why not give it a try but you're not…"

She didn't finish the sentence and he said, "Not what?"

"It doesn't matter." He started to speak but then stopped and shook his head slowly, knowing when he was beaten. When he did speak, his voice stayed low in deference to the surreptitious interest of the barman and a couple who had just come in.

He leaned towards her and said spitefully, "Okay. So go back to your shallow little life of shopping and X Factor and changing your hair colour every week. You don't know what you've lost." He stood up as the beginning of tears formed in her eyes and he went to his wallet and threw two twenty pound notes on the table, suddenly feeling a sense of relief. The last hour had not been pleasurable. He said quietly and sardonically, "Missing you already," and then turned quickly without looking at her and walked, almost ran to the hotel car park.

The night was now wet again and his wipers throbbed softly as he drove to an area of dockland. Cobbled streets, shiny from rain and the reflection of streetlamps were fringed by vast derelict buildings reaching up mournfully to the black sky above, their broken windows a dismal echo of such a different time. Dotted along the pavements were isolated figures, alluring in silhouette, and he drove up and down the road, peering out, trying to discern the reality behind the illusion before finally stopping alongside one of them. The passenger door opened and slammed and he sped away with his cargo to a desolate spot where he parked up and sought to ameliorate his rage and frustration on the back seat of the car with the booby prize.

***

He'd checked out of the hotel early the following morning and back at the flat he set about assembling the glass furniture. An unrealistic target time of 11:00 a.m. came and went and he cursed and spluttered in impotent indignation at the unhelpful and confusing instructions. Constantly losing tools and screws and nuts amidst the chaos of the flat, he moved from job to job without ever quite completing anything, ploughing knee deep through the mounds of cardboard and plastic and expanded polystyrene. When he over-tightened the screw affixing a table top to a leg a crack appeared in the glass and his nagging vexation boiled over into rage. He stood up and petulantly kicked aside the packaging, searching for the hammer which he took to the treacherous glass, smashing it into a thousand shards. He threw the hammer down, further damaging the already chipped and scratched marble floor, and went through to the bedroom and swept the clothes from the bed with a savagery that continued with a bare-handed assault on the wrapping of the new linen. Perhaps it was then a mistake to allow thought to encroach on demonic action as he sunk to his knees with his elbows on the bed and his head in his hands, swamped by the magnitude of the tasks ahead, incapable of putting them in any order, his grasp slipping agonisingly away from the precipice of motivation.

It was well after dark when he came back and the frame shook as he slammed the door behind him. He threw down the carrier bags overflowing with books and CDs and clothes and belched to release the gas from the beer in his stomach, before inspecting the fingers that had explored the tender nostrils. The nose had stopped bleeding. He tried Catalina's mobile again and this time responded to the goad of the infuriatingly cheerful sounding Spanish answering service with a terse, aggrieved message. When he threw himself onto the bare mattress with the music playing, the oven on and a tap running, his escape from himself was sadly only temporary.

***

The next day was Monday and Prior stood at the bar of a favourite watering hole near his newspaper office. His fourth pint of lager sat on the counter as he spoke over the heads of three men who sat laterally to him on tall stools, staring ahead. It was late morning and the rain of the last three days had mercifully relented, giving way to spring sunshine that streamed through the open doors of the pub. Without any discernible prompt and to no-one in particular, he poured out a discourse on his perception of the ills of the modern world, starting with his specialist subject.

"Football. Let's not even go there. We've heard it all before. We know; but what do we do about it? Bugger all. The national obsession. Everybody's got an opinion, everyone's an expert. The idiots making inane calls to daft phone-in programmes sounding so self-important as if they're discussing nuclear physics. The smug 'cats who got the cream' sitting on their sofas making it sound as complicated as nuclear physics to keep the illusion going to justify their cushy jobs and large salaries. I love football but I'm sick to death of it. The over-exposure's killing it. Where I come from, even in the summer all you get on local radio is bloody football. All the kids play in the park is football. What about cricket? Well there's another thing."

He remembered his drink and drained the glass, holding it in the air and tapping it in the barmaid's direction. "Yes, same again." He hadn't shaved since Saturday morning and his dark stubble rasped as he drew a hand across his cheek. Spittle had formed on his lips and some clung to the thick growth at the edges of his mouth. His face was red and some capillaries had burst on his upper cheeks.

"The Ashes. The broadcasters have turned that into the new obsession. I don't know why we bother to play the other teams. Just a bit of practice I suppose for the real thing."

He leapt without apparent connection to the subject of racism.

"Kick racism out of sport! You must be joking. I can remember the treatment of the early black players. Do you think people's attitudes have changed that much in the forty-odd years hence? Do you think your average white fan has turned into William Wilberforce? No. They just know they can't get away with it now but it's still there. You get the football commentators and analysts who've never got a good thing to say about a black player. The vitriol for a black player going back to his old club ten times worse than for a white one." The other men at the bar looked uneasy. A few attempted interjections had been steamrollered by Prior's insistent diatribe. He shook his head. "My dad would be turning in his grave if he was still alive."

The barmaid could not suppress a giggle and she smiled at the other men for corroboration. Prior's eyes narrowed and he stared at her.

"What are you laughing at?"

She looked nervously at them this time and replied, "Well if he was still alive he wouldn't be in his grave." Prior's lip curled in a sneer.

"Oh aren't you so clever. We've got women like you on our paper. Only one agenda – the gender agenda. Using isolated stories to slag off all men. The one percent assuming the other ninety-nine percent are all man-haters like them."

The man at the other end of the bar, furthest away from Prior, spoke up.

"Leave her alone mate, she was only having a joke." Prior looked across at him down his nose, noticing his walking stick leaning against the wall.

"Oh, we've got one of the stick brigade with us have we? Hobbled down to the post office and got your invalidity benefit this morning? Now going to spend the day pouring it down your gob at the taxpayer's expense. Well why not if you can get away with it?" Something in Prior's demeanour caused the man to laugh submissively and shake his head, avoiding further confrontation, and he went on, "We've all been feminised, you see. We've gone soft. Our parents' and grandparents' generations hid affliction and they sure had enough of it living through two world wars; and they were all conscripts. Nowadays even the regulars are bleating if they get a sore finger. Health and bloody safety, speed cameras everywhere, grotesque pictures on cigarette packets, bloody units on bottles of alcohol, sell by dates on food, counselling because somebody looked at you the wrong way – I'm bloody sick of it! I think I'll emigrate."

He was interrupted by his mobile ringing. He fumbled in his pocket, dragged it out, and pressed the wrong button, turning it off by mistake. He waved the phone at the men.

"And these bloody things – don't get me started. What they're doing to your brain – now that *is* something to worry about; and all these idiots on trains and walking about spouting their petty nonsense – 'Look at me, I know someone who wants to talk to me.'"

He howled his exasperation, "For God's sake!" And at that moment his phone rang again. This time he pressed the right button.

"Bob?" It was Dave Partridge. "Where are you? You missed the Monday meeting." Prior walked out onto the street and lit a cigarette. He heard one of the men at the bar say something that included the words 'Alf Garnett' followed by laughter and stored it for revisiting on his return.

"I am at present in one of our excellent local hostelries imbibing their excellent brew and putting a few of the peasants right on a few things."

"Are you alright Bob?"

"Couldn't be righter old boy."

"Have you seen our paper this morning?" Prior hadn't bothered to get one today. "Well if you had you'd have noticed that there's nothing by you in it. What in heaven's name was that crap you did on Saturday? Quite apart from how strange and rambling it was, it was libellous about four times. No editor in the world could have got more than a couple of coherent lines out of it. Listen Bob, we need to meet. Get yourself up here." He took a deep drag on his cigarette and glared at a passing youth talking into a mobile, raising his voice as he turned back to his own.

"No – you listen. I won't be in today. I'm off sick or something. Sick of the lot of you in fact." He ended the call and remained outside watching the passers-by through hollowed eyes rimmed by dark grey skin. After a few minutes a cab drew up and the large figure of Dave got out. He spotted Prior and moved towards him tentatively, shocked by his appearance.

"I guessed you'd be here. Blimey mate, you look terrible. What's been happening?" Prior stood on the pavement and looked at his colleague. His white shirt was stained with lager and the beltless trousers had slipped down so their bottoms bunched over his dirty brown shoes and revealed the elastic top of his boxer shorts, into which the shirt was tucked. His flies were open and the spittle had now dried on his lips and face.

"Didn't I tell you I was sick and wouldn't be seeing you? Don't you speak English? I know you don't write it very well. That's why you're jealous of me. I'm the best bloody writer in Fleet Street on any subject and you damn well know it. How dare you not print my articles… how dare you!" He pushed his face close to that of his editor and Partridge backed away from the stale beer and nicotine tainted breath as another youth talking into a mobile careered towards them, his downturned face grinning as he babbled animatedly into the device. Prior held his ground stubbornly and at the last second the youth skipped to his right to detour him. He took one step onwards and Prior lashed out with his foot at the trailing back leg, sending him sprawling onto the pavement. He quickly pocketed his phone and was up in a blur, leaping at Prior, and the two men wrestled each other to the ground, punching away with their free hands.

The manager of the pub had seen what was happening through the open doors and came out and together with Dave, managed to prise them apart and hold them until the arrival of a police car summoned by an observer. The youth, clearly the wronged party, gave vent to his righteous indignation to one of the policemen and anyone else that would listen but Prior continued to struggle with both the interceders who pinned him against the building. Their grip loosened slightly as the other policeman approached them and he took the opportunity to launch his forehead at the officer's nose, a mop of hair rising and falling in a vaguely comical manner above his wild, desperate eyes. He was restrained and cautioned and then placed in handcuffs and pushed, almost thrown into the back seat of the police car with one of the officers getting in beside him. Before they could move off, Partridge knocked on the driver's window and he wound it down.

"This is not him officer. I'm his boss and know him well. He doesn't know what he's doing. He needs some help, not locking up, take my word for it."

The policeman thanked him for the information and looked at Prior in his rear view mirror. He was mumbling to himself, his labile expression changing from sad to amused and back to sad, and he said to his colleague, "A&E on a 136 I think, don't you Jim?" Jim agreed and the driver put on his siren and pulled out of a line of vehicles. Not because there appeared any fight left in Prior, whose eyes were now closing; just so they could negotiate the turgid city traffic as they headed for the nearest hospital.

CHAPTER 4

On the following Thursday twelve people sat on easy chairs round a centre table scattered with bulging case files and other paraphernalia. The small room had not been designed to accommodate this number of personnel and the March wind blowing outside was in the wrong direction to penetrate the one window, resulting in the room feeling stuffy and airless. The ward consultant, a middle-aged Scottish woman, yawned and referred to a list of names.

"Robert Prior. What can you tell us about him, Suresh?" The young Indian Senior House Officer shuffled through the files and pulled out a relatively slim volume.

"Forty-two year old man, admitted Monday on Section 136 from A&E. Now converted to Section 2." For the benefit of the medical and nursing students he added as an aside, "That's a twenty-eight day section for assessment." He continued, "He was apparently causing a disturbance in a pub. Police were called and took him to casualty. Presented as hostile and agitated on arrival on the ward and was given intramuscular tranquillisation and placed in a side ward on close observations. Now on lorazepam 1mg. TDS, haloperidol 5mg. TDS and 5mg. PRN. As you suggested Dr. Mckay, we've done an ECG and bloods for U&Es, LFTs, TFTs, FBC and calcium, glucose, and cholesterol with a view to starting on a mood stabiliser. The results have come back okay. Hard to get much background leading to admission as he lives alone. A neighbour who came to see him apparently said he's been noisy through the night recently and he noticed him playing air guitar at a window, bare-chested, one afternoon which seemed a bit out of character. Next of kin is his mother who lives up north and hasn't seen him for years. The ward staff have spoken to his ex-wife who also lives up north and she's going to come down to see him in the next few days. Jenny will tell you more about what she said." He looked at the ward nurse, a woman in her early thirties who took his cue.

"She also hasn't seen him for years. Apparently he's a journalist, quite a successful one. No previous history or involvement with psychiatric services up to his moving to London although she did say he was very difficult to live with. He was very moody and drank a lot and I think it got a bit too much for her eventually. They've got three children who he never sees. She said she'd tell us more when she comes on the ward. As Dr. Nehra said, he was quite a handful on admission but he's quickly gone the other way and is pretty low in mood. We've still got him on close obs as we're worried about the suicide risk. He's also been found smoking twice on the ward, presenting a fire risk." She looked at the consultant hesitantly, not wanting to sound above her station. Whilst in the main approachable, Dr. McKay was intolerant of uninformed opinion.

"I don't know if he's going into a psychotic depression but he came out with something that sounded delusional yesterday morning." She looked at the sea of faces and continued, "There was a picture on the front page of one of the papers of a footballer coming out of a club in Spain with a girl. He's married and the paper was going to town on him calling him a 'love rat'. Robert stared at it for ages and then started crying and muttering to himself. When we asked him what was wrong he said that this player, Darren Johnston, had pinched his girlfriend – the one in the picture." There were a few smirks and titters around the room, quickly interrupted by Dr. McKay who now spoke to wind up the discussion of Prior before moving on to the next patient.

"Well keep an eye on that, Jenny. I haven't actually met Robert yet. I'll do that tomorrow at the ward round. We do need to try and get more of a history. At least two episodes of mood disorder are theoretically required for a diagnosis of bipolar disorder. At the moment we're guided to see this as a single manic episode although I think the suspicion is that Mr. Prior has a type one bipolar disorder. We'll continue with current medication and I'll decide on a new regime tomorrow."

***

Earlier that morning a woman stepped from her large detached house and got into her car to drive to the Cheshire village station. She was of early middle age, just past forty, and everything about her, from her mid-brown hair to her undemonstrative expensive clothes, was understated and looked just right. She changed train at Manchester and settled into her seat on the London express, breathing an inward sigh of relief as it drew slowly away from the station. Not that she wanted to be leaving or was looking forward to the next twenty-four hours. She just felt that this start was at least the beginning of the end. She had bought papers and magazines and taken a novel she was halfway into and enjoying but hardly looked at them. Instead she spent almost all the journey in soporific contemplation.

Her mind took her back to a time she barely thought of these days and she was surprised at how easily she could evoke the atmosphere and feelings of those distant times. She first remembered the night Robert came into her life in the students' union bar at Cambridge. It was three weeks into their first term and they had a natural starting point for their conversation because they both came from North West towns thirty miles apart. Prior covered his insecurity and homesickness with an aggressive bravado, playing up his working class Northern roots and developing a barbed edge to his personality that dared his more privileged peers to cross him at their peril. He latched onto Caroline as would a drowning man to a buoy, his disillusionment uncoiling slowly at his realisation that their geographical empathy was not matched by any similarity with their socio-economic status. His father was a baker, his mother a housewife, while Caroline's parents were both solicitors. In his confused adolescence he saw her as a traitor somehow. Nevertheless, they maintained an on-off relationship over their four years of study characterised by rows and reconciliations. There was some mutual attraction that seemed unbreakable, however, and their union was inadvertently cemented when she became pregnant towards the end of their final year. Prior graduated with a first in English and Caroline with a 2:1 in History. He began working for a national newspaper at their Manchester office and their daughter Laura was born soon afterwards. Their son Graham was born the following year and Helen completed the family two years later. Caroline put her career on hold to bring up the children with Prior playing the traditional role of breadwinner. Although naturally maternal and a good, loving mother she became worn down by the drudgery and constant fatigue and more and more frustrated at the lack of energy or opportunity to satisfy the creative needs of an intelligent person and her husband's lack of support. He was a kind father but left everything to his wife, throwing himself into his career and getting sucked into the laddish drinking culture of the sports journalist. The chasm between them grew gradually wider and when he left for a promotion to the London office she was surprised at how quickly she got over him and found a relative peace and fulfilment.

***

Caroline reluctantly resumed meaningful activity following the blessed suspension of obligation on the train and walked quickly through the station to the taxi rank. It was now 2:00 p.m. The ward had told her she could visit at any time and stay as long as she wanted given the distance she had travelled. Her apprehension at visiting a psychiatric ward was assuaged somewhat by its context as part of a general hospital.

As a girl she grew up close to one of the old asylums with its massive, forbidding Victorian buildings, its sense of being a world within a world, and of distant screams of torment. As she got out of the taxi in front of the automatic glass doors of the neutrally named Nathan Centre, she couldn't help feeling that Euston was more like Bedlam and she had found sanctuary. The impression remained as she was greeted by a friendly receptionist and directed to the ward her ex-husband was on. She pressed the buzzer and was taken to a small office off a corridor and asked to sit down by a young male charge nurse. Caroline was heartened further by the contemporary conventionality of the pleasant-looking man and his open, easy manner. A far cry from the slightly sinister-looking people she used to see going in and out of the gates of the asylum of her youth. He was the first to speak.

"I believe you've had some background to Robert's current circumstances. We were wondering if you know of any previous similar episodes."

"Well, nothing so extreme as to warrant hospital. You have to understand that I haven't seen Robert for ten years now. He was only thirty when he moved to London and thirty-two when he stopped coming up to see the children. He was always a bit complex, a bit of a contradiction, one day happy, charming, full of life – the next morose, brooding, irritable. Sometimes he would change from one minute to the next; but never anything that stopped him functioning, nothing to ever suggest that he needed professional help. One thing I wanted to ask you; if he has got bipolar disorder is it usual for it to come on so late?" The nurse took his jaw in his left hand and looked pensive.

"There's no definitive age of onset. A first episode would normally be earlier but I've known people to develop the illness later than Robert. From what you've told me he has probably experienced a condition known as cyclothymia in which continual hypomania is interspersed with depressive symptoms without either meeting a threshold for clinical diagnosis. A full-blown manic episode could be sparked by some kind of extreme stress or combination of circumstances. Or even something very good or exciting happening to them. Sleep is the real key. In layman's terms the person becomes too excited to sleep which in itself perpetuates the mania. I hope that sort of answers your question." He smiled diffidently and went on, "Presumably you won't know of his recent situation. We may be able to speak to his employers but obviously there are confidentiality issues. I believe you mentioned a problem with alcohol to my colleague, is that right?" Caroline returned the man's earlier smile.

"I don't suppose a wife exists who doesn't think her husband drinks too much; but yes, I did think he might be developing a problem. He always had a good capacity for it. At university he took great stock in being able to drink the 'soft southerners' under the table. In the latter stages of our marriage I noticed the conscious effort he had to put in when, for whatever reason, he was constrained from drinking and a sort of edgy preoccupation which only went away when he could start again. He tried to be a good dad, I will say that for him, and he knew the alcohol got in the way of that but you could see it was an effort to stop. Why? Is that relevant?"

The nurse cleared his throat and said, "His blood results show evidence of liver damage," instantly regretting a breach of Prior's confidentiality. He went on hurriedly, trying to dilute his error. "Nothing too alarming and certainly reversible at his age but something he needs to be aware of. To answer your question, alcohol certainly can influence mood disorder and as with lack of sleep can heighten and perpetuate the manic symptoms and indeed the depressive symptoms in the aftermath of a drinking episode." His professional mask slipped a little and he suddenly looked vulnerable. "To be honest Mrs…"

"Ross; but call me Caroline."

"Okay. Well I shouldn't really have given you clinical information without his permission, especially as you're not even his next of kin or a relative. I'd be very grateful if you'd forget I said it." Caroline looked sympathetic.

"Of course I won't say anything. I know how careful one has to be nowadays. Not that I could see Robert giving much of a damn. He always prided himself on how frank and honest he was and he hated cagey people. At least when he was drunk anyway." They both sensed a completion of the exercise and stood up at the same time. Caroline spoke.

"I'm afraid that's all I can tell you. As I say, what's been going on for him in the last ten years, I wouldn't know. I read his articles and he's obviously kept things together judging by how well he's done in his career. He's even been on telly a couple of times. He's in the past now, for me anyway, but he's the father of my children and I felt a duty to come to see him, just once."

The ward was on the first floor and had been purpose-built as part of the mental health unit in the nineties. The dayroom sat at the end of the corridor and its large windows of toughened glass looked onto a lawn where people sat on benches smoking and drinking tea from paper cups. Framed by the window stood a male figure with his back to the room dressed in tracksuit bottoms, a grey T-shirt and slippers. As Caroline drew closer she recognised the way the hair grew haphazardly on the man's neck above broad shoulders. Prior must have sensed her presence and turned round sharply. They looked at each other awkwardly, weighing up for a brief moment an appropriate form of greeting. Prior took away her uncertainty by wrapping his arms round her neck and resting his head against hers, and she felt a wetness on her cheek. She was glad she was facing away from the other patients in the room so they couldn't witness the discomfort on her face. She exerted gentle pressure away from him but he clung on, not wanting to relinquish his hold. He finally raised his head and looked at her through moist eyes. His voice was low, almost a whisper.

"You look wonderful." There was a hint of awe in the way he said it and his expression was cowed and submissive. She had never seen this in him before; but then she had never seen *this* man before. His loose clothing could not disguise the weight he had lost. His yellowish cheeks were sunken and his hair uncombed and too long. The dark rimmed eyes held an alarmed furtive look.

"Where can we go Robert? To talk, I mean." The question didn't seem to register and he continued to look at her, his arms now hanging loosely by his sides. "Robert?"

He motioned to two chairs and began shuffling towards them, bending his knees agonisingly slowly like an old man and manoeuvring his backside between the arms, sitting back with a jolt and a sigh. Caroline remained standing and said, "I'll be back in a minute Robert," and went back to the corridor in search of a nurse. She found two in the kitchen making tea.

"Excuse me. I'm Mr. Prior's ex-wife. I was wondering if there was anywhere private we could go to talk; outside maybe?"

"Well, he's on close observations and a sectioned patient so a member of staff would need to go with you. They could be discrete and just keep an eye from a distance."

"Yes, thank you. It would be nice to get some fresh air. Robert doesn't look like he's got it in him to escape even if he wanted to. He does seem awfully sedated."

"I'm afraid he needs to be at the moment, Mrs. Prior." Caroline didn't bother to correct her.

"I'll come down with you in a minute, I'll just finish this." She went back to the dayroom where Prior was staring blankly ahead and in due course the three of them went down in the lift and crossed the garden to an empty bench by a bed of deciduous shrubs, their buds beginning to form. An early flowering clematis climbed a trellis behind them and she remembered how this time of year used to lift his spirits. She wondered idly if there was any connection to his current circumstances or whether it was just coincidence. The wind was light and the afternoon warm and sunny in contrast to the near freezing nights. The nurse moved to a spot on the grass about forty metres away and sat down, leaning back on her outstretched arms, closing her eyes as she raised her head in the direction of the sun. Her long brown hair cascaded onto the ground behind her and her skirt rode up over her thighs to reveal a nice pair of legs to which Prior was oblivious. There was a long silence as Caroline rehearsed an opening line. Her emotions were confused. She only felt the detached compassion one would feel for a disadvantaged stranger and yet she saw the faces of her children in his and perhaps she cried inwardly for them. Graham was now about the same age as Prior had been when they first met and although facially more similar to his mother, he was showing the same prickly, rebellious traits. To her surprise Prior spoke first.

"How's Doug?"

"Doug?" She looked puzzled at the irrelevance of the question.

"He's okay. Why?"

"Just wondered that's all."

"Let's talk about you, Robert. I've not got too long – I'm going back this evening. Do you want to talk about what's been happening?"

He gave her a tortured look and said simply, "No." The silence returned and Caroline looked across the lawn at a man sitting on a bench opposite, holding his knees and rhythmically rocking backwards and forwards, laughing to himself. The nurse was now flat on her back, an arm across her eyes. She would have liked to have told him about the children but was wary of doing so in the absence of his inquiry. She never quite knew the depth of his feelings where they were concerned. He seemed to have closed the book on them. She had married Doug two years after Prior left and he had been an exemplary stepfather. The children had tried hard not to like him but slowly and grudgingly his patient turning of the other cheek won first their respect and eventually an affection close to love. He was solid and practically minded, everything their biological father wasn't.

"Well that's okay," she said, and immediately felt foolish. She sounded like one of those 'right on' counsellors she so despised. Actually it wasn't okay to come all this way to hear he didn't want to talk about anything. He began to speak haltingly as if every word was an effort.

"It's just good that you're here Caroline. You're doing me good just being here." His face suddenly contorted and he leant forward and put his head in his hands. "I just feel so ashamed. Such an idiot." She put her hand on his back and his own hand immediately clamped over hers.

"Have you got everything you need Robert? Can I get you anything?" There was another long pause. Caroline was gradually attuning to the pedestrian pace of the conversation.

"I've only got these clothes the ward gave me. And I've got no money or cigarettes left." She sighed at what she might be drawn into. Her train left in three hours. She hoped he hadn't heard.

"So someone needs to go to your flat?" He looked at her and nodded and she felt again the irritation at the helpless, canine eyes followed by the same self-reproach.

"The staff told me a neighbour had been to see you. Couldn't he help?" Prior took an age to reply, gazing absently at a blackbird flying into a laurel hedge and then a brief fluttering commotion before its swift exit back into the skies.

"I wouldn't want him in my place. Certainly not when I'm not there. All he ever wants is to borrow money." She started to reluctantly consider some preliminary adjustments to her schedule.

"I thought yesterday that he had brought me something from the flat. My sponge bag appeared in my locker. It turned out that I'd picked up somebody else's. I don't know why I thought it was mine – he's not got a key." He turned back to her and said, "My head's a mess, Caroline."

"Can't the ward help? With your things, I mean."

"They're too busy." She couldn't help a brief glance at the prostrate figure on the grass, now lying on her side.

"Have you got your bank card on the ward?"

"No, it's in the flat." He looked imploringly at her. "Could you go for me Caroline and get me some clothes and cash some money, and buy some cigs?" It was her turn to be silent. She inwardly cursed him for the predicament he was putting her in. The long-buried animosity began to rear its head but she looked at the pathetic figure alongside in the baggy uniform of the underclass and the scuffed slippers a size too large and felt some pity return. She thought for a few more minutes and then said, "I'll have to stay in London overnight. If you give me your flat key I'll go now and get your things and drop them in later. If you want to trust me with your pin number I'll draw some money out and get your cigarettes."

Prior came as close to a smile as was possible given his current state. He said quietly, "Thanks. I've got no-one else, you see." Their eyes met, tacitly acknowledging the paucity of his life. "Of course you can have my pin. The card's in the wallet in a North Face coat." He suddenly remembered the state of the flat.

"Place is in a bit of a mess but that's a long story. Coat's in the rear bedroom I think and clothes on the bed in the first bedroom. Just bring what you want." He looked wistful. "You always did know what I look best in."

Caroline became businesslike in response to this attempt at nostalgia and was shortly sitting in a taxi on the way to Prior's flat. She felt a surprising elation. She was over the first hurdle and the decision to stay overnight had released some pressure. She had taken tomorrow off from her job as an HR manager with a large department store chain and then there was the weekend. She began to plan her evening as the taxi ground its way through the traffic going south towards the river. She'd need to find a room. She'd try the Premier Inn by Euston and change her ticket at the same time. Then she'd need a change of clothes and some nightwear and toiletries. She was at a stage where she didn't have to worry about money. It would be nice to have an evening pampering herself away from the noise and energy of three adolescents.

The taxi driver agreed to wait and she fiddled with the keys, eventually finding the one to open the outside door. The concrete steps echoed loudly from the contact with her heels as she went up to the first floor and entered Prior's flat.

She had been prepared for a bachelor's pad, a bit untidy and in need of a 'woman's touch' but not what confronted her now. Thank goodness, she thought, for the strong smell of fresh paint. She dreaded to think what it was masking. There wasn't an area of carpet or floor that wasn't covered with something. Unwashed glasses and cups and half-eaten plates of food littered the windowsills, and full ashtrays and wet towels were everywhere. Half-assembled furniture sat amidst mountains of packaging. A tasteless mural flapped gently when her movement created a slight flurry, the Blu-Tack on one top corner having come away from the wall. The noise of a running tap drew her into the kitchen and she stepped over boxes and full bin bags, untied and festering, to turn it off at the sink. She crossed the bathroom to use the loo and her never quite forgotten frugality, honed in the early days of marriage, caused her to open the cupboard housing the electric immersion heater. The switch was down. She flicked it up and washed her hands at the basin, the steam rising from the scalding hot water. She was tempted to investigate further and begin a cursory attempt at restoring some order but discretion prevailed and she found his coat and put it in a travel bag along with two changes of clothes, a pair of shoes, and toiletries she found in the bathroom.

How long would he be in hospital she wondered? The section two was for twenty-eight days, she had been told, but could be converted at any time up to then to a section three which would then be in place for another six months unless he successfully appealed to a Mental Health Review Tribunal for discharge of the section. The charge nurse had said that he would be ready to leave when his mood was stable and he didn't present a risk to himself, others, or of self-neglect. Well that wasn't her problem, she thought, as she closed the door and returned to the taxi. Someone else would have to attend to his longer term needs.

Back in the cab the driver found her the number of the Premier Inn and she was relieved to find that a room was available. However, when they returned to the hospital she glanced at her watch and did some rapid calculations and was in two minds to ask the man to wait again, cancel the room, say a brief goodbye to Robert and try to make that train. She was not used to feeling so indecisive. In the end she stayed with her original plan. She would be glad when the train had gone and there was no decision to make.

It was now late afternoon and the ward was more or less deserted. A nurse told her that the patients were down in the dining room having their evening meal. Prior however, suddenly appeared at the door of the dayroom. They had the room to themselves and found two seats in the corner where they hoped they could maintain some privacy even when the patients returned.

"Aren't you eating, Robert?" He shook his head. There was something childlike about him. The pursing of the lips; the dependency on others his position had placed him in.

"I've got your cigarettes and some cash, and here's your card. She immediately realised she should have given them to the nurse but it didn't matter. He made no attempt to accept them and she quickly put them back in the holdall. He made no offer to pay her taxi fare and she didn't ask for it.

"I won't stay long now. I've got to do some shopping if I can find anywhere open and get another train ticket."

He spoke without looking at her in a strange monotone. "Come back tomorrow Caroline."

She experienced an uncomfortable, dreamlike sensation of being powerless to resist an unwelcome clutch. The anger returned. She would not be a prisoner of conscience. She had done more than enough already. Was he so obnoxious that an ex-wife he hadn't seen for ten years was the only person he could count on? She said as sympathetically as she could, "No Robert. I really can't."

"But you said you were staying overnight now. When's your train tomorrow?"

"I don't know – I haven't booked it yet. I'll try and make it as early as possible. I need to get back for the children."

"They'll hardly be children now." He looked into space. Caroline hoped he might be trying to picture them.

"No, they're young adults but they still need a lot of input. It's not fair on Doug."

His voice went back to a whisper that sounded eerily melancholic. "It's not fair on Doug." She didn't know if he was parodying or agreeing with her. He started again. "How do they….?" and then tailed off, not completing the sentence.

"How do they what, Robbie?" She had inadvertently reverted to her old name for him when they had been together.

"It doesn't matter." She realised that if she waited for his permission to leave she would still be here until he was discharged. She was put in mind again of the passivity of a child, the being swept along on a tide of events decided by others. She took his hands in hers and looked at him from her sideways position.

"I'm going now. I'm so sorry to see you like this. You *will* get better – you are in good hands. I'll phone the ward and keep up to date with how you are." She stood up and took the holdall from the floor. People were starting to return to the ward and it was slowly coming alive again with the sound of doors slamming and laughter and chatter. A man entered the dayroom singing loudly and tunelessly in a basso-profundo voice. Prior's eyes held the fear and abandonment of those of a four-year-old left by his mother on the first day of school as he watched her walk away and down the long corridor to the locked doors.

CHAPTER 5

He spent a fitful night tossing and turning between dreams, conscious, and half-conscious thought. In his conscious state he tried to piece together the betrayal of Catalina. How had Johnston been able to trace her? He recalled his whispering in her ear, his attempted look of amused unconcern at her rejection, and remembered reading he'd been injured for Sunday's game. Oh how it must have hurt his superstar's ego – turned down for a journo fifteen years his senior. Bayliss, the little shit! He'd shown unusual interest in her at the airport that morning – her name, where she lived, where she worked. Prior had been only too keen to give him the details, to bask in the glory of his conquest. They must have found her on Twitter or Facebook or something. That's why she didn't answer the phone on Sunday night.

His dreams were vivid – a cat digging its claws into him, biting at his neck and face. The pain was almost real. He was stronger than the cat, smarter than the cat, older than the cat, but he couldn't get it off him. He dreamt of waking in the bedroom of a large Victorian country house. At the window, her face framed by ivy overgrowing onto the panes from the red brick walls, was the staring face of a middle-aged woman in black-rimmed glasses – judging, disapproving, inexplicably terrifying. He was fully awake at 4:00 a.m. as he had been on every morning since Tuesday and he then drifted into a semiconscious state where reality and fantasy became blurred.

Work anxiety floated in and out of his thoughts; unfinished articles, failure to meet deadlines; intractable abstract problems he wrestled with before returning to full consciousness at six. He experienced an overwhelming sadness and despair far worse than any physical pain, with its capacity to be communicated and alleviated. All he could see and feel was loss. Caroline and the children, his job and comfortable way of life, his unthinking certainty. Less importantly, Catalina – not so much the loss of her herself – more the esteem and sense of desirability she had revived in him. All he could see ahead was failure, loneliness, and tribulation. And the present didn't bear thinking about.

He lay there until eight, his negative thoughts building to tidal waves of anxiety. The lorazepam had worn off and his head hurt. Not so much a conventional headache, more a raw, exposed sensation. He recalled a sketch from a 1960s alternative comedy programme where half-wits staggered about clutching their heads, saying in guttural, Neanderthal voices, 'My brain hurts.' That was how he felt. The words of Caroline came back to him. 'You *will* get better, you're in good hands.' He wished he shared her faith but he sensed instinctively the problems of communicating a disease of the mind. How could he put into words this feeling he had where he couldn't focus, couldn't carry a thought through, this awful disconnection. That's it – 'I'm losing my mind.' That's the phrase. That's the best anyone's come up with after all these years.

When a nurse entered the dormitory he was the only man still in bed. There was no impulse compelling him to rise. Neither was there an impulse to stay in bed. He felt becalmed. If he'd been at home he would have stayed there all day. In the end, at the nurse's cajoling, he drew back the bedcover and swung his feet onto the blue linoleum floor, laboriously peeling off the white vest and pulling yesterday's T-shirt over his head. He took the tracksuit bottoms from the chair and stepped into the legs, drawing them up over the underpants he had slept in. The bag Caroline had brought remained under the bed untouched. He avoided breakfast and after his morning medication he sat in the dayroom waiting to be called to the ward round where he would be meeting his consultant psychiatrist for the first time.

At 10:30 he was taken to a room in which six people sat. A woman motioned to the one empty chair, smiled at him, and said in a reassuring Scottish accent, "I'm Dr. McKay. Do sit down Robert. Do you know everyone in the room?"

He looked down at the floor and muttered, "I think so." He felt intimidated and failed to see why there had to be so many people there. He thought he would just be seeing the psychiatrist.

"Now tell me, Robert. What's been happening for you?"

He felt an acute anxiety. Something in his conditioning urged him to speak. This was a meeting. A game that grown-ups play in work, loving the sound of their self-important voices. He'd become quite adept at it; but now his mind felt numb. Without looking at anyone he said, "I don't know."

The psychiatrist allowed the statement to settle on the air before saying, "You seem very low in mood, Robert, is that right?" She had quickly realised the need for closed questions.

"I am, yes."

"Okay, let's go back to the beginning. This feeling low is a new thing. You weren't like that when you came in. You were the opposite in fact weren't you?"

Prior nodded.

"Do you remember the first time you started feeling unusually happy?" Prior felt this was all a waste of time. What was it going to achieve? He looked at the woman for the first time since his initial entry to the room.

"Do you mind if we stop this? I'm really not up to it."

She looked back at him and said, "Yes Robert, I do mind. I know it's difficult for you but if we're going to help you we need to understand a bit more about what's happened. You're a journalist I believe?"

"Yes."

"Well you know better than anyone how important background information is, collection of data, isn't that right?" He found her tone patronising but he was too vulnerable, too slowed to react. He lowered his head again and said nothing.

"Okay. So you began to feel very happy. Was this because something happened?" He felt he was running on autopilot. The thoughts were there but he couldn't vouch for their veracity. Nothing was certain.

"I met a girl."

"Right. When was this?" It felt like about a hundred years ago.

"Last Wednesday."

"And where was this?"

"In Barcelona. I met her after the game I covered."

"I see; and it made you feel very good about life?"

His hackles started to rise. *What business is this of anyone's?* He looked round the room now at the faces – curious and interested. Who the hell were they to be hearing about his private life? He didn't even know who any of them were. He felt like he'd been subpoenaed to appear on the Jeremy Kyle show. His anger rose in a crescendo but at its apex it changed to a gut-wrenching anxiety and turned inwards.

"What was the question again?"

"I said it made you feel very good about life, meeting this girl."

"I think so. To be honest, after that my memory goes a bit hazy." Dr. Mckay paused and changed her line of questioning.

"Have you been in hospital before? For a mental health issue, I mean."

"No."

"And is this the first episode of the kind that you've experienced?"

Prior looked pensive. "I don't know what this 'episode' is. I was hoping you were going to tell me. I feel like I'm losing my mind."

"Yes, Robert, I'll come to that in due course; but it will help me to have as clear a picture as possible. How do you feel about your life in general? Before becoming unwell, I mean." He said nothing and she prompted him, "Good, bad, indifferent, curate's egg?"

"All those things at different times."

She chanced another open question. "So what sort of a social life do you have?" Prior appeared to be about to speak on a few occasions but said nothing and the doctor continued, "Do you have many friends?"

"No."

"We've noticed your liver function tests were deranged Robert. Do you drink a lot?"

He was tiring of this questioning and just wanted to return to his bed and to shut out the world.

"I suppose so."

"So you drink on your own do you, if you haven't got any friends?"

"I drink on my job, with colleagues. Sometimes on my own. My job is sort of my life."

"Okay. Well you'll need to address your alcohol consumption but we can talk more about that closer to discharge." She smiled and said, "You won't be getting much chance to drink in here." He didn't join the others in the room in their polite smiles. She changed the subject.

"I believe you were very upset about something you saw in the papers. Why was that?"

Prior sighed. *Is there nothing they don't notice in here?* he thought. "It was nothing. Just someone I knew. The one I just told you about."

"Would you like to expand on that?"

"No."

"A nurse told me the girl in the pictures was your girlfriend, have I got that right?"

He rubbed his eyes.

"If you don't mind Dr. Mckay, I'd really rather not talk about it."

"Sure. We'll leave it there. If you ever change your mind just speak to one of the staff." She asked him some more questions about sleep and appetite and then suddenly became businesslike and her voice took on an autocratic edge.

"Well Robert. I'll let you go now. I'm sure you must be very confused and worried but you don't need to be. We know how to help you. You have had what we call a manic episode and you've now developed a clinical depression. This suggests that you are suffering from a condition known as bipolar disorder. I'm going to get you started on a mood stabiliser called lithium carbonate at 400mg daily. We'll monitor the level of lithium in your blood weekly and increase it until we have a stable therapeutic level in your blood. The ward staff will give you a leaflet explaining all about it. I'm going to add an anti-psychotic drug, aripiprazole, also known as abilify. We'll start at

15mg. We'll stop the haloperidol but keep the lorazepam PRN, i.e. for if and when you need it. I'm not starting an anti-depressant yet but it is a future short-term option if your mood remains stubbornly sub-euthymic, sorry, low."

Prior looked alarmed.

"Anti-psychotic? Are you telling me I'm psychotic?" All the connotations of the habitual misuse of the word in the press and society disturbed Prior even in his psychomotor retarded state. Was he being compared to deranged maniacs? The consultant picked up on his lay perception of psychosis.

"Bipolar, although primarily an affective mood disorder, is also classified as a psychotic illness. Psychosis can be described as a disorder of thought. We now have very sophisticated drugs to correct this, Robert, and the one I am prescribing for you is probably the least prone to side effects. Nearer to discharge, I'm going to ask our community mental health team to allocate someone to help you, probably a CPN – that stands for community psychiatric nurse. In the meantime, try to keep as busy as you can on the ward. I know what an effort everything seems at the moment but the sooner you engage with occupational therapy and perhaps the gym, the sooner your recovery will start. And my staff are there to talk about anything that's worrying you at any time." He had a brief image of Rankin, who he had to admit had thankfully turned out to be the exception, not the rule.

"Now is there anything you wanted to ask?" Prior cleared his throat. In spite of his lassitude there still remained one passion he clung on to; his need for freedom to control his own destiny, however bleak that may be.

"I'm told I can appeal against the section." Dr. McKay looked disappointed. Another report to write.

"You can, yes."

"Well I will be doing that."

"Of course, Robert. That is your legal right. I would hope however, that even if the tribunal discharged you from the section you would agree to stay as a voluntary patient until a comprehensive care package could be set up before discharge." She resisted the pressure to use the word 'robust' instead of 'comprehensive' that current terminology dictated.

"Anything else?"

"No, that was all."

Prior got to his feet and went back to the ward where he sat until lunchtime gazing into space.

***

The previous night, Caroline had got a taxi from the hospital to a large all-night supermarket. She had bought a small suitcase, a new outfit, toothbrush, toothpaste, shampoo – everything she would need for an overnight stay, and checked in to her hotel just before seven. The temptation to sink into a hot bath and soak away the travails of the day was alluring but she forced herself to make the short walk to the station to re-book her train for tomorrow. She managed to get a seat on the one leaving at 11:00 a.m. at exorbitant cost but she didn't care. The rest of the evening was now hers. After her bath she poured red wine from the bottle she had bought into one of the glass tumblers and sipped at it as she dried her hair and put on make-up. She felt a warm glow as the alcohol released the serotonin and took away the slight discomfort at being alone and female in an unfamiliar city. She put a music channel on the TV and perused the menu, deciding on what she would have later. Before she went down to the restaurant she phoned home and all was well. She felt unselfconscious as she ate her meal alone with two glasses of chilled white wine, enjoying the anonymity bestowed by a big city and the mature indifference to a woman dining on her own. Her main worry in coming to see her former husband was that it might upset her equilibrium, rekindle her long-lost feelings for him. His vulnerable state might have made her more susceptible to this happening. She was pleased, however, to feel nothing but relief that it was all over and that she could return to where she belonged with her duty done. She still thought him physically attractive even if his fleshy good looks had turned gaunt and angular. It was his neediness, his submission that ruled out any hint of regret. She lingered over her coffee, enjoying the furtive looks from the men and the friendly atmosphere of the restaurant, and the sense of the commune of travellers. It was also a welcome departure to be looked after and pampered for a change and it was with some reluctance that she eventually got up and took the lift back to her room. She read for a short time before falling into a deep, contented sleep between the starched white sheets.

She woke with a feeling of slight melancholy which could only be partly explained by the wine of the night before. She got ready quickly and fretfully and got to the station two hours before her train was due to leave. She thought of Robert's imploring eyes and toyed with the idea of going to see him again – there was just enough time – but she consciously delayed the moment with a coffee and croissant and an unnecessary visit to the loo until she could tell herself it was too late. The train pulled slowly out of the station and she looked out on the receding metropolis, wishing she knew how she felt.

CHAPTER 6

One week later Prior sat in the garden on a sunny early April day reading through the reports on him that had been written in preparation for his appeal to the Mental Health Review Tribunal. It was his legal right to see the reports, although third party information which might be deemed to put a third party at risk if the appellant had access to it could be removed at the discretion of the tribunal judge. The first two were the views of his consultant psychiatrist and a nurse on the ward and more or less described diagnosis, treatment, prognosis and risk, which Prior already knew about. They both recommended continuation of the section which by now only had two weeks to run anyway. The other, more in-depth file, was the social circumstances report.

He had been visited by a social worker from the community mental health team that would be responsible for his care on discharge. She was young – Prior put her at about twenty-eight – and filled him with a sense of unease. Her dark hair was cropped short and she wore carefully tattered jeans tucked in to desert boots at the calf. Her face was adorned with piercings and garish make-up. He liked to pride himself on not judging a book by its cover but her unsmiling expression and lack of any social graces was slightly unsettling on top of her appearance. She imparted an attitude of absolute indifference to him as a human being, of just seeing him as a vehicle to complete an objective. Her veneer, if that's what it was, was impenetrable and he had become morose and monosyllabic in response to her questions.

He shaded his eyes from the sun and began to read. Under the heading 'home and family circumstances' she had written:

'I met the patient on Oak Ward, Nathan Centre on Tuesday, 29th March, 2011 and interviewed him for approximately sixty minutes for the purpose of writing this social circumstances report. I have not met him before or since this one occasion.

Robert Prior was born on 27th October 1968, in Formby, Lancashire (now Merseyside). He achieved all normal milestones and attended grammar school, gaining A Level results which enabled him to attend Cambridge University from where he graduated with a first class honours degree in English. He is the elder of two brothers. His father died from a myocardial infarction in 1980 when Robert Prior was aged thirteen. In 1990 he married Caroline and they had three children, Laura born 1991, Graham born 1992, and Helen born 1994. In 1999 he moved to his current address, a two-bedroom flat in an East London suburb, following a job promotion. His family did not join him and his divorce was made absolute in 2001.

Mr. Prior was a poor historian and the author has based her report largely on access to case records and the testimony of those who know him, including ward staff and GP. With his permission I have spoken to work colleagues and his ex-wife to assist me in building up a picture of his life and formulating a plan for discharge. I attempted unsuccessfully to obtain the views of the nearest relative, his mother Mrs. Ethel Prior, but they are estranged and have not spoken to each other for twelve years.

Mr. Prior's pre-morbid personality indicates a male entrenched in pre-feminist attitudes. His work colleagues are almost exclusively male and his work genre appeals predominantly to the male gender. Since his divorce he does not appear to have had any relationships or made any close friends. He lives alone.'

Under various other headings she had written:

'His attitude towards me was obstructive and antagonistic. I was unable to build a rapport, and based on one relatively brief and unsatisfactory assessment I would defer to the opinions of my ward based colleagues regarding Mr. Prior's current mental health. I can confirm from his GP that there is no record of any previous psychiatric history. Regarding a discharge plan, I would envisage follow-up from the community mental health team which would include allocation of a care co-ordinator from the team to make regular home visits to provide monitoring, education and support as appropriate. He would be required to attend the lithium clinic for three monthly blood tests and to see a consultant psychiatrist at regular intervals.

Mr. Prior is in receipt of full pay at present up to a maximum of six months after which he goes onto half pay for a further six months. I spoke to his manager who indicated that he hoped a phased return to work, possibly in a reduced capacity, could be arranged when his mental health has stabilised.'

Under recommendations she had written:

'In view of the violence contained in Mr. Prior's index offence I would assess his risk of harm to others as high whilst his mental health remains an issue for concern as indicated by ward staff in my discussions with them. Mr. Prior also continues to be nursed under close observation due to potential suicide risk. It is therefore my opinion that it would be most unwise at this point to consider regrading him to informal status.'

Prior had been starting to feel a little bit better over the last day or two. The change in medication had sown some seeds and he experienced fleeting sensations of the person he really was. Brief flashes of optimism illuminated the possibility of a return to a life beyond this present purgatory. The report plunged him back to tremulous apprehension. He felt like a cork on top of a turbulent ocean at the mercy of the arbitrary currents beneath it. The cold dissection of his circumstances by a seemingly malevolent force with a mandate to influence the course of his life stunned him and in his vulnerable state he felt he could no longer count on any certitude.

He was joined on the bench by a patient from his ward, Steve, a large lugubrious man with a loud voice and a diagnosis of schizophrenia. He was a 'revolving door' patient, a fifty-year-old who had spent all of his adult life in and out of hospital. With the mutual telepathy of the mentally ill he discerned that all was not well with Robert. He spoke in a hoarse cockney accent.

"What's up Bob?" He looked at him with staring, ingenuous eyes, his concern authentic and empathic. Prior sighed.

"I've got my tribunal tomorrow. Just been reading the reports. These people think they own you." Steve suddenly took on a knowledgeable air. Prior could see the pleasure he felt at being on one of his own subjects. He thought to himself, *The poor guy's been forced to make a career out of his illness.*

"'Ad more tribunals than you've 'ad 'ot dinners Bob me lad. Now my advice to you is don't fight the section. Two is it you're on?"

Prior assented.

"Right. Well what you want is to get it made into a section 3. That way you'll be on section 117 aftercare which means you'll get more benefits. You'd qualify for severe disablement premium and..." Steve looked triumphant as he prepared to deliver the coup de grace, "the best thing is, if you have to go into a residential home you can keep your benefits – they don't have to go towards your care like they do for the poor sods not on 117. They get about £15 pocket money a week and that's it. Doesn't even cover their baccy." If Prior had been close to deflation, Steve had just totally exploded the balloon of optimism. Residential home? The gradual erosion of his self-determination had just taken a giant leap forward. His tenuous hold on reality was being sorely tested. He started to speak his objection, his expression a mixture of incredulity and anguish, but he stopped himself as he looked at Steve who was now staring ahead with a satisfied smile on his face, crowing in the wealth of his wisdom and obviously not listening to Prior. *Leave him with his dubious status intact,* he thought. *It's all the poor bugger's got.* Steve turned to him again.

"Now I didn't have to put anything on Bob. I was as mad as a box of frogs when I first went on a three. You might have to lay it on a bit if you know what I mean. You only have to be on a three once to get 117 for life so it won't stop you being able to appeal in future if you come back in on a three. Section 3 is for six months at first and after that for a year, but you can be regraded to informal at any time if you're better so don't worry about that." Prior stood up and patted his companion on the shoulder.

"Thanks for that, Steve. I'll keep it in mind."

Lunch was now being served in the canteen that looked out onto the garden he was in but he walked past it and took the stairs back to the ward and flopped onto his bed. He had no appetite for the food on offer, nor for the battles ahead.

***

Prior entered the meetings room off a highly polished corridor outside his ward and took a seat at a large mahogany table. The antiquarian elegance of the room contrasted sharply with the modern furnishings of the ward – it was as if a deliberate attempt had been made to foster a judicial atmosphere. Sitting opposite to him sat the three tribunal members. The chairperson in the middle was a retired solicitor, an elderly distinguished man in silver framed spectacles resting on the end of his nose. To his right sat a female GP and to his left another woman who was introduced as the lay member of the tribunal. Prior's own solicitor sat to his right and on his left were the social worker, ward nurse, and Dr. McKay. A minute taker and the clerk to the tribunal sat in a corner away from the main table.

The chairperson outlined the forms and procedures the meeting would follow and invited Prior's solicitor to advocate on behalf of his client. The overweight, shabby-looking man shuffled papers around the desk, dropped his pen and grunted as he groped for it on the floor, banging his head on the underside of the table as he rose. The legs of the trousers of his worn grey flannel suit rode up onto his fleshy calves during the commotion and as he began his address in a voice slightly breathless from his exertions, Prior closed his eyes and sighed in irritation. As he spoke however, Prior became gradually reassured.

"My client would like me to stress that he is most grateful for the opportunity to come here today to show that the continuation of his detainment would be entirely erroneous. He acknowledges that he experienced a breakdown of sorts and that he acted quite out of character due to various stresses occasioned by work and his domestic situation. I am sure you are aware that he is a highly intelligent individual with a first class honours degree from Cambridge University and a successful career. However, everyone has a breaking point and he had reached his. Again, he would like me to offer on his behalf his extreme gratitude to the ward team for their excellent work in restoring him on the road to recovery. He appreciates he is not quite there yet but as he can tell you in his own words later, he now feels 'one hundred times better' than when he was admitted. The grounds for detention under the Mental Health Act are clear and unequivocal. On the grounds of impaired mental health the patient must present a risk of harm to themselves, others, or of self-neglect, or their mental health itself must by its nature, degree, or both, be of sufficient concern to justify detainment.

"I submit that Mr. Prior presents no such risk, is entirely stable on medication, and that it would be in direct contravention of his human rights for him not to be discharged from section 2 immediately."

Get your retaliation in first, thought Prior as the chairman looked up and said, "Thank you Mr. Blake. We will now hear the views of the people involved. Dr. McKay, I'll start with you." He took out her report which he had read beforehand and asked, "You state your opinion that Mr. Prior should remain subject to the section. Could you expand on your conclusion, perhaps by outlining Mr. Prior's progress since admission and his current mental state?"

The consultant spoke concisely in her no-nonsense fashion chronicling Prior's traumatic arrival on the ward, his rapid tranquillisation, and subsequent descent from mania into depression. She ended by saying, "I have no doubt that with medication and the support of the community mental health team Robert will be able to regain his life and put this episode behind him. However, it has to be understood that he will be subject to relapse given unfavourable circumstances. I would partially agree with Mr. Blake that there are signs of improvement but in my opinion Robert remains profoundly depressed and there is some way to go before I would feel comfortable with him leaving hospital. He is only two weeks into a first admission for a severe mental illness and I feel it is too early to conclude that he have finished our assessment."

The chairperson invited questions from the two colleagues either side of him. The GP wished to clarify issues relating to lithium testing in the community and the length of time it was envisaged that Prior would need the support of the community team before being discharged back to the care of his GP. She also sought Dr. McKay's opinion on the nature and degree of his illness which she classified as bipolar affective disorder type 1 of quite severe degree.

The lay member had no questions but, in the way of meetings, wished to establish her presence by saying something so she explained in a rather long-winded fashion that the questions she was going to ask had already been answered. The chair turned to the solicitor again. "Mr. Blake. Is there anything you wish to ask Dr. McKay?" Blake, who had been slipping further and further down his chair, pulled himself up abruptly.

"Yes indeed. Thank you Mr. Chairman. Dr. McKay, you

acknowledge that there has been some improvement in my client's mood but you say that he remains profoundly depressed. From my position as a layperson in these matters would you be able to enlighten me as to the symptoms and signs you would be looking for on which to base this assumption?"

She launched straight into her reply. "Primarily physical symptoms – loss of appetite and sleep disturbance are the most common and these are both present in this case. Psychological symptoms can be numerous but we are looking at low mood, obviously, feelings of guilt and worthlessness, absence of hope for the future, suicidal ideation. In comparison with unipolar depression, bipolar depression is more likely to feature the melancholic symptoms mentioned. There will also be a greater tendency towards psychosis, and Mr. Prior has exhibited signs of this."

"You mention suicidal ideation and I understand this has been a concern on the ward. I am not aware, however, of any attempt by Robert to harm himself in any way."

"That's right. Unfortunately in my line of business we deal with uncertainties and unknowns in a culture of blame and recrimination. Not least from the learned people in Robert's own profession. Suicide rates are comparatively high in bipolar disorder, even when compared to those in unipolar depression, and the optimum period of likelihood of a suicide attempt is in the very early days of a sign of recovery. Risk predictability is exceptionally difficult in psychiatry. One's intervention always has to set the balance between the rights of the individual and the risks to themselves and others. In Robert's case it is the view of myself and the team that the risk of him harming himself is high at present and the ward environment and level of monitoring have reduced the opportunity for self-harm to virtually nil."

"And risk to others – is that a factor?"

"Currently, no. Risk based on previous history is now a feature of his risk assessment but I would only consider it to be a valid concern during an episode of mania."

"And self-neglect?"

"At both extremes of the illness self-neglect is a relatively high risk. Yes, at present I would hold concerns about Robert's ability to care adequately for himself."

Blake looked pensive and then addressed the chair. "No further questions."

The ward nurse supported the consultant's opinions and it was now the turn of the social worker to be questioned on the contents of her report. She stressed the brevity of her dealings with Prior and her deferment to the greater involvement of the ward team. She expanded on the form the community support would take and then answered questions from the tribunal members. In her facial expression and tone of voice she seemed to convey a bewildered impatience at the self-evidential nature of her replies. Blake was then invited to speak. He smiled engagingly at her and said, "You are a social worker I believe. Do you have any training in psychiatry?" She glanced to her right to look at him briefly before turning away and answering without looking at him.

"Yes, I am a mental health social worker, also an approved mental health practitioner."

"I see. So were you the practitioner who made the application for Mr. Prior's section 2?"

"No. It's done on a rota system and I wasn't on duty that day."

"Right. I just wanted to clarify that." He looked intently at her. "You don't like my client much do you Ms. Connolly?" The room seemed to come alive from its official torpor. She instinctively looked at the lay member of the tribunal whose eyes motioned her towards the chairperson who addressed the lawyer.

"I'm assuming, Mr. Blake, that your question bears some relevance to your client's interests?"

"Certainly more relevance than abstract judgements on Mr. Prior's supposed views on gender issues."

The chairman sighed. "You may answer the question." The social worker turned a viperous look on Blake.

"Like or dislike is immaterial. I'm just a professional person making an objective assessment on a patient."

"So on what grounds do you make this assumption about his 'entrenchment in pre-feminist attitudes' and how on earth is this relevant to his mental health?" He could see she was struggling to keep her temper.

"A number of things. His manager's patronising tone when I spoke to him, and his and Mr. Prior's use of trite, impertinent endearments when addressing me. Mr. Prior's inability to sustain even fundamental relationships with females. His refusal to co-operate with my assessment."

"Correct me if I'm wrong Ms. Connolly but I was under the impression that my client is supposed to be profoundly depressed. Wouldn't that impact on his ability to co-operate? The consultant has even referred to a degree of psycho-motor retardation." She was looking sideways now at Blake across her two colleagues.

"I thought your argument was that he wasn't sufficiently depressed to remain on the section."

"So Ms. Connolly, you are saying that he was sufficiently…" he searched for a word, "'undepressed' to be able to decide not to co-operate for whatever reason."

She did not try to conceal her exasperation.

"I've already told the tribunal that I defer to the opinion of Dr. McKay and the ward staff on Mr. Prior's mental health."

The chairperson's professional propriety had slipped in allowing the exchange to go as far as it had out of a purely human instinct to enjoy a good fight and he said belatedly and authoritatively, "I don't think this bickering is leading us anywhere. Have you any more questions Mr. Blake?"

"No."

He turned to Prior and smiled warmly. "Thank you for your patience. It can't be pleasant to have to listen to your life being dissected by us all. However, it is your turn now to make any comments you wish." Prior looked blank, his eyes focussed on the wall between two of the tribunal members. He had rehearsed this moment in the days leading up to it but now it had come he couldn't think of a thing to say. Everyone looked down uncomfortably except for Ms. Connolly, who trained her gaze on him. He turned his head towards her and concluded that she was relishing his discomfort. It acted as a spur.

"Thank you. The whole experience has not been pleasant, no. You all make your judgements on people guided by the behaviour you see but you have your own prejudices, values, preconceptions, agendas. It's not objective and psychiatry's hardly an exact science is it? How the hell do any of you know what's going on in my mind? I can't even put it into words. You've said it's a disorder of mood. Mood is feeling. By definition you can't put a feeling into words can you? Perhaps, given my circumstances, my subsequent behaviours and reactions were the only sane response. Who was it who said you'd have to be mad not to be depressed in today's world?" He paused and the brief window of lucidity fed by his antagonist had passed. His brain began to cloud again and he said haltingly and unconvincingly, "I'm not going to hurt myself or anybody else."

He felt tears welling up from nowhere and inwardly cursed his weakness, fighting not to show it externally. "I can look after myself, honestly."

The chair invited questions from his colleagues and the GP established Prior's spoken agreement to take his medication and accept help from the community team if discharged. The final question was from the lay member.

"If you were to be discharged from the section today, Mr. Prior, would you decide to leave immediately?" He looked at her suspiciously as he contemplated the question.

"I don't see why not. Yes, when my medication was ready. As I've said, I don't think I need to be on a section."

"Yes, I know, but there are people who are in hospital voluntarily who are not formally detained. You wouldn't consider listening to the opinions of the medical and nursing team then that you would benefit from a longer period on the ward?" Prior shifted in his seat.

"Well yes, I suppose I would think about it."

The chairperson thanked everyone for attending and instructed them to leave the room while they deliberated on their decision. After half an hour the clerk to the tribunal invited them to return and the chair addressed him directly.

"We've made our decision Mr. Prior, and that is that you will remain subject to section two of the Mental Health Act." The glint from the spectacles perched on the end of his nose now gave him a

Teutonic look. He was no longer the stern but kindly solicitor with whom he had sensed an earlier rapport.

"I can understand your disappointment and I can assure you we have deliberated at length. Ultimately we have concluded that it is in your own best interests to remain in hospital to continue the assessment. We all hope, and indeed expect, that your return to health is not far away and we wish you all the best for the future."

With that, he stood up and normality returned in place of the formality of the past hour as briefcases were snapped shut, chairs scraped, and tensions released in an outpouring of relieved chatter.

CHAPTER 7

Dominique's eyes opened at 5:00 a.m. as they did every morning without the need for the prompt of an alarm clock. She threw back the sheet covering her lithe naked body and crossed the stone floor to a bucket sitting in a corner. With an economy born out of habit and necessity she washed herself with the lather from a small bar of soap and rinsed the suds with an impossibly small amount of water which she pushed with a broom towards a small adjacent drain hole. From the top of a rudimentary chest of drawers she took the clothes that lay carefully folded and soundlessly slipped into underwear and a short smock dress, mindful of not waking her younger sister, asleep on the other mattress.

She stepped into flip-flops and went out into a yard enclosed by a ramshackle arrangement of wood, bricks, and metal. In one corner stood a makeshift fireplace with a base of corrugated iron. Beneath a grate supported by bricks was a small pyramid of paper and kindling wood which Dominique now lit with a match, and she watched fascinated by the daily conundrum of whether her construction of the night before would allow the paper to burn for a sufficient time and in correct proportion to ignite the wood above. It did, and when the flames were at their height she took some larger pieces of wood and placed them carefully on top. Her three young brothers were entrusted with the task of procuring the wood which they did with a keen enthusiasm, knowing their meagre pocket money was dependent upon ensuring a constant stock. After school they would comb the beach and construction sites for the lifeblood of a home without electricity. One of the few small advantages of living in a place where it hardly ever rained was that it could be stored outside without trepidation. When the flames had died and the logs glowed red, she placed an iron on the grate and took from a washing line four sets of school uniform, one female and three male. When the iron was hot enough, she pressed the clothes on a rectangular table and then filled a pan with water which she put over the fire.

The concrete single-storey house contained four rooms which were all fluid in function. It stood in a congested residential area of disparate properties where expedience and survival supplanted any aesthetic considerations. Nevertheless, the women were constantly to be seen using their precious water to scrub the front steps in a ritual of pride. Dominique's invalid mother had the luxury of a room where she could sleep alone but in the day the mattress was leant up against a wall and the room became their lounge until the woman returned to her bed.

Dominique now entered the fourth room – the smallest in the house – and went to a cupboard from which she took various items of food, carrying them outside and placing them by the fire. Into the now boiling water she dropped maize and beans which boiled for ten minutes before she added herbs, sweet potato, and cassava. When this was ready she left it simmering on the corner of the grate and covered the bread she had bought yesterday with a cloth to protect it from the flies which were now appearing as the temperature rose with the rising sun. She allowed herself the luxury of five minutes on a stool, squinting at the sun, imagining a day not filled with obligation and service.

Her large brown irises were encircled by clear, luminescent whites set in a long angular face of coffee colour below black glossy hair tied back in a ponytail. Its beauty was in its impression of unassuming benignity. She was nineteen, tall and slender, with a languor which belied her strength and tenacity. She began loading a wheelbarrow with empty twenty-five litre flagons which she trundled out of the yard and along a track of sand and dust towards the reservoir where water was dispensed from a large tank in return for some money. The sun was hot now and dogs littered her path, slumped in front of their houses waiting hopefully for the promise of breakfast. She joined the scrum that had formed, even at this early hour, struggling to maintain her place in the queue amidst the jostling throng, impatient to fill their containers and get on with their day.

She took a detour home via the bakery, her sinuous hands and forearms tensing against the weight of the laden barrow, where she bought bread and cakes. On a whim she purchased some bananas and tomatoes from the women sitting on the ground opposite in the long flowing gowns and headscarves of West Africa, dropping the money into an old tobacco tin without discourse. The haggling would come later with the arrival of the tourists.

Back at home the house had come alive. Her sister and brothers were sitting in the yard of the compound eating their cachupa povera with bread, dressed in their blue uniforms. They had taken food through to their mother who sat on the one easy chair they possessed, her head propped on one arm, picking unenthusiastically at the food on her lap. She grimaced in pain at each movement and eventually put the unfinished bowl of food on the floor and flopped back in her chair, her eyes wide and bemused as she stared up at the ceiling.

***

Dominique set off again in the direction of the town through the narrow, unnamed streets, arriving at the small Italian-owned hotel where she worked just after nine. She went through to the tiny staffroom and changed into a pink, candy-striped pinafore and began her routine of cleaning the guest rooms, changing beds and mopping corridors and public rooms until noon when she went to the small bar and served drinks to the customers sitting on the terrace and took their lunch orders. When lunch was over she returned to clean the rooms of the late risers and worked in the laundry until six, when she changed back into her own clothes and commenced the half-mile walk to the offices of a property company, a large glass-fronted one-storey building on the edge of the town, close to the beach and the more up-market hotels. In a large open-plan office, ten people of divergent nationalities sat at computer desks around a reception area of couches and easy chairs. Fans whirred as background to telephone conversations in various languages and the soon-to-set sun glinted on the west-facing windows. A thirty-something Caucasian woman yawned and stretched as she turned off her computer and leant back in her chair, calling across the room, "Hi Dom, that time already." Dominique smiled. Her Italian was almost fluent but she was still learning English. She tried to practice it at every opportunity.

"Oi Zina. Yes is already six o'clock. Time for you to go have funs." Two men were sitting at an adjacent desk and one made a remark in Portuguese followed by mutual laughter but Dominique didn't pick up what had been said. Zina swivelled her chair away from the desk and stood up. She was an inch taller than Dominique. Her wavy light brown hair was streaked with ash blonde and her thin lips and aquiline nose in a bleached, unblemished face gave her an intrinsic haughtiness that was further suggested by the shrewd pale blue eyes. She raised her voice.

"C'mon boys and girls. Dom wants to clean up."

Over the next half hour people gradually packed up and left as Dominique mopped and dusted and polished around them. She cleaned and restocked the lavatories and closed the blinds and at 7:30 p.m. she locked the front door with her set of keys and stepped wearily from the concrete veranda in front of the office onto the dirty sand below.

Back at home her sister and brothers sat round a candlelit table covered with paper and pens and books doing their homework. The two younger boys whooped with joy when they saw their sister and clung onto a leg each as she stroked their dark heads.

The oldest boy and the sister smiled at her, and they chattered about their day as Dominique kindled the ashes of the fire and put some more wood on, dragging the pan of cachupa back to the centre of the grate. Another two large covered pans of water simmered gently and she emptied them into an iron bath and threw in some washing powder and the pile of clothes that her younger siblings had discarded after school. She went into her bedroom and changed into shorts and a bra and threw her own clothes into the water, mixing it with the end of a broom and allowing the clothes to soak until the water was hand hot. She could hear her mother's snores from the house and she looked briefly pensive before returning to the practicalities of her existence. She rinsed and hung the clothes on a line strung high across the yard and settled the younger boys in bed, reading them a story before kissing them goodnight and blowing out the candle. The other two were still at the table, playing a board game now, and listening to the music coming from a battered little radio which crackled on the last legs of its batteries.

At last she could eat. Alone and in semi-darkness she sat on a stool in the yard and voraciously finished the remains of the stew, her natural demureness eclipsed by the strength of her hunger, and she treated herself afterwards to a small cake and a banana. With food came the instant exhaustion that cautioned her to leave it as late as possible and she doused the fire and re-laid it before moving her tired legs through to the bedside of her mother. She kneeled down and looked at her, torn between wanting to speak and not wanting to disturb her deep sleep. She bent to kiss her softly on the forehead, her tears rolling down her cheeks and falling onto the face of the prostrate woman beneath her, grown old before her time.

***

Abdulai N'Jie wandered back towards the town along the small jetty from where he had been scanning the beach for early rising tourists. He walked with a loose-limbed swagger and exchanged affectionate insults with the other young men who hung around a square of sand and rubble fringed by offices and shops. His own shop was on one of the corners and he mounted the step in front of it and walked through past the wooden carvings and paintings to a room at the back where he lit a cigarette and opened a can of Coke. Photographs of people in formal groupings dressed in full African costume adorned the walls and he looked at them again for the umpteenth time.

The emptiness of the day stretched ahead of him and he sat back in a chair and put his feet up on a chair on the desk in front of it, trying to think of new ways to fill the void. He was barely surviving. Four years ago, aged twenty-three, he had left his village in West Africa with plans of making enough money to support not only himself but also his extended family. He had imagined triumphant returns to his homeland and being met at the airport by his grateful kinfolk laden with gifts and money and a new sophistication. He had not even been able to scrape up the airfare to go back and they were becoming a distant memory. Most of the stock he had brought with him still sat growing dust in the shop. Hackneyed and unwanted, he was sick of looking at it. Cumbersome, weighty carvings of elephants stood at the entrance to the shop. Vast paintings of sunsets and fishing boats filled the walls. Who on earth would be putting them in a suitcase or taking the trouble and expense to ship them home? The expatriates had bought a few items when he first arrived but now his merchandise had become passé – a joke even, and he had taken on the resigned pessimism of the ill-fated angler.

He locked the shop's door and began a leisurely walk along the main shopping street of the small town. He passed the bank and coffee shops and stopped at one opposite the catholic church where an Italian girl he knew would give him a cup on the house. They exchanged pleasantries in her mother tongue, bound by the commonality of being strangers in a strange land. He moved on past the plethora of property businesses – buying, selling, renting, managing. A new landscape was being fashioned on the island and the sharks weren't only confined to the sea. The craft shops were dotted here and there, anachronistic and irrelevant. African women sat chewing on sticks at the side of the road, selling cigarettes and sweets. Their turnover was slow but at least they were selling something that people needed. On a corner where a business hiring out quad bikes stood, he turned left and walked along the dusty tracks separating the rows of shacks that passed as roads. At a junction he entered the incongruous refuge of a cyber café and spent the remainder of the morning trawling the internet. The café was owned by a friend from his own country who allowed him free access when computers were not being used. In turn, Abdulai would steer tourists wanting to send emails or make phone calls in his direction by handing out cards. At one o'clock, when the café closed for the afternoon, he joined his compatriot and his family in the yard and they grouped round a large oval plate of benechin, a dish of predominantly rice with a spiced stew running through it amongst isolated pieces of chicken and vegetables. They all ate from the same plate, plunging their fingers into the mound, talking and laughing in their own Wolof tongue. In the way of his culture he felt no embarrassment at being a recipient of this charity and no grudge was even considered, let alone held.

The town had shut down in the afternoon heat and an air of serenity, broken only by the occasional bark of a dog, pervaded the air as he walked back to his shop. He stretched out on a makeshift bed and dozed, soporific from the heavy meal. His morning surfing had brought no enlightenment, no eureka moment. He had all too quickly turned from exploring ideas for business ventures to the football websites where he pored over the week-end results from around the world and looked at the goals. He was himself a good player, fast and strong with an innate control fashioned from practising with almost anything vaguely spherical from when he first learnt to walk. It was still a dream he held – to be a professional footballer – but it was receding with the years. He was twenty-seven now and opportunity was scarce.

At four o'clock he opened the shop again and spent the rest of the 'working' day in the company of his fellow traders, hanging around the square, kicking a football, laughing and shouting, breaking off abruptly when a white figure passed by. The absence of any competitive jostling between them was striking as tourists were cajoled in a seemingly random rota. Abdulai had one bite and slipped the ten euro note exchanged for a small painting into his back pocket. He would treat himself to a few beers tonight at one of the bars showing a game. He had been brought up in the Muslim faith but was selective with its impositions. At seven thirty he once again closed up his shop and jumped from the stoop, wistfully admiring the curvaceous figure he had grown used to seeing walk gracefully away from the office opposite at this time of the evening.

CHAPTER 8

Prior woke and almost immediately felt something was different. Not the smell of feet from the man in the next bed. That was as inevitable as death and taxes. No alteration to the stark perspective of the dormitory where he had been incarcerated for the past five weeks. No. He had regained consciousness in something approaching daylight for the first time since admission and he was aware of an almost forgotten feeling akin to that of a Saturday of his schooldays or a last day of term.

He might be going home today, and the fact that he had enjoyed a good night's sleep without waking at four to a sense of dread and apprehension was proof that he was ready. He almost threw back the covers and swung his legs off the bed. He even felt hungry, but he wouldn't change the habits of a lifetime by taking a breakfast of anything heavier than his usual cup of coffee and a cigarette. He shaved carefully with a steady hand and dressed in what he had called the demob suit that Dave Partridge had brought in – black trousers, white button-down collar shirt and grey V-neck pullover. The black brogues felt uncomfortable on feet spoilt by weeks of slippers and trainers but the smell of the polish he had applied last night and the black stains on his hands evoked the memory of the excitement of occasions – weddings, christenings, the award ceremony when he won sportswriter of the year.

He walked down the stairs and got a cup of coffee from the machine, taking it out to the garden where he sat down on a bench and lit up, mercifully free now of the necessity for the accompaniment of his nurse jailer. He exhaled, looking into the sun that was rising above the little community to the East that he called home and to where he prayed he would be returning later today.

He was no longer a sectioned patient. After twenty-eight days the section two had lapsed and Dr. McKay had not applied for the six-month treatment order, section three.

Prior could have taken his own discharge one week ago which would have been against the medical advice offered by his consultant who felt that although he was not detainable, he would benefit from a little longer in hospital. He also knew that a qualified nurse could impose a six-hour section five/four to have him reassessed if he decided to leave and he didn't want to tempt the wrath of the Gods or that of a particularly unpleasant male nurse who seemed to have taken a dislike to him. They had you all ways but this was no time for negativity.

The sun was quite hot and he took off his pullover and rolled his shirtsleeves to the elbow, and undid the second button of his shirt, looking with affection at the isolated figures on different stages of their journeys through insanity. A girl he had not seen before lay on her front a few yards away from him, her legs bent at the knee, her bare calves moving rhythmically side to side. The pallor of her colouring and the lightness of her red hair, augmented by her pale grey tracksuit, gave her a ghostly look. He could hear her talking to herself, the expletives slightly alarming coming from a face so young and ostensibly innocent. She turned her head to look at Prior and her watery green eyes conveyed an indescribable other-worldliness that he had come to recognise as being a result of opiate addiction. She said in a childlike voice, "Got a fag, mate?" He went to his top pocket and pulled out a cigarette which he offered to her. She took it without any expression or thanks and said in the same toneless voice as before, "Got a light, mate?" He offered her his lighter which she used and then put in her pocket. He felt awkward. Why can't life ever be exclusively good for more than ten minutes? Hell truly is other people.

"I'll need my lighter." The girl, who had now resumed her position facing away from him, did not turn round and raised her clenched right hand above her head with the middle finger erect by way of reply as the smoke wafted towards him. He felt faintly ridiculous. To bicker over a lighter with a young patient would be undignified. To walk away without saying anything would involve submission, loss of face. He sought a compromise and pulled out another cigarette.

"Have you got a light please?" The question did not seem to register and he repeated it. The girl seemed to be miles away but as Prior was about to accept defeat and leave, she surprised him by going to her pocket and throwing the lighter in his direction. He lit up and the glow of satisfaction returned. As he smoked he glanced at her and felt the same stab of compassion as when Wesley was retreating from his flat. Her lank greasy hair had parted to reveal an angry-looking teenage spot on her neck. Her pink ankle socks and white trainers were filthy and her face, now turned to one side and supported by a bony hand on the end of an emaciated forearm, looked resigned to a life of inevitable misery. He got up and laid the lighter on the ground near her face with another two cigarettes. Her eyes moved to the objects without a movement of the head in a childlike way that made him feel further vindicated.

At 11:00 a.m. he once again entered the meeting room with its sea of faces all trained on him as the object of their attention. They had become all too familiar to him with the exception of a heavy man in his fifties, too big for the chair he was sitting in, his face pink and moist from the hurry to be there on time and the padded anorak he had not removed.

"Sit down Robert," said Dr. McKay, smiling at him in what he could only describe as a maternal way. He found it comforting and reassuring rather than condescending. He spoke cheerfully, conscious of an impulse to convey an impression that all was well.

"Isn't this jolly? I'm going to miss our little meetings." He instantly regretted the slightly facetious tone – she might think he was on the way up again. He tried to attenuate the remark with a hint of gravitas in his smile.

"Yes, so am I Robert. How do you feel now?"

"Almost there, Doctor. Obviously a bit shell-shocked but nothing that anyone wouldn't feel after five weeks away from the world in a place like this." He looked suddenly perturbed. "Not that I mean that as a criticism. Of course not. I've been very well looked after on the whole and I'm just pleased to feel more like my old self."

"Well, I'm glad to hear it. I plan to discharge you today – are you comfortable about that?"

He suppressed a smile and answered, "Very comfortable." She looked happy. Another freed-up bed awaiting some other poor sod, he supposed.

"Right then." She gestured to the man Robert didn't know. "This is Charlie Vaughan. He's going to be your Community Mental Health Nurse or CPN for short. Did you want to say anything Charlie?" Prior correlated the P in CPN to the originally inoffensive 'psychiatric' and mused on the need to change terms applied to disability; not because of the words themselves so much as the cruel human attitude to infirmity. Psycho, maniac, spas, mong. He wondered how long it would be before 'bipolar', 'Down's syndrome' and 'cerebral palsy' would need changing in the light of a new slang connotation.

The man had been sitting uncomfortably, waiting for his lines with a nervous smile on his lips, and he appeared relieved as he held out a large, muscular hand. His voice was deep, the accent not pronounced but immediately identifiable as Welsh.

"Yes indeed. Hello Robert. Is it okay to come and see you at home or would you prefer to come to our office?"

Prior thought briefly.

"You could come to my flat I suppose."

"Okay then – I'll give you an appointment after the meeting. Basically I'm there to help in any way that's necessary and to give advice and support. You'll have to come to our lithium clinic every three months to have your bloods done and you'll be seeing the community consultant psychiatrist periodically. I'll explain my role in more depth when I next see you."

Dr. McKay took over again.

"So Robert, we just need to order your take-home medication." She looked at the ward nurse who confirmed it was ready.

"You'll receive two weeks supply and we'll fax the prescription to your GP. It should be ready to collect before our supply runs out but if not, tell Charlie. I urge you to take it, Robert; it's going to help keep you well." She added with a wry smile, "And out of places like this." She stood up and they shook hands and an appointment was made for the CPN to call the following week. Prior went to his bed and put his meagre belongings into the grip that Caroline had brought in what seemed like so long ago. He went to the office to collect his medication, said his goodbyes and went down the stairs and through the automatic doors to resume the illusion of freedom.

***

On the top deck of the bus he surveyed the machinations below with a slight sense of awe at the synchronous order but also with a detached, disconnected feeling that caused the beginnings of a spiral of anxiety. This was a world which he no longer felt a part of – at least not on the same terms as before. His isolation was reinforced by the self-containment of his fellow passengers and his certain knowledge of their complete indifference to the concerns and welfare of anyone but themselves beyond that needed for their own survival. That his knowing this was as a result of it being his own attitude was no consolation. He felt an unexpected nostalgia for the ward, with its slavery to the rituals of time and tasks, the abdication of responsibility, the 'caring' of one human being for another. Only motivated by remuneration, of course, but like the supermarket chain that imposes on its staff an insistence on trite platitudes of civility – 'sorry for your wait', 'have a nice day' – the brain has the capacity to suspend reality and imagine a genuine altruism. To what extent the germ of institutionalisation had taken hold would be revealed in the days ahead.

The nearest bus stop was half a mile from his house and the journey was arduous. He felt weak and slowed by the drugs and the noise and speed and fumes from the vehicles on the A-road he walked alongside made him uneasy after the relative tranquillity of the hospital. He crossed at a junction in trepidation, his mind not quite trusting what his eyes were telling him. He felt a little better as he turned off to walk through the suburban streets of semi-detached houses. The bag felt heavy to his unused right arm and he transferred it to his left for a few yards. As he came to the park gates his flat became visible in the distance and he felt ambivalence; pleased that refuge was in sight; despondent at the chaos he knew awaited him.

He let out a sigh as he closed the door behind him. He had entertained a faint hope that Caroline might have restored some order but she hadn't. He held no grudge – he knew she had done more than enough for him. It was worse even than he had imagined.

If he had doubted the justification for his incarceration it now confronted him in sordid admonishment in the sights and smells that assaulted his senses. There was no chair to sit on so he cleared a space in the living room and sat down on the floor. It was 2:00 p.m. on a Thursday and he had a lot of thinking to do.

He felt confused. The anti-psychotic drugs had compromised his intellect, dulled his cognitive function, and he was out of the habit of making decisions. How was he going to cope again? The rug had been pulled from under his feet. The instinctive spontaneity, the certainties of his previous life were no more. He was an accident waiting to happen. The words of the charge nurse came to him and pulled him back from the brink. He began to practice the square breathing and tried to replace negative with positive thought. He had never been a list writer until the episode of mania but he felt in his pocket for a pen and ripped a scrap of cardboard from one of the empty boxes and wrote down: 'contact work, sort flat, take medication, phone bank, shopping, clean car.' He drew a line to form a supplementary column and headed it 'Flat', which he underlined. He felt a bit better already. He paused for a few minutes, his eyes circumnavigating the wreckage, and began to write under the heading: 'bins, assemble furniture, blinds, tip, sort rooms, clean'. He went to the phone to listen to his messages. There were only two – one each from his gas and water suppliers touting for insurance business.

At eight, showered and changed, he poured his first alcoholic drink for five weeks and sat back on his new couch warmed by a small glow of satisfaction. He felt he had made good inroads and he gave himself the rest of the evening off. He had tackled the most onerous job first by phoning his sports editor who told him to enjoy a long weekend and come in on Monday morning for a chat. He then started on the kitchen, carrying malignant, foul-smelling black bags down to the bin until it was full and then loading the remainder into his car along with the mountains of packaging and going to the tip. Something was nagging away at the back of his mind, depleting the pure satisfaction he customarily felt at converting his unwanted paraphernalia into someone else's problem and as he started the car to return home he remembered what it was. Dr. McKay had been vague and ambiguous about whether he could keep his driving licence but had sown seeds of doubt based on his diagnosis and medication or a combination of both. He couldn't recall if she had said she would inform the DVLA or whether the onus was on him. He made a mental note to research it online later and he added this to his list back at the flat. He managed to squeeze the rest of the rubbish into the car to make it his last journey for the moment and he sat hemmed in and close to the windscreen, gears one, three, and the handbrake only operable by fierce pressure to repel an encroaching broken mirror sliding about on the front passenger seat. He was able to park fairly centrally and walked diligently to the various skips putting the appropriate waste into its allotted place. The workers sat around a table outside a shed drinking tea and smoking as they always seemed to when Prior was there, unconcerned by what was going where.

He had then sorted what items needed to be in which room, tuning in the TV in its rightful place in the sitting room and setting up his new music system. He rebooted the computer and sifted and opened the tiny percentage of pertinent emails from the mass of irrelevance and then finished assembling the flat-pack furniture. He cleared the mound of clothes from a bed so he would have somewhere to sleep and after going through his post, his final job for the day was to put up the louvre blinds. He approached this task with great trepidation based on previous vexatious experience, knowing it could develop into one of those early hour of the morning nightmares, but to his surprise and delight it went smoothly and he played with it like a child, opening and closing the slats with a sense of wonderment at his proficiency.

His second drink went quickly to his head and he made it the last of the evening. He was going to fight this demon and live a life on his own terms. He made a coffee and ate the sandwiches he had bought in the garage on his way back from the tip and began planning his tasks for the next day, drawing lines through those already completed. He saw no reason why everything wouldn't be finished by this time tomorrow and he got into bed and lay down feeling as good as he had felt in an awfully long time.

***

Dave Partridge welcomed him into his office with a wide smile on his large face, one hand on the open door, the other on Prior's shoulder. Prior had come up on the tube and felt frail and anxious. He had walked quickly to the editor's office looking straight ahead, trying to avoid catching the eye of the people who knew him.

"Sit down old lad." When the normal pleasantries had been completed, Prior could see that Partridge felt uncomfortable. He was out of his comfort zone and had a very antiquated attitude towards mental illness despite paying lip-service to the politically correct dictates of the day. He acknowledged as much.

"Now I've got to confess Bob, I'm not on very solid ground here. The bottom line is you're a damn good journalist and I don't want to lose you, so you can rest assured there. I've had a word with occy health and they're happy to leave it between myself and your mental health care team. You can of course go to see them if you want though. I've also spoken to HR who will set up a more formal meeting after we've had this little chat. Now I'm going to run my idea past you and you say what you think." He paused for effect and said, "The cricket season is starting." His voice took on a wistfulness laced with sarcasm. "Ah… the sound of leather on willow, the starched creams, the sense of fair play. Well, we both know that's all gone. Cricket's cutting edge now with 20:20 and betting scandals and the decline of the Aussies and our resurgence. I want to raise its profile on the paper. It has more appeal now for the common man and who better to be our new cricket correspondent than your good self. As before, Bob, you've got a free rein to go whither you want but obviously you'll take in all the international games and big domestic one-dayers. We've got the Sri Lankans and Indians this summer and then two 20:20s with the Windies in September. Barry will carry on in your old job as chief sports writer – I think he's doing pretty well."

Prior remained impassive. He had been tracking his replacements since he began to emerge from the darkness. Dave himself had taken over initially as a stop-gap. Dull, pedantic dirges about various, to Prior, trivial issues that he had a bee in his bonnet about. Then Barry Noble. Prior winced daily at the superficiality and the bias towards football and he had now stopped reading him – it was too painful.

"So to my way of thinking, Bob, this will break you back in gently and we can reassess in early October before the winter tours. Tony's been doing the bits and pieces of cricket in the close season but it's not really his forte. As I said, I've spoken with HR who envisage a phased return, gradually building your hours back up to full time. Tony can fill in when you're off until then. So what do you think?"

Prior had been listening intently, his emotions darting in different directions. It was a demotion and loss of status but he loved cricket and it was an easy option for him. His pride made him angry – he was being punished for being ill – but discretion told him he was now in uncharted waters and maybe this was the sensible option. He tried to sound buoyant.

"Sounds good to me Dave. What if I'm back to feeling A1 by October? Is the old job still open?" Partridge looked doubtful and cleared his throat.

"Er… well of course that's something we'll consider when we review things." He picked up the phone and spoke to someone in Human Resources. "Just a minute." He looked at Prior. "Friday, 10:00 a.m. okay for you Bob to see HR?"

He nodded.

"Okay, see you then." He put down the phone and stood up. Prior sensed an unease in him, a distance. "Got to go for our Monday meeting now Bob, so I'll see you Friday. Just settle back in at home 'til then." He forced a smile and offered his hand. The invitation to attend the meeting, even briefly to reacquaint, was not made and Prior's anxiety dissipated with the relief. Partridge said heartily, "Good to have you back on board," but the darting eyes conveyed a different message. On their way out through the newsroom they couldn't avoid bumping into some of his colleagues and the lack of a previous rapport and their suspicion and unease at the latter developments was emphasised by the polite handshakes and remarks and the absence of any bonhomie or empathy. Bayliss shifted uneasily and smirked self-consciously and there was further relief all round when he left the room and took the stairs down to the foyer.

The tube was relatively tolerable after that ordeal and even the deluge that fell on him from a capricious April sky on his way home from the station could not dampen the warm feeling inside as he contemplated some return to normality in his new palatial home.

CHAPTER 9

Charlie Vaughan sat at his desk in the large carpeted office waiting for the computer to let him in. The other nine desks were unoccupied and he was alone. He liked to get in early and have half an hour of peace and tranquillity with a cup of tea before his colleagues arrived. He was becoming increasingly aware of feelings of alienation from them. They were almost all a good deal younger than him and he had to struggle to suppress an almost constant irritation when he was around them. He spent his working life now in a state of quiet desperation and cursed the lassitude that had stopped him from pushing for promotion when the opportunities had presented themselves. At least now he would have been able to dictate to these people from the blessed isolation of his own office. When the last of them had dribbled in at 9:30 they turned their chairs round to face each other and a short meeting ensued as they shared their itineraries for the day and discussed potential problems. Vaughan had a day of five home visits ahead of him. This was the part of the job he enjoyed most, vastly preferring as he did the company of his patients to that of his workmates. The only drawback was the mountain of reportage that had to accompany any patient contact, necessitating marathon spells in front of the screen. He walked a tightrope where every line typed had to be imagined in the context of a subsequent enquiry into the care and treatment of X. He left his third call of the morning at midday and drove to one of his usual haunts where he parked in a quiet setting and ate his packed lunch with his newspaper and half an ear to the Radio 2 lunchtime programme. He looked forward to this small comfort throughout the morning and resented passionately the occasions when other obligations necessitated alternative lunchtime arrangements. The worst scenario was when he had to attend some mind-bending day course and make forced conversation over a cholesterol-laden buffet with people he felt he had absolutely nothing in common with. How he longed for the sanctity of his car at those moments. It was customarily with a deep sigh and heavy heart that he dusted the crumbs from his shirt and trousers onto the floor mat and turned on the ignition. Today, however, he did so with slightly more enthusiasm than usual. His first appointment of the afternoon was a new patient who promised to be an interesting case.

It was a constant source of irritation to him that mental health patients always seemed to live at addresses that were impossible to find. Today was no exception as he searched vainly for flat 4, 113, Dulwich Road. He found 111 and 115 alright and assumed the un-numbered house between them must be 113. There was no entrance from the front of the building and he opened a large double gate at the side and walked round to the rear. Cars were parked on a tarmac area rimmed with unkempt gardens bursting free from the constraints of a severe winter. The numbers below the six bells on the red brick wall to the side of a communal door had faded and become completely illegible. Charlie made a guess at number four and was about to try another bell when he heard footsteps on the stairs. The door opened and Robert Prior stood before him with a baffled look on his face. He didn't recognise the bulky stranger on his doorstep. Vaughan introduced himself and his face lit up in recollection.

"Of course, Charlie. I'm so sorry – I'd completely forgotten you were coming. Come on up." The CPN accepted Prior's offer of a cup of tea and sank back into the comfortable cushions of the very new and very expensive sofa, soporific from lunch and the early afternoon testosterone dip of the middle-aged male. He closed his eyes fleetingly, teasing himself with the fancy of sleep and opened them quickly at a sound from the adjacent kitchen. It wasn't Prior coming back though and he looked around the room, admiring the opulence and its clean orderliness. Most unusual in a male living alone. He compared it favourably to the jaded, over-cluttered house his wife had turned into a monument to their departed children, parents, youth, and person she could have been if she hadn't wasted her life on him.

Prior kicked the door open and set the drinks down on mats which matched the black and gold wallpaper and Charlie experienced a familiar feeling of ineffectuality. He was here to try to help this man but whether he could was another matter. He was conscious of not only the physical intrusion but also that of supplying false hope with very little substance with which to back it up. It wasn't so bad if there was a clinical intervention such as giving an injection or taking blood to validate his presence but words alone often felt empty and inadequate. He had been reading Prior's column for years and this only added to the pressure. He spoke rapidly, searching for an articulacy and economy that would appease the dubious expression of the wordsmith opposite.

"I'll tell you a bit more about why I'm here, Robert – I'm not sure how much you know about the role of a community psychiatric nurse."

Prior smiled. "Absolutely nothing."

"Right. Well at its most basic level I'm the link between you and your consultant psychiatrist, Dr. Patel. You'll see him about once every six months but I'll see you regularly to monitor your mental health and if there are any concerns I can get you an earlier consultation. We hope to build what we call a therapeutic relationship whereby there is two-way trust and hopefully allows you to talk to me about anything you want without fear of judgement. See me as a support mechanism both emotionally and practically. We can have a wide scope of intervention, taking in mental health, physical health, finances, accommodation, leisure, employment, medication, substance abuse, risk. That's the overview but obviously everyone is an individual and we'll be making a care plan that is tailored to your particular situation and needs at some stage soon. In bipolar disorder the current thinking is that it's useful to compile a checklist of prodromal relapse signatures, if there are any, so we can maybe nip a manic episode in the bud. I'm also here to provide education on healthy lifestyle options for both your physical and mental health." Vaughan paused and saw Prior's pensive expression. He felt a slight embarrassment at how patronising his ritual blurb may sound to some and said hurriedly before Prior had the chance to speak, "I'm sure a lot of this is teaching my grandmother to suck eggs Robert but bear with me and tell me to shut up when you've had enough." Prior smiled.

"Where the hell does that come from – 'teaching my grandmother to suck eggs'? I'm sure my rag has explained its origin at some time along with a lot of other curious idioms. While we're on the subject – prodromal's new to me." Charlie looked vacant. It was an example of the newspeak of his profession that he trotted out with little regard to its meaning and he thought quickly, anxious to preserve some credibility.

"Er… prior to breakdown – early signs of or triggers to relapse." He searched in vain for the term in a dictionary later so needn't have worried about the faint whiff of charlatanry in the air.

Prior continued, "No, don't worry Charlie – is it Charlie or Charles?"

"Charlie's fine."

"No, don't worry, that all sounds good. Any help greatly appreciated at the moment but hopefully not forever." Charlie picked up on the implicit question.

"It's a bit early to say how long you'll need secondary mental health care. If you keep taking the medication I see no reason why you won't be discharged back to the care of your GP in the future."

"So keep taking the tablets." He looked upwards and pictured a lifetime of battling to keep his weight down with a head that felt like it was stuffed with cotton wool instead of a brain.

"What about when I go back to work full-time – how could you see me then?"

"Is that on the cards?"

"Oh yes. I'm seeing my HR department on Friday to discuss a phased return to work. I should be full-time in about two or three months maximum."

"Well I suppose if you're well enough to be working full-time we would regrade your care level. You'd just see your consultant periodically and have your bloods taken every three months. You could go to your GP for that." Prior took a sip of coffee and took out a cigarette, offering the packet to Charlie as an afterthought. The latter looked sheepish but manoeuvred his bulk to the front of his chair and stretched out a hand to take one.

"Thanks. I'm trying to give up and don't bring any into work. Just the odd one at home." He took a deep drag and smiled. "Luxury. A cigarette indoors with a cup of tea. How we took such simple pleasures for granted not so long ago. My wife would scalp me if she caught me smoking in the house or the car."

Prior glanced at his balding pate and said, "Looks like she already has," and they both let out a belly laugh in genuine amusement. After the preliminary appraisals both men seemed to have decided that they liked each other and the atmosphere felt relaxed. Vaughan reluctantly steered the conversation back to its professional purpose.

"So how are you feeling now, Robert?" Prior had grown to hate this question, thrown out so casually and so often in the past few weeks. How to find the middle ground between the glib and the self-obsessed. He knew they had to ask it but somehow it emphasised the gulf in their respective human status with its absence of reciprocity.

"Better I suppose. In one sense. I'm not making an arse of myself. But then again, when I was, I've never felt so 'happy' in all my life. Now I feel sort of flat. Not miserable like I was on the ward – just finding it a bit hard seeing the point of anything. A bit slowed, mentally and physically."

"Don't expect too much of yourself. You've been through a lot. You're still getting used to new medication, new circumstances. Things will fall back into place." A silence ensued. The platitudes hung in the air. Prior's face hardened and his head turned to seek out eye contact.

"If you really want to know how I'm feeling, I'm feeling that my life's not my own anymore. Controlled by dullards at work. Controlled by you people and your bloody sections and sub bloody sections. Controlled by chemicals. Controlled by the guesswork and uninformed opinion that seems to pass for psychiatry." His head dropped. He had expressed the thoughts that had been crystallising for some time. He was sorry that Vaughan had borne the brunt. Charlie's hangdog face looked even more doleful as he prepared a reply. He was becoming slower to respond to the unexpected these days, falling as he was into the habit of turning the job into a rote whereby he could do as little thinking and working as possible based on the wealth of his experience. He was becoming burnt out. He still however held a candle for the mentally ill and his ire rose out of a sense of betrayal.

"Nobody wants you to have this illness, Robert. And I can assure you nobody wants to curtail your freedom one iota more than is absolutely necessary, least of all me. We've come a long way from the days of the asylum; and let's be honest, that's almost entirely down to these drugs everyone so despises. Alright, it's an old cliché and I'm sick of saying it, but if you've got diabetes you take insulin. You've got a simple imbalance of brain chemistry so you take something to correct it. Because it's the brain, okay some of the side-effects are a bit numbing but it has to be better than the illness. In time I'm sure we'll be able to reduce the Abilify or even stop it altogether." He paused for emphasis. "You suffer from bipolar disorder Robert – a proper clinical manifestation and not some kind of chattering classes designer accoutrement. Now that *will* control you and wreck any kind of order in your life if you leave it untreated. See it as the treatment giving you your autonomy back rather than taking it away. If you want to value self-determination above mental wellness that is your choice but in my opinion it is the wrong choice." Prior had been staring out of the window through the new louvre blinds as Vaughan spoke. He turned his eyes towards him again.

"Have you ever taken any of these tablets?"

"No. I don't have bipolar."

"So how do you know what they make you feel like?" Charlie was disappointed. He had been here so many times before and he expected better from Prior. He shook his head and declined to answer. He would have liked to have reeled off his anecdotal experience of the results of people not complying with medication but he felt the conversation had gone far enough for a first session. He had to build a relationship and work with this man. Prior felt better for expressing his previously undefined feelings of discontent despite appreciating some of the inescapable logic in Vaughan's replies. He too felt disinclined to continue the sparring. They could take it up on a subsequent occasion. He gave the nurse a conciliatory look.

"I'm not getting at you Charlie, I'm really not. You asked me how I felt and I've told you, whether I'm right or wrong."

"Sure – and very normal feelings in your shoes. I'm sure we'll revisit the subject." The work of the call was over and he enjoyed reversing the roles for the remainder of his time. "Can I say, Robert, that I'm a big fan of your writing." Prior gave a self-deprecating shrug and smiled. He had been wondering if Vaughan was aware of him.

"Thanks. Yeah I'm looking forward to getting back to it. You like sport then do you?"

"Very much. Rugby union mostly, being a Welshman, but all sports really."

"Where are you from?"

"Llandudno. Not exactly the heart of the rugby culture but Welsh nonetheless. And you?"

"I'm from a place called Formby. It's about thirteen miles from Liverpool."

"Yes, I know. Hotbed of football." They talked about sport and Charlie listened spellbound as Prior spoke with the knowledge of the insider. It was with a sharp jolt that he glanced at his watch which showed that he should have been with his next patient ten minutes ago. He scrawled the date and time of their second appointment on a scrap of paper and hurried off to his car, a munificent smile on Prior's lips as he watched his new friend take his leave.

***

For the remainder of April and throughout May, Prior's changed life took shape. His editor went back on a promise to allow him freedom to set his own agenda. At their weekly meetings he was given specific assignments for the week ahead and Partridge appeared intractable and autocratic in the face of any alternatives he suggested. He sensed instinctively the satisfaction his colleagues were deriving from his reduced status. He began to feel like a cub reporter again but he knew that he was on slippery ground and had to keep quiet and go along with it. He couldn't decide whether his boss was exercising a prudent caution or extracting retribution for the abuse he had received during the incident at the pub.

A damp and disappointing June did not improve his situation and on the limited occasions when international cricket was possible the action was anticlimactic, a graceless England proving embarrassingly superior to the opposition. Prior felt even further alienated from his jingoistic, gloating colleagues. He wanted to see proper competitive sport irrespective of who won. An article he wrote to this effect was binned by Partridge who preferred Barry Noble's 'barmy army' perspective. He had an intuition that he was viewed as a renegade and he thought he heard the words 'haw haw' on one occasion when he entered a press box which went ominously quiet in his presence. Throughout this time and into a July and August that got even worse on the weather and professional fronts – India of all people were decimated by a rampant England – Charlie's visits helped him to just about keep things together. They seemed to help him as much as they helped Prior. They both poured out their jaundiced views on an increasingly imperfect world, their periodic pauses for a conciliatory reference to 'grumpy old men' allowing them licence to continue their diatribes against the usual suspects – the health and safety culture, political correctness, IT, and Charlie's favourite bugbear, the criminal waste and inefficiency of health and social services. The mounting discontent of the previous months and years took flight in the presence of a similarly embittered listening ear and the words came in a cathartic stream. He paused now and again for a cursory question related to Prior's health before ploughing on again, his guilt over his self-indulgence assuaged. Robert spoke mainly on work-related subjects too, conscious of a whine in his voice he was unable to dispel. On a daily, hourly, basis he was reminded of his diminution in status and he worked in a limbo of impotent rage at a discrimination he felt unequipped to deal with. Charlie urged patience, tried to massage his ego and suggested a counselling referral which Prior declined through an instinctive mistrust of talking therapies that Vaughan felt unable to argue against. They tacitly acknowledged the insolubility of his situation and Charlie encouraged him to put out feelers to contacts on other papers. A common theme emerged in their conversations of the contrast between working in the public and private sectors. Vaughan was a lifelong socialist but he was becoming increasingly disillusioned with the National Health Service. In common with most of his compatriots – of whatever political hue – he was fervently in favour of the principle of a health service that was free to all at the point of access. As an insider though, he felt uneasiness at the growing inability of his service to meet demand and the low morale amongst his colleagues. Not that he necessarily felt over-burdened which in itself hinted at a failure to effectively manage resources. Half the time he felt that no-one seemed to know or even care what he was doing. As long as paper targets were achieved he was largely left alone. At fifty-two, even with only thirty years of his maximum forty-year pension entitlement, he could leave with a grossly inflated sum under the anachronistic final salary scheme. He was seriously considering taking it and finding something else to supplement his pension income that would give him back some of the enthusiasm and will to get out of bed in the morning that he used to have. Prior spoke of the pressures created by the profit motive and the creative need. The constant stresses of deadlines, maintaining a reputation and the transparency of his work. Unlike Vaughan, his performance was there for all to see and assimilate on a constant basis.

One morning, early in September, Prior answered the doorbell and bounded back up the stairs with the sound of Charlie puffing and wheezing behind him. Prior noticed that he looked downbeat and preoccupied when returning from the kitchen with their coffees. Charlie took two cigarettes from the packet and held one out in a new unspoken ritual. They lit up and he began to speak.

"I'm afraid this will be my last visit, Bob." Prior experienced mixed feelings. He would be sorry not to see Charlie anymore but it would represent a step in the direction of autonomy.

"Oh? Why?"

"I'm going next month. I'm taking my pension and am going to boost it with a shot at taxiing." Prior looked at Charlie and pictured him as a taxi driver. He envisaged the large hairy hand on the gear stick, the cable knit cardigan. The blessed relief of small talk without having to come up with a solution that wasn't there. He would feel useful again.

"Good on you, Charlie. I admire your enterprise. I'll miss you though." Charlie's face took a melancholy turn. Prior was not sure if it was genuine or contrived in deference to the feelings of a vulnerable person.

"I'll miss you too, Bob. And all my patients. I've thought long and hard about this, believe me. In the end there was no argument. They've rumbled us in the public sector and it's time to cash in on the pension. It's probably worth more now than it would be if I took it in ten years' time. My children are off my hands, both working. I've paid the mortgage. But it's more than that. It's the job itself." He saw Prior's questioning look. "Oh not the patients. More the morale, covering for sick colleagues; the way IT has made it twice as long to do anything, the obsession with box ticking ahead of proper care. You know, what we've talked about ad infinitum." Prior put a cigarette in his mouth and threw another across to Charlie, who was up to twenty a day now.

"So where's your patch going to be?"

"I'm going to do airport runs Bob. My own boss. I'm buying a minicab out of my lump sum. There's a good catchment area – Heathrow, Gatwick. I can even go out to Stansted, Luton. I know someone who does it and he seems to do okay. I'll see how it goes anyway."

"Well, good luck. I'd love to know how you're getting on. I could even put a bit of business your way probably. Are we allowed to keep in touch?"

"Of course. I'll have nothing to do with the NHS then. If I was just discharging you and staying on in my job then it would probably be a bit awkward; some potential for conflict of interest or something; but no, certainly I'd like to keep contact." Prior smiled.

"We'd be equals."

"Well we always have, Robert. You'll be able to help me with *my* problems now." They laughed but their eyes contained the suspicion the remark was not entirely in jest.

"So is that it now, am I discharged?" Vaughan shifted uncomfortably.

"Er… no. Not quite yet. I did recommend that you could revert to what we call standard care, i.e. just see the psychiatrist every six months and have your lithium bloods done every three months. The consultant's a bit cautious though and thinks it's too soon after your discharge. He wants you to still be seen regularly in the community." Prior gave a sigh of exasperation.

"But I should be working full-time in about four weeks."

"I know – I told him that but he reckons the nature of your work should allow enough flexibility for you to be seen now and then."

Prior's voice rose. "What the hell does he know about the nature of my work?" He shook his head and looked at the floor with a pained expression.

"Who's it going to be anyway?"

"It's a woman. Marie Connolly. She's a social worker in our team." The last few minutes had taken on a sort of rhythmical downward spiral and the nadir had been reached.

"Oh I know Marie Connolly. She wrote that bloody report." The anxiety began welling up again. "Why her?"

"She's the only person with caseload capacity at the moment, Bob. I'm sure it will be okay – she's very up on all the new thinking."

"Oh, I'm sure she is but why a social worker? I thought you keep telling me I've got a medical problem, a chemical imbalance, no shame in it etcetera, etcetera. What am I now, some sort of inadequate?"

"No, of course you're not. Some time ago mental health services integrated – social services and health combined in community teams. Initially the roles were separated with nurses and social workers concentrating on what they were best at, trained to do. There's been a gradual blurring and now the care co-ordinator, as we're labelled, does everything for the people on their caseload. I don't personally agree with it but that's the way it is." Prior looked defeated and neither spoke for some time. They knew each other well enough now for the silence not to be oppressive. Eventually it was Prior who spoke, softly and morosely.

"You know the worst thing about that Connolly? She talked about Caroline as if their affinity, based solely on gender, was superior to that of me and my ex-wife. It was as if gender trumps everything – even all our time together and the life we created between us. She only spoke to her once on the phone. It bothered me so much I mentioned it in a letter I wrote to Caroline after I left hospital and she wrote back, 'Oh, rather like you when we first met at university and you thinking our both coming from the north west overruled any relationship I had with anyone not from the north however long I'd known them for.'"

"What did you say?" He'd forgotten that the exchange was by letter.

"I didn't write back. I'd only written really to thank her for coming to see me. I suppose if I had replied I'd have said there are a few more women in the world than people from the north west of England. Do you see what I mean though?" Charlie knew he'd made a rod for his own back by making a friend of a patient and he felt uncomfortable. Whatever he really thought, he still felt he had to display a professional loyalty to a colleague.

"I do but I suppose it can work both ways." Prior's face wore a tormented look, reflecting the confusion his mind was wrestling with.

"Listen Charlie, I love women – it's only the feminists I have a problem with. I'll admit our fathers' generation and before them, men didn't know how lucky they were. Things had to change. But don't you think it's gone a bit too far. Misogyny is somewhere up there with paedophilia and drink driving but the radical feminist, the female equivalent of the misogynist, can say whatever she wants in the media and no-one dares to oppose it. Tell me what the modern western woman has got to complain about. Instead of twisting the knife into perceived chauvinism here why don't they try to do something for women in other parts of the world?" Charlie glanced at his watch as Prior went on, "There was an article in one of the Sundays saying women had won. Have they been to Saudi or Pakistan or Afghanistan recently?"

Charlie hoped his smile was philosophical as he tried to lighten the atmosphere.

"You'll be alright with Marie, Bob, and it won't be for very long. Besides, she's a lot easier on the eye than my ugly mug. I'd better be off. I'm late already. As usual."

Prior's eyes had a faraway look and he appeared not to heed his visitor's time constraint.

"You see, I feel bad now. It's ridiculous but I do. It's not 'manly' to whinge about the opposite sex. It's exclusively the female prerogative. We're supposed to be above that. But isn't that the most condescending attitude? Isn't that sexism?"

Charlie stood up and rubbed his eyes, his hand concealing an involuntary frown.

"I really must go, Robert. Vive la difference is what I say." He smiled and gave Prior his personal mobile number and they walked together to his car. They shook hands and Charlie opened the door and stooped and shifted awkwardly into the low seat. Prior watched the car as it drove through the double gates at the side of the flat block and as it receded in Prior's view past the park and towards the main road, he turned and shuffled back towards his flat, feeling that another brick had been removed from his precarious wall.

CHAPTER 10

The notes from the tenor saxophone were carried away across the shops and houses below in plaintive, impeaching waves The noise emanated from a rooftop bar in the centre of the town, its origin to be found in the full lips of a tall Caucasian woman. Ringlets of red hair danced alongside her protruding cheeks as she leant forward to coax a soulful, powerful sound from the gleaming instrument. Behind her, two black men and one of Mediterranean appearance supported her on keyboards, guitar, and drums. To her left another man in dreadlocks stood swaying at a microphone waiting for the completion of the solo and his cue to sing.

The bar was above the third storey of a concrete building, the tallest in the immediate vicinity. There was a small wooden dance floor in front of the low stage that held the performers where a few couples gyrated to the music. Easy chairs and sofas were arranged randomly in a square seating area fringed by a metre-high parapet that provided the only protection from the sheer drop to the street below. Vast ceramic pots stood in the corners, their tropical plants lending a dimension of height and an insinuation of jungle in the sticky, breathless heat.

At a long, low table almost entirely covered with bottles, glasses and ashtrays, Zina Stannard sat in a chair, her legs swung over its arm. She was talking to a Portuguese man in his language and she threw back her head at a whispered remark and laughed. Her expression then hardened abruptly in a sneer of mock indignation and she slapped him softly across his grinning face. She said in English, "Naughty boy," and got up and walked to the wall where she looked down onto the street swigging from a bottle of beer. Her fine hair was damp with sweat and clung to her face and neck. She wore flip-flops and a tight fitting pastel kaftan down to her ankles and she imagined the hungry eyes of Ramon as she leaned her thighs against the low wall, swaying her hips gently to the rhythm of the music. It was nearly midnight on a weekday but the small town was alive with conflicting music, noise, and nationalities. Western European tourists, overdressed in long trousers and sensible shoes, meandered slowly up and down in small groups, assailed, even at this late hour, by locals attempting to scratch a living. The Catholic church opposite was set back a few metres from the dusty road, its doors shut against the sin being played out around it. It looked lonely and forlorn, lost and out of place with all its congregation tucked up in bed leaving it abandoned to an alien tribe.

She turned and moved to her table, taking Ramon's hand and pulling him to the dance floor. The band were having a break and a deejay was playing tamla motown records, her favourite dance music. She danced for an hour with various partners and then at one thirty left without a word to anyone, continuing her sashay at the end of a song in the direction of the stairs. Ramon noticed her departure from across the room and followed her hurriedly down the steep narrow stairway. He caught up with her on the way to her car, parked on a path leading down to the shore. The beach was deserted and they went to the sea's edge, where the last small waves were tumbling, and coupled briefly under cover of the water, all but their heads hidden from the unforgiving luminescence of the full moon, their clothes strewn dangerously close to the extent of the incoming tide.

Zina left him struggling into his clothes without a farewell or kiss or backward glance, her body visible through her wet dress as she started the car and drove away from the still throbbing town.

***

Her home was fourteen miles from her office and at eight thirty she got back in the car she had left only six hours earlier. She was tired and her head ached but business was slow and she could probably while the morning away playing on the computer, restoring her hydration with endless cups of coffee.

As she travelled south, skirting the west of the island, she passed little traffic – a few lorries laden with more fuel for the building explosion in the tourist area where she worked and the usual minibuses. She compared it to the journey to work in the provincial town in the south of England that she originated from – the horns, the mercurial flow, the angry faces.

She had worked for a big four high street bank as a financial advisor, quickly moving her way up through the hierarchy. Joining straight from school she had a head start as she viewed it on her contemporaries who went to university. By twenty-two she was buying her own semi and had a nearly new car. She had boyfriends but no desire to settle down or start a family, eschewing emotional commitment and abruptly cutting the ties as soon as anyone showed signs of getting too close. During a holiday to where she now lived she made contacts with the ex-pat set and returned there to work shortly afterwards, keeping up the mortgage on her house in England which she rented out for a figure considerably in excess of her monthly loan repayments. Her job title was senior sales executive which meant she basically had a free rein in generating business via property management, rental, sale and purchase. When she had first arrived, business was booming with disaffected Europeans following their dreams of a place in the sun. The six hour flight from most European capitals ensured a destination with high temperatures for twelve months of the year and the beaches were impressive. However, the market had begun to slow two years ago and now in a world recession, times were hard. Despite over-building contributing to the downturn, the developers continued to press ahead with new builds with the island's infrastructure trailing woefully behind, unable to keep up. A result of this was that the main area of development contained many half-finished houses as funds dried up and many completed houses were empty due to nobody buying them. At the same time, a large proportion of the indigenous population lived in shanty town accommodation with no electricity or water.

The morning brought in no new business and she was able to recover in relative peace. At one the office closed for siesta until three thirty and she followed her usual routine of changing into a bikini and heading for the beach, picking up a sandwich and a Coke on the way. She walked until she reached a spot away from close proximity to anyone and laid out her towel and ate her lunch. The desire for sleep was overwhelming but she forced herself into the reviving sea in continuation of her hangover therapy. After drying off she covered her lean body with the factor 50 sunscreen she meticulously used to protect her fair skin and then lay back and fell into a deep sleep within minutes.

Her internal alarm clock woke her at three and she sat up and rubbed her eyes before turning onto her front to doze for a little longer. She felt fully revived and began to contemplate how she would spend the evening. The will to go out was always strong – there was so little else to do. This morning she had promised herself an early night after a DVD but the lure of the nightlife began to pull again. She would decide later. She waded back out beyond the breakers and plunged head first into the clear turquoise water before lying on her back, relishing the sun on her face as she watched the windsurfers. A Brazilian man she knew shouted her name as a strong wind hurtled him across the surface and she raised a hand in acknowledgement.

Her bikini dried quickly on her walk back to the office along the shore and then up through the softer sand, picking her way between the huddled tourists. Before stepping onto the track that led away from the beach she brushed some of the sand from her feet and put on her flip-flops. The preciously scarce fresh water supply on the island precluded the provision of any taps. Back in the office she washed the last traces of sun block from her face with warm water and put on some lipstick and straightened her hair before changing back into a skirt and blouse. The late afternoon shift until six was always relaxed and sociable, the easy banter an indication of the length of time she and her colleagues had worked together. There was no manager on site and no-one held superiority over her. Their manager had responsibility for offices on this and four other neighbouring islands and he based himself at one of these, only visiting Zina's office once or twice a month. Although she was on a par with three other senior colleagues, her knowledge and ability to manipulate people gave her an unspoken authority that she now took for granted.

She left the office at five telling the others she was going to meet a developer and view the progress of a new coastal development but drove straight home, flicking on the air conditioning and lying naked on the bed for an hour in a pleasurable limbo of suspension of thought and decision. As the cold water from the shower washed over her came the moment of resolution, not that there had ever really been any doubt; she would go out. She dried herself in front of the full length mirror, admiring the unblemished ivory skin covering the thirty-seven year old body that would be the envy of a girl fifteen years younger. She applied cologne and the allure of alcohol to heighten the mood was irresistible, conditioned by the rapidly declining sun. She stepped onto the terrace in her towel and luxuriated in its last rays, the vodka and tonic immediately hitting the spot. The beach ahead was unpopulated, the veneer of the sea calm in its deceit, masking the power and activity lying below. She fixed another drink and sipped it more slowly than the first while she dressed and then locked the house and got in the car, heading back to the tourist town for the evening. It was one of the advantages of life here that she rarely had to make plans or arrange to meet people. She could count on there always being someone she knew at any of her regular haunts and if not she was friendly with all the proprietors and staff. Failing that, she was always happy with her own company anyway.

Tonight she chose the bar restaurant at the end of a small jetty where people ate and drank surrounded by lapping waves on three sides of the open terrace. She bought a beer and joined a table of three men and two women. They were all British and worked for rival property agencies. The man sitting next to Zina smiled broadly, his suntan accentuating the brilliance of his white teeth. His long blond hair had obviously been lovingly arranged around a face which under closer scrutiny was older and harder than the impression given by the cosmetic camouflage. His shrewd darting eyes did not match the mirth of his smile and strayed inquisitively around the restaurant before returning to Zina's face.

"So how's business?" Zina had been observing the people at a nearby table – a middle-aged man in black trousers, white shirt, and tie, charming and attentive to the older couple sitting opposite.

"Slow. And you?"

The man, Terry, smirked enigmatically and said, "Oh you know. Win some, lose some. Can't complain." His vanity wasn't confined to his appearance. He oozed self-satisfaction. He leaned towards her and said with a sneer, "Sold three white elephants today. Like taking candy from a baby." He sat back in his chair and shook his head.

"Stupid divvies." Zina looked at him and said nothing and the conversation gradually became general. The man in the shirt and tie passed their table on the way to the bar and formed his thumb and forefinger into a circle indicating a sale to the couple who now talked animatedly, their heads close together, their excitement tangible. The people who came and went as the evening wore on belonged mainly to the expatriate contingent involved in the purveyance of property, and a dispassionate observer could hardly fail to arrive at an unsettling impression of a neo-colonial sub-class peopled by mavericks and chancers.

The alcohol was not having its desired effect on Zina this evening and she knew she had reached the point where a period of abstinence was necessary rather than desirable. She had surmounted the hill of inhibition and was on the downward slope but instead of the usual gaiety it was now releasing an irritability unchecked by normal restraints. She felt detached from the people around her and listened to their triumphal self-aggrandisement with unconcealed contempt as she affected a sneer of disgust that she shared a profession with them. She pushed back her chair and stood up and said, "You lot want to get over yourselves," before covering herself with an exculpating smile and walking slowly away from the quizzical group. She meandered from bar to bar, released by the knowledge that her brain and liver would be taking a well-earned period of R&R after tonight. In the early hours of the morning she reached her final watering hole, a dissolute nightclub with a piratical theme where everything could go, and usually did. Her dance partner was a Scandinavian tourist at least twenty years her senior and she delighted in the incredulous envy of the younger men at the bar as his hands roamed her angular body and his tongue sought her slackening mouth. The obstinate lucidity of her mind was not matched by the movement of her legs and when her partner let her go as he went to get them drinks she swayed a little unsteadily in the direction of the ladies and then on out into the night. As she moved towards her car she enjoyed the thought of the man sitting waiting for her return. His gradual realisation that it had been too good to be true and the gloating scorn of the men at the bar.

She supposed there were drink drive laws on the island but she had never seen any evidence of their enforcement. It was not something anyone gave a second thought to. Her vision was impaired by the alcohol and she drove home slowly, forcing herself to concentrate hard on the road ahead. She left the car out of the double garage and fell fully clothed onto the bed, tossing and turning against the vertiginous, nauseous sensations until they finally gave way to unconsciousness.

***

She woke at nine with a blinding headache and voracious thirst and called the office to say she was going straight to an apartment with the developer she met yesterday and would be in later – probably at three thirty. She went back to bed and spent the morning in a fitful state of unrewarding half sleep. The room was light and hot and in a rare moment of nostalgia for her mother country she pined for its cold gloom and a nest in which to hide away. At twelve she showered and ate scrambled eggs, the evolutionary antidote to the deathly hangover, and drove to a beach near where she lived on the west coast of the island. The rocks and force of the waves ensured she would be alone and she immersed herself in a rock pool of restoring sea water, allowing the salt to dry on her skin, forsaking her usual sun cream. At three o' clock, by an effort of will, she forced herself back onto the so familiar road to be assailed again by the noises and charades and activity that sought to give meaning to the futility of existence.

Her unanswered emails and telephone messages had accumulated rapidly in her absence and she worked through the calls efficiently, her voice assertive and unequivocal, her prose precise and brooking of no argument. Most of them were from disgruntled customers, their dream turning sour as an axis of malevolence closed around them and disappointment took root.

One woman had phoned from UK in her desperation and Zina's colleagues smirked at each other as they listened to one half of the conversation.

"Well if you buy an apartment in a condominium you will expect to pay condominium property management fees. "It may only be a shoebox in a slum but it's *your* shoebox in *your* slum and *you've* got to pay for it." Zina continued to parrot the woman for the benefit of her audience. "I'm sure I did tell you there were management fees – even if it had slipped my mind, I advised you to read the small print.

"Six hundred euros per annum is very reasonable actually

compared to our competitors but of course if you would like to take your business elsewhere then you have the opportunity at the next condominium meeting." She acknowledged the silent applause of her colleagues.

"You had no electricity or water when you last came over because your contract had not been signed with the electricity company.

"No, we liaise with them on your behalf post-contact – it's your developer who is responsible for the initial contract.

"We charge one month rent for finding you your tenant, yes, and yes; this is chargeable every six months at renewal of contract in addition to our monthly fees.

"Twice the initial quote, you say. Well you'll have to take that up with the solicitor himself. Yes, I did recommend him and he's very well respected. I'm sure you must be mistaken." A colleague opened his eyes wide in mock admonishment of her description of the shyster Morales.

"You were categorically informed pre-purchase of post-sale expenses over which I have no control. It's the law of the land." Her voice took on a sinister intonation. "I hope you're not implying anything negligent on our behalf. No, well good."

She had taken control and finished conciliatorily.

"I'm so sorry that you feel like that. Really we only want to help people realise their dreams, fulfil their ambitions. You have my assurance that we will carry on…" (she heard a colleague in the background say 'Bleeding you dry.') "...working towards the fulfilment of that dream." She put the phone down and they all laughed.

The middle-aged Englishman from the bar the night before shouted across the room, "Oh you old philanthropist Zina – you brought tears to my eyes," before letting out a hoarse laugh and returning to his computer screen. His heavy nicotine-stained fingers on the end of hairy, muscular forearms seemed out of place on the keys. They looked as if they would be more suitably employed clasped around a tool or immersed in a tub of grout. Time passed quickly and she soon experienced the warm feeling of official home time in the form of Dominique coming through the open glass doors with the customary shy smile on her lips that evoked in Zina, not for the first time, an uncanny sensation that her conscience had arrived.

Back at home she quickly filled her stomach with food to forestall the urge for alcohol and spent a self-indulgent evening on the couch watching two DVDs she had borrowed, gorging on chocolate and fizzy drinks. After a shower she snuggled into bed in a room artificially cold from the air conditioning on full power, elated at the prospect of waking tomorrow fresh and revived and ready for the conflicts ahead. Experience told her there could only ever be one winner.

CHAPTER 11

Marie Connolly sat in Prior's living room sipping from a bottle of water having declined his offer of a drink. Another woman she had introduced as a support worker sat alongside her, gazing with wide eyes around the room which Prior, with time on his hands and a return of good taste, had turned into a space that would have formed a sublime backdrop to the visits of Catalina. He rested his jaw in his left hand with his elbow on the arm of the chair and looked at Marie. She wore a short black leather skirt over black leggings tucked into boots. Her dark brown hair was cropped short and the black lipstick and mascara together with the piercing gave her a vampish look. Prior had been determined to start afresh, to erase the memories of their previous acrimonious contact, but there was an immediate bone of contention as he lit a cigarette.

"Did you not read the appointment letter I sent out?" He felt a pang of anxiety in his stomach.

"Yes I read it. Why?"

"There is a reference to the Trust's policy on passive smoking. We ask service-users not to smoke when we visit." Prior was incredulous at being dictated to in his own house.

He said haltingly, intimidated by the blank stares from the settee opposite, "But this is my home – surely it's up to me?"

"Of course you can smoke in your own home but not while I visit – or for two hours before I'm due. I can see you at our office if you'd prefer."

Prior weighed up the alternatives. It would be a hassle but on balance preferable and he said, "Okay. I'll come to you in future," and ground the cigarette into the ashtray.

"Fine. Apart from the risks to myself and my colleague though Mr. Prior, as a health professional it is my responsibility to remind you of the risk you are placing yourself under and to offer you help from smoking cessation services."

Aah, she cares about me, he thought caustically as she continued.

"I'm sure your previous care co-ordinator will have discussed that with you." Prior had an image of a breathless Charlie mounting the stairs.

"Yes, he did, but I declined. It's the last thing I need at the moment – to be deprived of nicotine."

"Well that's up to you. While we're on the subject, did Charlie address your alcohol problems?"

"I haven't got an alcohol problem." For the first time since he had met her, Marie's face creased into something approaching a smile.

"That's not what your blood results indicate." He sighed and raised his eyes to the ceiling. He didn't know if this was a legitimate professional concern or just irrelevant bating. He gave her the benefit of the doubt and kept his temper in check. Something about her calm, steady demeanour unnerved him and he answered as neutrally as he could.

"What, the recent ones?"

"No – I haven't seen any since you left hospital. I'm talking about the bloods you had done on the ward."

He went quiet again as he wrestled with the complexity of why his liver results might be deranged – not least as a side-effect of his new medication – but he didn't want to get into that discussion and said instead, his voice raised and more authoritative, "Look, I've been over this so many times. Yes, I did used to drink too much. Yes, in the week before I was sectioned I hammered it like there was no tomorrow. But since I left hospital I've hardly touched it and don't intend to. Three or four beers once a week and that's it." Her eyes seemed to bore into him.

"To drink more than six units in one session, even once per week, still classes you as a binge drinker, Mr. Prior." She was unrelenting and he cast his caution to the wind.

"Listen, I thought you were here to talk about my mental health not nag me about drinking and smoking. If I wanted that I'd get married again." He entreated them with his eyes and a desperate smile to take the remark with the humour that was intended but it obviously had the opposite effect. The support worker looked apprehensively at Marie as soon as he said it, fearing instinctively her internal reaction. For a second time she betrayed a glimpse of emotion and Prior could see the struggle she was having between her human anger and her professional role.

She said icily, "Alcohol has a large influence on mood disorders. Of course I'm here to talk about your mental health. I don't know what you've been doing with Charlie but I'll be looking at such things as early intervention and risk strategies, identifying trigger factors and relapse signatures, mood charting, life stress inventories, family focussed therapy, cognitive behavioural therapy to look at challenging thoughts and beliefs contributing to mood disturbance, coping skills, interpersonal and social rhythm therapy. Medication is helpful up to a point but needs to be used in conjunction with psycho-social interventions. Did Charlie do any work in this area?" Prior felt a requirement to protect a friend and give nothing away to the enemy. The trouble was he couldn't remember talking about much beyond sport and their mutual bugbears. A phrase filtered back from an early exchange.

"Um… he did something around pre-dromal signs."

"Prodromal signs." She looked at her colleague and raised her eyebrows. "Well, I suppose that's a start. So you came up with a list then?" He felt oppressed. There was simply no hiding place from this latter-day Nurse Ratched.

"Er… we didn't come up with much to be honest. We sort of concluded that it just came out of the blue – the manic episode I mean." Marie briefly closed her eyes and shook her head.

"I'll also be looking at your diet and exercise regime." She looked at him and his eyes moved down to glance at his rapidly expanding stomach, now hanging over the belt of his trousers. He had been truthful in his report of drinking only once per week in relative moderation and he was eating no more than before but he was nevertheless steadily accumulating weight.

"Excuse me for asking, but why are you here?" He looked at the support worker who had not said a word up to now. She was an older woman with dyed blonde hair and a full figure.

"Oh, it's our lone worker policy. Females don't do lone visits to male patients. At least not the first time anyway."

"Right, I see."

Marie jumped in quickly. "And sometimes there is a role for a support worker. That brings me to another area, Mr. Prior."

He interrupted her. "I'd really prefer it if you called me Robert." Her face showed no flicker of acknowledgement of the attempt at social bridge building and he was reminded of the lack of warmth he had felt on first meeting her. She carried on as if he hadn't spoken.

"We'll look at your lifestyle – your social network, level of activity, level of social skills and see if you might benefit from some input from Valerie."

She hasn't done much for your social skills, he thought before saying didactically, "I won't need any help in that area thanks. I'm meeting my boss next week and I'll almost certainly be going back to full-time work." The phased return had been drawn out longer than expected and he was still working part-time. He had the feeling that the less Partridge and his colleagues saw of him the happier they were, but he knew that HR would sanction a return. Political correctness could be a double-edged sword and he knew his situation should only be enhanced by the more enlightened contemporary attitudes towards mental illness. However, as Charlie had suggested, he had put feelers out to other papers to be met with a wall of disinterest he suspected had more to do with stigmatisation than lack of ability. Marie looked doubtful.

"Have your employers discussed this with Dr. Patel?"

"I don't think so. Why, should they?"

"I'd have thought so. I'll speak to him and see what he says. I'm thinking more of the stress it might put you under."

I'm sure you are, he thought as she rummaged in a canvas bag and pulled out a diary worn and dog-eared from nine months' use, flipping the pages on to a date in the middle of October.

"Friday, 14th alright, 11:00 a.m.?"

"I don't know. I might be working. Can I let you know after I've seen my editor?" Prior waited for the inevitable negative response but was pleasantly surprised by a softer tone and a semblance of a smile.

"Fine. We'll keep that date in and unless I hear from you I'll see you at our place. If you can't make it phone me on this number," she handed him a card, "and we'll rearrange to a suitable time." He showed them to the door and as he was about to close it she called out, "Oh Robert, I forgot something," and skipped back up the stairs, the sound of her boots echoing heavily on the concrete in the confines of the stairwell. He felt another little flutter of optimism at her use of his first name.

"Are you still driving?"

He looked at her as if she had asked if he was still breathing and said, "Yes."

"Well I'm not sure you should be. That's another thing I'll mention to Dr. Patel." She levelled her eyes on his – she was as tall as him – and he recoiled almost physically from the hate he saw in them. The surge of anxiety constricted his voice.

"Why on earth shouldn't I be driving? My job virtually depends on it."

"Well I think Dr. Patel will have to inform Swansea. You suffer from Bipolar Disorder 1, a notifiable illness, and you're also on tranquillising medication, you see."

Prior couldn't help himself and started a parodying reply, "Oooh, I seee," before stopping in alarm at this self-destructive move. He tried to let his voice return gradually to normal so she wouldn't notice his attempt at sarcasm. "I see. Right, well let me know. Please inform him how important my licence is to me." In the virtual conversation that had been running alongside the real one he heard himself say, *Like hell you will*, as he closed the door without a further goodbye.

That night Prior got blind drunk. He deliberately omitted his tablets for the first time and reacquainted himself with spirits before walking to the nearest pub where he propped up the bar until closing time, lost in his own morose thoughts, talking to no-one other than to replenish his glass. He replayed Marie's visit over and over in his mind, trying to be objective, telling himself he was overreacting, seizing on the sparse moments of comfort, but it was no good. His gut feeling told him that he was in a war he couldn't win. All the power was in the hands of his antagonists. What he now appreciated as the privileges of his former existence were being slowly taken away. He bought fish and chips on the way home and ate them voraciously, wiping the grease from his hands on his coat. He tripped on an uneven paving stone and cursed loudly as chips spilled onto the ground and he ignored the bellowed abuse from some youths at the bus stop over the road. His dreams that night were confused and disturbing with a long manic drive like a car chase in a film with him at the wheel of an out of control car searching for something or someone he couldn't find.

He woke early despite the alcohol and tossed and turned with his thoughts from yesterday. Why hadn't Charlie mentioned the driving and the job? What were the rules? He would do some internet research tomorrow when he wasn't hung over. Encouraged somewhat by having set himself a minor goal, he got up and got ready and felt a bit better as he washed down his morning medication with his coffee and spent the day relaxing before the first of two meaningless 20:20 internationals at the Oval versus the West Indies scheduled for that weekend. He went up to the ground on the tube and watched a West Indies team woefully weakened by the lure of the IPL lucre capitulate dismally. It was a fitting end to a woeful summer of cricket. The majority of the crowd didn't seem to care what happened on the field and were more concerned with drinking themselves insensible to the point where they resembled a football crowd. Prior knew the article he would have written previously but that under the present editorial climate it was a waste of time and effort. With his meeting with Partridge in mind he penned a suitably triumphal piece and headed home. He was surprised to feel not the slightest inclination to drink and he took his medication and fell into a deep undisturbed sleep, waking on Saturday morning feeling more energetic and optimistic. His time was his own until tomorrow evening's second game and he spent the morning at his computer downloading information concerning his illness and related driving and employment issues. He printed off articles by mental health charities MIND and the unfashionably entitled Manic Depression Fellowship and felt an upsurge at the clarity and support offered via the Disability Discrimination and Equality Acts. He highlighted some of the text such as 'the DDA makes it unlawful for an employer to discriminate against those with a disability in areas of applications for employment, training and development, terms and conditions, benefits and the dismissal process', underlining 'terms and conditions' and 'the act prevents the treating of a disabled person less favourably for a reason related to their disability'. He looked forward to showing it to Partridge. The driving issue was less clear. He established that it was an offence under the Road Traffic Act not to notify the DVLA of any medical condition which may affect safe driving and he printed off an M1 form, a questionnaire assessing medical fitness to drive. He felt he could answer no to most questions with a reasonable veracity but would be in a quandary over question 6 – 'in the past six months have you regularly misused alcohol?' Question 8 was also a negative, relating as it did to his hospital admission for psychiatric treatment. He divined from a very vague system that his consultant, Dr. Patel, was probably the final arbiter. He felt a little better disposed towards Marie Connolly. Perhaps she was not acting purely out of malice. He would give her the benefit of the doubt for the moment. He retained, however, a nebulous mistrust of statutory mental health services and was reassured by the existence of charitable organisations that were on his side. He wondered why he had had to discover them by himself.

With his mood further heightened by the morning's work he had lunch and drove south with no particular plan in mind, only an instinctive desire to make the most of the pleasant late September day and enjoy the countryside. He drove as far as the coast and walked for miles along the promenade of a seaside town in shirtsleeves, stopping for a cup of tea along the way, wistfully regretting the lack of the company of a woman and feeling a little envious of the men with their partners. He began the journey home at five, driving cautiously and correctly, responding to an unconscious sensation of being watched, assimilated by an unseen examiner. He stopped at a pub in north Kent and drank a pint of real ale in the beer garden, enjoying the innocent play of the young children, and went home with a sense of renewal, a feeling that he was in control of the beast within him. He showered and had three lagers while he listened to music and got into bed feeling sad that the day had ended.

***

The following evening he returned to the Oval and rejoiced inwardly as the, again, virtually unrecognisable West Indian team beat a jaded English side that fell at the final hurdle of the season. The month of October was defined by a series of appointments. He met with Dave Partridge and HR and a return to full-time work was agreed. Partridge however, would not budge on his refusal to restore him to his previous role and status although he reluctantly kept Prior on his previous salary. He was to continue as the cricket correspondent but would not be going to India to cover the imminent tour of five one-day internationals and a twenty-twenty as it was now too short notice and someone else had been allocated. His next overseas assignment would be in January to cover the games against Pakistan in the United Arab Emirates. Until then his staple would be football reportage and maybe some rugby at the editor's discretion. Prior contacted his union and protracted discussions began. Partridge and his seniors argued that the decision to, in effect, demote him was based, not on his mental health, but on performance whilst accepting the argument that the two were inextricably linked. They cited the articles he submitted just before his 'breakdown' as they called it. The union argued on Prior's behalf that he had not been given the opportunity to show that his previous expertise had returned to which the paper replied that he had, and had been found wanting. Prior's problem was that it was such a subjective judgement. He began to tire of the wrangling and to sense that he was on a sticky wicket. His union lacked power and were losing the argument and he stalled on seeking legal representation.

He saw Marie and she inundated him with mood diaries and charts and graphs and lists until his head spun. She set him homework which he hurriedly turned to in an anxious frenzy an hour before he was due to see her again and sat in trepidation as she appraised his work with an expression somewhere between disdain and disgust. He habitually tried to move their relationship onto at least a more human level by asking her where she lived and other personal questions but she abruptly implied that it was none of his business and that they were there to talk about him, not her. The contrast with Charlie could not have been greater and without ever directly maligning him she made her low opinion of his practice obvious. He had to confess that for whatever reason, he felt better. He was more inclined to think this was due to getting used to the medication and reaching some kind of closure and acceptance of his work situation rather than Marie's cognitive approach, but who really knew with psychiatry? He met his community consultant psychiatrist, Dr. Patel, for the first time and instantly warmed to him. He proved supportive both of a return to full-time work and his retention of a driving licence and Prior was hopeful that the DVLA would reach a decision in his favour. His medication was left unchanged as his lithium bloods showed a level of 0.70 m/mols per litre of blood – right in the middle of the therapeutic range. The anti-psychotic, Abilify, was continued despite Prior's tentative request to have it stopped or at least reduced. Dr. Patel gave him the carrot of a review of the decision at his next appointment. This was not until next April but he knew that it was an academic exercise as he was self-medicating. He was weighed and measured and alarmed to discover that his height of five feet, ten inches or 177.80 centimetres and his weight of sixteen stones (102kg) gave him a Body Mass Index of 32 indicating apparently that he was clinically obese. He had never been this heavy in his life. His blood pressure was also high and he was advised to see his GP.

The clocks went back and the days grew shorter but he managed to avoid a plunge into a depressive episode. He turned forty-three on the twenty-seventh of October, cursing again the fates that had decreed the anniversary fall at a time of year he loathed more than any other. He had looked ahead to November with trepidation but the continuation of a mild autumn helped to assuage his apprehension and he immersed himself in his work and began to grow used to his new circumstances. If his employers wished to pay him a very generous salary for an undemanding job that he found ridiculously easy then that was their concern. His colleagues continued to keep him at arms' length but that didn't worry him as the aloofness he had previously maintained ensured the absence of any great contrast. He was not naturally thick skinned but the medication seemed to dull and neutralise emotion. Nevertheless, he replaced some of his previous haunts where he was known personally – local shop, pub, garage – so as to not be continually humiliated by his reduced status and he built a new, more anonymous terrain.

One cold Monday afternoon in mid-November he drove into the car park of the hospital where the community mental health team was based and walked hurriedly from his car to his appointment with Marie Connolly in the single-storey purpose-built brick building where he saw her. He had been in a meeting in work which had run over time and he was now late. His homework had not been looked at and he felt anxious and angry at what he was now viewing as an intrusion into his busy life. He waited in reception and eventually the electronically controlled door clicked open and Marie asked him to go through. She looked different. Her calfskin ankle boots and long multi-coloured cardigan in pastel shades made her look softer somehow, vulnerable almost. She brushed aside his apologies for lateness and absence of homework with an air of indifference and said with a thin smile.

"I have some news which I am sure will please you. Dr. Patel has decided to regrade you to standard care. That means this will be our last appointment." Prior did his utmost to suppress a smile but was unsuccessful. He tried to imply that it wasn't personal.

"That's very good news. I am finding it increasingly hard to get away from work. I'm sure there's someone else waiting who's far more in need of your expertise, Marie." He left it to her to work out whether he was being ironic or not. She looked at him coldly.

"We're always under pressure to rotate our caseloads, yes." He had the feeling that she would have preferred to prolong the agony for him if it had been her decision. He decided to take the plunge – he didn't feel he had anything to lose.

"Why don't you like me, Marie?" She had been looking at the wall, apparently lost in thought. She continued to gaze at the same spot before slowly turning to face him, her mouth and eyes fixed in contempt.

"I'm sorry?" The strategy of the skilled mind worker had its desired effect and he was forced to repeat himself, less confidently this time. "I've been asked that before if you remember, by your solicitor at the tribunal and the answer remains the same."

"Well we know that's all a bit false and stage managed. Nobody can really say what they are thinking. Honestly, no hard feelings. I really would like to know – it might help me to understand myself better." He looked at her imploringly, beseeching her for once to drop her professional guard, but she stood up and as she pushed her chair in to the table with her back to him he noticed that her neck was flushed. She turned round to look at him and he held his breath, longing for an insight into the person behind the persona even if it inflicted hurt on him.

For a moment his hopes were raised by her downward glance and fleeting hesitation but ultimately she held out a limp hand and said tersely, "You'll continue to see Dr. Patel but I'll arrange for you to have your blood tests at your GP surgery. You can phone our team with any problems in office hours and you know how to access the crisis team out of hours." She walked with him to the door separating the offices from the reception area and pressed the pad to let him through. The look on her face as she said goodbye chilled Prior to the bone and he walked slowly away, shaking his head with incomprehension at what it was about him that inspired such a reaction.

CHAPTER 12

Manna from heaven dropped through his post box one morning in the form of a letter from the DVLA informing him that he could keep his licence and he drove up north to cover an evening match with something akin to his old abandon, released from the prying eyes of his internal arbiter by the welcome news. The game was taking place near to Caroline's home and he left early, harbouring a thought of dropping in if his mood on arrival allowed him such a giant step on his path of renewal and regeneration. He left the M6 in Cheshire and drove absently in the direction of the village where his ex-wife and Doug had bought a house he had never seen. He knew the address and he felt a flutter of excitement as he exited a sharp bend of the hedge-flanked lane and came upon the nameplate of the village where a large part of him dwelt. The austere tones of the voice on the satnav guided him 0.8 miles along the main street where large detached houses were set well back behind mature trees at various stages in the process of shedding their leaves onto the broad pavement. He turned left at a point just after the main lifeblood of the community – a pub, and general store and post office – and followed the instruction to drive 0.3 miles to his destination on the left. The chequered flag appeared and he pulled up at an open gate at the beginning of a long drive of at least sixty metres in length. It was flanked by enclosed fields of grass in one of which two horses grazed. The house that he could see in the distance was Georgian, large and impressive, and fronted by gravel on which was parked a 4-by-4 vehicle and a new-looking saloon car.

He drove back to the high street and had a late lunch in the oak-beamed pub, sitting as inconspicuously as possible in a corner with a newspaper he had bought in the general store. In mid-afternoon he drove back to Caroline's house and parked under a tree in front of the house next to hers and sat in a sea of indecision, gradually appreciating the stupidity of a cold call. Nevertheless, he didn't want to leave. Once he had reached the relief-giving decision he hoped at least to make some kind of human connection in compensation and this came in the late afternoon as the increasing mist was turning into the premature dusk of late autumn. A car drew up ahead of him at the end of the drive and a young woman got out of the rear passenger door. She bent at the waist and said her thanks and goodbyes to the other three occupants through the open window before stepping back to wave them off. She wore a heavy navy blue coat and carried a large bag, from the top of which protruded files and books. Although he hadn't seen her since she was seven, ten years ago, he knew at once that it was Helen. She was the most like him of the three facially and a lump came to his throat as she glanced briefly at him without recognition and began walking away towards the house. He sat at the wheel for some minutes watching the fall of leaves in the gathering wind through damp eyes before turning on the lights and pulling away in the direction of Manchester.

For the next two weeks he focussed on his goal of weight loss with a steely resolve and was surprised and gratified by his powers of self-discipline. He exercised obsessively, puffing and grimacing in a kind of cloistered hell, eating only small amounts of low fat food and cutting out alcohol altogether. At the end of a week of this he stood on the top of the range digital scales he had bought and waited in excited anticipation for the numbers to appear. If the drop in weight had been proportionate to the plummeting of his spirits he would have been happy. He had lost three quarters of a kilogram.

He fought against a petulant self-pity that urged rebellion in the form of beer and chips and doughnuts and continued with his Spartan regime for another week. His stomach had shrunk and the food craving was marginally less. He mounted the scales again one Saturday morning at the end of the second week without trepidation. He had decided on a response to another disappointment. It predictably appeared in the same reading as last week. He looked ahead and pondered a future of living in a perpetual state of near starvation and exhaustion just to remain in the same place. He imagined the misery of an existence without sensual pleasure. He hadn't taken his dose of medication the previous night and he felt vindicated as he stepped back onto the ivory coloured bathroom tiles. His next blood tests were not due for two months so he had a window of opportunity. He would continue to collect his prescriptions – issued weekly because of suicide risk – so as not to invoke suspicion and see how things went without the cosh.

Throughout the day he felt the subtle stirrings of a lifting of spirits. Whether it was the liberation from the chemical or the psychological strictures he couldn't be sure, although it was probably the latter as the drugs would still be in the system. Whatever the reason, he left the press conference at a London Premiership ground after the game with a lightness of step and uncharacteristically joined some colleagues at a pub. He still felt like the outsider but it didn't bother him. He joined in with their laughter and his inward contentment seemed to draw him into the group. They still appeared guarded but the tacit derision was less apparent, and was it his imagination or could he detect a little of the old respect and veneration for his undisputed ability? He bade breezy farewells and walked away quickly to guard against the mutter or snigger that would burst his bubble. He took a tube to Leicester Square and entered one of his old haunts, an Italian restaurant where he was greeted like a long lost friend. Full of lasagne and ciabatta and Chianti and bonhomie, he took a late train home and fell into bed where he was consumed quickly by a descent into a sleep filled with benign dreams.

He retained the contentment over the following days. The Saturday night lapse was an isolated event and temperance returned but without the previous level of compulsive zeal. He ate and drank sensibly, in moderation without going hungry and on the following Saturday the dial showed a loss of three kilograms. As he drank a coffee and smoked a cigarette he felt an exquisite delight at the prospect of two weeks' annual leave ahead of him, starting from today. He made out a Christmas shopping list and set off for the city, parking in a multi-storey near Oxford Street. In previous years he had bought what little he needed online but today he felt like mingling with his fellow humans and getting caught up in the ill-tempered frenzy that was now the precursor to the celebration of the birth of Christ. He shopped with a single-minded resolve that only just stayed the right side of the recklessness of his flat makeover and he ferried the goods back to the car when they became too heavy or cumbersome with an intense satisfaction at the suitability of his purchases and the amount of exercise he was getting from the brisk fetching and carrying.

For the first time in years he bought presents for his children rather than the usual impersonal cheque to Caroline for distribution. He bought perfumes for the girls at exorbitant prices, enjoying the attention of the beautiful young sales assistants with eyes only for him until his money was secured and their eyelids fluttered at the next customer. He bought them scarves, hats and gloves picked out by girls of roughly the same age, an item of jewellery for each in diamond and gold and he completed their gifts with vouchers for £500 at a department store with a branch in Manchester. For his son he bought top of the range men's cosmetics, a leather wallet, cuff links and a Rolex watch in addition to a £500 voucher for a men's clothes shop. He had decided to send Caroline and Doug a Harrods hamper and went into the store to arrange delivery. By mid-afternoon he was finished and for the remainder of the day he turned his philanthropy on himself in the form of a cashmere overcoat, two Italian wool suits and a selection of shirts, ties, jumpers and shoes. He returned home, exhausted but exhilarated and resisted a nagging urge to begin wrapping the presents, spending the evening instead drinking and listening to music before falling asleep in front of Match of the Day. He woke in the early hours of the morning in his armchair and got up with the intention of moving to the bedroom but by the time he reached his bed he felt wide awake so he washed and shaved and spent the day busying himself with Christmas chores, experiencing a pleasant feeling of satisfaction in the early evening as he surveyed the parcels wrapped in their brown paper and the illuminated tree and decorations that he had decided on for the first time since he moved in.

Throughout the following week his satisfaction rose by the day. By Tuesday he had despatched the parcels, written and sent cards, and fine-tuned his apartment and he felt entirely justified in indulging himself with some 'me time', cringing inwardly at the awful expression. This took the form of dressing sharply in his new suits and shirts, getting out and drinking more and revisiting his old haunts. He admired himself frequently in the full-length mirror and enjoyed caressing the returning keenness of his jawline. By Thursday he felt that his suits and coat were too big and he dropped them into a charity shop before going up to the city to replace them with a smaller size. He began waking early, feeling refreshed and without a hangover despite drinking heavily the night before. He was not totally without what his mental health workers called 'insight'. He could have ticked most of Marie's list of prodromal signs of relapse. He knew that rebound mania following rapid cessation of lithium occurs in fifty per cent of patients. He imagined the voice of Charlie urging him to take medication but wild horses wouldn't drag him back to that purgatory at the moment. He told himself he would know when he had reached the point where he had to resume the drugs. The big difference now was that it was a devil he knew and he was going to be its master.

***

Prior relieved himself at the urinals and enjoyed the reflection of his face in the mirror above the basin as he washed his hands. It was Friday night and he had been at the country club for most of the day, having joined that morning, paying his annual subscription in one sum. Motivated largely by the reminder of the paucity of his social life when writing his Christmas cards he thought this would give him the opportunity to meet and mix with the type of people who had the means to afford the exclusive fees and to indulge himself on the nine-hole golf course and in the gymnasium and swimming pool. He had started with a swim followed by a sauna and after a light lunch he had enjoyed a round of golf with a stranger he had struck up conversation with. He was now ensconced in the saloon bar and he felt a warm glow of pleasure as he returned from the gents' to the group of seats where his golfing partner and two of his friends were sitting. One of them had recognised Prior and they listened avidly as he regaled them with indiscreet anecdotes and insights into the world within a sporting world. The rounds of drinks came at increasingly shorter intervals and the raised voices and laughter turned heads from nearby tables. Outside, the early evening was laden with damp, the dark clouds heavy with the impending deluge which came after thunder and lightning and intensified the relative luxury of the internal surroundings. As he bade farewell to his new comrades and watched them saunter away he imagined the evening ahead of them. The recrimination, the icy retribution, the heavy meal repeating on them as they fought a losing battle with the premature onset of gratuitous sleep in front of some drivel on the TV. It was at times like this that he counted the lucky stars of his self-determination.

Three women in their late thirties were sitting at a table by the wall and Prior had fancied that one of them had been taking a particular interest in him. She was his type – an angular brunette with a bobbed hairstyle and shrewd blue-grey eyes full of worldliness and the promise of immoderation. He went to the bar and pulled his wallet out from the inside pocket of one of his new suit jackets, paying for a bottle of champagne which he instructed the barman to take over to their table with four flute glasses. As the barman pointed in his direction, he glanced briefly at them and smiled engagingly before turning in profile to study the array of bottles behind the bar. The man returned with a message that they would be pleased if he would join them. He returned to the gents, delaying his gratification, confirming his irresistibility as he refreshed his face and hands with cold water.

Their table was set in a booth with four seats, the springs and backing covered with plush red velvet. The brunette moved towards the wall and Prior eased in alongside her opposite a blonde woman and a redhead to her right. Words came fluidly to his tongue and he effortlessly opened the bottle and proposed a toast to a celebration of life and the moment and the thought of no tomorrows. They all wished time could stand still and leave them in this blissful state of feeling both soporific and energised at the same time. The conversation was light and skittish and mainly involved Prior talking and the women laughing. They were three old friends. They usually went out with their husbands as a sixsome but the three men were in Portugal on a golfing weekend. All their children had been inveigled into arranging sleepovers with friends and the women had enjoyed a pamper day of saunas and massages and beauty treatments. Prior felt privileged to be sharing some of their evening time. He had assumed that Della, the girl who had been looking at him, would be the most logical choice in his quest for amore but he was a little disappointed to find her frustratingly irritating. He felt a more immediate rapport with Carol, the blonde woman opposite, and he experienced an increasing fascination with the quiet, enigmatic redhead who sat next to her whose name was Naomi. He had just completed a long joke that he told expertly with the nuance and timing of a professional. Ordinarily he was incapable of remembering any when a situation called for one, or if he could, he got hopelessly muddled when he reached the punch line stage, often needing help to finish his own joke which rather spoilt the effect. He basked in the approval of his companions, Della's coarse cackle further confirming his earlier impression. The waiter brought over another bottle of vintage champagne which Prior poured before standing up and taking cigarettes and lighter from the pocket of the jacket folded between him and Della.

"Another of my vices I'm afraid, ladies. I won't be long. Anyone joining me?"

Naomi, who was looking at him with eyes that were beginning to glaze, her head propped in her hand, stood up in affirmation and they walked out together, Prior taking her arm and negotiating her through the obstacles of furniture and people in their way. They passed through a glass revolving door and turned left towards a covered smoking area warmed by halogen heaters, their fierce irradiation illuminating the wet surrounds following the storm, the heat feeling uncomfortable and unhealthy in its honed-in artificiality in the context of a cold December night.

Naomi looked beautiful in the harsh glare. Her wavy light auburn hair was glossy and her henna-painted lips contrasted attractively with her ivory skin, taut over a spare, high-cheekboned face. Prior sat alongside her, as close as he could get his chair to hers, and lit the cigarette he had offered and then his own. She dragged deeply and exhaled, blowing the smoke towards him. The combination of the smell of tobacco and her perfume evoked an intense nostalgia in him. As a small boy he seemed to remember all women smelling like that. He was further in awe of her alluring femininity as her cigarette stuck to a dry top lip as she attempted to pull it away from another puff and her tongue swept briefly from one corner of her mouth to the other to lubricate it. His arm moved along the back of her chair and his hand rested on her shoulder. He felt an innate certainty that he would not be rebuffed and at his slight pressure she turned to him and kissed him lightly on the lips.

"Merry Christmas," she whispered, perhaps to keep an innocent option open.

"And a Happy New Year," replied Prior, who drew her head towards his and their lips met again in a more elongated and animated convergence. She broke away as hurriedly as she could without conveying a rejection she didn't seek. The small percentage of discretion not engulfed by inebriation caused her to remember where she was and she glanced anxiously at the other tables. To her relief they were all empty apart from a couple on the fringe of the terrace who she didn't know and who anyway only had eyes for each other. She stubbed out her cigarette and stood up unsteadily, smiling at Prior whose eyes were intense, his face serious, concentrated by lust.

"Better go back Bobby or they'll be talking about us." In answer to her enquiry he licked his fingers and wiped away a smudge of lipstick on her face and then guided her back, his arm this time around her narrow waist.

Della was on her mobile talking coquettishly to someone on the other end who Prior assumed was her husband. She made wide eyes at Naomi and Prior as they slipped into the booth, Prior this time sitting next to Naomi in the seat vacated by Carol who was talking to some friends. His hands wandered in the concealed space beneath the table, Naomi's face impassive as his groping became ever more adventurous. She put up no resistance until a point when the surface of the millpond was about to ripple and she gently took his wrist and placed it on his lap. Della was off the phone and relayed the news from the men in Portugal to Naomi and Carol who had now returned. Looking at Naomi with the conspiratorial self-importance of the messenger she said, "You'll never guess what's happened, Nay. Paul missed the flight." She felt a sting of anger and couldn't restrain her impulsive reaction.

"Oh what an idiot. What's he doing then?"

"Barry and Roger have gone on ahead – Paul can't get a flight 'til tomorrow morning."

"So what's Paul doing?" Della looked quizzical.

"You two not talking or something? I feel like the go-between here." Naomi shook her head.

"We had a row this morning. He's so pathetic. I had to pack his case for him and find his passport and iron his shirt and trousers and he knew I'd had today planned for ages. Honestly, he's worse than the children. So I suppose he got Barry to pass on the news through you. Did he say if he's staying overnight at the airport or going home?" Della shrugged,

"No. Why don't you call him, Nay?"

Naomi sighed deeply and rummaged in her bag for her phone. She raised her eyes to the ceiling as it rang. Her voice was slightly slurred but glacial nonetheless when he answered and the conversation played out in staccato whenever there was a need for more than a monosyllable.

She concluded with, "Well don't wait up," and pressed the button sharply to end the call.

"He's not going at all now. Sulking because they went on without him. What the hell did he expect them to do?"

"How come he missed the plane?" asked Carol.

"Got a puncture and then stopped for speeding. Okay that's bad luck but he never leaves enough time for something going wrong. Always last minute."

No longer the centre of attention, Prior's erstwhile showing off had now disappeared to be replaced by a look of preoccupation and an air of impatience with the women's conversation. Naomi went quiet again as the other two dissected the new development and she chewed her lower lip, her perturbed face betraying the emotions within. She was now drinking Coke in an effort to regain some sobriety but she knew it was too little too late. Before an acceptable time had elapsed they could wait no longer and Prior stood up and took out his cigarettes, nodding at Naomi who followed him through the swing doors. Once outside he took her hand and steered her gently to the right, away from the smoking area in the direction of the car park. They walked briskly towards a small hut in the distance whose roof they could make out above a laurel hedge, still lush and verdant in the mild winter they were experiencing. On closer inspection the hut was a clubhouse in front of a bowling green. To Prior's delight there was a gap of about three feet between the hedge and the back of the clubhouse where they could not be seen. Beyond the green was blackness but as their eyes became more accustomed to the dark they could make out the silhouettes of fences dividing fields. If there was any life immediately beyond them it was not human.

They freed themselves below the waist and connected effortlessly, their heights compatible as Naomi leaned against the shed, protected against a now biting wind by Prior dressed only in slacks and a billowing white shirt. The events of the last few minutes had created an urgency that was both tacit and mutual. A sudden noise of approaching footsteps caused Naomi's heart to flutter and Prior placed his hand softly over her mouth and cocked his ear. The steps were coming closer and he withdrew quickly and they moved soundlessly around to the side of the hut, just before two youths took their places and relieved themselves against the hedge. When their departing footsteps were barely audible, Prior took her hand and for the first time he sensed a resistance. He looked at her and she looked away.

"What's wrong?" His voice carried a trace of indignation. She felt suddenly sober and clear minded.

"I'm sorry Bobby – I can't go on with this. I'm going back." She was into damage limitation. Just what constitutes adultery? Had she already crossed the line? Obviously. Even to think about sex with someone other than your spouse was adultery by strict application of the law of the bible. She could still salvage a grain of mitigation from the denial of the ultimate; the self-restraint could only count in her favour. Contrary to the evidence of tonight's behaviour she was a Christian. Prior felt the surge of rage and disappointment he had experienced in that ridiculous hotel. The fundamental frustration of thwarted sexual desire. His turbulent emotions materialised in a look of incredulous outrage but he remained silent. He couldn't find the appropriate words to express his devastation. Unlike the previous occasion he felt something for this woman beyond lust and he felt not just a peevishness at the rejection but a hurt. He held her by the shoulders and looked down at her in the moonlight. Her lipstick was smudged again and there was some on her front teeth. Her hair had stuck to her face and forehead in the thin drizzle that was now falling and her eye shadow was running. She looked small and vulnerable and broken. He was momentarily disarmed by the poignancy of the sight and the irretrievability of the situation. He rehearsed a number of responses but they were either hostile or ingratiating – what else could they be? – and he relinquished his grip and walked quickly away towards the car park without another word, the distance between him and the pursuing Naomi lengthening with each bitter stride.

***

He woke abruptly to the sound of crashing and shouting and thumping followed by what sounded like a herd of elephants coming up the stairs. It took him a few moments to discount dreams and other tenants before the thunderous bangs on his front door confirmed the commotion concerned him. He flicked on the bedside lamp and looked at the clock which showed it was 3:17 a.m. Before he could get out of bed to put some clothes on his bedroom door burst open and six policemen appeared complete with Taser guns. Prior raised his hands to signal acquiescence and to forestall their need to exercise their itchy trigger fingers. He was instructed to get off the bed and get dressed, and in answer to his request for an explanation one of the men answered, "Robert Prior, you are under arrest for the suspected rape of Naomi Thompson in the vicinity of the Pinewood Country Club on Friday, 16th or Saturday, 17th December, 2011. You do not have to say anything but it may harm your defence if you do not mention when questioned something which you later rely on in court. Anything you do say may be given in evidence." The colour drained from his cheeks and he sat down heavily on the bed. He looked up at the arresting officer and then down to his bare feet and pulled on a pair of odd socks and stepped into a pair of slip-on shoes with a gathering realisation that his brief liberation was over, perhaps never to return.

The events of the next hour or so between being manhandled down the stairs in handcuffs and hearing the custody suite cell door slam shut felt surreal. He endured the formalities of arrest – the fingerprinting, photographing, and confiscation of personal property with a sense of detachment as if he was observing this happening to somebody else or playing a part in a film. He sat on the low bunk only inches from the floor, the state issue pyjama bottoms and tunic providing scant protection against the chill cast by the spirits of the thousand godforsaken souls who had preceded him in this tomb.

He took his mind back to when he had stopped taking medication and remembered telling himself that he would know if he was becoming unwell and when to resume it. Had he unknowingly gone past that stage? The happiness had been tangible, the spending a bit extravagant and impulsive, yes. The drinking had escalated, the libido had returned in spades, okay. But no, he thought, not at any stage was he not in control. Why shouldn't he have behaved like he did? It was Christmas, he'd been to hell and back, he'd lost his family, work had turned into a crock of excrement. He deserved a bit of fun, dammit. Okay, she was married but for how much longer, given the way they seemed to be getting on? She was as willing as he was and the bottom line was that they pulled back from the precipice and by an extreme effort of will he had let her go without entreaty. And now this. His thoughts went round and round in chaotic circles as he tested the reality of his recollection. He allowed for every possible misapprehension he may have been labouring under but by the time the heavy door cranked open he was convinced of his own innocence.

The male orderly looked at him pleasantly enough. Innocent until proven guilty? Prior was glad to see another human face.

"FME wants to see you. Follow me."

Prior sniffed and said mechanically, "What's an FME?"

"Forensic Medical Examiner."

"Why?"

"No idea mate. I just do as I'm told." He was taken to a room resembling a clinic off the main custody area containing a bed, desk, scales, medical paraphernalia. The pale blue paint on the brick walls was barely visible beneath the plethora of charts and notices. A tired-looking woman in jeans and a low-cut blouse with a stethoscope around her neck looked up at him from her chair at the desk.

"Hello Robert. Please sit down. I'm Dr. Blethin." They shook hands.

"I've been asked to see you because Sergeant Donaldson mentioned that you're in contact with mental health services. That may have an impact on police procedure." Prior was invited to outline his recent mental health experiences and this he did with a vengeance, the words pouring out with hardly a pause for breath, his recollection sharp despite the ordeal and the lack of sleep. He sensed a potential ally in the kindly woman sitting at right angles to himself, leaning back with her hands clasped behind her head, and his tone was collaborative in its assumption of her sympathy and support. She stopped him abruptly as he began a description of yesterday's events.

"That part of it is for the police, Robert, not me." He looked at her with a troubled expression, not welcoming the interruption. The whites of his eyes were red and watery, the expression on his unshaven face conveying his trepidation at the thought of the unequal, virtually hopeless battles ahead. His voice was urging, insistent.

"But you believe I didn't do it don't you? You must have a gut feeling about people in your job." Her unassuming manner which had given him comfort now provoked him.

"You know I can't possibly make a judgement on that."

No 'Robert' this time, he thought.

"I know nothing about the facts of the case. I'm just here to give an opinion on health matters. Now you gave the sergeant a list of your medication. Have you been taking it?" The same old question again.

The way he answered, "No I haven't," seemed to dissuade the doctor from continuing on that topic.

Instead she said, "You seem a little agitated, Robert, and quite understandable in the circumstances. Would you like a little diazepam to help you relax?"

He shook his head without looking up.

"I'm sure it would help you cope with the day ahead a bit better."

"Thanks for the offer, Doctor, but no. I want to be as clear headed as I can because I am going to fight it all the way." His voice rose almost to a shout as he said, "I didn't do it. I promise you I could never do something like that. I'm being made out to be some kind of animal. I've got two daughters…" Dr. Blethin put her hand on his arm.

"You've only been arrested, not charged. Your solicitor will help you. What I think I'll do, Robert, is ask the Criminal Justice Mental Health Liaison team to see you. They attend the custody suite and they are a specialist service more suited to your needs I think." Prior sighed as he contemplated yet another assessment by yet another service in this myriad bureaucratic profligacy. *No wonder the country's nearly bankrupt.* He kept his thoughts to himself and watched her try to stifle a yawn. He smiled sympathetically.

"Tired? When do you finish?" Her professional mask disintegrated with what looked like relief.

"Eight. I came on at eight last night."

"Straight to bed when you get home?" Prior instantly regretted any mention of bed to an attractive woman in his current circumstances.

"I wish. My husband passes me the baton and goes straight to work. I've then got two children to take to school and a three-year-old to drop at nursery. I'll grab what sleep I can before it's time to pick them up again." She looked suddenly embarrassed and stood up and pressed a buzzer on the wall and the civilian orderly appeared at the door almost immediately, and Prior was taken back to his cell.

He sat on the bed for half an hour, leaning in the corner against the two adjoining walls with his arms resting on his knees, staring absently at the wall opposite. At eight thirty a furtive-looking man was ushered into his cell and he was asked the usual questions. He had lost count of the number of times he had been asked them even in his, up to now, brief sojourn in the twilight world. 'How do you feel? Are you taking your medicine? If not, why not. Rate your mood on a scale of 1-10. Have you any thoughts of harming yourself or other people?' The list was endless and he answered impatiently, petulantly at times. When an eight-page form was complete, Prior asked, "So what are my alternatives?" The man, Robin Graves, was about Prior's age, dressed in a suit and tie that somehow failed to make him look smart – worn under sufferance presumably due to the necessity of attending court daily.

"There are a number. You could be bailed to return here on a specified date. You could be interviewed during the next forty-eight hours and then be either charged or released without charge. If you are charged you'll go to the Magistrates Court at the next sitting. Given the alleged offence, bail is unlikely to be an option. I'm pretty sure you will be interviewed today. Regarding the mental health angle, I could refer for a Mental Health Act assessment but to be honest I haven't seen evidence today that that's justifiable. I would concur with Dr. Blethin that you are fit to plead and fit to be interviewed but in view of your mental health problems I would recommend the presence of an Appropriate Adult.

"A what?" said Prior.

"A sort of advocate to advise, clarify, help communication, ensure you're treated fairly during the interview process."

"No thanks." He shook his head. "It just doesn't stop, does it?"

"What doesn't stop?"

"This patronising bloody nannying. I'm not some sort of half-wit if that's what you're implying. The powers that be say I've got a 'mental health problem'. Even if that's true I've still got a first from Cambridge and am quite capable of speaking for myself thank you." He was not in the habit of blowing his own trumpet unless he felt he was backed into a corner. The man looked belligerent rather than apologetic and his reply ignored the content of Prior's rant.

"Our team will keep tabs on your progress through the system. Someone will be in court if it comes to that. See you."

Only a few minutes passed before the door opened again and his solicitor, Blake, was shown in. *Better the devil you know*, Prior had thought when opting for him over the duty solicitor he was offered. He sat down heavily and noisily on the low bed and loosened his tie.

"Oh dear, oh dear, Robert. What a mess." In spite of his predicament, Prior couldn't restrain an involuntary grunt of amusement. There was something unintentionally comical about Blake. He reminded him of a boxer dog. His affection turned to irritation as Blake's doleful eyes roamed the grimy cell. What the hell was there to look at in this mausoleum that was surely depressingly familiar to him?

"Before I say anything else, I want you to know that this is a complete fabrication. I totally deny it and will be pleading not guilty." He maintained an oppressive eye contact to reinforce the truth of his words and it was Blake who looked away first.

"Okay, okay Robert, slow down. You haven't even been charged yet. They've set the interview for one o'clock which has taken account of your eight-hour rest period. I've seen the arrest sheet and the complainant's claims. What's your version?" Blake shifted back to lean against the wall. His lower legs stuck out from the edge of the bed, the trousers riding up to reveal again the pink hairless calves, his arms folded across his large belly as Prior explained the events of the previous evening. It seemed so long ago now, framed as it was in such a diverse circumstance. He could remember everything down to the last detail and was incredulous that the ecstasy of some of the moments he described could have turned so quickly to this abject despair. When he had finished, Blake stroked his chin and looked passively at the wall.

"So it's really your word against hers unless there are witnesses. Your DNA will be all over her by your own admission but your argument is that it's consensual." He put his hands on the bed and shuffled clumsily forwards until his feet touched the floor and he straightened with some effort and some heavy breathing.

"I'll go and see if I can find anything else out, Robert – I'll see you later."

At 12:40 p.m. a female orderly collected him from his cell and led him through a maze of low corridors past numerous closed doors to a small ill-lit room where two people sat behind a desk. Blake sat on a chair against the wall to the left of the door alongside a middle-aged woman. The woman behind the desk smiled and said, "Good morning, Robert. Sit down." She gestured towards the one empty chair in front of the two plain clothes police officers and the male officer immediately took two new cassettes from their wrappers and loaded them into a twin deck recorder. He informed Prior that the interview would be recorded and clicked the record button. The woman identified herself as Detective Sergeant Willis followed by Detective Constable Higgs.

Willis nodded towards Prior and Blake who gave their names and then the other woman who said, "Hazel Williams, Appropriate Adult." Prior exhaled in exasperation.

"I made it clear I don't want one. I'm an adult and I'm appropriate." There was a pause as they all looked at each other. Detective Willis was the first to speak.

"You don't have to have one if you don't want. The system is there only for your own protection. Mr. Blake, have you got a view?"

"I'm satisfied that my client has the capacity to understand the proceedings." She turned to the social worker. "Sorry to have wasted your time, Mrs. Williams." She stood up looking rather disappointed to be cheated out of one of the few cushy and interesting assignments in her largely thankless job.

Prior felt a bit sorry for her and tried to convey it in his look as he said, "Nothing personal. That bloke can't have passed on my instructions." When she had left, Higgs stated the time of commencement and place of the interview and explained to Prior the procedures relating to the master tape and the working copy before saying that he was now turning it off to replay a portion of it to check it was functioning correctly. He smiled coyly as the room listened to a brief reprise of his nasal south London drone.

"I hate hearing my own voice." The flash of resonance Prior felt at the commonality of the emotion was quickly replaced by his growing awareness of an insidious exclusion from the membership of that universal communality. The machine was turned on again and Willis took over, formally cautioning him with words which cut through any illusions that may have been germinating and confirming the gravity of his predicament. They were the same words he had heard at his flat a few hours ago but this time, in this environment and in the absence of any suspension of reality, they chilled him to the bone.

She leant back and looked at him with a faint smile on her lips. There was however no hint of mirth in her green eyes.

"Okay Robert. Is it alright to call you Robert?" Prior nodded and was told to verbalise his assent for the benefit of the record.

"Right. Well could you describe the events of Friday, 16th December. Say, from about lunchtime."

He felt relief that he could finally begin the process of clearing his name.

"I joined a country club yesterday morning and had a round of golf with a guy I met. We teamed up afterwards and had a few drinks with a couple of his mates before they went home; about seven I suppose it was. I thought I'd hang around so I had a bite to eat and then got talking to these three ladies in the bar."

Willis interjected, "Do you remember their names?"

"Yeah. Their first names anyway. Della, Carol, and Naomi."

"Okay, carry on."

"It was nice. We were all happy and we had a laugh. What I needed to be honest after the time I've had recently. I'm going to be completely up front with you because I've got nothing to hide. Well nothing illegal, anyway. I went out for a smoke with the one called Naomi and we hit it off. I mean there was a chemistry. We'd both had a lot to drink and we're only human. It was wrong though because I knew she was married."

Higgs interrupted him. "What was wrong?"

"We kissed. That was all." He paused before saying, "Until later anyway."

Willis nodded at him. "Carry on."

"We went back in. Shortly afterwards we learnt that her husband had missed his flight to Portugal. He was back at home. It sort of panicked us I suppose. Now or never. If he had gone what happened might not have. We'd have probably got so drunk as to have been incapable. As it was, in our uninhibited state but with the remains of some control it made us concentrated and determined."

Blake cleared his throat. "Can I ask something?"

The police officers looked impatiently at him.

"Yes?" said Willis.

"When you say you were 'uninhibited', was this down to the alcohol or as a manifestation of a manic state given your diagnosis of bipolar disorder?"

Prior thought for a few seconds, trying to discern the relevance of the question. He looked at Blake with a hint of annoyance. No-one was going to suggest mitigation of a non-existent guilt by throwing in the mental health card.

"The alcohol. I'm perfectly well at the moment."

Blake looked vaguely uneasy but said, "Okay. Thanks Robert." The policewoman seemed irritated by the break in her concentration and looked sharply at the solicitor.

"If you remember Mr. Blake, an Appropriate Adult was declined with your approval. You'll have an opportunity to speak when we're finished." She turned back to Prior. "So what happened then?"

"We went out again – ostensibly for another smoke but we had something else in mind. We walked across the car park and found a private place. At least we thought it was private – behind the bowling green clubhouse." His embarrassment at his description of what happened next was tempered by the need to clear his name.

"We started intercourse."

Higgs put in hurriedly, "Full sexual intercourse?"

"Yes. No preliminaries. We were disturbed though. Some lads were looking for somewhere to take a leak and we stopped what we were doing and hid. By the time they'd gone Naomi had changed her mind."

"So what did you do?" said Willis.

"Well you can imagine how I felt. Well I'm sure Mr. Blake and Detective Constable Higgs can anyway. What could I do? I accepted her decision. Disappointed? Yes. Angry? Yes. Frustrated? Yes. Rape?" He shook his head. "Never in a million years. I didn't even argue with her. You might not believe this but I had actually started to feel something for her – you know, beyond the lust thing. I just walked away and she followed some way behind." He stopped to ponder his next quandary. He could probably be done for public lewdness or something on his testimony thus far and he had then broken the law again that night. He decided that to lie about this might prejudice his chance of being believed about the far more serious allegation.

"Okay. I'll hold my hands up. I then did a silly thing. I collected my jacket and then went straight to my car and drove home. Probably over the limit." The Detective Sergeant's face took on a stern countenance.

"More than 'probably' I would imagine. That's not something I could do anything about now as I'm sure Mr. Blake would tell you." She looked at Blake, who carefully avoided being lured into the smile that the script called for. He knew how much she hated drink driving. He had appeared slightly disconcerted throughout the interview as if preoccupied by an insoluble conundrum. He turned his eyes from her steady gaze and she continued, "Carry on, Robert."

"That's it. I went straight to bed, about midnight I think, and the next thing I knew all hell was breaking loose with your friends bursting in on me."

There was a natural pause in the proceedings and Higgs turned off the tape and both police officers jotted some notes in pocket books. Prior reflected on his account and felt generally pleased with it. He appreciated the importance of the accuracy of his first statement and the damage to his case of any subsequent need to alter it. He had said nothing that he wouldn't stick by. Just how Naomi had twisted those events had him completely baffled. And anyway, why? He could only assume that her husband had got wind of something and she was protecting her reputation by impugning him. It seemed out of character but then he'd never been much of a judge of a person on first impressions as Caroline had frequently pointed out. His thoughts were interrupted by the click of the recorder being restarted and Willis looked up and spoke.

"Right. We are now going to ask you a few questions. You say you went straight to your car after you left Mrs. Thompson. Can you recall what time this was?"

"Not exactly. I should think about elevenish."

"Where was your car parked?"

"I wasn't in the main car park as it was full when I arrived in the morning. I was in a side road adjoining the club's grounds. I kept meaning to move it into the car park through the day but never got round to it."

"How did you go to your car – I mean what route did you take?"

Prior couldn't understand the line of questioning.

"I just vaulted a small wall into the road I was parked on. The entrance gate on the main road would have taken me about five minutes. I just wanted to get home as quickly as possible."

The detective paused and made a note.

"Okay. You told Dr. Blethin you have stopped taking your medication. Why and when was that?"

Prior cursed himself for his honesty. "About two weeks ago. I was piling on weight. My brain felt like cotton wool and I'm trying to do a creative job. I just thought I'd give it a try."

"And how do you think the trial has gone?" He sensed a note of cynicism.

"Good. I was actually starting to feel happy and normal again. Until this."

"So you didn't think you had become or were becoming unwell again?"

"No."

"When you made an unprovoked assault on a member of the public, assaulted a policeman and resisted arrest last March – would you say you were unwell then?"

Prior was puzzled. A vague notion that this was inadmissible crossed his mind but maybe he was confusing the police interview with the courts. He was also surprised that this information must have been on their database. He looked at his solicitor for support or clarification.

"Can I speak?" said Blake, a little tentatively in the light of the previous mild admonishment.

"By all means."

"Regarding that incident, Robert, you were perhaps fortunate to have it disposed of by way of a section 136 – that's the police power of removal to a place of safety of a mentally disordered person found in a public place. The young man involved did not wish to prefer charges and you weren't arrested or charged. Reports were obviously made out however, and that's how the officer is able to refer to the incident."

Willis continued, "Yes, thank you Mr. Blake. So Robert you can quite justifiably dispute my version of those events. Do you?"

"I don't remember much about it. I suppose I have to accept other people's testimony. I was under a lot of pressure at the time."

"So is that your way of admitting you were unwell?" Prior looked heavenwards. He felt again the implicit coercion towards an admission of a state of mind that would deplete his credibility.

"Unwell? To me unwell is a dose of flu or diabetes or cancer. I'd describe my behaviour as a proportionate response to external circumstance rather than anything internal."

"And what were those external circumstances?" He felt foolish. The pressures sounded so pathetic now – overwork, affairs of the heart, loneliness – just the stuff of life. He despised the current stress culture, the knee jerk excuse for deficiency.

"Nothing really – my business." Willis looked pensive and Higgs took over the questioning. He took Prior by surprise by actually smiling at him.

"You'll be pleased to know Robert that Mrs. Thompson has more or less replicated your account word for word." He paused to allow the impact of the words to sink in. Prior waited for the inevitable sting in the tail.

"It's what happened after you say you left her that concerns us." He fixed Prior with a stony glare.

"Mrs. Thompson was found semi-naked and weeping in undergrowth adjoining the smoking area and the side road you say you parked in at twelve fifteen a.m. on Saturday, 17th December, 2011. She had incurred traumatic injuries to her face, bruising to her body and had been forcibly raped." He continued to stare with an intensity that caused Prior to reluctantly look down when he could bear its oppression no longer.

"What do you say about that?"

"It makes me sad. And angry."

"Why's that Robert?"

"Because I told you, I cared for her. I'd like to get hold of whoever's done this."

"So you deny that it was you?"

It was Prior's turn to glare and he said with as much emphasis as he could, "Categorically yes."

Willis leaned forward and her tone was sympathetic.

"You're not doing yourself any favours, Robert. My colleagues are at this very moment checking CCTV, DNAs, forensics. You had motive, opportunity. You have no alibi. You were present in the vicinity. It's not looking good. An admission of guilt is going to stand you in good stead. And you're not well, Robert – that's obvious even to me as a lay person in medical matters. I'm sure your legal team will look at pleas in mitigation and diminished responsibility. It needn't be so bad for you."

Prior mirrored the detective and leaned forward towards her.

"Watch my lips. I didn't do it."

They concluded the interview and sealed the master tape in Prior's presence, keeping a second tape to be used as a working copy. He was offered the opportunity to clarify anything he had said or to add anything which he declined. He signed the label Higgs had put on the tape and was given a notice explaining aspects of its use. Finally, Willis informed him that he would be asked to sign the interview record later.

Prior felt drained and desperately in need of a smoke. He had had to surrender his cigarettes on arrival in custody but thankfully Blake was a smoker and the orderly allowed them access to a small, uncovered yard where they both lit up, inhaling deeply. Blake leant against a wall with his left hand behind his back, his cigarette cupped surreptitiously in his right hand as if he was trying to conceal it while Prior transferred his weight from foot to foot, swivelling his hips as the cigarette's orange glow in the dim light scarcely had time to turn to ash before it was finished, such was his voracity.

He flicked it away and begged another and said, "What do you think?"

Blake spoke in a barely audible voice. "I think we need to speak privately," and he jerked his head in the direction of the door where the orderly was waiting.

Blake went into the cell with him and waited until the door was closed.

"I thought you did very well. I certainly believed you. There doesn't seem to be any doubt that the woman was raped. The injuries make that pretty indisputable. The fact that she's admitted the shenanigans between the two of you suggests she's got no ulterior motive."

Shenanigans, thought Prior. The description somehow conveyed the resentful envy of an involuntary celibate.

"The assumption has to be that someone else got to her after you'd gone, in which case his DNA will be present."

"So what do you think will happen now?"

"You're entitled to another eight-hour rest period before you can be interviewed again; if they need to. You came in at what, 3:45 a.m.? They've got to charge you within twenty-four hours or release you – either altogether or on police bail. They could ask for a twelve hour extension on the twenty-four hours though. As they told you, they'll be doing some investigative work. It's anyone's guess what they'll come up with. DNA's going to be crucial in this case and that can take time. Try not to worry about it – have a rest. They'll bring you some lunch in a minute. I'm getting away now. Is there anyone you want me to phone?" Prior had been offered a phone call shortly after being arrested but declined. If he wasn't charged, the less people who knew about it the better. Why give the 'no smoke without fire' brigade any ammunition? He shook his head.

"Oh, one last thing, Robert. If the worst came to the worst and you were charged I would strongly recommend you avail yourself of all the help that's available – Appropriate Adult, the mental health people." He waited for the predictably animated response but Prior's reply was muted, diffident. He suddenly looked weary and almost defeated.

"Okay Bernard – I'll think about it. But it won't come to that will it?" Blake patted his arm by way of reply to the rhetorical question and left him alone as the impenetrable door closed again on his liberty.

He lay on the hard bed consciously fighting sensations of claustrophobia which had not registered earlier, and anxiety escalated into near panic as he contemplated the totality of his present non-determination and the limit of his movement. Outside, the world went on, its populace by and large engaging in activity voluntarily within the dictates of the need to survive and play the necessary games for survival. With the benefit of relativity he wanted to scream out to them to value every second of their precious freedom. He began the breathing exercises Marie had taught him and gradually felt calmer. He even felt a surge of affection for her, although he knew that the law of relativity was at play again. Right now he cherished anything and anyone that preceded and had nothing to do with this Godawful mess he had found himself in. An extreme fatigue came on him and he fell into a fitful sleep that was disturbed by the arrival of lunch. He waved it away and finally, with his body curled in the foetal position and his head close to the smeared wall there came a sleep deep enough for dreams.

CHAPTER 13

Dominique turned the corner and trundled her barrow along the forty metres of path to her home. It felt lighter this morning and her spirits were high as she anticipated the excitement of her younger sister and brothers. It was Christmas Day and the queue at the reservoir had been shorter. Added to the fact that the bakery was closed, Dominique's arrival home was earlier than usual. They all embraced and wished each other a happy Christmas and she put a large frying pan on the makeshift range and added the remains of yesterday's cachupa povera to a little oil and fried it. When it began to caramelise she transferred it to a plate and fried six eggs before dividing the mixture onto six plates and placing an egg on top of each for a celebration breakfast of cachupa guisada. When that was finished she would go over the instructions again with her younger sister, Veronique, for the cachupa rica they would be having this evening with the treat of some added chicken. Veronique would be cooking as Dominique had to work as normal in the hotel, although she would be home early as the property agency was closed for the holiday. She covered one plate and left it warming on the edge of the grate while she ate her meal and when she had finished she took it through to her mother. She doubted she would manage more than a mouthful or two before it was given to the dog but she would be pleased with its appearance, garnished with tomato and the addition of the egg to denote the difference of the day. The woman on the mattress did not stir as her daughter entered the room and Dominique put the plate on the floor and gently shook her mother by the shoulder. Her face was obscured by the white sheet that covered her frail body and Dominique peeled it back and looked at an ashen face whose staring eyes and anguished twist of the mouth gave a clue to an uncomprehending, solitary departure some time during the hours between now and the kiss her eldest girl had placed on her clammy forehead the night before.

Dominique struggled with her shock before burying her head in the sheet and sobbing in soft plaintive gasps. She closed her mother's eyes and placed her carefully on her back. Rigor mortis had not yet set in so her demise must have been recent. Covering her face with the sheet, she got wearily to her feet and stood pondering on how to break the news to her siblings who she could hear chattering excitedly in the yard. She could hardly bear the thought of it. They still pined for their father, killed in a construction site accident two years before. There was no need for words. Her tear-stained face and halting step were enough to impart the tidings and the five of them linked in a huddle. The grief was restrained, moderated by its inevitability but made more poignant by the happiness around them as the sounds of the awakening town increased. After they had paid their respects they gathered in the yard to re-plan the day.

So strong was Dominique's work ethic and need to earn she even considered turning in but she was dissuaded by Veronique who made her see that this was one day when she would be needed more at home. At fifteen, four years younger than her sister, she was used to deferring to her invariable rectitude and was pleased at this small victory. The boys, Amilcar, eleven, Christiano, nine, and Edson, eight, shuffled around the yard, heads down, their emotions confused and in disarray at the unexpected turn of events, periodically gripping tight to their sisters for the comfort of a vicarious maternal osmosis. In a cupboard in the house a bag full of presents, lovingly wrapped by Dominique, sat untouched, forgotten. She called them in from their meanderings and spoke authoritatively in her Creole tongue with a wisdom beyond her years, trying to force a radiance she did not feel.

"Let us be happy on this wonderful day of our Lord's birth. Let us be grateful that our dear mama is now free of her pain and safe in the arms of God." She turned to more practical considerations. "This is what we shall do. Veronique – wash the dishes and put them away. Boys – change into your clothes for church and stay clean until I get back. I am going to phone my work and then go to the church. They will know what arrangements to make for Mama. When I come back we will all go to church together to thank our Lord for all the things He gives us. Then we will come home and have our presents and enjoy the remainder of the day."

Buoyed by her attitude, the children immediately made themselves busy and she slipped onto the sandy path and walked to the cyber café owned by African Muslims and open as usual. She called the hotel owner who was sympathetic and considerate, reassuring her that she would still be paid for today given the circumstances and to come back when she was ready. Dominique assured her that it would be tomorrow.

As she entered the church on the main tourist thoroughfare just after nine, a few isolated figures were in leisurely preparation for the Mass at eleven. She approached a bespectacled woman arranging flowers by the altar who gave Dominique an enveloping hug when she told her the news.

"Father de Freitas has not arrived yet but he will be here soon." She took Dominique's hand and they went into a small office in the church's annexe where a young man in a white shirt sat at a rudimentary table serving as a desk. She explained what had happened and he belied his languorous demeanour by making a series of efficient phone calls. He had obviously done it before.

"The doctor will be at the house within one hour to certify death and he will inform the undertaker when this has been done. They will then bring your mother to the Chapel of Rest. We will arrange the funeral and meet the expense. Don't worry about anything; we'll take care of it."

Dominique was relieved at his calm assumption of control and she went back into the church and knelt at a pew for a few moments before approaching the woman who was arranging hymnbooks and service sheets on a table at the entrance of the church.

"I need to go home now, Madame Gracieth. I very much want to come to the service but I cannot leave my mother alone if the undertaker does not come before eleven. Can you suggest anything?" The woman thought for a few seconds.

"I will send someone to the house at 10:45 to sit with her. You go and I will see you later."

She made the short walk back and changed into a clean dress and they sat in uncharacteristic serenity, mostly lost in their own thoughts and recollections. At 10:15, a knock on the door revealed the figure of Father de Freitas standing on the step. He was a short Portuguese man in his early fifties, sturdy and swarthy with thick black hair greying at the temples. He smelt of soap, cigar smoke, and the communion wine he had finished off at the nine o' clock Mass he had conducted in a nearby town. He covered three parishes and the heavy workload meant he had little chance to become intimately involved with his parishioners, including Dominique and her siblings who knew him only by sight. They were slightly awed by his presence in their humble dwelling and the boys giggled nervously as Dominique showed him to the room where the dead woman lay and he said some prayers over her body. The girls gushed their gratitude at his finding time on this busy morning for them and he raised a hand to stop them.

"Hush-hush. God will always find time for His children. I am only a medium for His love." He blessed them and went quickly away to prepare for the service and the doctor came shortly afterwards, followed by two girls from the church as promised. Dominique felt torn in respect of where she should rightfully be at this moment but was reassured by the knowledge that she would be seeing her mother in repose in the Chapel of Rest. The service was emotional but they were strengthened by the unspoken support of the congregation who were made aware of their mother's departure in the Intercessions.

Back at home the body had gone and they drank Coca-Cola and ate the cakes they had bought from the bakery yesterday. The capucha rica was cooked and Veronique took it off the heat to be warmed up later. Dominique then brought out the bag and emptied the gifts into the middle of the yard. The boys fell on them and she raised her voice and took control, handing out the few packages to the appropriate recipients. She had managed to buy them two presents each and they had scraped together their meagre resources to buy her one between them. There was a new polo shirt each for the boys and for Veronique a dress and a small battery operated CD player. Amilcar had a football, Christiano a compendium of games, and Edson, a promising artist, paper and paints. They were all genuinely thrilled with their presents and there was no need to feign satisfaction. They knew their sister could not afford to waste her precious salary on unwanted things. She opened hers last and smiled with pleasure at the bag she needed. She could now dispense with the plastic bags she currently used. One present was left unopened and she picked it up and carefully undid the paper. It was the small manual fan and cotton nightdress she had bought for her mother. They all embraced and began preparations to go to the beach for the afternoon. Given the simplicity of their existence, these were mercifully few and they set off on the kilometre walk, the girls in bikinis with towels wrapped around their waists and the boys in shorts and flip-flops. Amilcar clasped his precious football and Dominique's new bag contained only a bottle of water and a battered radio. The boys ran on ahead, passing the ball to each other as the older two walked behind. Dominique couldn't remember the last time they had all gone to the beach together.

At the edge of the town they joined the wide road which ran alongside three of the hotels and led to the beach. The road was formed by a neat mosaic of bricks fashioned from volcanic rock mined from below the sea and then laid laboriously by hand, brick by brick. To the right were apartment blocks in various stages of construction and the seawater marshland between the road and the semi-completed buildings gave concern as to the potential stability of their foundations. The whole town seemed to be in a permanent state of development with little sign of an elusive workforce. To the left the family looked through to the contrasting hotels. The main hotel buildings with their glass-fronted air-conditioned lobbies backed onto a labyrinth of asphalt paths separating rows of guest chalets, their verandas fringed by exotic tropical plants watered by seemingly infinite supplies of water. Tourism had replaced salt as the main industry of the island and it could be argued that this profligate use of a precious commodity was part of an investment. The boys, however, gazed in incomprehension as they thought of their sister's daily excursions to the water tank and her ferocious monitoring of its consumption. They reached the end of the road and moved past the hotel's uniformed security guard, positioned at a junction between the beach and the entrance to the hotel complex. They all removed their flip-flops and put them in Dominique's new bag and the feel of the soft warm sand and the sight of the clear blue sea gave a lift to their subdued mood. One of the boys kicked the ball far ahead and they began a frantic chase to be the first to reach it while at the water's edge the girls chose a spot in that curiously considered yet arbitrary way that leads almost immediately to a sense of possession and territorial ownership. They watched the boys rushing headlong into the waves, their yells at the sharp contrast in temperature carried on the warm stiff wind that blew sand onto the towels around their bent knees.

Dominique leant back on her straight arms and squinted at the wind and kite surfers beyond the dark bobbing heads of her brothers. The waves here were relatively small, although an occasional rogue giant could take one by surprise and she kept a watchful eye. Further along the coast towards the Hotel Rui, the waves grew progressively larger and stronger. She felt confused in her emotions. She didn't feel as upset as she felt she should be and was not convinced the reason lay in the brave words she had used to lift the spirits of her younger siblings. She felt guilt at a slight relief as she contemplated a return to the house that would not involve washing and changing and feeding her mother, but defended herself with thoughts of the blessed alleviation of the distress that had accompanied these tasks, the natural role reversal much too premature. She enjoyed idly watching the people passing by between her and the sea and experienced an increasing recognition of the female figure walking hand in hand with a red-headed male, his milk white skin turning pink in the hot afternoon sun. When she was about twenty yards away she saw it was Zina. Zina had spotted her too and the couple veered off diagonally and trudged up the slight incline through the softer sand. They stood smiling at the two sitting figures below them, shielding their eyes from the glare of the sun.

"Oi Dominique. Happy Christmas. Oh, this is... Craig." Dominique sensed that she had needed to concentrate her mind to remember his name.

"Oi Zina. Please to meet Veronique." She pointed at her sister who smiled engagingly.

"How is your Christmas?"

"Okay." Zina grimaced and tapped her head.

"Be better when my hangover has gone. And you?" The split second the brain has in conversation to form a response evidently decided her against complicating the exchange and she said nothing.

"We're going up to watch the surfers – I think there's a

competition. Might try a hair of the dog." The man let out a cynical laugh. Whether he was amused by the debauch or Dominique's blank incomprehension at the colloquialism was unsure. He appeared bored with the conversation and eager to be going.

"Okay Dom. Nice to see you. See you on the…" She did some mental arithmetic. "The third isn't it? Enjoy the rest of the holiday." The girls watched the retreating figures, Zina's buttocks gyrating on either side of a black thong, the man's guttural laughter growing gradually more distant as they waded along the edge of the increasing swell of the ocean. The girls walked to the seashore and gingerly moved through the water, rising onto tip toes as each wave encroached on a higher portion of coffee-toned body. When she was waist deep, Dominique joined her hands and arrowed below the surface, squealing softly at the relative cold as her head emerged although the sea temperature was a pleasant twenty degrees. Veronique lowered her top half under the water and her look of panic turned to a smile of relief that the delicious torment was over. They lay on their backs just beyond the breakers, rising and falling with the swell, and lifted their heads to make out the silhouettes of their brothers engaged in a football game at the end of the beach near the town. Veronique went to a pocket on the inside of her bikini bottoms and took out the remains of a small bar of Camay soap, making a thick lather in her hands and massaging it into her face, hair and body before rinsing it off and passing it to her sister who repeated the exercise.

They came out of the sea and allowed themselves to dry naturally by walking slowly towards the footballers and watching the impromptu game which had now developed into something more organised, with pitch markings scratched out in the sand and driftwood serving as goalposts. Their brothers and three European-looking tourists were being soundly beaten by a team of four West African traders who were toying with the opposition. The girls were drawn in particular to one the others were calling Abu, whose lithe athleticism and skill set him above the others, even to their untrained eyes. Dominique thought she had seen him before near to the property agency she worked in. The game continued throughout the rest of the afternoon and into the early dusk experienced on the island. The personnel were fluid and transient but the three young boys remained the constant, which was fortunate as they were the proud possessors of the ball. Their energy appeared limitless and their enthusiasm mercifully allowed them to detach from the earlier events of the day. For once Dominique was grateful to football in its capacity as a channel for the males' arrested emotions. She dreaded the darkness which would soon follow the beauty of the pastel sunset and the solitary thoughts of the orphaned boys.

They walked home in the last minutes of dusk as the solar lights fringing the hotel paths came to sporadic life, skirting the edge of a town whose levels of noise and activity were starting to build as the tourists and expatriates began their nightly quest for sensual pleasure. By candlelight the boys played snakes and ladders from the games compendium while the girls prepared for the next day. The atmosphere was restrained and they all felt emotionally and physically spent. They ate the capucha rica ravenously, savouring the rare treat of unrationed chicken, and the boys went to bed with Dominique's fears thankfully unfounded as they succumbed almost immediately to the overwhelming sleep of childhood. She mustered the energy to complete her last jobs before making the customary check on her siblings. Amilcar clutched the ball to his chest and did not stir as she bent down to kiss him. She thought briefly about claiming her mother's room for herself but this was not the time and she stooped down to the mattress that Veronique had pulled next to hers and slipped beneath the sheet, the two girls entwined in defiance against the diminution.

CHAPTER 14

He was covered in sweat when he woke and the recollection of his dream was still vivid. He had been in a boxing ring with a faceless opponent and had marvelled at his own skill and stamina. He had ridden the other man's heavy blows with fortitude, returning them with interest, doing all but drop him. The man just wouldn't fall but no matter – his was the victory. At the end of the bout he offered his arm to the referee who walked past him and grabbed and raised the arm of the other. He couldn't understand the acclaim for his adversary and his own invisibility now in what should have been *his* triumph. As he slunk unnoticed through the crowd on the way back to his dressing room, he made eye contact with only one person and he recoiled in horror at her face, bleached white with black eyes and a crimson mouth creased in a sneer of contempt. His fear of her was matched only by his lust, each emotion seemingly fed by the other. His awakening coincided with the return to the dressing room and was synchronous with the stark cell of the reality he opened his eyes to. The time was six-thirty p.m.

He lay on his back trying desperately to preserve reason as his thoughts slipped into a vortex of persecution and despair. He could not imagine anyone else in a worse position than him, all locked into their smug worlds of complacent disregard for the vagaries of misfortune, their undeserved intuitive avoidance of calamity. He chastised himself for only appreciating in retrospect the comfortable little atmospheric zones lasting a few weeks that we realise too late to be happiness. Ahead now, he could only see darkness.

At eight, having earlier refused his evening meal, he was escorted again along the corridors that now resembled underground tunnels to the same interview room where five people lay in wait. The same two officers and Blake had been joined by a custody officer and another woman who had been designated as the Appropriate Adult, who Blake had assumed he no longer had an objection to. The police officers wore blank expressions that gave no clue to what they were going to say. Prior thought his solicitor looked flat, resigned, but then he was naturally hangdog whatever the circumstance. He was asked to sit down and the custody officer handed a piece of paper to the Appropriate Adult and began to speak. It was like one of those letters informing you that you didn't get the job or had been caught exceeding the speed limit. The little pulse-raising words the eyes extract instantly from the verbiage – 'regret', 'unsuccessful', 'warn', 'prosecute'. As the circumstances were itemised and the caution and his right to legal representation repeated, all that registered were the words 'charged' and 'rape' and the incongruous 'Naomi Thompson'. Even now the name still instinctively conjured a faint sense of the allegiance and 'us against the world' unity that he had felt so strongly on that fateful night. He took the charge sheet from the outstretched hand of the Appropriate Adult and scanned it blankly, unable to take in the words or summon any objection to her unexplained reappearance. He was dehydrated and dry spittle had left a white deposit on his lips. He was asked if he understood the charge and he shook his head almost imperceptibly from side to side, staring at the Custody Sergeant, his eyes a weapon to deflect their own pain onto him. The intensity of his look disturbed even a person of the policeman's experience.

"Is that a yes or a no?"

Prior's voice was almost a whisper. "Yes, I understand the charge. No, I don't understand why I've been charged. I didn't do it."

He looked around the room at each of the faces. The bloated solicitor growing fat on the carcass of wretches like him, the rebuke implicit in the sour countenance of the Appropriate Adult, the impenetrable confederacy of the police. He felt sick to death of other people and just wanted to be alone again. He was taken back to his cell and an interminable night finally gave way to the longest Sunday of his life. He was seen by a custody nurse who was concerned by his low mood and lack of appetite and he was persuaded to see a doctor who took advantage of his passive malleability to get him to agree to start accepting nourishment again under the supervision of custody staff. He flatly refused to recommence lithium or start an antidepressant but his request for a sleeping tablet that evening was granted. He was deemed to be a suicide risk and watched closely. The thought had indeed crossed his mind but all avenues had been closed, even down to the paper underwear that was his only apparel. At nine a.m. on Monday morning, the start of the week leading up to Christmas, Prior was incarcerated in the dark windowless vehicle that transported him to the Magistrates' Court. The claustrophobia was even worse than in the cell. At the courts he swapped his mobile cell for another dingy tomb in the damp, echoing bowels of the building, and he was joined after a short time by Blake and Robin Graves in a shiny maroon suit and matching navy blue shirt and tie which made him look like a dodgy bookmaker.

"You two know each other I think," started Blake, and Graves nodded in the absence of any response from Prior. The sleeping tablet had worked well in sending him into a deep dreamless sleep at nine but he had woke at three and been unable to go off again. His brain felt taut and unrested but he blessed the absence of the mind-numbing mood stabilisers.

"How do you plan to plead?" continued Blake, who knew the answer anyway.

Prior spoke without looking up.

"Not guilty."

Blake and Graves looked at each other and the former said, "Fair enough, Robert. However, it is my duty as your solicitor to give you as much information as I've been able to glean from the prosecution. This is not confirmed, but the word I've had is that they've worked very quickly on the DNA taken from Mrs. Thompson. Semen and saliva samples have shown only one DNA – yours." Prior started to speak but Blake interrupted him, "Yes, I know you say you didn't go all the way but there can be seepage." He continued, "You were captured on CCTV walking past the foyer of the clubhouse at 11:11 p.m. The time of the rape is estimated at 11:30 p.m. That raises the potential of you still being in the vicinity. The CPS will argue that you had strong motive and no alibi. Unfortunately there are no CCTV cameras covering the street you were parked in. Have you any questions?"

Prior looked blankly at the wall behind Blake and said nothing.

"Again unfortunately, the woman was unable to provide any identification of her assailant. She was grabbed from behind by someone who then dragged her into the bushes adjacent to the area where she was standing smoking. At no stage during the ordeal was he visible or audible to her. The prosecution will rely on DNA and the circumstantial evidence alluded to."

Prior grudgingly spoke. "So what will happen today?"

"Today's appearance in court will be very brief. I can assure you bail will not be granted so there will be no application for bail. Your intention to plead not guilty will be noted and a date will be set for you to return to the Crown Court for a plea and case management hearing. That will be quite soon, although a bit longer away than normal due to Christmas – probably two or three weeks. At Crown they will give you a trial date and you don't need me to tell you that will be in the long distant future – probably towards the end of next year." He paused to allow Prior time to digest the information. "But this is where it gets complicated and why I'm grateful for the assistance of Robin here."

Graves took his cue and spoke with the quick voice of the busy, Prior would say dismissive, person. His original instinctive dislike of the man remained.

"Whether you like it or not you have a diagnosis of severe mental illness, you're under a psychiatrist and have recently been detained under a section of the Mental Health Act. Your mental health is relevant, guilty or not guilty, ill or not ill at the time of the alleged offence. As Bernard says, it is quite complex in terms of the plethora of options. On the one hand it's simple – if we don't play the mental health card you'll go to prison on remand until your trial. There are of course mental health services in prison and you can be medicated but by and large you're treated like any other prisoner."

Prior mustered a plaintive interruption. "But I haven't done anything. And why no bail?"

Blake spoke again. "I'm afraid, Robert, that it's for the protection of the public. The CPS feel they have a very strong case against you."

"Do you?"

The solicitor shifted uneasily and averted Prior's eager gaze.

"I'm not saying I don't believe you but yes, I do think they have a strong case. They will almost certainly have DNA evidence, or shall we say the lack of it, which gives them the trump card."

Prior took the opportunity to express a thought that had emerged from his feverish ramblings of yesterday.

"Haven't you heard of condoms?" The question took Blake by surprise and he took some time to answer.

"Very unlikely in a rape case."

"But not impossible."

"No. But in the absence of any other identified suspect it's only conjecture and a pretty flimsy defence."

"It's the only explanation if Naomi was raped."

Graves interrupted the conversation of the two other men.

"I'm sure this will all be discussed in more detail before the trial." He looked at his watch. "The mags will be starting shortly. I need to outline the options I mentioned. Rather than spending your remand in jail I think there is a case for you needing to be in hospital." Prior winced at the thought. The admission was still too recent, too raw for him to appreciate its relative advantage. He spoke on an impulse of emotion.

"No. Not hospital." Graves narrowed his eyes.

"With respect, that decision is out of your hands. You undoubtedly had a manic episode prior to your arrest, albeit not as intense as the previous one. Your mood has very quickly reversed and you are clinically depressed. Part three of the Mental Health Act governs patients involved in criminal proceedings or who are under sentence." He looked at his watch again and spoke even faster. "We'll ask the magistrates to consider either a section 35 – Remand to Hospital for Assessment, or a 36 – Remand to Hospital for Treatment. A section 48 – Remand to Hospital of an Unsentenced Prisoner might also be an option. This may be accompanied by a section 49 restriction direction meaning you can only be discharged from the section or allowed leave at the discretion of the Home Office." The words came easily off his tongue as if by rote. "49 would probably apply in a rape case. Looking a long way down the road, if you are found guilty we would look at a section 37/41 – a Hospital Order with restrictions meaning you would spend your sentence in hospital as opposed to prison."

Prior looked up slowly, struggling to assimilate the dry terminology of numbers and protocols charting his immediate future. He felt an unexpected stab of pity for this strange-looking man spending his working days in the gloomy cells of custody suites and prisons, derided, Prior imagined, for being a fringe member, a bit part player in the massive theatre of the law. If his brain was not numbed and enfeebled by the crippling absence of serotonin he would have acknowledged that he too was a parasite feeding off the glory of the main players in the drama, but there was no comparison between the relative terrains. His was vastly preferable.

Graves continued, "My suggestion will be to go for a 35 initially, mainly because we only need one doctor to make the recommendation which will save time. If the mags are a bit wary we can reassure them that a 48 or 49 will be the probable option after a fuller assessment. To be honest they don't have much idea about the Mental Health Act. The Clerk to the Court doesn't either. They're usually happy to be guided by us."

Blake asked Graves, "So I am right in saying he can't go straight from the court to hospital today?"

"No. He'll have to go back to custody. I'll arrange for Dr. Patel to see him ASAP and then on to hospital if he agrees to make the recommendation which I'm sure he will."

"So when you say hospital… what sort of hospital?" said Prior.

"Good question. Today I'm looking at the Nathan Centre at the Imperial." His heart sank at the thought of a return.

"I checked earlier and there's a bed on Juniper, the lock-up ward. That will only be very temporary and we'll be looking at 48 or 49 as I said and medium or high secure forensic."

Blake looked puzzled and asked, "So they have prisoners on remand at secure forensic hospitals?" Graves nodded and Prior felt dizzy, anxiety welling up in his abdomen as images of Broadmoor, Rampton, and Ashworth flooded into his mind.

He could only say again in an agonised whisper, “But I didn’t do anything.”

An orderly opened his cell half an hour later to inform him that his case was called. He was taken up a seemingly never-ending flight of winding concrete steps and finally found himself in a reinforced glass booth in the centre of a court room. He sat down and recovered his breath before an elderly bespectacled man in the centre of the three people opposite asked him to stand and confirm his name, address and date of birth. Beneath the magistrates sat a female Clerk to the Court and facing her at a long table with their backs to Prior were Blake and four other lawyers. Graves sat in a pew to their left and behind him were an assortment of people in the gallery, one of whom, with an internal gasp of horror, he recognised as a reporter from his own newspaper. The room was heavy and oppressive to Prior, the weighty polished wood of its furnishings and the hierarchical structures lending an aura of majestic gravitas.

Despite the setting there was an air of informality about the events played out in front of him, the bemused magistrates apparently at the mercy of the legal brains, the Clerk attempting to decipher the complexity of the alternatives and translate for their benefit. Beyond the self-righteous pomposity of the upstanding citizen, Prior wondered what qualification they had to sit in judgement on their fellow man.

Although Crown in itself indicated the more serious nature of the offence, he was hopeful of a less arbitrary arbitration further along the line. The CPS advocate had no objection to the course of action suggested by Graves and put to the bench by Blake, and with his plea noted and no application for bail he was informed that he would be returned to a cell at the custody suite to return to the Magistrates’ Court at the first sitting following the psychiatrist’s assessment and recommendation.

Dr. Patel saw him early that afternoon and duly decided that he required hospital on the basis of deterioration in mental health manifested by severe depression and his being a high risk of harm to self by suicide. He promised Robin that his report would be typed that afternoon and in the hands of the magistrates the following morning.

He lay on the bed for the rest of the afternoon contemplating the next few days, months, years. They didn’t bear thinking about. From the last vestiges of an evaporating survival instinct he thought of others in similar positions – the Iranian hostages, those serving long sentences erroneously; they had somehow found the will to fight on and eventually regain what remained of their lives. He lamented the lack of a faith which might have supported him at a time like this. His only crutch was the anger he felt, indiscriminate and bitter. He knew it was all that stood between him and oblivion, probably at his own hand, and he needed to nurture and sustain it without the destruction of self-pity. He had been vaguely comforted to see Dr. Patel again, a reminder of a time of the green shoots of recovery, and he had agreed to restart lithium which was brought to him early that evening. Now under section, he couldn't refuse it anyway. He was reassured by the fact that he was exactly the same in his attitude towards him as on their previous meeting. The doctor urged him to accept the hospital option when it was offered throughout the ensuing months. He should not feel stigmatised by his diagnosis and cut off his nose to spite his face. He tried to allay Prior's hellish perception of secure forensic hospitals and reminded him of the treatment an alleged sex offender might receive in prison. That night he closed his eyes and in his desperation, offered up a prayer to an unknown God like a sceptical fisherman casting a line in the vain hope of getting a bite.

***

He returned to court the next morning and a section 35 Remand to Hospital for Assessment document was issued along with a date of 11th January 2012 for his first Crown Court appearance. He was taken from the court through the streets of the capital by a car containing three policemen, one of whom sat alongside him in the back. He felt that to all intents and purposes he had already been found guilty. As the car pulled up in front of the hospital's psychiatric unit he remembered his journey in the opposite direction eight months previously. Oh, if only in the tremulous, uncertain frame of mind of that day he could have appreciated the jewels he possessed. If only that elusive foresight contained a fraction of the certainty of hindsight. He would give all his worldly goods now to be standing in the same spot looking out at the uncharted horizon rather than being escorted through the glass doors back to another purgatory. At the top of the stairs they turned left towards Juniper Ward. He glanced right at the doors of Oak Ward and in continuation of the theme of relativity the sight evoked an unexpected nostalgia as he remembered the better times – the later sense of renewal rather than the early despair. One of the policemen pressed the buzzer and the reinforced door was eventually opened by a fat nursing auxiliary, his belt buckled beneath a vast overhanging stomach, his head shaved. *Welcome to the asylum*, he thought, and then tempered his cynicism with a recollection of the dangerously disordered souls this ward gave refuge to, and society protection from. There would be times when the presence of this sort of fellow would be reassuring to both staff and patient alike. As long as his heart was in the right place.

He was put on level one observation which entailed his always being within eyeshot of a member of staff, which was tedious for both parties but at least the nurse had the advantage of being relieved after an hour by a colleague. As he sat in front of the television taking nothing in, what had started as the germ of an idea late that morning had taken root and grown inexorably through the afternoon to culminate in the decision he had now reached. He had noticed that patients were allowed to leave the ward to smoke accompanied by a member of staff. At 4:30 p.m. a chatty, ebullient woman took over his observation and he took his chance. He knew that time and opportunity was short and that the vultures of an impenetrable incarceration were hovering. The fact that day had turned to the premature darkness of late December was in his favour, as was the nearly new moon, and he walked slowly down the stairs alongside the woman, checking an impulse to bolt there and then as he remembered the security staff who hung around the unit's entrance. They turned left at the bottom of the stairs and went through a hall, past the gymnasium and into the canteen which looked out onto the garden which was the designated smoking area whatever the weather. The woman went ahead of him and unlocked the French window, holding it open for Prior before turning to answer the banter from one of the cooks filling the bain-marie with the patients' evening meal.

He took off from the blocks like an Olympic sprinter, heading across the damp lawn towards the bushes without looking back. He knew the layout well from his time there in the spring and headed straight for a perimeter wall he knew he could vault at about five feet in height. He dropped onto the pavement below and resumed his sprint, the adrenaline feeding his pumping legs. The back of the hospital receded into the distance behind him and he turned into a street of suburban semi-detached houses, slowing to a trot and gradually allowing his breathing to return to normal. His brain was alive with the excitement, the depression evaporating in the all-consuming preoccupation with survival. He crossed the wide tree-lined avenue to a house in darkness with no car outside and no gate to the alleyway that separated the side of the building from a parallel brick wall that he assumed led down to the back garden. He risked it and breathed a sigh of relief as he discovered he had access to a garden with flower beds on either side of a lawn with mature shrubs and trees at the bottom. He moved stealthily across the grass and found a spot where he could crouch unseen between an evergreen bush and the wooden fence behind. He held himself tense and watchful but after some minutes he relaxed a bit and leaned back against the fence, his anorak just long enough to provide protection from the wet, mossy ground. It was thankfully mild for the time of year and Prior hadn't begun to feel cold yet, still insulated by his long run. He breathed in deeply the comforting smell of bark and soil and rotting leaves and allowed himself the luxury of briefly forgetting why he was sitting where he was and the tortuous, almost certainly doomed life of the fugitive that lay ahead.

Out of habit he felt in his pocket for the cigarettes he knew he couldn't risk even if he had any. All of the possessions that normally filled his pockets – wallet, change, keys, cigarettes, lighter – had been passed to the ward staff by the police for safekeeping. The nurse would still have the cigarette she had taken from his packet and at the memory he pondered on the likely aftermath of his escape – the recriminations, enquiries, apportioning of blame. He hoped the poor woman would not be used as a scapegoat for a flawed system that had given him the window of opportunity. He shifted to a squat position and his hand went into the back pocket of his trousers and he pulled out a brown envelope which he opened. It contained nine twenty pound notes and, unable to see them, he counted them by touch, comforted like a soldier feeling his gun. He had not implored Blake to advance him some cash for incidentals for later payment along with the rest of the fee with his current situation in mind, but he now basked in his inadvertent ingenuity. Blake had huffed and puffed in jobsworth fashion but eventually relented and slipped him the envelope after this morning's court appearance. He had secreted it in his underpants and waited in trepidation for a strip search on the ward that never materialised.

Each of the sirens that penetrated the now wet night air caused a momentary rise in heartbeat but only in their reminder of the presence of the new enemy. His greater concern was for the heat-seeking helicopters whose appearance would cause him to rethink and perhaps relocate if he was that high a priority. He put up his hood and pulled the drawstrings tight around his face so only his eyes, nose, and mouth were visible as he looked up into the sky out of which the rain was falling increasingly heavily. None were there, yet at least, but his neck jerked sharply and his eyes moved in the direction of the house as the beam of a set of headlights travelled down the alleyway and across the patio followed by the banging of a car door and lights flicking on in the house.

He began to take stock of his situation, aware that he was entering an intricate mind game, the rules to which he had not a clue. He nevertheless felt a warm glow of conviction that he had taken the right course. He had little to lose aside from a possible argument that his action increased an implication of guilt. He felt he could argue the opposite. He analysed the minefield that he would have to negotiate to reach his ultimate goal and a picture came into his head of the game of pick-up-sticks he and his brother used to play and which he introduced to his own children when they were small. He could not afford for any of the sticks to move, even infinitesimally, if he was to retain his freedom. Doubts and unknowns flitted through his mind. How high a priority was he to the police? Would they be watching airports, train stations, coach stations? What would be the level of media coverage – local, national, front page, four-line footnote? He should have known that one but didn't. In the absence of any answers to his questions he decided on a policy of ultra-caution in everything except where risk was absolutely unavoidable. He knew what he was going to do next and with the knowing came an impatience he knew he must fight.

His watch showed nearly seven. He had been there two hours and the temperature was falling rapidly. He exercised his body as best he could without noise or outward movement by clenching and then relaxing his muscles in rotation and tried to occupy his mind with lists of sports teams comprising players with the same initial. It was an old habit he used to combat insomnia, a kind of creative sheep counting, and when he tired of that he made lists of his favourite films and books and albums in order of preference. His thoughts were occasionally interrupted by sounds from the house – a raised voice, a back door opening and the shuffle of a bin, and as the door closed again his anxiety was replaced by a melancholy yearning for the normality of the existence of his unwitting protectors.

Gradually the minutes formed hours and at just past eleven o' clock the last light in the house went out. The fence behind him adjoined the back garden of another house so the only exit was the way he had come in. He got up gingerly and stretched and then moved quickly through the garden back towards the house. His heart began pounding as he tiptoed along the alleyway, pausing at the end to look out at what he could see of the street beyond the front garden. He heard the sound of footsteps and voices and waited, pinned to the wall, until they were out of earshot and then he was across the front drive and out into the street in a few strides and walking quickly in the direction of the North London suburb where he knew there was an all-night Tesco. He kept his hood up and moved with his head down, avoiding eye contact with people he passed. He enjoyed the warmth and enticing food smells of the supermarket as he took the escalator up to the clothes department where he chose a pair of tan chino trousers, navy blue rugby shirt, fawn cashmere pullover for warmth and a bottle-green hooded anorak. They provided a stark contrast to the clothes he had left hospital in and he added a pair of brown boots to his trolley and went downstairs where he supplemented the clothes with a pair of thick tortoiseshell framed reading glasses, scissors, razor, mirror, travel bag, wash bag and contents, sandwiches, soft drinks, cigarettes and lighter. Before going to the till he grabbed a copy of the *Evening Standard* late edition, glancing at the first few pages with relief at the absence of any picture or reference to his escape. He then ensconced himself in a cubicle in the gents and set about changing his appearance as far as he could.

He changed into the new clothes, and propping the mirror on top of the lavatory cistern, he hacked at his hair with the scissors until it was short enough to shave. For this he had to take the distasteful option of wetting the stubble with the water from the lavatory bowl but the all-consuming survival instinct outweighed any fastidiousness concerning hygiene. He flinched as he patted aftershave lotion onto his smooth head to close the pores and finished by arranging the glasses on his nose. He was startled by the image he glimpsed in the large mirror over the basin as he headed for the door. Reassuringly so. He contemplated dumping his old clothes in a bin on the short walk to the tube station but thought better of it and kept them in his bag. He was dogged by choices in every aspect of this new situation. The wrong choice, a seemingly trivial lack of attention to detail could scupper him instantly. He took a tube train south on the Northern Line and got off at Euston and his pulse increased and he felt dizzy as he took the escalators up to the mainline station. His blood sugar was low and he knew he needed to eat and drink. He also knew he was taking a chance by coming here but he had considered the alternatives and decided that rail was the best option in terms of speed and anonymity.

He had twenty-twenty vision which the glasses were blurring so he pushed them down his nose, giving him an incongruously donnish air given his shaved head and day's growth of beard. As he stepped off the escalator and into the station he searched the throng for the florescent green jackets of the police, spotting two over by the entrance to the platforms and he walked anxiously towards the ticket office. The next train to Manchester was not until 6:17 and the digital clock on the wall showed 12:47 a.m. He had hoped that there would have been an earlier train. He bought a single ticket with a sigh of relief that he had just enough money left and picked the most unobtrusive seat he could find, washing his sandwiches down with a can of Coke and scanning the paper in more depth. There was nothing beyond a brief description of the morning's court appearance. He pictured the chagrin of the editor at just missing the opportunity to describe the escape that would be all over tomorrow's dailies and he hoped he could get one before his train departed for some enemy intelligence.

The five-hour wait was interminable. He closed his eyes but knew it was futile. The Coke was counter-productive but he was glad of the increased alertness it gave him given the impossibility of sleep in these circumstances. People flitted to and fro in front of his eye line – curious dispossessed figures brought to this wretched place in the middle of the night by an absence of planning, foresight, intelligence, luck or whatever. The floridly mentally ill were in relative preponderance and Prior had a momentary horror of someone from the hospital recognising him. He buried his head in a crooked arm but it was no good. Sleep would have to wait for calmer waters.

In the stark transparency of his conspicuousness among the public he was unable to while away the hours in conscious mental exercises as he had in the shelter of his previous nest. Instead, alternatives to his chosen course of action encroached from his unconscious mind and he began to agonise over more expedient decisions he could have made. Why on earth come to such a predictable place? The safest thing would have been to walk all the way. He wasn't exactly short of time. Or at least walk to a less high-profile station away from the glare. Or hitch. Would a coach have made him less visible? He went round and round in circles as opposing arguments in support of his decision gave him some relief. He was unrecognisable; if he could just get on the train unmolested he'd be far away within a couple of hours – the net was going to be tighter around the metropolis. By five thirty a.m., having resisted multiple impulses to stand up and head for the exit, his mind was made up and he'd risk the original plan.

He bought a first edition of three papers – a quality one, his own middle-of-the-road tabloid, and a red-top tabloid. He turned first to the one he worked for, its front page headline story a scare-mongering, self-pitying description of the 'snow hell' and 'arctic blasts' on the way, a stock subject on a list that also included miracle cures for stubborn illnesses, house price increases and immigrant bashing. The weather-related articles seemed to be more dependent on the time of year rather than any actual meteorological evidence. At this particular moment he had never disliked the selfish, small-minded, middle-England mentality his paper represented more. He flicked through and on page seven a large picture of himself, a blown-up version of the one usually above his articles, stared back at him. Under the headline, 'Top Sports Journalist on Run from Rape Charge' was a brief article relaying the facts and that was it. He imagined his colleagues chafing at the bit to take advantage of their insider knowledge and the discussions with the lawyers over the *sub judice* implications. He was sure there would be more in-depth coverage tomorrow. He wondered if, and where, he might be reading it.

The red-top article had included a standard 'police are watching all potential escape routes' sentence which heightened his unease as he made his way through the ticket barrier, although the two policemen in the vicinity didn't appear to be taking any particular interest in him.

He had decided that to have his anorak hood up might, on balance, be more incriminating than to have it down and he risked the latter under cover of the shaven head. He chose the opportunity to merge into a group of young men who were passing through and drew some comfort from the insulated nature of people these days, their blinkered self-absorption heightened by the earliness of the hour and his own intimidating appearance. He ensured that he was one of the first onto the train and was relieved to discover there were a few seats not separated by a table where it was easier to hide his face. He put his bag on the rack above and settled in to a window seat, turning his gaze towards the platform as the kerfuffle of seat procurement and baggage positioning played out around him. When at last doors slammed, whistles screeched and voices shouted followed by a slow, powerful surge of movement, Prior experienced the first sensation loosely akin to happiness that he had felt in what seemed like an age.

The journey was mercifully uneventful. The train's motion and the tranquillity of the countryside almost induced sleep a number of times but there was an unconscious barrier to exposing himself to the vulnerability of oblivion. His only moment of anxiety came with the cry of "Tickets please," but the interaction was negotiated with a minimum of eye contact. It was with a sense of disappointment that Manchester approached after what seemed an implausibly short time and he had to leave the relative security of the vacuum in which he had felt cocooned. He had considered his next move at length and eventually settled on completing his journey with another train. He just made the connection and in the late morning stepped into the gloom of a Cheshire village station and set out on the five-mile walk to his hoped-for asylum, a taxi obviously being out of the question.

The dank air moistened the hibernating hedgerows and fields as he trudged towards the first of two villages that separated him from his destination. He was aware that his travel bag made him mildly more noticeable but an appreciation of its link to himself via contents, and more particularly fingerprints, caused him to doggedly hold onto it. The lanes were largely without pavements and he walked close to the hedge on the side of the oncoming traffic, fatigue gradually eclipsing the adrenaline that had sustained him thus far. It was four days to Christmas and the first village was alive with the voices of excited children from gardens and a large green where boys played football and a group of girls talked and giggled and shrieked. He walked past the pub with a mournful longing to be inside, with its warmth and beer, and the enticing smell of the food teased his nostrils. An impulsive whim to cast care to the wind was resisted easily with a philosophical smile. The recovery of freedom would be made sweeter by recollection of the moments of self-restraint such as this. Between the two villages Prior's pace slowed and his shoulders slumped and the driver of a tractor pulling a trailer in the direction in which he was walking slowed and called out, "Jump on mate, have a rest."

Damn, he thought. Apart from buying his tickets and paper he hadn't needed to talk to anyone since his escape. He held up his free hand.

"It's alright. I'm trying to lose a bit before Christmas. Thanks anyway." The driver looked a little confused. The bag, he supposed.

"Please yourself," he shouted and the engine revved to a roar and he pulled away.

The road sign at the next junction indicated a mile to the next village and he cast a wistful look at the tractor climbing the steep hill ahead that he would shortly have to mount. To his left and right the incline revealed fields of winter wheat stretching expansively towards woods of evergreen trees on the limits of his horizon. The tractor went out of his eyeshot as it passed over the brow of the hill and he followed in laboured pursuit, his thighs and calves aching in protest as they hauled his tired body upwards. At the summit he waited by a copse of sycamores and horse chestnuts, restoring normal breathing before rewarding himself inappropriately with a cigarette. The quintessential Englishness of the countryside was reinforced by the next village he came to – a hamlet of grassy knolls and stone dwellings that couldn't have changed much since the Middle Ages apart from the infernal speed caution apparatus. He cut an unlikely figure as he shuffled through in his new clothes and intimidating haircut, his ugly spectacles dotted with the raindrops he had now tired of wiping away. He would have felt more in keeping in the guise of a hobo.

As he left the village behind, a sign told him that it was two further miles to his terminus. A watery sun began to emerge from behind the higher clouds but he felt a sudden downturn in his mood. He dragged himself on at the point of complete mental and physical exhaustion, his mind urging him to keep putting one foot in front of the other while his body longed to collapse into the roadside bush and go into shutdown. With his mood of despond came an appreciation of the risks contained in this course of action and the final hour of his hike was spent in a torment of apprehension as the odds against a Panda shortened with the passing of each car. At last, however, he arrived unscathed at the village street and his step quickened as he approached the general store and post office and turned left into Caroline's road. He paused at the foot of her long drive and pondered his next move. It was now nearly two thirty – about two hours 'til dark. In the distance, to the left of the house, there appeared to be some outbuildings and he moved quickly up the drive, past the horses and round to the back of the building where he found a courtyard enclosed by stables and various outbuildings of indeterminate purpose. He tried the door of one of these and was relieved to find it open. It appeared to serve as a storeroom for all kinds of paraphernalia – harnesses, saddles, garden implements and the like. Leaning against the wall in one corner was a rusty sun bed which had seen better days but its canvas was still intact and Prior opened it out. Using his grip for a pillow and covering himself with some horse coats, he stretched out and at last felt secure enough to fall almost immediately into a deep sleep.

It was dark when he woke, pitch black in the windowless building, and he fumbled in his pocket for his lighter which he used to illuminate the dial of his watch. It said 7:47 p.m. He had been asleep for five hours and he could quite easily have gone straight back off but there was too much thinking to do and besides, he was aware of a raging thirst and hunger. He eased open the door, wincing at the creak, and was at once drawn to the large window opposite, across the courtyard and at the back of the house. A bright light shone out and he could make out some heads around a table. He edged towards what must be their kitchen, staying close to the perimeter, and found a vantage point behind a kaleidoscope of bins where he could look up at the figures in the room without being seen himself. With his back to him with greying hair spilling over the neck of a thick mustard-coloured jumper, he identified the figure of Doug. Caroline sat opposite, drinking wine and laughing. Standing in the background, also laughing and alive with energy was Graham, the son he hadn't seen for more than nine years.

Prior stared, transfixed. It is almost impossible to be objective about your own children's looks when you are seeing them all the time but for the absent father it was easy. He saw a striking young man – facially more his mother with her fine, sensitive features – but with Prior's broad build, chestnut hair, dark colouring and something of his prickly, rebellious mien discernible even at this distance. He guessed he probably topped his own height by a couple of inches. He felt an intense pride as he watched him shadow box and swivel, unable to keep still or suppress the surging lifeblood of the well-adjusted adolescent as he swigged lager from a bottle. Prior imagined he was having a few mood enhancers at home as a prelude to a pre-Christmas night of revelry.

For a moment he forgot his own parlous circumstances and was vicariously back in his own younger days, with their bliss of the unmindfulness of the morrow which only changes gradually in the light of painful and bitter experience.

He waited for him to leave the room and then moved out from behind the bin and inched towards the house, crouching so his head was below the level of the kitchen windowsill. When he reached the wall he slowly drew himself up until his face would be visible to the couple still sitting at the kitchen table. He could now make out their muffled voices. Doug was only about two metres away from him and was talking. Caroline opposite was looking at him, her face slightly flushed from the wine, her thin lips forming the sardonic smile he found so infuriating or so attractive depending on its context. The bromide of familiarity had long since dissipated and he felt again a stirring of the passion of all those years ago. Her expression suddenly changed to one of shock and she let out a noise somewhere between a shout and a scream. She pointed at him in answer to Doug's enquiry and he turned round quickly and then stood up. He opened the top window and in as intimidating a voice as he could muster he said, "What the hell are you doing on my property?"

Prior spoke in an urgent whisper, standing back from the window and looking up through the superfluous spectacles he still had on out of newly acquired habit. "It's me, Doug – Robert." He noticed Caroline putting her hand to her mouth in surprise as realisation gradually dawned on Doug's bemused face. He told Prior to wait a minute and spoke to Caroline before closing the window and opening the door onto the yard. They both stepped out and the three of them looked at each other for some moments, unsure of what to say. It was Caroline who broke the silence.

"We can talk, Robert, but not in the house. Graham's getting ready to go out and Helen's in. There's no way the children are to know you're here."

Prior held up his hands in submission. "Of course, of course." He turned his head and beckoned towards the harness room. "I've set up camp over there." His presumption caused her to give him one of her looks and against her better judgement she couldn't suppress an involuntary snigger.

"You look absolutely ridiculous." For some reason she was reminded of Leonard Rossiter as Reginald Perrin when he hit the road after his breakdown. All it needed was the false teeth. Doug did not appear to share her amusement and she quickly composed herself as she remembered the circumstances and the gravity of the charge that had been assailing her in the media since yesterday. Prior returned to the outhouse and waited while she went in for her coat and the beer and cheese sandwich he had requested. Doug stayed in the house in case Helen came down from her coursework. He was to say that her mother had nipped next door.

The moon was a thin crescent in a blue-black cloudless sky as she tiptoed across the yard, the gathering wind fluttering the debris of hay and leaves. The inevitable frost was not far away. The room was wired for a rudimentary ceiling light but she lit a candle and closed the door to avoid drawing any attention to its occupancy. She brought two cans of cold lager and he drank the first in two gulps, pausing only to draw fleeting breath before draining the can. He opened the second and looked intensely at his ex-wife.

"You've heard, I suppose."

"Yes. It's been in the papers and on the news." Prior had temporarily dispensed with the glasses. In the candlelight with his shaved head and almost two days' beard growth he had the authentic look of the desperate fugitive. Caroline felt both pity and anger. Anger that he had disturbed their idyllic run-up to Christmas. Anger at the stupid, stupid mess he was making of his life. Anger that he had no qualms about making them potential accessories to a heinous crime that for all she knew he may have committed. Pity for this relic of the past made even more of a stranger by its cloak of mental illness. Pity that in the ten years since he had left he hadn't managed to find someone he trusted enough to displace her.

Prior had been vaguely rehearsing his opening gambit since his decision to come north and with his tongue loosened and his brain relaxed by the alcohol, the words came easily and convincingly.

"First of all Caroline, I am completely innocent. I would not have come anywhere near you and the children and put you in danger if I wasn't and I'm sure you know that."

Her face remained impassive.

"I know what you're thinking – I'm ill, I don't know what I'm doing, I've changed, I could do things without even knowing I've done them. Believe me, I've thought of all that. But no. On my children's lives, Caroline, I didn't rape that woman." He could see the perplexity in her eyes and continued, "I've been well actually. I'll admit I got a bit 'excited' a few weeks ago. Things started picking up at last but I was in control. Then of course my mood plunged back to the depths when I got arrested – whose wouldn't?"

Caroline interrupted, "So what did happen on the night she was raped?"

Prior repeated the account which was almost word-perfect after all the practice he was getting. As he described the more intimate details he searched her face for a hint of jealousy but none was there – only a suggestion of distaste. She quizzed him as the police had done, asking the insightful questions, unsettling him with her look of scepticism at some of his answers. When the incident had been dissected in all its detail and there was nothing left to say she looked sideways at the wall to avoid his urgent gaze, chewing her bottom lip with her face a picture of confusion and unease. As in the old days he jumped into the void, taking advantage of her temporary vulnerability to try to enforce his will.

"You've got to help me, Caroline. I've got no-one else." She turned her eyes on him, her mind in disarray. She had hoped that by looking at him she could form a snap judgement based on whether she felt pity or anger but as before she felt both in equal measure.

"What sort of help?"

"Money, fake passport, refuge until you can get me a flight out of the country." She screwed up her face and let out an involuntary gasp.

"So not much then. Bloody hell, Robert. We could go to prison if we were caught doing all that." Prior looked down. Her anguish had finally contaminated him.

"I know Caroline, I know." He spoke softly, sadly, understanding her dilemma.

"I'll obviously need to speak to Doug and then we'll sleep on it. You can stay here tonight." Prior began eating the sandwich.

"Thanks. Whatever you decide I'll accept. No grudges if you kick me out." He was not sure he meant that but saying it might further his cause.

"So have the kids talked about it?"

"A little. The girls have cried. It's just made Graham even more angry with you."

Prior wished he hadn't asked. He had to keep a cap on the geyser of guilt that perpetually bubbled below the surface.

"One day, if I ever reach calmer waters, I'll make it up to them if they'll let me."

"Laura's taken it hardest – she was always 'Daddy's girl'." She looked coldly at him and added in admonishment, "If you remember."

He changed the subject. The sandwich had opened the floodgates of his appetite and he said, "Could you get me a flask of coffee and more to eat and then I'll get my head down." She sighed and went back to the house and half an hour later Doug appeared with the flask, more sandwiches and some chocolate biscuits. He returned to the house and came back with a newer camp bed, sleeping bag, blankets and a pillow. Prior ate all the food and drank most of the coffee, leaving just enough for a cup the next morning, and after a last smoke he nestled into the bag, its warmth and shelter removing him quickly to a place there is no pain.

***

Doug and Caroline lay on their backs in the king-sized bed looking up at the white ceiling.

"So how did you find our Magwitch?" said Caroline and they both smiled.

"Okay really... considering." His voice was deep and reassuring. His meteoric success in business had occasioned no compromise of his broad Northern vowels.

"You didn't think he was... well, mad, for want of a better word?"

"Well he looks a bit strange and he was a bit edgy but the guy's obviously been through a lot. How did you find him compared to the hospital?"

She thought for a while.

"Better. He's reacting appropriately to his circumstances. Even given the bloody awful situation there's a light in his eyes. They were dead in hospital and he had this air of detachment – of belonging to a different species almost." She tried to think of more but was unable to. She dreaded the next bit but knew they couldn't put it off any further. He had been patient for long enough in waiting for her to lay out the territory.

"He wants us to shelter him until we can provide money, a fake passport and a ticket to sanctuary." Doug pursed his lips and then exhaled through his teeth. He declined the trite remark and stayed silent. He tended to only speak when he had to and even then, only after a good deal of thought. Caroline also said nothing, allowing him time to respond, her toes curling under the feather duvet. At last he spoke.

"The bottom line is did he do it? And the answer is we don't have a clue. If he didn't, then we have to have faith that our justice system will clear him. If he did do it then we are aiding and abetting someone who's committed a despicable crime and who might do it again. So looking at it like that it's a no-brainer." Caroline flinched inwardly. They had found enough of a common denominator to have forged a very satisfying relationship but sometimes his use of irritating modern parlance grated on her. She vindicated him by allowing that it was perhaps the sort of language necessary in the phoney, cut-throat business world he moved in.

"So that's the bottom line." Doug was warming to his subject. He could have been discussing the relative merits and defects of a new product. "Assuming then that he didn't do it. What would be our justification, if any, for shielding him? One – he's the father of your kids. Two – he's your ex-husband. Three – you feel sorry for him. Four – you don't trust the legal system. Not very convincing reasons to be honest. You have to assume, and I'm sure I'd be massively backed up by statistics, that in ninety-nine cases out of a hundred the CPS prosecutes the guilty, not the innocent." He turned and saw her unhappy look. "I'm sorry to sound so negative, sweetheart. I'm just being logical, realistic, whatever you want to call it. At the end of the day if you decide to help him I'm with you." Ten years ago she would have flinched at 'bottom line' and 'at the end of the day'. Now they were just part of the language as she supposed 'no-brainer' would be in time.

The brain acts in mysterious ways sometimes and at this moment of extreme and agonising conflict she started to consider the 'H' question. When verbalising the letter itself she had always known, in her middle-class fashion, that the 'U' way of expressing it was as 'aitch' with the 'H' silent. Now though, due she supposed to the legion of poor souls castigated for 'dropping their aitches', the taking of the wrong end of the stick had resulted in the misconception that the letter was 'haitch'. She, and others like her, were now the new linguistic plebiscites. The absurdities of the English class system never ceased to amaze.

"Anyway, what does he say happened?"

Caroline paraphrased his account and when she had finished Doug thought briefly before issuing his next pronouncement. She knew that some people found him pompous and pedantic but to her he was just filled with enthusiasm to make things better for others – especially her, who he worshipped. There was something in his solidity and consistency that she needed. She liked the pragmatism that caused him to look to repair rather than complain – to shape life rather than be shaped by it. He was the owner of a large engineering company, a self-made millionaire who got to where he was by his own efforts and, unusually in business, a predominantly honest approach.

"His only defence is that the man who did it used a condom. Against that is a weight of forensic and circumstantial evidence. The prosecution will argue he was drunk, mentally ill, had motive. I don't think it looks very good."

"The forensics don't prove anything. They both agree there was consensual contact. The rest of it is supposition and not enough for a safe conviction in my opinion."

"But there's no doubt she was raped – she didn't inflict those injuries on herself – and there's absolutely nothing linking anyone else." Caroline got out of bed and opened the window an inch and as she got back he said, "So honestly, what's your opinion – your gut feeling?"

"I don't think he did it. Whatever his faults that is just not in his nature."

"But he's changed, Caroline. You've seen him once in ten years. He's ill now. To our knowledge he's not had another partner since you split up. Goodness knows in what sexual direction he's gone. You've said yourself he can't handle relationships with women – that deep down he doesn't really like them, is frightened of them." He saw her pained expression and said quickly, "Look, I'm just playing devil's advocate, looking at what an objective view might be. I'd love to believe it wasn't him."

The ticking of the bedside alarm clock emphasised the silence that followed as she gazed back up at the ceiling and he took some tablets from his bedside locker and washed them down.

"If, just if," said Caroline, "we did help him, the odds on our being implicated would be very small wouldn't they?"

Doug considered the risks.

"I suppose so, if we were very careful. You would think the police would call here at some stage to ask if we know anything. Whether they would search or not I don't know. That would be the biggest risk and you'd think it would be sooner rather than later. That's not really the point though is it? Risk to us, I mean. The issue is right and wrong." He paused to let the words sink in and then said, "Look, there's absolutely no obligation on us to help him – he wouldn't even expect it himself if he was honest." He got up and went into the en suite bathroom to relieve himself and then climbed back into bed and turned off his bedside wall light.

"Let's sleep on it now. We'll feel clearer in our minds after a good night's sleep."

They kissed and turned away from each other to face the walls on their respective sides of the bed. Doug was snoring softly within minutes but Caroline endured the opposite of the good night's sleep that Doug had advocated and was obviously enjoying. In her mind she moved from one position to another, deciding emphatically on one course of action only to find her descent into sleep hampered by insidious arguments from the other direction. She heard Helen going to bed at one and Graham coming in at four. Laura was staying at her boyfriend's house. At five she was fully awake, incapable of estimating the meagre hours of sleep she had managed, and in her maddening state of simultaneous exhaustion and tension she got up and washed and dressed and went down to the bitterly cold kitchen where she flicked on the boiler and made herself tea and toast.

She tried to think of ways to use the unaccustomed two hours between now and her usual rising time productively, and decided to prepare the vegetables for the evening meal and tackle some of the ironing that had built up. She normally slept so well. The experience was new to her and she felt a tenuous empathy with Robert. She had read up on bipolar disorder at length and was aware of the pivotal role of sleep disorder in the condition. The effects of the wine she had been unable to sleep off were causing a stabbing pain at her temples but at the same time she peeled and chopped vegetables and pressed clothes with a ruthless efficiency comforted by the time she was buying herself for later. By seven, as she heard Doug stirring above, she had decided what she was going to do.

She crossed the yard and gently opened the door of the guest suite. By the light of her torch the torment she saw engraved on the face of the man child, even in sleep, served only to confirm her decision.

CHAPTER 15

Prior stooped to open the door of the fridge and removed another can, which he took out to the rocking chair on the veranda of the summer house. Warmed by the bars of a little electric fire, he peered out into the blackness beyond. He had to be selective in his use of lighting and was glad of even the scanty illumination from the fire. He had been here for three weeks and already felt at home. With each passing day since the police had come he had felt a little bit more secure. The wooden structure lay in a three-sided thicket on the edge of Caroline and Doug's property about seventy-five metres from the stables. The veranda was south facing and beyond the picket fence in front marking the perimeter of their land were the fields of their neighbour Wallace's farm. It was a cloudless evening and Prior gazed up at the stars, drawing comfort from the insignificance of himself and his problems compared to the vastness and wonder of the universe.

Two policemen had called on the same day that Caroline told him they were going to let him stay. She had darted out to warn him while they spoke to Doug and he had hastily folded the camp bed and put it with his case and bedding in one corner, covering the evidence with the horse coats before crawling under a tall cupboard which conveniently had legs and stretched along the length of wall behind the door. Tightly wedged against the wall, he heard the footsteps on the cobbled yard and he closed his eyes tight and held his breath as he heard the door open. He was a little heartened by the voice of Doug, calm and matter of fact.

"Just junk really, gear for the horses – have a look if you want." The next voice sounded young and almost apologetic.

"No it's alright Mr. Ross. I can see there's no-one here. Just got to go through the formalities, you understand."

Prior gradually allowed his breathing to return to normal as he listened to the three men walking round the yard in what was obviously becoming a cursory inspection. He was immensely grateful at this moment for Doug's wealth and standing in the community, his Rotary Club membership, his friendship with a senior police officer. Prior had always suspected he was a mason as well.

That evening was by far the best he had experienced for as long as he could remember. Ensconced in his new home, he and Doug had shared the best part of a bottle of whisky as they charted out the future territory. The summer house had mains electricity and contained two rooms approximately three metres square in addition to the veranda. Prior made one his bedroom and the other a living room whilst being careful that they gave no clue to his occupancy. The time of year was a Godsend, with a summer house holding very little in the way of attraction for some months yet. Until the end of the Christmas holiday his toilet and washing arrangements were difficult, with at least one of his children invariably being at home, but on the resumption of a return to normality he could go up to the house as soon as they had gone out to shower and change into a clean set of Doug's clothes that were two sizes too big. There was only one close call in relation to his being discovered when he looked out of the window at the back of his living room one afternoon and spotted Helen approaching. He hid in some undergrowth as she thumped about looking for something, silently cursing the blowing of his cover. Caroline told him later that Helen had alluded to a dirty mug and ruffled sofa bed but that she had bought her rather unlikely story that Doug had slept there after they'd had a row.

Before Doug staggered back to the house he fixed Prior with a gaze and stood up, pointing an index finger at him.

"Understand this, Robert. None of this is my idea. I'm doing it for Caroline and I don't feel comfortable with it. You'd better not have done this, mate." He didn't say what he would do if it turned out he had but Prior gathered it would not be pleasant and would run consecutive to and not concurrently with the sentence of the court.

His mental health was good but as Doug grew closer to finalising the arrangements his mood began to dip and anxiety was never far away. As he sat on the veranda in the sharp mid-January air, insulated by the warmth of the alcohol, he conceded to himself that he had reverted to childhood and he had to reluctantly admit that he was enjoying it. He had no responsibility, nothing to do, and was waited on hand and foot by Caroline out of the necessity of the situation. Meanwhile, in the background, Doug laboured away to secure a better future for him. He took another deep swig from the can and licked the foam from his now thick moustache. He had shaved off the stubble on the rest of his face but left a Mexican bandito-style growth on his upper lip. He continued to keep his head shaven and Caroline had bought him another pair of spectacles with gold frames which still changed him but gave him less of a bizarre look for the passport photograph. He heard footsteps followed by the low wolf whistle that was code for Doug's approach and they went into the living room and sat on two of the cane armchairs.

"It's all set for the day after tomorrow. Your flight is at 10:40 a.m. from Ringway, check-in from eight. Arrive 16:40 p.m. our time but 15:40 there – they're an hour behind GMT. I'll take you to the airport – you'll need to be ready for seven." His tone was impersonal, his distaste for both Prior and the situation implicit.

"Your passport and ticket are in the name of James Hudson, date of birth 03.02.64. I've added four years on so try and act your fucking age for once." Prior's half smile was not returned and his look was cowed as Doug carried on, "I've got one hundred and twenty thousand euros in cash which I'll give you tomorrow in your hand luggage. Caroline has packed a suitcase for you. You'll need to get a tourist visa on arrival."

Prior was in an unfamiliar position. He was not used to being beholden and gratitude and humility did not come easily. Neither did submission in the face of an aggressive or superior attitude but this tangible realisation of his wishes left him genuinely touched. He wrestled for the right words.

"You'll get every penny back, and more. And I swear you'll not regret this, Doug. You'll go to your grave happy that you made the right decision, I promise you that." Doug grunted in a way that managed to convey contempt, scepticism and his astonishing forbearance all in one. He said nothing and turned away. As Prior watched the tall broad-shouldered figure retreating towards the house he felt insignificant and diminished by its strength.

He couldn't decide whether the next day felt like the last day of term or the last day of the school holidays. In his restless apprehension he paced and fidgeted, chain smoking and feeling there should be so much to do but unsure of quite what. He had become used to his surrogate parents up in the main house taking his decisions for him. The thought of being back in control of his own destiny tomorrow and the vast uncertainty of the void that lay ahead caused a consistent level of anxiety that peaked at intervals to something close to panic. He was engulfed by relief at the sight of Caroline early in the evening on her return from work. He felt a strong urge to wrap her in a hug and lay his head on her shoulder but Caroline, sensing this, folded her arms and moved out of his range. He stood looking blankly at her with his arms hanging limply by his sides and her now habitual ambivalence was reflected in her confused expression.

"I'm doing roast chicken – your favourite. I'll bring it down around seven." Her voice carried an insinuation of a deliberate attempt to subdue any affection.

Prior said mechanically, "Thanks."

"And Robert." She looked suddenly severe and entreating. "I really don't think you should drink tonight – you're going to need all your faculties tomorrow." He looked away and sniffed, saying nothing. She sat down on one of the armchairs and he followed suit in the other chair.

"Did you get the will?" Prior had asked her to pick up an instant will, having remembered that he was intestate. She nodded and produced it from the pocket of her coat. He filled it out, leaving everything to her.

"Damn. I forgot my signature needs two witnesses." She looked at the rudimentary form and read the small print.

"It's okay. I'll get that done later." Prior looked pained. She could see it was an effort to concentrate.

"I need to talk about my financial situation, Caroline. It's all a bit of a mess, I'm afraid." She let him gather his thoughts. "Everything's gone a bit haywire lately and now my hands are tied as to access my accounts is going to incriminate me, attract unwelcome attention.

The mortgage is paid on the flat. Thank goodness I decided to do that early. I bought it for £75,000. It's probably worth about three times that now. My current account's in credit by a few hundred. Salary is paid in arrears and I'm due holiday pay. There should be a full payment at the end of January but it'll stop after that, I imagine. I've been transferring the surplus of salary after taking out what I need to live on to a savings account by standing order each month. It was very healthy up until the beginning of last year but then I went a bit… you know." He didn't want to use the allegorical words that in his case were too literal.

"I did have about £200,000." He looked down guiltily. "I think it's less than fifty grand now." He sighed deeply. "Oh God Caroline, everything's so up in the air. If I snuffed it the will more than takes care of what I owe you. So the other alternatives. If I manage to evade capture and live out my days in some remote outpost, then again, the will covers it. If you went first obviously it would then go to the children. That reminds me – I'll need to add that." He took a pen and made the addition.

"I don't know how I'll live when the euros run out but I'll cross that bridge when I come to it. I'll have to try and get a job of some kind I suppose. While I think of it, you'd have to say I sent you the will otherwise they'd know you've been harbouring me. That doesn't explain the witnesses though." He went back into thought, his brow creasing with the effort, and Caroline tried to spare him this line of thought which was opening up more questions than it was providing answers.

"The money's really not important. And even if you did die intestate I'm sure your assets would pass to the children."

"It's important to me. Going back to what I was saying. I could get caught of course. I'd be looking at a long stretch if found guilty. I could even be kept in a secure hospital for the rest of my life." He lowered his eyes as he contemplated that prospect. "Then I'd sell the flat and pay you out of the proceeds. Or I could get found not guilty. I'd get another job, no question. Not with my current paper but with the highest bidder." His face lit up. "Imagine the pull I'd have – my ordeal serialised exclusively in their rag. It would be quite a story. I'd set up a standing order to you and Doug and have it paid off in no time."

She started to speak and he held up a hand to cut her off, "I feel better now I've covered all the bases. Allow me that little satisfaction. You've no idea how I feel for putting you in this situation. Anyway, how the hell did Doug manage to get the passport?"

She had wondered about this herself. She knew him to be a kind, honest man but suspected there was a harder side to him. He spoke very little about his work but had often surprised her with his autocratic tone when she overheard the occasional phone calls he made from the house. She supposed that he hadn't got where he was without knowing the wider, seamier picture even if he had no wish to be part of it himself. She said simply, "Money talks," and smiled.

"Money doesn't talk, it swears." The now hackneyed line from a Bob Dylan track took them back to over twenty years ago at university and their mutual discovery of music. Another song came into his head and he began singing Peter, Paul and Mary's 'Leaving on a Jet Plane'. Caroline smiled ruefully. It was a song that evoked memories of their previous partings – not the final one accompanied by silences and slammed doors but those temporary schisms of a few weeks when he was going away to cover an Olympics or a World Cup.

"Those were the days weren't they Cazza?" She hated the abbreviation and he used to say it to provoke her in a playful way. She smiled politely and changed the subject, steering it away from a nostalgia she was not quite sure she could trust herself to be detached from.

"How are you going to manage your mental illness over there Robert?"

Prior visibly bridled.

"Mental health not mental illness please. It makes us nutters feel less stigmatised and excluded, don't you know." She ignored his sarcasm.

"Sorry. Mental health then."

"I'll be okay. I'm sure there's treatment there if I need it. I've not had a tablet for four weeks and I'm okay aren't I?"

"I've been searching the net. It sounds a bit nebulous – all healthcare I mean. Anything more serious than a cold and you have to fly somewhere else for treatment."

Prior looked exasperated.

"Look Caroline, that's the least of my problems. What the hell can I do about it now anyway – change the tickets to New York? There's probably not much call for bipolar disorder in the third world – too busy trying to bloody survive. I'm sure I'll be joining the scrum to put some rice in my bowl sooner rather than later." She didn't respond and they sat in silence for a while. Prior began craving a beer but something held him back. She finally got up.

"I'll go and finish off the meal."

He tried to insinuate conciliation into his brief reply. "Okay… thanks."

She returned half an hour later with a plate covered with silver foil and he pulled it off to reveal a chicken breast and leg, bacon rolls, chipolatas, bread sauce, roast potatoes, sprouts, peas, and carrots, all covered in gravy. His voice was restrained as he said, "The condemned man ate a hearty meal."

She flushed with an embarrassment that she didn't know the origin of.

"I'll say goodbye now, Robert. I'll get the plate in the morning after you've gone. Doug will come down at about 6:30 to check you're awake." Prior grabbed her upper arms before she could turn to go and looked down into her face. She looked up fleetingly and then turned away.

"I still love you, Caroline. I may never see you again. I just wanted you to know that." She looked up and pecked him on the cheek and there were tears in her eyes. She put her hand on his shoulder and gently pushed away and he relinquished his hold.

She said quietly, "Look after yourself Robert," and clunked across the wooden stoop in the high-heeled work shoes she hadn't found time to change. The steam continued to rise from the food as he watched her through the window as she went back to the house, the skirt flapping around legs still as perfect as those of his memory of all those years ago.

PART 2

REBIRTH

CHAPTER 16

The idyll of the six-hour suspension of reality was marred only by the nicotine deprivation. Squeezed into a window seat on the budget flight, the hum of the engine drone and air conditioning formed a backdrop to the snatches of conversation he picked up from adjacent holiday-makers, the volume of noise and good will rising in proportion to the progress of the drinks trolley down the aisle and the lengthening distance they were putting between themselves and the January gloom they had left behind. He resisted the temptation to engage in conversation with the Mancunian couple in the seats alongside his. Caroline and Doug's repeated cautions about keeping a low profile were still fresh in his memory, as was the sadness he had felt at leaving, although this was now easing with the aid of the emotional emollients he was pouring down his throat. His only slight anxiety had been caused by the stare of a middle-aged man in the departure lounge and the longer than usual eye contact between them as the man journeyed between the seats on his way to the toilet. Prior had noticed that he was reading a copy of his newspaper at the airport. An hour before landing a stewardess handed out immigration forms and he put down his folding table and closed the blind against the now harsh glare of the sun. He had a return ticket and was ostensibly entering the country as a tourist, although his holiday was flight only and he would be making his own accommodation arrangements. Doug had found the immigration policies and laws complicated and Prior sensed he had grown impatient and not applied his usual diligence and tenacity to the research. He knew that he would need to apply for a visa on arrival and Doug thought this would be valid for ninety days. He felt on balance that possession of a return ticket would provide proof on arrival of an intention to depart, which would outweigh the potential disadvantage of the flagging up of his failure to get on his return flight. He planned to clarify the immigration issues after he arrived. He suspected that he would be able to merge easily into the tourist and ex-pat communities without drawing attention. As long as he stayed out of trouble…

As the aircraft began its descent he fastened his seat belt with some regret at the passing of the flight. Like the recent train journey, there was something about the motion and the commune that diminished the reality of his plight. In a few moments man would revert to type in the unseemly jostle to be first through the bureaucratic formalities. The unaccustomed heat would fuel the nicotine withdrawal and alcohol-induced dehydration and smiles would turn to scowls, at least until the renewal of elation at the seat on the coach.

When the plane emerged from the lowest cloud Prior saw an aquamarine sea meeting the shoreline of the island of Sal, Cape Verde. One of an archipelago of ten islands and five islets in the Atlantic Ocean, three hundred miles off the coast of West Africa, he was immediately struck by the sparse aridity of the brown land and the absence of vegetation. In the distance he made out what appeared to be black mountains of volcanic rock which had left this legacy from the eruptions of millions of years ago. He sensed a confused disappointment on the faces of his fellow passengers, most of whom seemed to be coming here for the first time. Perhaps they were searching for tropical rain forests and palm trees but Cape Verde lay just above the doldrums and rainfall was in pitifully short supply.

The landing was smooth and his smile at the woman next to him as the aircraft went into orgasmic reverse thrust was returned. As he stepped off the gangway with his hand resting on the precious cargo in his shoulder bag he was pleasantly surprised by the temperature. It must have been about twenty-five degrees. Very warm compared to the frost he had left behind six hours ago but, cooled by the northeast trade wind, not the oppressive blanket he had been expecting.

The predictable chaos in the arrival hall ensued. There were two queues – one apparently for those with visas already procured and one for those without; which queue was for which was unclear, however, and there didn't appear to be anybody to ask. Prior joined the one the consensus of opinion had identified as being for those without but it was shorter and, inexplicably, faster moving. His passport was stamped and the money taken for his visa and he waited for his suitcase in eager anticipation of the cigarette he would soon be enjoying. His only worry as he collected his case was if he was asked for an explanation for all the cash he was carrying but he crossed the hall and stepped through the airport exit doors without being apprehended or even seeing any evidence of Customs. He lit up and the mixture of nicotine, excitement, and apprehension hit him like a blow. He was reminded of his early attempts at smoking when he was about thirteen – the anxiety and nausea he would experience, and not for the first time he cursed his dogged persistence in cultivating a habit with such negative connotations for future health and pocket.

Coaches and minibuses dominated the forecourt and the throngs of disorientated tourists were herded onto the appropriate vehicles by smart-suited reps exuding charm and control. Prior watched them abstractedly, the sun beating down on his shaved head, sweat beginning to dampen his heavy moustache. Local boys weaved in and out of the bedlam grabbing bags without invitation, laying claim to the worthless coins they would attempt to hustle back to the tourists on the other end of their journey in exchange for their superfluous local currency. Prior lit his second cigarette and waved away the insistent attentions of a boy of about twelve who lifted his twenty kilo suitcase in one deft muscular movement.

"No. Taxi." The boy was not easily dissuaded. He released the case and gestured towards a car a few metres away.

"Okay, come."

Prior felt in his pocket and pulled out the five euro note he had received in change from the fifty he had proffered for the visa and the boy took the case and then the note without a thank you or a change in expression as he hurried away in search of further prey, leaving Prior to reflect on another example of his alienation from society as he got into the taxi and observed the last stragglers climbing into their transport. As far as he could see he was the only person in his position. He had enjoyed the isolation when it was voluntary. At this moment he would have given anything to be a part of that ovine mass.

It became quickly apparent that his choice of taxi was not ideal. The driver spoke no English and after some fruitless bandying of words and phrases the man left the cab and returned with another driver who spoke rudimentary English. Prior hoped he had managed to convey his need for a low budget hotel and they set off on the dual carriageway towards Santa Maria. He leant back in his seat and took in the view. The tarmac road was virtually empty and ran through a valley flanked by the mountains of volcanic rock he had seen from the plane. Between the road and the mountains lay what could only be described as wasteland – a scorched expanse of earth and stone with a thin covering of plant life fighting to maintain its existence with minimal nutrition from the elements. After about ten minutes they reached the outskirts of the town and to the right he looked at modern looking apartment blocks and hotels, the sea visible between the buildings. He sat in the back, his immediate fate in the hands of the coffee-skinned man in a maroon polo shirt. He envied him his familiarity with the surroundings, the simplicity of his decisions as he changed the CD. The music carried a mournful Latin quality that seemed somehow in keeping with both the geography and his own precarious circumstances. Northwards, to their left, lay the vast wastes of saltpans on which the island of yesteryear had depended so much for its meagre existence. The road doglegged sharply to the left and they followed the southernmost coast of the island for a kilometre before coming to the oasis of a garage set in a wild west hinterland of dry earth and rubble waiting to play host to the next capricious whims of the developers. They turned left again at the garage and drove slowly along the wide avenue of compressed sand. With increasing unease Prior surveyed the depressing vista. Half-finished buildings sat amongst completed dwellings of disparate size and style. Pastels of pink and blue vied with vivid browns and terracottas. Dogs were everywhere – more plentiful than humans. The majority were the indeterminate pie dogs of West Africa but he was surprised to spot the occasional pedigree breed. People moved around sporadically, their purpose unfathomable, their faces opaque, their barrows laden with paltry cargo as they picked over a terrain bereft of the hope that had inspired its origin.

The car pulled up at a sign reading 'Ventura Hotel' and the blue sea, wind-surfer, and palm tree painted onto the board seemed a sad parody of the reality of its setting. He paid the ten euro fare and checked in. The hotel itself was surprisingly welcoming given the pessimism of his approach. Set back from the road, a white pebble-dashed wall topped by bougainvillea growing from long wooden tubs was separated from the main four-storey building by a long patio of tables, chairs, and parasols. A group of two bearded men and two women with their hair in plaits sitting at a table drinking beer smiled and greeted him as he hauled his case through, feeling faintly ridiculous in his white shirt, black, belted trousers and brown lace-up brogues. The foyer was air conditioned and he leant against the bar top which also served as a reception desk and spoke to the proprietor, an Italian woman. He paid for a first-floor room for two nights in cash and they agreed that he would be given the option of extending his stay before the room was offered to anyone else who was interested. The price was forty euros a night. After some internal debate he decided he would unpack and he then turned off the AC and opened the French doors which led to a small veranda where he stood smoking, surveying the horizon visible between the last buildings in his view to the west. He flicked the butt skywards and watched the stern breeze carry it beyond the flat rooftop below delaying its eventual fall to earth.

He lay on the bed in his underwear and took some mental stock as he looked through to the spacious shower room that was almost as big as the hotel room itself. The sight of the black socks on the end of hairy white legs caused him to consider his appearance and he pulled them off and pondered on whether he could let his hair grow again and dispense with the awful moustache. The disturbing look from the man at the airport haunted him and he concluded that his vanity would have to wait. He thought about his mental health, a hard thing to do dispassionately, and concluded that he was okay. He clung to a conviction that his behaviour was dictated by external and not internal factors. Any fears of lapsing into depression were tempered by a comparison with where he would be now if he hadn't taken this course. And relatively better though his situation was, he doubted the months and years ahead would contain much in the way of stimulus to mania. It was now late afternoon and he resisted an encroaching feeling of fatigue and forced himself off the bed and took a cool shower. He feared that if he succumbed to sleep he may end up waking in the middle of the night, hungry and bored with the dark hours before the dawn stretching ominously ahead of him. He changed into a pair of khaki knee-length shorts and blue and white short-sleeved shirt that Caroline had bought and packed for him, and slipped on a pair of leather sandals. He fell between two sizes and Caroline, being Caroline, had opted for the larger of the two, which he fastened onto the last buckle hole. He shaved and splashed on some cologne and went downstairs with a renewed spring in his step.

The sunset came early in Cape Verde and he sat on the terrace drinking bottle after bottle of Portuguese Superbok beer, watching the sun falling gradually towards the horizon, leaving trails of pink and gold which fringed and overlaid the milk-white clouds. If this was to be his last night free from captivity he was damn well going to enjoy it. He was attended to by a tall, graceful girl whose beaming smile frequently lit up her artless, pretty face. Prior was disappointed when she left early and he called soon after for the menu from which he played safe and ordered cheese omelette and fries with a side salad. It was only after he started to eat that he realised how hungry he was and they brought him bread and more potatoes. The tiredness of earlier turned to exhaustion as the oxygen was diverted from his muscles to his digestive system and he abandoned the idea of investigating the town which he had entertained during his celebratory pre-dinner mood. He had slept fitfully the previous night and been up since five thirty. To his body it was an hour later than local time and he mounted the stairs in happy anticipation of the greatly underrated sensory pleasure of the twilight before sleep, although he knew it was only a precursor to the onset of an unpredictable dawn.

He woke at six from a disturbing dream and a bolt of panic caused him to sit up abruptly and swing his legs off the bed. He paused to hold his throbbing head in his hands and began a fevered search for the money, the whereabouts of which he couldn't recall. With a sigh of relief he remembered the safe in the wardrobe and opened it just to make sure. Banking it would be his first task. He stood in front of the mirror above a basin encased in a long marble shelf brushing his teeth and recalling his dream. Between himself and the promise of blissful conjunction with a faceless girl were littered untold obstacles and diversions. A labyrinth of snarling dogs and vacuous faced humans obstructed him, pushing him towards the margins of irrelevance, dissuading him from a goal that became increasingly unattainable. A pair of copulating mongrels, their tongues hanging lasciviously from open mouths mocked the impotence of his hopeless quest. When he finally reached the house of the girl he searched for her in vain and awoke to the sadness of unfulfilled passion.

He took a chair out to the veranda and sat for an hour drinking coffee and smoking, watching the sun and feeling the temperature slowly rise. Isolated shouts and engine noises grew slowly to what became a cacophony of sound by 8:00 a.m. It seemed they started early but, judging by yesterday, ran out of steam by the afternoon. He reflected idly on what had brought him to this particular place when the world was his oyster. Doug and Caroline had come for a package holiday three years before when the children had reached the stage of being old enough to leave alone and when the idea of holidaying with parents filled them with horror. Billed as the new Canaries with the added advantage of twelve months of sunshine and warmth per year, they had enjoyed the absence of sight-seeing distractions to prick their consciences and divert their attention from sun, sea, and sand. There really wasn't much else to do apart from visiting the volcano crater and salt lake of Pedro de Lume and see the harbour at Palmeira, with its lobster storage facility. With its apparently relaxed immigration laws and comparative obscurity, they thought it as good a place as any for Robert to make his new life.

He went downstairs and the girl from the previous night served him a breakfast of fruit and more coffee. He still felt full from the large dinner. He found it difficult to take his eyes off her as she shuffled to and fro in flip-flops, the short primrose skirt barely covering her behind and showing off her perfect copper-coloured legs. Was she the girl from his dream? He assuaged his sense of loss by imagining she was. He finished his fruit and she anticipated his need for an ashtray without his asking. He thanked her and smiled.

"*Mane k'e nom d'es kosa?*" He had used a little of the time in the summerhouse to learn by heart a few phrases of the Barlavento

Creole of the Northern islands. Caroline had suggested that any attempt at the language would generate goodwill.

She looked surprised and laughed, her dark brown eyes lighting up as she responded, "*Nha nom e Dominique. Bose?*"

Prior extended his hand in mock formality. "James."

Dominique carried on speaking in her language and he held up his hands to stop her and said, "I'm sorry. I only speak minuto creole," holding his forefinger above his thumb as he said it. "Do you speak any English?"

"A little."

"Where is the nearest bank?" She described the route in broken English, standing by his table with one foot behind the other, her left hand cupping her chin in concentration. Prior had a rough idea and it didn't sound very far.

"Where do you live Dominique?"

"I live here in Santa Maria. We moved from Espargos where I am come from. You know?"

Prior shook his head. "I've never been, but near the airport, yes?"

"Two kilometres from the airport."

The proprietor emerged through the fly drape and walked slowly onto the patio smiling benignly at the breakfasting guests. Dominique took her cue and moved away to clear a nearby table and Prior went back to his room to get the money.

He stepped out onto the dusty road and had only gone a few metres when he was greeted by a young black man. He had been coming from the opposite direction but he turned and began walking alongside him in the direction of the town. He spoke with a heavy West African accent.

"My friend – where are you from?"

"England." Prior had travelled the world enough to know the way the conversation would go.

"Which part of England?"

He felt listless and his breathing was laboured. He resented the requirement to talk at all, let alone the interrogatory nature of this discourse. However, he gritted his teeth and replied, "From near to Liverpool but I live in London." He could almost see the cogs of the filing system in the man's brain sorting the information.

"Ah… Stevie Gerrard. Wayne Rooney." The familiar names in this remote and unfamiliar land touched off a brief wave of nostalgia. They talked a bit about football, the common world religion, but as they traversed a large square the man, whose name was Abdulai, steered him to the right, away from the town, and applied the sting.

"Please come and look my shop, Jimmy. Because you are from England I give you very good price." He had abbreviated Prior's name autonomously, based no doubt on some footballer. Prior was vulnerable due to his disorientation and hangover and didn't put up much of a fight; the shop was dark and cramped and he eyed the merchandise with an air of bored distaste. He supposed it would have been kinder in the long run to have not given Abdulai any hope at all. He buzzed around him like a fly, holding things in front of his face, going through his hackneyed repertoire, filling his head with deals and offers. By an effort of will Prior mustered the resources to cut off the babble.

"Listen Abdulai, you have a very nice shop but I'm not a tourist. I don't need anything – I'm living in a hotel. Before I go back to England I will make sure I buy from you." The trader's face took on a pathetic look of disappointment, rehearsed no doubt by years of practice. In a final desperate gambit he took a picture from the wall of a boat in the foreground of an impressive sunset that Prior had shown a passing interest in.

"For you – twenty euros." It had come down from an improbable fifty. He thought of the hundred and twenty thousand in the shoulder bag and felt a twinge of pity for the young man in the hopelessness of his vocation. Besides, it would be worth twenty euros just to escape his clutches. He handed over the money and established that he would pick the painting up later on his way back to the hotel.

The scrum in the large bank dissuaded him from entering and he found another smaller one at the beginning of one of the roads leading into the town where he opened an account and deposited the money. Buoyed by the lightening of his load and the pleasant efficiency and transparent trustworthiness of the girl in the bank he stepped out into the sun and replaced his cap and sunglasses with a renewed optimism, walking a few metres up the street and stopping at the first café he came to. He went through the glass fronted entrance, raised a little above the street, and took in the comfortable furnishings in brown and bronze as he waited for his coffee. The interior was cool and dim, yet to be illuminated and warmed by the passage of the sun and he took his drink out and sat at a small table overlooking the street. The enormity of the vacuum in his life was starkly emphasised by the earliness of the hour. How on earth would he fill the remaining hours in *this* day, let alone the days, weeks, years ahead? He had discussed this with Caroline who, with her usual pragmatism, had urged on him the clichéd 'day at a time'. How he wished that she was here now with her wry sense of calm and their similar senses of humour.

He wandered slowly up the street, his creeping sense of isolation and futility emphasised as others talked and laughed or moved on their way with the sense of purpose he so envied. The only blessing was the absence of the infernal dogs, for whom this hub of the town seemed to be a no-go area. He stopped opposite the church and then without conscious decision crossed the road, drawn by the notice board showing the service times. The church was Catholic and he had read that Catholicism formed ninety-five per cent of the island's religion. Prior was nominally Church of England but he had no faith. He carried on walking to the extremity of the high street marked by the welcoming smells coming from a bakery that greeted people entering the town from the other direction. A throng of all nationalities queued and jostled as the West African women opposite sat on the pavement in colourful robes and headscarves, the abundance of fruit and vegetables at their feet fuelling the deception of plenty in this barren land. He tried to imagine the origin and journey of the lettuces and okras and tomatoes as he moved away from the town and once more into the hinterland of rubble and canines, seeing ahead of him a commotion of activity as people filled their plastic containers with the precious lifeblood of water. With the almost total lack of rainfall, water from desalination plants was tanked in daily to this central point and purchased at relatively high prices.

He spent the remainder of the morning walking aimlessly, choosing his direction on a whim and by noon, when the sun was nearing its zenith, and heat, fatigue, and hunger sapped his energy, he was hopelessly lost and seemingly miles from anywhere providing succour. His self-conscious enquiries for directions were met by incomprehension and looks of mistrust that heightened his sensation of alienation.

He eventually stumbled on a shop on one of the corners of a wide junction where a large group of men who looked like labourers drank grogue, the local spirit, and beer from the bottle. He guessed he may have stumbled on part of the explanation for the rapid waning of construction after midday. The darkest of the men, dressed only in a dusty pair of ragged shorts, spoke fluent English and although he didn't know Prior's hotel, he aimed him in the direction of the town's main street from where he thought he would be able to regain his bearings. The man was one of a horde of immigrant West African labour attracted from the mainland to work on the building sites. With increasing relief, dereliction gave way to more ordered signs of civilisation and at last he found himself in Abdulai's shop where he collected the painting – more out of consideration for the trader's feelings than any desire to possess it – and returned to the merciful sanctuary of his hotel room. As he removed his sweat-soaked clothes and pulled off one of the six pairs of £3 Primark plimsolls Caroline had packed, their condition and odour explained their mysterious proliferation. She thought of everything. He left them soaking in a basin of soap-lathered water and showered and changed and went down to the terrace, where Dominique brought him a lunch menu.

Her glossy black hair was tied tautly back into a ponytail held by a white hairclip and her wholesome freshness and simplicity made him feel renewed and invigorated somehow. They smiled as if they were old friends.

"And how was your morning?" Her weight was all on her left leg and her crooked elbow formed a triangle with her protruding right hip. He liked the way the enduring eye contact was not oppressive.

"Busy, always busy. All the bedrooms to clean. And you?"

"The same. Nothing to do, but busy. As we say in England – busy doing nothing."

She seemed to understand and laughed.

"Did you see the bank?"

"Oh yes. Thank you. I have an account now."

"Are you going to rest in Cape Verde?"

He thought for a moment.

"You mean 'stay in Cape Verde'?"

"Of course. I'm sorry. Stay."

"I hope you don't mind if I correct your English. I can help you to learn it properly if you want."

"Yes. Please. I would be very happy for that." She remained standing at his elbow showing no inclination to leave. The clothes he had worn for only three hours lying on the bathroom floor came to mind.

"I was wanting to ask you, Dominique. Would you be able to do my laundry for me if I pay you?" It was an offer she knew she couldn't refuse even though it would further add to her exhausting routine and she assented.

"So that means you are going to restée…" She put her hand to her mouth and giggled. "I mean stay in Sal, yes?"

He smiled, conscious of a desire to check an instinctive tendency towards the avuncular. "Yes, for some time. I have some business to do. But I won't be able to stay here for much longer. Do you know any place I could rent?"

She seized enthusiastically on her ideal position to be able to help him and said quickly, "Yes. When I finish here I go to other job to clean office of property company. I am pleased to show you. They have many apartments for sale and rent."

Prior took to his bed after lunch with the air conditioning on and blessed his luck in meeting Dominique. Their respective needs seemed to dovetail so perfectly and she was one of those people who he felt immediately comfortable with. He sensed she felt the same with him and he went to sleep on a rare peak in a life so full of troughs.

CHAPTER 17

A few days later at lunchtime on a Sunday, Prior sat at a table in front of a large screen showing an English Premier League football game. The setting was a new beach bar and the atmosphere was raucous. The tribal instinct seemed to dictate an obligatory affiliation to one or other of the teams, at least for the duration of the ninety minutes, and the audience, who were mainly tourists, roared their protestations and insults, seemingly suspending the reality that none of the protagonists could actually hear them. At half time as Prior queued at the bar for his sixth pint of lager, a man came to his shoulder and spoke.

"It's driving me mad. I'm sure I know you from somewhere."

Prior turned his head. It was the man at the airport. He stared at him levelly, the alcohol moderating the increase in heart rate. He tried to sound as matter-of-fact as he could and looked at him with feigned curiosity before saying in a broad cockney accent, "I don't think so mate." In his preoccupation with appearing innocent of the charge he was within a split second of sabotaging the deceit by revealing his real name. Just in time he remembered. "James Hudson. Ring any bells?" It didn't. They were served and moved away to stand in front of a bamboo screen separating the main auditorium from a beachfront seating area. Prior joined in enthusiastically with a tedious process of elimination, finally convincing him that the paths of an insurance salesman from Rochdale and a carpet fitter from Dagenham were unlikely to have crossed until now and they went their separate ways, the man's face still wearing a slightly pained look at the lack of fulfilment.

As a corporate bellow signalled the final whistle and Prior sidled past the bar in the direction of the seaward exit, the man once again approached him but this time he looked animated and grabbed his arm.

"I've got it! Robert Prior the sports journalist. I've been looking at his face every morning for the last ten years. You're the spitting image. Without the moustache and with a bit more hair you'd be him."

Prior hoped he didn't notice the momentary look of panic he knew must have crossed his face. He quickly replaced it with a wide smile. "Oh him. I wish I had a quid for every time someone's said that." He tested the man's awareness. "Wouldn't want to be in his shoes now."

The man's face hardened. "Aye. Hope they catch the bastard."

Prior entered wholeheartedly into a discourse on how to treat sex offenders, outdoing him in the severity of his proposed sanctions involving suspension and testicles and it was with an intense feeling of relief that he finally escaped his clutches and waded through the little avalanches of soft sand until he reached the firm, damp ground at the edge of the tide. He removed his shoes and shirt and began walking parallel to the beachfront hotels away to his right. It was a beautiful afternoon with the sun at its apex, the incessant wind now a gentle cooling breeze.

The beach was crowded but strangely quiet, with only an isolated raised human voice to compete with the soothing splash of the waves around his feet. The beer had filled his bladder again and he put his belongings just out of reach of the incoming tide and took off his shorts, running into the sea in the black trunks he was glad he had decided to put on instead of underpants. He swam out a few metres and felt the warm stream before turning onto his back and floating with his arms and legs stretched out in the shape of a star, his eyes half closed against the sun. The sea temperature was cool enough to be bracing without being uncomfortably cold and he felt considerably revived as he fastened his bum bag and set off again. He thought he would get beyond the beach chair rental hut which signalled the end of the more densely packed tourists and set up camp for the remainder of the afternoon. The nurturing of a tan would further alter his appearance. Just before he reached a spot ahead he had vaguely identified as his resting place a female hand waved at him from about twenty metres away. He didn't know who she was immediately but as he drew closer he recognised the woman sitting on the towel as Zina, the property agent Dominique had introduced him to on Friday. He grinned in genuine pleasure at seeing a familiar face and she squinted up at him, her lips parted slightly in a sardonic smile which disconcerted him a little. He noticed again the distinctive, and not unattractive, white enamel coating on her front teeth. Her fine ash blonde hair was still damp and darkened from a recent swim.

"Zina. Do you mind if I join you for a bit?"

She patted the sand next to her. "Of course not. Sit down."

He was conscious that the beer was becoming stale on his breath and he took a pack of chewing gum from his bum bag and offered her one which she declined. She smiled with a hint of mockery,

"Aren't we just the tourist," and she laughed softly in a gurgle from the back of her throat. He looked down self-deprecatingly.

"Oh, the bum bag. Yeah I know. Not really me." He thought of Caroline with a defensive pang. It was her who was being mocked and he felt an unexpected sadness in the self-protective need to affirm an alien present with the denial of a vastly preferable past.

"It's just that I've got cigarettes, lighter, chewing gum, money, sun cream, sunglasses, watch – my pockets would be bulging."

"I *am* only joking," she said before adding the word, "Wally," and moderating the insult with the weapon of her exculpating smile. He was disconcerted again – this time by the speed at which she appeared to think it was okay to be familiar. There was something about her that he found unsettling but intensely fascinating too. She changed the subject.

"So what have you been doing today?"

"Just finished watching the game. Was wending my way slowly back to the hotel. Then thought I'd stay on the beach for a while."

She grimaced. "Football." She made it sound like an accusation. "I came here to get away from the national obsession with it." They both laughed.

"And you?"

"I didn't get up 'til twelve. Then drove out here. I love the beach. Come every day." He looked surreptitiously at her white body. Her legs were long and her hips wide, the stomach flat beneath small, firm breasts and shoulders that were broad for a woman.

"You're not a sun worshipper though."

She looked at him down a long narrow nose.

"God no. Worst thing for your skin. I use total sun block. Factor fifty. You need to be careful – you're starting to look like a lobster already." Prior delved into the accursed bag and brought out his sun cream.

"Yeah. I haven't got round to putting it on yet."

She moved her neck to look at the bottle.

"Factor eight won't do any good – waste of time." He felt a rising resentment. What the hell was it to do with her? She seemed to read his thoughts and lay back on her towel with a sigh. "Do what you want – it's your skin."

She closed her eyes and Prior began oiling himself, the cream matting his copious leg and stomach and chest hair. He put some more on his hands and reached round to his shoulder blades, at which point Zina sat up and took the tube, squirting some onto her right palm.

"Lie on your front and I'll do your back." He had no towel and she told him to lie on hers and she then straddled him and rubbed the cream into his back in slow, sensuous movements down as far as the top of his trunks. She then shifted herself down to his feet in jerking zigzag motions and continued rubbing the cream into the back of his thighs and his calves. Prior's heart began to beat rapidly at this totally unexpected physical contact and when she had finished he had to remain lying on his stomach to hide his arousal. As if to defer the need to reclaim her towel and to allow him to regain his composure she went to the shore without a word and plunged headfirst into the sea.

Prior lay prone for a while deliberately trying to think of other things, and as soon as it was possible he bounded towards the waves in a vigorous attempt to expunge a curious feeling of emasculation. He swam muscularly in the direction of the floating Zina, going underwater as he neared her, and then nipped the back of her thigh with his fingers as he passed beneath her. He emerged from below the surface about five metres away like an enraged porpoise and watched her immobile, unresponsive figure, the pink and white bikini blending with the creamy flesh of the floating body on the surface of the deep blue ocean. He swam up to her and out of a need to restore a dialogue after the physical consummation more than anything else he said, "How long are you staying?"

She replied without looking at him, "What time is it?"

"About five I think."

There was a long pause before she answered, "Let's go for a walk to dry off and then I'll get going."

They walked west towards the Rui hotel as the sun continued its descent. It would be set in two hours. Prior noticed the greater proliferation of rock and the greater power and size of the waves the further they walked. Small sand dunes and scrubby, parched vegetation lay to the north between the shore and the massive hotel, a cloistered Western retreat of unlimited water and electricity, lush flora and self-indulgent luxury. He wondered how much of the island its residents saw apart from the hotel and the airport. After about two kilometres they turned and began walking back and Prior broached the subject of his accommodation.

"Any developments after I saw you on Friday?" The absence of eye contact somehow made their conversation more serious, less skittish. Or maybe it was just that they were tired.

"I've been thinking. I don't know how you're placed financially but it's worth considering buying rather than renting. Properties are dirt cheap here now, especially distressed re-sales. A lot of people bought hastily and are now regretting it. You could get a real bargain." He was silent while he thought.

"How do you think the market will go? Eventually I mean. Can you see the place taking off?"

"Oh yes, I think so. It's slow but there will be a boom. I'm sure of that. Once we're out of the world recession things will change. Now's the ideal time to buy. When you go home you can always rent it out as well. I can arrange that for you." He had been thinking along the same lines but didn't want to appear too keen.

"I could be in a position to buy for cash if the price was right. I'll certainly think about it."

"Okay, good. You said you are here on business. Do you mind my asking what sort of business?"

"No, I don't mind." He had prepared his answer during those long days in Caroline's shed.

"I'm in import-export. I thought I'd just come and do some research into markets, demand, stuff like that. I'm a bit of an entrepreneur really. I'll turn my hand to anything that makes money."

"Why Cape Verde?"

"Some friends of mine have holidayed here. They bemoaned a lack of certain items, or the expense if they *were* available. It wouldn't worry me if I didn't find any gaps in the market – I could do with a long holiday and let's just say I can afford it." He remembered the rudimentary nature of his hotel and felt a little foolish at the self-aggrandisement. Zina gave a long-suffering look.

"Well I can certainly add to your list of items. I'm experiencing severe grapefruit withdrawal symptoms for one. The new colonialists, the Chinese, have more or less cornered the retail market. In return for generous aid programmes their citizens don't have to pay import duty. Seriously though I could help you make some contacts – commercial, legal, government officials. And of course you'd need office premises which I could arrange." His mind wandered and he had to remember to pull back from becoming prey to his own deception.

"I like to do my own nosing about." He added enigmatically, "I have my own methods and they've served me well up to now. Thanks anyway though – I'll keep the offer in mind."

Caroline's words came to him again like those of a Guardian Angel – 'Don't get close to anyone, keep everyone at arms' length. The deeper you get the more they want to know about you.'

It was nearly six when they returned to their impromptu base camp and they sat back down and watched the dissipating rays of a declining sun cast shafts of gold onto a sea frothed by a hastening wind. Zina sat on her folded right leg, her left leg pointing at the horizon. She distractedly pulled her hair into a ponytail as she gazed off to the right, deep in thought. He sat with his arms folded across splayed, drawn-up knees staring ahead. The hiatus between now and the nine pints of lager he had drunk earlier would normally have induced a feeling of jaded melancholia that could only be prevented by carrying on drinking to a state of near collapse, with the reckoning postponed to the following day. Regenerated by the salt water, sun, exercise, and presence of Zina however, he felt surprisingly alive and responsive to the seductive call of the cocktail hour, never as enticing as when accompanied by the sunset of a warm, exotic land. The smell of burning charcoal hung on the breeze to evoke the comforting aura of humans uniting in a common gratifying goal. He imagined the hotels were preparing their barbecues and he felt suddenly very hungry, remembering he hadn't eaten since breakfast. Zina had been quiet for some time and Prior experienced the need to say something. The rapid intimacy they seemed to have established earlier had been attenuated by the reminder of the pragmatism of their relationship as they strolled along the beach and he felt confused and irritatingly gauche. He finally took the plunge.

"Do you fancy a drink and something to eat?" She continued looking out to sea and then turned her head slowly towards him. He noticed for the first time that her eyes were of the palest blue, almost grey, and a few light freckles had formed across her nose where the sun had breached her defences.

"Mmm?"

He repeated his suggestion with less conviction. The light, throwaway remark sounded more a submissive supplication in its repetition. She either *had* heard or cared not enough to listen. Either way he felt diminished.

"Hell no. I'm going home to have a shower and wash my hair." Prior tried to assume an air of indifference as he got to his feet and pulled on his shorts and T-shirt.

"Right, well I'm going to make a move – I'm starving." He was about to thank her for her company but decided against it. They ploughed through the soft sand together in their flip-flops, the muscles tightening in their calves, until they reached a place where their paths diverged and they slowed and stopped at the point of separation. He gave her a bright look but his evasive eyes conveyed a sense of rejection. Her own eyes focussed unwaveringly on him, commanding his eventual complicity, and he stood looking at her like a boy called to see the headmaster. She gave him her sardonic smile.

"You don't try very hard do you?" He felt a curious elation.

"I don't push myself on people, no."

"That's not what I've heard." The colour drained from his sunburnt face as if he had applied some of her cream. He managed a half smile and said as casually as he could, "Why? What have you heard?"

"Oh – you'd be surprised how quickly gossip travels in this little ex-pat community. It's all they've got in their boring little lives." He fought doggedly to keep the terror he felt inside from his face but feared he was not succeeding.

"Okay – so seriously Zina – what *are* they saying?" She threw back her head in the most energised movement he had yet observed from her and laughed loudly.

"Oh for fuck's sake, I'm only joking." She smiled at him. "Why? *Have* you got something to hide?"

The relief brought the colour back to a face that looked confessional as he said, "I'm a bit over-sensitive at the moment to be honest. Had some problems at home. Take no notice. It's hard to know how to take you sometimes though." There. He'd said it and he held his breath.

"Well Sigmund – I'm going now to get my shower and tart myself up and then I'm coming back to Santa Maria about ten to the Paradise Bar. Might I see you there?" Wild horses wouldn't stop him but he tried to feign tepidity, doubting at the same time that there was much point in this as she conveyed the impression of being able to read him like a book. She told him where the bar was and turned and walked away with Prior unable to take his eyes off her erect bearing and the hips that swayed beneath her tight ankle-length kaftan.

***

Dominique walked away from the hotel and turned out of habit in the direction of the site of her second job before remembering with a sudden glow that it was Sunday and the office was closed. As she turned back towards the town and her home she noticed out of the corner of her eye the figure of Prior trudging towards her from the direction of the beach. She carried his dirty laundry in a bin bag over her shoulder. The thought of throwing it in with the towels and sheets she had laundered at the hotel that morning had wistfully crossed her mind but she never seriously entertained this transgression of the rules. She would have to boil her own precious water and squeeze away the dirt with her sinuous forearms. Prior had insisted on paying her very generously and Sunday evenings gave her a window of opportunity.

She hesitated, caught in a moment of indecision over whether to wait for him or not. She wouldn't have expected him to notice her from this distance and decided on the latter, hurrying on so her back was to him and receding as he reached the end of the road. She thought of her mother as she entered the narrow streets approaching her house. She had been dead for a month and she couldn't avoid a sense of guilt that the raw pain of her bereavement had now turned prematurely to a dull ache of acceptance. She appeased herself with the knowledge that her grieving had started well before her demise as its inevitability gradually dawned on her. She felt the customary flicker of excitement as she turned into her road as she looked forward to the comfort of her own flesh and blood. She embraced her sister and the boys fell on her like a litter of puppies, falling away from her laughing protestations into a scrum of flailing arms and legs, into which plunged the dog, biting at her brothers with the innately judicious force of play. She set down the bag which distracted them and they clambered into Prior's clothes, parading around the yard striking arch poses which sent the dog into a further frenzy and caused Dominique to intervene before it could do any damage.

The hysteria gradually dissipated and they wandered out into the town leaving her to commence the mountain of chores. Her meagre supply of water was not sufficient for the extra laundry and she took her plastic containers to the house of a neighbour with mains water, handing over a few escudos to have them filled. As the water boiled she prepared her siblings' meal and started her preparations for the next day until it was cool enough to use. She washed his clothes first and then her own in the water that was now grey and tepid. She was thankful that there were no school uniforms to wash tonight but would have to remember to buy extra water next Sunday morning. At ten p.m. she finally lay down in her usual state of near exhaustion at the same time as a spruce and rested Prior was arriving at the

Paradise Bar a few blocks away.

He mounted the winding staircase and crossed a dimly lit floor to a circular bar where he ordered a gin and tonic from a young French woman. The night was young for the frequenters of this establishment and very few people were in. Zina wasn't there. He took his drink over to the walled parapet and leant over, watching the street below. After about fifteen minutes he heard the roar of a quad bike and a laughing, bearded ape of a man brought the machine to an abrupt halt outside the club and jumped off. He wore shorts and leather flip-flops with nothing on his torso apart from a heavy gold medallion and chain. Prior looked down at his chinos, socks and shoes and unbuttoned the cuffs of his long-sleeved shirt and the second front button, reminding himself again as he rolled up his sleeves that he must get out of this habit of overdressing. The man's female passenger swung her legs from the saddle and followed him off the bike, and in the glow of the bare sixty watt bulb above the door he saw that it was Zina. He felt an instantaneous envy and then told himself to stop being stupid. He turned to face the bar and watched them come in and their loud, showy, tactile greetings to the people there before they both leant over the counter and kissed the barmaid. He stood unnoticed, framed against the slate night sky feeling awkward and foolish. It was one of those nights when no matter how much more he drank he felt sober and serious, unable to cast off inhibition and act unselfconsciously and instinctively. He wished he could slip away but the one entrance was the only exit.

They sat on bar stools drinking bottled beer as a group formed around them and the chatter and laughter was incessant, their ease with each other obvious. Prior felt frozen to the spot but not to approach would appear churlish, odd even when eventually spotted, so he moved tentatively towards them and tried to mould his mouth into a grin. The barmaid looked up and smiled by way of enquiry as to what drink he wanted and Zina then looked round and saw him. She let out an affected shriek and threw her arms around his neck.

"Oh good. You came, Jimmy. I didn't see you skulking in the background." *Which probably meant she had*, he thought. The man she had come with looked at him with an air of contempt as if he was from another planet and Prior's hand went to the third shirt front button.

"This is Ramon. Ramon – Jimmy." Ramon's hand dwarfed his own but his handshake was limp and perfunctory. He ordered another gin and tonic and two beers and Ramon watched the ritual of merging a generous slug of gin with ice and tonic and lemon with a mannered incredulity as he removed the cap from his bottle with his teeth and drank deeply, nearly draining its 330ml contents. He belched loudly and then swung himself off the bar stool and wandered away to talk to the DJ. Zina visibly softened and patted the seat of the stool her friend had vacated. He climbed on and put his drink on the bar and she took his hands in hers and sought out his eyes. He noticed that her pupils were the size of pinpricks.

"I meant it Jimmy; I'm really pleased you came." He felt suddenly better.

"Yeah, so am I. But how do you do it? Haven't you got work in the morning?"

She laughed dismissively.

"Oh that. You have to be its master and not let it master you. Every night is party night in Sal." Then, as if remembering that he was her client she added, "No seriously – I'm on top of my job. I've got a cast-iron constitution." She looked disparagingly at the cigarette in his hand resting on the bar, the drifting smoke wafted by an adjacent fan.

"At least I don't use those things – they make a hangover twice as bad." She had a dismaying way of pricking a bubble before it became too big. He smiled at her.

"Well that's a conversation stopper. Live and let live is what I say."

"Not very appropriate given the subject matter, Mr. Hudson." He smiled again.

"Touché. But let's not have a diatribe about passive smoking. What about drink driving? The law here seems to be if you're capable of staggering to your car without falling over you're fit to drive." He recalled his own indiscretions and changed the subject. "So where do you live, Zina? You never said."

"Palmeira."

"Whereabouts is that?"

"It's a little port about halfway up the West Coast of the island – about seven kilometres west of Espargos."

They chatted some more in a light, easy way and Prior's mood continued to improve. He switched to beer and took off his socks and was pleased to see that the Neanderthal Ramon had latched onto a group of people sprawled across easy chairs in front of a low table close to the parapet. Zina showed no sign of desiring his company. The DJ finally managed to produce some music after an age of tinkering with the bulky, dated equipment – Zina told him that this was the only night of the week when there was no live music – and she pulled him onto the floor and they danced non-stop for an hour to a catholic selection of local and Western music. As with Catalina on the night in Barcelona that seemed now a distant memory, Prior danced with soul and energy and Zina looked genuinely surprised and impressed. He enjoyed what he thought were Ramon's furtive, slightly worried looks of reappraisal in his direction.

They replenished their drinks and joined a group of expatriates working mainly in the catering and property industries and he was as evasive as possible on the topic of his own line of work. They all shared a disdain for their countries of origin and an immense pride, bordering on smugness, at their ingenuity in fashioning a new life in this disparate setting. Prior guessed that nonetheless they clung to each other for company, paying an ostentatious but superficial lip-service to establishing meaningful friendships with other cultures and ethnicities. The high fives and convoluted coming together of hands and digits between the Europeans and Africans was nice window dressing for a state of affairs that seemed to still massively favour the former.

At three a.m. they danced to a slow record and he whispered into her ear, "Shall we go after this one?"

She pushed him gently away and said, "We?" He should have known it wouldn't be straightforward with this woman.

"Yes. We. Are we going?"

She shook her head slowly as they both swayed to the music.

"I left my car at Ramon's and he brought me here. It's about four kilometres away.

"Well, we can get a taxi."

"You won't find a taxi now. We're probably the last place that's still open on a Sunday night." He looked down at the floor.

"Well come back to my hotel. It's only a kilometre. You can get a taxi in the morning." She looked at him in a maternal way and shook her head again, a slight smile on her lips.

"No, Jimmy. No means no." She raised her index finger and waved it at him. "You're a naughty boy." He knew when he was beaten.

"Are you and that knuckle-scraper an item then?"

She looked shocked.

"Who? Ramon?" She carried on without waiting for his answer. "No. We're just friends. I've known him for years. Anyway, he's gay." They thought for a while and burst out laughing simultaneously. It was not possible for Ramon to be gay and they both knew it. She took her arms from his shoulders and took his hands in hers again as she had done when they were at the bar.

"Listen, Jimmy. I do like you but I'm not the kind of girl who does that on a first date. And I'm still on my own at thirty-eight. I've been hurt and let down too many times, Jimmy. Please respect my need to take it slow." He looked disappointed but resigned.

"I understand, Zina. I'm sorry I pushed you. I can still see you again though? Apart from through the business connection I mean."

"Of course. I want that. What about next Saturday? I'm off all day. I could show you the island."

"That would be great, yes. And what about the property side of things?"

"Well have a think about buying rather than renting. It really does make sense. If you want I could show you some properties for sale on Saturday but pop into the office any time before then if there's anything you want to talk about."

He left feeling buoyant, his respect for Zina increased and feeling more kindly disposed towards her. He would just have to get used to her quirky sense of humour. He was pleased that he was beginning to find his bearings and he found his way back to the hotel effortlessly along the network of dusty roads and paths. The town was deserted apart from the ever-present dogs lining the route or occasionally stepping into the road to scratch, their soft growls at his approach never materialising into anything more threatening. They were only issuing a warning as he passed the house of their owners, he supposed. He had never been particularly fond of dogs and thus far they were the only blot on the horizon. He held up a hand and bade a hushed welcome to an old night porter in the corner reading a magazine by a dim light and climbed the flight of stairs with a sudden realisation of how tired he was. He threw off his clothes, turned on the AC and fell naked onto the bed, falling almost immediately into the deep semi-coma of drunken sleep.

Back in the town the last revellers at the Paradise Bar bade their farewells and went their separate ways. The last to leave, a man and a woman, leant heavily against each other, overcome by helpless laughter as they made their way towards the beach in the dark hour before the dawn.

CHAPTER 18

He opened his eyes and his first observation was the barred shadows on the wall opposite cast by the light from the louvre windows. This was not a usual feature of his awakening and he felt clumsily for the bedside clock, cursing as he knocked over a glass of water. It showed five p.m. and he had been asleep for thirteen hours. He threw back the sheet covering him and sat up and then fell heavily back on the pillow. There was too much time lost for haste to make any difference now. Anyway, he thought, as he lay with his wrist across his forehead, what was the relevance of time in this limbo he had found himself in? The room felt chilly from the prolonged air conditioning and he got under the sheet and bedspread and stayed in bed for another half hour, comforted by the noises outside that affirmed that the world could carry on quite well without him. He got up and went into the bathroom and was pleased with the image confronting him in the mirror. His face looked tranquil, rested from the long, replenishing sleep, and the angry redness of the skin was turning brown. He showered in cold water and shaved and then listened to CDs on the little player that Caroline had packed, even remembering to throw in the round pin adaptor needed here. As he sorted and tidied his clothes and effects he was reminded of his arrangement with Dominique. He looked at the clock and it showed 5:56. He thought with relief that she wouldn't have left yet and went down and saw her in the corner of the patio talking to some guests. He fancied she sensed rather than saw his presence, and that the small talk had suddenly become onerous with his arrival. He smiled broadly, Dominique shyly, as he asked her if his laundry was ready.

"No. I wash it yesterday. Today I smooth it. I will bring

tomorrow." His look was affectionate.

"Press it – or iron it we say. Not smooth it. Although actually yours is probably a better description."

"Okay. Press it. Thank you. I'm sorry – no time to talk today Jimmy. I have to leave now. I'll see you tomorrow." He had a sudden thought.

"I'll walk over with you… if you don't mind that is. I need to see Zina."

At first he couldn't see her and assumed she must have cried off work today but then she came through to the main office from a room at the back. Dominique went away to fill her bucket and collect her cloths and cleaning materials and they stood looking at each other. She looked pallid and listless and for the first time carried a hint of vulnerability. Prior knew he looked good in the last of his unworn shirts, a sparkling white Henri Lloyd polo, and his eyes willed her to acknowledge his irresistibility. When she broke the silence her voice was a little hoarse and perversely, of a higher pitch than normal.

"Why do you have that awful moustache James? It makes you look like a tubercular Mexican. Either that or a refugee from the 1970s gay scene." He supposed that his vanity had deserved that. He looked around the room at the figures sat in front of their screens. No-one seemed to have heard. He searched for the witty retort but none was there so he muttered a rather pathetic 'thanks'. Her smile was conciliatory.

"I hate to see a silk purse being made into a sow's ear, that's all." She ran her tongue across her upper lip disarming him again and rekindling his longing. He didn't feel in the mood for verbal jousting. Maybe it was the conditioned work ethic that lamented his Monday spent comatose and unproductive that made him want to claw something back by being businesslike and practical.

"I really dropped in to say I've been thinking it over. I've decided I would like to buy here."

Despite her fatigue at the end of a long day her look was calculating.

"Wise decision, James. I hope I'll be able to help you find what you want." She glanced at her watch. "We can start the process right now if you want, with you buying me a large Bacardi Coke and me mapping out the territory."

The nebulous angst and insidious shame of the hours since awakening dissipated in a moment as they drove the short distance to a bar/restaurant on the end of a short pier. She had the top down on her convertible and the refreshing draught and sight of the darkening ocean erased the last traces of anxiety.

They sat on the terrace listening to the waves crashing onto the rocks and the shore behind them, watching the fishermen in the distance away to the right bringing in the daily catch. She kept her sunglasses on against the weakening rays of the setting sun and Prior glanced at the slenderness of her neck and the neatness of the small, almost lobeless ears revealed by her wearing her hair up for the first time in his experience. He sensed a small, indefinable sea change in her. Her look was more tender and her waves and greetings to the fluid acquaintances meandering this little idyll of sensory excess were friendly but muted, her loyalties firmly anchored to the mysterious man sitting at her table. He looked out at the last of the wind-surfers hauling their contraptions onto the beach, comfortable in their silence, confident of her growing interest in him. The tourists had all retreated to their hotels to apply the after-sun and prepare themselves for an evening of eating and drinking and the hotel 'entertainment'. He thought of where he should be now – the bleak forensic setting, the therapy now laced with a caustic edge of judgement and distaste, and he quietly urged himself to appreciate moments like this without the taint of thinking of what could lie ahead tomorrow. He listened inattentively as she outlined the complex-sounding procedures related to the sale and focussed absently on the figures she bandied at him – the six thousand euro solicitors fee, two thousand for IUP property purchase tax, the 0.2% stamp duty, fifteen hundred euros for Notarial and Registration fees based on his proposed purchase price of sixty thousand euros.

He cut her short, bored with the detail,. "Okay – about ten thousand euros solicitors and taxes. Where do I find a solicitor?"

"You can leave all that to me if you want. In fact I can make the whole process easy for you – just shove bits of paper in front of you to sign now and then. There are no agency fees of course as you're the purchaser. I know an excellent firm of solicitors and I can probably get you a good discount." He looked at her shrewd, intelligent face. She was not beautiful – the down-turned nose a little too long, the lips a little too thin, but there was something about her that fanned his desire into a perpetual, almost painful longing.

"I'm glad I've met you, Zina. You have my full permission to handle all the negotiations. I know people in the UK who've bought abroad and the hassle they've had – before, during and after."

"Good. So all that remains is to choose a property. I've a few in mind within your price range. What about tomorrow?"

"I thought you said Saturday?"

She widened her eyes.

"No, Saturday was for pleasure. This is business."

"Tomorrow's fine. I'm in your hands. Let's shelve the subject now anyway. Same again?"

Prior felt they had reached a point of tacit acknowledgement of an escalation of feeling and they began the exquisite exchange of life stories that he felt the occasion now warranted. He kept as close to the truth as he could without incriminating himself, transposing real events into different places and situations. They had a meal together with a bottle of wine and just after midnight she drove him back to his hotel. As the engine idled on the dust track outside he looked intensely at her but said nothing, waiting for her to speak first. She turned off the engine and said softly, "Goodnight, Jimmy. That was a lovely evening." She put her hand on his shoulder and moved her face towards him and their lips met in a kiss they held for several seconds. She broke away with an anguished sigh as his hands began to roam and said, "Not yet, Jimmy. Be patient with me. I'll see you tomorrow at ten." He kissed her again lightly on the lips and opened the door and got out and waited to watch her turn in a tight U, waving until the red tail lights disappeared as she turned right at the garage and joined the coast road.

***

He was first in for breakfast the following morning and he sat on the terrace, smoking and drinking coffee in the shade of an orange tree lovingly nurtured as if it were a prized pet. He hadn't slept a wink but wasn't surprised or concerned given how late he had got up.

He noticed a lack of the usual friendly smiles and greetings from his fellow guests and in due course the proprietor approached his table and addressed him privately in low tones.

"I'm sorry Mr. Hudson but I have received a number of complaints about the noise from your room last night." He gave her a look of perplexed innocence.

"Oh? What sort of noise?"

"Music. Loud music throughout the night." He scratched his chin and looked thoughtful. He felt nothing but contempt and a slight irritation at the accusation but he reined in his feelings.

"Yes, I confess I did play some music, but very quietly, I thought. I couldn't sleep. It was so hot and my air conditioning wasn't working." He felt no guilt at the lie.

"Well, I'm sorry about that. I'll ask my husband to look at it this morning. Please no more music after ten p.m. Okay?" He didn't feel disposed towards backing down but he knew she was a good, peaceable woman and he relented.

"Please pass my apologies to the other guests and I will be more considerate in future. I think I will be leaving soon anyway. I am going to look at properties today." They exchanged some stilted pleasantries and with her job done she went back into the hotel with a slight disquiet still on her face. Shortly afterwards Dominique arrived with his bag of washing all neatly ironed and folded. She put it down next to him and then her hand went to her mouth and she let out a soft exclamation of surprise.

"Oh. The moustache is gone. You look very different."

"Better?"

The jury appeared to be out on that. Eventually she said, "Mm. I think so. When it is the same colour as the rest of your face." He laughed. He too had been alarmed by how comparatively white the skin was above his upper lip when he had removed the bush at five a.m. He took the washing up to his room and showered for the second time that morning, picking out his favourite shirt and shorts from the laundered clothes to put on. Today was an important day. He sought out Dominique and forced thirty euros on her – ten more than he had originally said and more than a week's wages. Despite the massive difference to her life that regular amount would make she still felt guilty accepting it and tried to return the ten euro note. Twenty in itself was way above the real local rate. Prior laughed loudly enough for people to look up and then he ran from the patio and out onto the road, walking away quickly and turning just once to thumb his nose at her.

He walked to Zina's office and when they were out of eyeshot of her colleagues on the way to her car, they kissed and held hands. He had rehearsed a smart answer to the anticipated contrary comment about his moustache but he should have known not to second guess her and she commented favourably on his new look. She smelt of expensive soap and shampoo and wore a short mid-green dress with a wide white belt. He knew he was falling in love. By lunchtime this had been severely put to the test and as they had a beer and a sandwich in the Cultural café on the terrace looking out onto the main square he could not disguise his disappointment. His expression was hard and admonishing and she chewed and looked into space as he sulked.

She finished her sandwich and wiped her lips and said, "Get real, Jimmy. Sixty thousand isn't going to buy you front line. The only properties you could get within a mile of the coast for anything like that are very dodgy. I wouldn't trust the developers as far as I could spit. You wouldn't know what was in the bricks or what the foundations were like. The one's I've shown you might not exactly be Malibu but they're good solid apartments, built to last and with excellent rental potential. Not for the tourist maybe but definitely the ex-pat or indigenous market. You could ask four hundred per month quite realistically which, believe me, is a good return on a sixty thousand investment." He drained his bottle and called for another.

"Okay Zina, I know, I know. But these are in half-finished ghettos. Unfurnished. Tiny terraces. Not that there's anything to see from the terrace anyway apart from scaffolding and dogs. Millions of bloody mangy, flea-bitten dogs." He sighed and took another long draught of beer. "I mean with furniture and solicitors and God knows what else I'll be looking at close to ninety grand. For what you've shown me? No way." She gave him a perplexed look.

"Well walk away then. Rent. You were only considering an investment weren't you, not a long-term home? I've shown you what's available within your budget. It makes no difference to me."

He realised for the first time that his reaction had been inappropriate and that he was in danger of betraying an ulterior motive. His voice was conciliatory as he said, "No – you're right. I'm being stupid. It's just that the game's sort of changing. I like it here and I like the people. One of them anyway." She looked pensive and then put both her hands on his cheeks and smiled into his troubled eyes.

"Ooh Jimmy – our first row. Don't get too down darling, I've thought of something."

"What?"

"It's a long shot I admit. But worth a try. There's a front-line apartment in a fairly new development owned by an English guy who's gone bankrupt. It's up for sale with us for eighty-five thousand euros. Absolute bargain – cost a hundred and twenty two years ago. Fully furnished as well. I know he's desperate for a quick sale, or at least I expect the Receiver is. Even at that price there's not been much interest. He's in the UK now. What about I show you round and if you like it – which I know you will – we put in a silly offer, say sixty for starters, and see if he bites." Prior's expression changed to one of cautious interest.

"Yeah. Of course I'll look at it. Can we see it today?" She nodded.

"I'll just have to pick up the keys. Tell me, what's the absolute maximum you could go up to? That's if he rejects our first offer. Prior thought aloud.

"Well I suppose if it's furnished that's saved me ten grand. I could go to seventy but that would be stretching it. There are the leeches to pay off as well."

"Right. Well drink up. I want to try and phone him before close of business today and they're an hour ahead in UK." He waited in the car while she went to get the keys and soon they were heading west along the stretch of coast away from Santa Maria. After about three kilometres she turned off the road and parked in front of a large archway above which a sign read 'Miramar Apartment Complex'. They walked through and at once Prior felt he had found a place he could call home. Mature flowers and bushes lined tarmac paths, their thirst sated by a plentiful array of sprinkler hoses. The long three-storey apartment block was set back about fifty metres from a sandy beach. She opened the main door to the block with one of the two keys and they climbed the flight of stairs to the first floor where the apartment was situated. Prior wore the awed expression of the child in a large toy store. He muttered, "First floor, perfect," as Zina opened the door to the flat and they were hit by a radiant wall of light that shone through the large glass doors that opened onto a long south-facing terrace. It was spotless, with tasteful furniture and furnishings in excellent condition, and there was not a hint of the thick dust of the ones he had viewed that morning. Off from the living room were two good-sized bedrooms and a kitchen and bathroom with elegant well apportioned fitments. An involuntary smile appeared on his face and he hugged Zina tightly.

"I've seen enough. I want it. Let's go and put in the offer now." She laughed tenderly, pleased for him in his enthusiasm.

"Wait a minute; you haven't even seen the view properly." She unlocked the glass door and slid it across and they stepped out, ducking under an inconveniently placed clothes line on which there hung a white bikini and a towel. *That will have to go*, he thought, as they went to the parapet and gazed at the sea. They were close enough to hear the powerful waves crashing on the shore. The beach was practically deserted and she saw his quizzical look.

"It's a little rough here for swimming to be honest, unless you're very brave. But it's only a short walk back along the beach to the calmer waters. Besides – keeps the tourists and beach bums away and you're okay dipping on the edge. Just don't go out beyond the breakers. There's quite a current." His voice rose almost to a shout.

"I'm sold. Hook, line, and sinker. I've come home. Now let's get the hell out of here and seal this deal honey." He laughed a little too loudly and took the stairs down two at a time with Zina following in his wake. She agreed to his request to drive and was nerveless in the face of his speed, laughing at his recklessness and unaffected by his inexperience of the locality which even stretched to driving on the wrong side of the road on one occasion.

The office was empty as it was the siesta period and she sat him at her desk and got him a Coke from the fridge before going through to a room at the back to make the call. She returned to the main office about ten minutes later and Prior tried to read her expression as she crossed the room towards him. She quickly satisfied his curiosity.

"He's completely rejected sixty K. Said he felt insulted. Nearly put the phone down on me. After a lot of haggling he would settle for eighty but not a penny less." Prior's eyes glazed in a look of intense concentration and she gave him all the time he needed to respond.

Eventually he said, "I'll put my cards on the table, Zina. I want it and I'll pay eighty if I have to. What about trying seventy-five?"

She shook her head.

"No, honestly Jimmy, he's gone as low as he'll go. I think that would just kill the deal altogether. Let's be realistic – you're getting it for forty thousand less than it's really worth – thirty-three percent discount. I can confidently say a property like this will grow in value. And think of the rental potential. This is definitely tourist market and you would be looking at a lot more than four hundred – four figures probably. Look. Say the worst came to the worst and you did stay here and then found you weren't cutting it. You could rent out the Miramar apartment, get yourself something perfectly good for three or four hundred and live on the difference. That would go a long way here I can assure you. I could arrange all that. And say you decided to sell – I'd get you a lot more than eighty."

"So why aren't you getting this bankrupt more than eighty?" Her eyes narrowed and she looked away with a suggestion of irritation before turning her look back on him.

"Because he's desperate and can't wait and because I'm doing you a favour, don't forget at our expense. We're losing commission." He had one last question before the crescendo was reached.

"What could you get the solicitors and taxes and everything down to?"

"Oh. Probably get you a couple of grand off. Say eight thousand."

He appeared to be inflating in front of her eyes. It was so logical, so unarguable and the joie de vivre came back to him in a wave. He marvelled at her capability and kissed her suddenly before breaking off to shout, "Two fat ladies. Go for it. Tell him he has a deal."

She said, "Wait here – I'll be back in a moment," and went into the back again. He wondered idly why she didn't use the phone on her desk and asked her when she returned. She informed him brusquely that she couldn't use Skype from the main office and then smiled and held out her hand.

"Mr. Hudson, you will very shortly be the proud owner of apartment 136, The Miramar Apartment Complex, Ponta Preta, Ilho de Sal. Congratulations."

He whooped and hugged her again before asking, "How long do you think, Zeen?" She went into a long discourse on searches, promissory contracts, tax cards, notary, deeds of conveyance and he held up a hand to interrupt. "Just how long?"

"The best thing would be to give your solicitor Power of Attorney. That will speed everything up. I'll help you with your electricity and water contracts. I think at the outside we're looking at two weeks. It helps that the vendor is in a hurry as well."

"Wow. Is that all? You could teach the UK a thing or two about conveyancing."

She looked at him benevolently.

"This is what I do, Jimmy, and I'm good at it. I'll make it smooth and painless for you. Your main job will just be to transfer the money for us to forward it on to the vendor. It would be best if you do that as soon as possible as the solicitor will need money up front for searches and legalising and translation of documents. I'll give you the Iban and account details for the transfer now." She wrote them down with a reminder of the total amount, €88,000, and the formal business was concluded.

Prior experienced a moment of anti-climax. He was tired of waiting. He asked tentatively, restraining his impatience with difficulty, "So what are your plans?"

She looked at the clock on the wall.

"Back to work I'm afraid. No beach for me today thanks to you."

"What about later?" She yawned on cue.

"Quiet, early night for me, Jimmy."

He waited for the invitation for him to share it with her and see where she lived but it never came.

"Aren't you going to ask me over then?" He tried to sound light and jovial but knew the hurt and rejection was in his voice and on his face.

"Not tonight, Jimmy. I will do soon. I'm just shattered today and need a night on my own. Please don't take it personally." He remembered he hadn't got her phone number. He didn't use his mobile but could phone her from the hotel and she gave it to him so he could call her that night. They parted with his elation marginally tempered by this mercurial woman. He wanted everything and he wanted it now.

***

Later that day as Dominique turned the key to lock the door of the property company office she almost jumped out of her skin as a football thudded into the window close to her head. The reinforced glass thankfully did not shatter and she turned and watched the ball bounce off the raised concrete platform in front of the office and back towards the feet of its launcher, Abdulai N'Jie. In the fading light before the imminent sunset she recognised what had become quite a familiar face, although they had never spoken. Between them they spoke a variety of languages. Noting the straight hair and her colouring and features he assumed she was Cape Verdean and he spoke to her in Portuguese Creole. Holding up a hand in apology he called over, "I'm sorry sister. You okay?"

He flicked the ball up as it reached him and kept it effortlessly in the air as she replied with a shy smile, "Yes, but you should be more careful. You could have broken the glass."

He flicked the ball over his head and stooped to catch it in the crook of his neck before letting it roll down his back and away. He drew himself straight again and called over, neither inclined to break the distance between them.

"Anyway, what's your name sister? I've seen you around a lot."

"Dominique." The shy smile returned. "And you?"

"Abdulai."

"Well it's nice to meet you. I have to run now."

"Okay – I'll see you again. Take care."

She said with a smile, "I need to with you around," and he walked back across the yard to his shop with his eyes glued to the elegant retreating figure. Although it was the last thing he would have admitted to his friends, he experienced a small thrill as she turned and looked back, giving him a brief wave before turning the corner and going out of sight. Usually the chase held no terrors for him but with her it was different somehow. He couldn't explain why he had needed the deliberately wayward kick to break the ice but now it was done he closed his shop and walked into the town in search of a hustle to help him to celebrate this small triumph.

CHAPTER 19

Sixteen days later he stood on the terrace of his apartment. It was late afternoon and he really could now call it his own. The contract had been finalised the previous day and he was awaiting the arrival of Zina with the certified copy of the deed and the land registry and tax certificates. He replenished his gin and tonic and glanced at his reflection in the glass doors as he returned to the terrace. Dressed only in white shorts, he noted the spare, bronzed body with satisfaction. He had barely had time or inclination to eat over the past fortnight and sleep was an irksome interruption to the magic of the waking hours. He smoothed the hair on his scalp which was regrowing quickly in the heat and stroked his face against the grain of a two-day growth of beard producing a sharp rasping noise. He doubted he had ever felt or looked better. The flat was immaculate, a situation greatly enhanced by its almost total lack of possessions. He looked through the lengthy shopping list and added some more items which he had just thought of. His mind went back to the refurbishment of his flat at home and he enjoyed the contemplation of the comparative simplicity of the task in hand, with its enforced restriction of lack of choice and decision. A hired Range Rover sat in the communal car park waiting to transport him on his purchasing spree and he could barely contain his excitement and impatience to be back at the wheel. Standing against the parapet, too animated to sit, he contemplated the events of the preceding days with a sense of gratification, the scorn for his adversaries unmitigated by the victory that was his. Perhaps they would like to come and survey his current circumstances and then hazard a guess at who had won. He threw back his head and let out a noise that was somewhere between a guffaw and a howl of triumph before going back inside to turn up the volume of the CD.

Ten days earlier Dominique had loaded bed linen and towels into the giant washing machine and then paused to wipe away tears from her eyes and blow her nose. She could not erase the image of a struggling Jimmy being wrestled from the hotel and into a car by two policemen. He was shouting her name, his tormented eyes locked onto hers, imploring perhaps some kind of mediation based on their friendship and her commonality of nationality with the officers. With each holding an arm they dragged him backwards to the car, their small statures belying a wiry strength while the driver opened the door to the rear seat and helped them push him in. They sat alongside him in their dark blue uniforms and he stopped struggling as they travelled the short distance to the police station. He tried out his small repertoire of Creole on them, which in spite of the circumstances still induced a surprised and friendly response. That evening, after her paid work was done, she delayed her journey home and called at the station where a desk officer directed her to a holding cell at the rear of the building. Prior lay on the floor in the foetal position and he stirred slowly and got onto his knees at the sound of the cell door opening and his name being called. He looked up to see her face as the cell was locked behind her. Tears welled and then ran down his cheeks, carrying away the sting of the sweat as he got to his feet and enveloped her slender body in his arms. She felt awkward at this unexpected intimacy with a strange white foreigner of divergent gender and generation and she stood with her arms hanging limply by her sides, not knowing what to say or how to react physically. She was relieved when he let go of her and looked at her face but disturbed by the intensity of his gaze and the aura of unpredictability in his eyes that she had not witnessed before. He spoke hoarsely, his throat tight with aridity and emotion.

"Thank you, thank you, thank you for caring enough to come, Dom. I will never forget this." She would look up 'caring' in her English-Portuguese translation book tonight. Now was not the time for the light conversation of the terrace. He had been there for half a day and had no idea of what was happening and only hazy recollection of what had led to his being here. Dominique called out and the guard appeared and they spoke at length in Creole, Prior's eyes moving furtively from face to face trying to divine meaning from body language and tone of voice. When he left them alone again she spoke in her pretty, halting English.

"You will come before the court in the morning. He thinks you will have to pay money but then you can go."

"But what is the charge… what do they say I have done?"

"You don't know?"

"No. I don't remember committing any crime." She made further mental notes in her sponge of a brain of words to look up later but had caught his broad meaning. "The German man. You push him when he complain of the noise. Then he hit you. Then manager call police."

"So why don't they arrest him? He hit me – I only pushed him."

"Arrest?"

Prior's mental thesaurus could not come up with a simpler alternative in one word.

"Why they no bring him here also – the German man?"

"Ah. You start it with noise and push. He only protect himself."

"Okay, I see." He smiled at her and was touched by the reciprocation, with its implicit lack of judgement, loyalty even. He wanted to hold her again but stopped himself, recalling her earlier stiffness. Platonic or not, she was still about the same age as his youngest daughter.

"You must go now. I've made you late. Please do one thing for me. Tell Zina first thing tomorrow what has happened. She can get me a lawyer if I need one." He held out his hand which she took with a shy laugh and then she was gone, leaving him greatly buoyed by her visit and relieved at the possibility she had opened to only a fine and not the horror of an incarceration within an incarceration.

The following morning at the small courtroom he was assigned a lawyer who spoke rudimentary English and who treated him with an irritation he might have shown to a bothersome fly. He had evidently not been sent by Zina and after a brief appearance in front of what Prior assumed was a magistrate, his lawyer informed him he had pleaded guilty to something akin to a breach of the peace and been fined 10,000 Cape Verde escudos plus court costs and the lawyer's fee, totalling a further 10,000. A policeman escorted him to the bank where he withdrew the amount and some more to settle his hotel bill and they returned to the court where he paid it to a clerk who issued him with a receipt and he was free to go.

Back at the hotel he threw his belongings into his case and paid the manager the debt outstanding. She took the money and completed some paperwork, her hands trembling slightly in the face of his belligerent attitude that implied a miscarriage of justice to which she had been a party. Thankfully the German was nowhere to be seen. He demanded to see Dominique before he left but was told that she was sick today. He made a point of swaggering away from the hotel with his head high and his back straight, carrying the heavy suitcase in his right hand until he was out of eyeshot before putting it down and wiping his brow with an aching forearm. He pulled it as far as Abdulai's shop, the plastic wheels fraying quickly on the rough terrain, and he allowed him to leave it there while he went to look for another hotel. He sensed that the word must have gone round on the bush telegraph and the first three he tried said they were full despite appearing extremely quiet. At the fourth attempt he found a small guest house owned by a French woman who offered him a basic room. It was situated in a side road only a few metres from the high street and within earshot of the clubs and bars which presumably carried the advantage of being able to drown out the decibels attainable from Prior's small, low wattage CD player. Not that this was in any way something that he had considered. The taciturn woman took the two nights' pension he proffered in advance, studiously ignoring his feeble attempts at schoolboy French and conversing in good English in a Parisian accent. Abdulai insisted on pulling his case for the entirety of the distance from his shop to the guest house and accepted the comparative fortune of a ten euro note with surprise and barely contained delight.

The next nine days passed in a blur of alcohol, visits to governmental offices, and a seemingly endless stream of official papers in Portuguese thrust in front of his nose by an impatient Zina for him to sign. In the relative cool of the dim and dusty buildings he watched her with a mixture of awe and lust as she spoke in fluent Creole, in obvious control of any situation she was in, the ordinarily supercilious bureaucrats making an exception of her with their ingratiating smiles and the uncommon brevity of the mysterious transactions. Her attraction went beyond the merely physical. Her complete inability to be fazed or made to look even faintly uncomfortable was a compelling aphrodisiac and Prior had never desired a woman so much.

He continued to try everything he could to move the relationship to a carnal level. He swam daily, allowing the salt to dry on his skin under the sun's rays, inducing a deep and uniform tan on a body taut and honed by the swimming of obsessively long distances. He swam laterally beyond the breakers, just within his depth from a point where the savage power of the sea was just abating, towards the jetty and the tourists and then back again. He tried to be witty and alluringly enigmatic by turn but none of this altered her position that she needed time. He dreamt again the boxing dream where nothing he could throw at his opponent could win for him the prize and finally his frustration gave way to a release that left him feeling diminished by a shabby sense of betrayal. She was a young West African girl plying her trade from a single-roomed hut on a dust track running parallel to the beach. Despite his post-nocturnal shame, he sought her out again the following night, reluctantly enfranchised by Zina's excuses not to see him, and this time sneaked her into his hotel. After a debauched exchange the girl's mood turned ugly in the face of the insufficient money he had readily at his disposal and a loud disturbance ensued resulting in his being asked to leave the next morning. He cast any last vestige of frugality to the wind, and after lugging his case back to his friend's shop, he booked a room at one of the upmarket beachfront hotels at $200 a night, more for the anonymity than the luxury. The wheels on the case had completely worn away and the muscles in his shoulders and arms ached for days from the burden he had been carrying. He vowed to hire a car as soon as he moved into the apartment.

As promised, Zina gave him a tour of the island. She picked him up from the hotel in a four-wheel-drive she had borrowed from a friend and they turned left at the beginning of the road to Espargos and bumped along a rough track parallel to Algodeiro Bay where the beauty of the turquoise water contrasted with the disturbing power of the waves and the indomitable black rocks that lined the coast. They stopped for a coffee at a fish restaurant and she showed him a pool where rescued turtles, common in the seas surrounding the island, were given sanctuary after becoming stranded on the rocks. They then re-joined the main road and drove up to Murdeira, a small development of villas and apartments, taking a left turn at the top of the bay and travelling west until they reached Monte Leao and got out to stretch their legs and look at the small mountain in the unmistakeable shape of a lion.

She continued to drive northwards on a coastal track that explained the need for a 4-by-4 and after about ten minutes they reached the small port of Palmeira where he hoped he might be invited to acquaint himself with her dwelling. She didn't stop though and they pushed on up to look at the frothing pools enclosed by lava rock at Buracona in the shadow of Monte Leste and saw the Blue Eye, an underground pool from which the more intrepid divers can swim through a tunnel to the sea.

They were getting hungry by now and drove south back to Palmeira and then took a main road east to the island's largest town, Espargos. They found a restaurant and he broached the subject of where she lived again but she made an excuse about some building work going on. After lunch they continued east to Pedra de Lume and he witnessed the impressive pastel shades of the salt flats in the crater of a long extinct volcano which had formed the lifeblood of the island in the years gone by. She turned down his suggestion of immersing themselves in the volcanic mud with its reputed benefits to mind and body, although with heavy innuendo she made it known that she wouldn't be averse to the idea in future with some more preparation. The infertility of the island was emphasised by his first sight of birdlife since he had arrived in the form of some wading birds, their mournful cries a lament to the rusty cables and machinery and the ramshackle wooden frames that spoke of an industry now replaced by the gawping representatives of the one that had succeeded it. They spent the rest of the afternoon driving around the island's northern coast, spending some time on the beach before returning via Pedra de Lume to Espargos where they met the asphalt road that took them back to Santa Maria.

At the end of a long and tiring day in the exclusivity of her company, a wave of melancholia came over him to impede the euphoric mania of the past few days as she drove him back to his hotel. He knew that its source lay in the now familiar feelings of rejection and frustration and the approaching need to ask the question yet again and wait in resigned trepidation for her response.

He tried a different tack.

"You know, Zina; I'm starting to have a few second thoughts about the apartment." She glanced sideways at him with no change of expression and turned her focus back to the road.

"Oh. Why's that?" He felt a little deflated by her air of indifference but perhaps the eyes, shielded by her sunglasses, would have given him more hope.

"It's a lot of money. And a big commitment when I'm not sure about my future plans." They were approaching his hotel and she pulled in by some railings on the left about twenty metres from its entrance. She switched off the ignition and turned to look at him.

"Has our little tour put you off?"

"No, it's not that. The island's okay. Alcatraz would be okay if you were on it. Just a bit of last minute panic I suppose."

"Well yes. We're close to exchanging contracts. It's not too late to pull out though, Jimmy." She put her hand on his and took off her glasses. "It's a lot of money and you've got to feel it's right."

"I almost do. Ninety-five per cent. It's that five per cent that's nagging away." He looked at her. Her face was softer; concerned, empathic even. Her voice was also soft but authoritative.

"It's the best deal by far on our books at the moment. No question. But I would say that wouldn't I? You'd just have to trust me on that one." She paused and her expression betrayed an uncharacteristic vacillation as she said, "From a professional viewpoint, Jimmy, as I've said before, it really doesn't matter to me if you pull out. Someone else would snap it up tomorrow. I'd be disappointed only because I wanted you to be the one to benefit. From a personal viewpoint, I'd be sad to think you wouldn't be staying." With a lowering of her eyes she conveyed a sense of understatement.

Prior took his hand away from hers and moved it to the nape of her neck, fighting an urge to kiss her. Instead he said, "I know I'm being daft. Of course I want it."

She anticipated his next question and said quietly, "I'm so happy Jimmy. I know we want to be together tonight but I'm up at five a.m. for a flight to Boavista. We'll probably be able to complete the day after tomorrow so what about a little flat warming on Friday evening?" He was surprised by the lasciviousness of her look as she added, "Just the two of us. Perfect timing cyclically and weekend wise." It took him a moment to decipher the message and then a broad grin covered his face before they said their goodbyes and he went to his room to change into trunks and enjoy a pre-cocktail hour swim in the hotel pool. As he floated on his back his mind returned to the night with Catalina and how he thought it couldn't get much better than this. He said aloud, "Oh yes it can," and then let out a laugh that was audible enough to turn heads that quickly looked away as he revolved his eyes towards them from a head as still as stone.

***

He woke on Wednesday from three hours' sleep and paced and fidgeted away the time until the rest of the world was able to join him. He was in the car rental office as soon as it opened at ten and spent most of the morning filling in forms and arranging the transfer of the deposit. The Range Rover would be available from Friday. He broke his record for time spent swimming that afternoon and lay down exhausted on the warm sand and slept heavily for two hours before being awoken by the incoming tide washing over his feet. He moved back and sat with his arms resting on his knees, inspecting his body. If he could have looked into a future of twenty years hence he would have appreciated the uniformity of the brown hair on his legs – not yet stifled by the remorseless pressure of sock and trouser; he would have gloried in the unblemished skin, unsullied as yet by the sinister visitation of mole and outsize freckle purveyed by the double-dealing friend above. He would have positively crowed at the firm, flat chest, untainted by goodness knew what constellation of hormonal and environmental factors waiting around time's cruel corner to compromise his masculinity.

He rinsed off the sand with a final swim and grabbed a snack at the hotel before setting off in the direction of Dominique's house. He had not been in before but she had explained to him where it was. He found the street easily enough but needed help from neighbours to locate the house itself. He used the excuse of collecting his laundry for the visit but in truth he was curious to see how she lived, and part of him longed for a glimpse of familial domesticity after the antiseptic isolation of his life in hotels. They greeted one another with a brief hug that felt natural in comparison to the awkwardness of the embrace in the cell and he surveyed her primitive abode with pity in his eyes and a feeling of shame at the comparative luxury of his own apartment-to-be. The boys stood in a semicircle in front of him, gazing up inquisitively, and Prior suddenly leapt forward. With a downward punch he knocked a plastic football from Amilcar's hands and kicked it hard against the wall. The ice was broken without a word being spoken and a wild disorganised kick-about ensued. When Prior grabbed the ball and the game metamorphosed into rugby with the boys jumping on his back, the slavering dog, demented with excitement, sank its teeth into his thigh in a misguided gesture of protectiveness. Prior howled and the females took charge, admonishing the confused beast and tending to the wound. Before arriving he remembered reading that rabies was not on the islands but he didn't know the date of his last tetanus. In his current state he couldn't have cared less anyway.

He stayed 'til late, accepting Dominique's apologies for not giving him her undivided attention as she went about her chores accompanied by his admiring glances at her boundless stamina and languorous dexterity. He told the boys a bedtime story of the three pigs, they seemingly fascinated by the unfamiliar words coming from the mouth of this unexpected visitor, beguiled by the narrative flow and his energetic sound effects. When he finished he reached in his back pocket and took three ten euro notes from his wallet, handing one to each of the boys with a forefinger to his lips and a glance towards the yard where the girls were working. At last, as the time approached ten, their work was done and they sat down to eat their longed-for reward. Prior forcefully repelled their exhortations for him to share the meagre fare and asked Dominique how her day had been and told her the outcome of the court appearance. Veronique sat away from them, glancing furtively at him and turning away with a shy smile when his eyes met hers. Dominique's yawns finally stirred him and he took the bag of laundry in one hand and offered the other to Veronique who took it with a similar giggle to that of her sister in the police station. He took a fifty euro note from his wallet in the dim light of the yard and pressed it into Dominique's hand in payment for the washing. He kissed her lightly on the cheek and turned and moved hurriedly away before she had time to inspect it, ignoring her eventual squeals of protest as he turned the corner and headed for the sound of music on the main street.

***

He stirred with excitement at the virgin ring of his buzzer and bounded over to the intercom which crackled with the husky, feminine voice of Zina. He pushed a button to let her in at the main entrance and opened his apartment door and heard her light step mounting the stairs. They embraced and he held her tight, drawing her towards him with the urgent pressure of his hand against the thin cotton skirt covering her bottom. She allowed the contact to remain and returned his long kiss but then gently extricated herself and walked through to the living room, placing a carrier bag on the flowered cushion seat of the cane settee, part of someone else's choice of furnishings which seemed inevitably more tasteful than his own would have been.

"Business before pleasure, Mr. Hudson." Her hands delved into the bag and she pulled out a wad of documents in Portuguese with impressive official stamps which she passed to him one by one, explaining what each related to. Prior gave them a cursory inspection. Zina laughed.

"Try to look a bit more interested, Jimmy. They're your proof of ownership. Make sure you keep them safe." She suddenly looked serious and troubled. "You'll never guess what. I'm still on. It's been really heavy this time."

He visibly deflated like a beach ball cut by a shell and then the futile anger welled up in him and he said savagely, "Oh come on Zina. What bloody excuse are you going to think up next? We're hardly at the headache stage yet." She gave him a sharp look that implied both hurt and indignation. The literality of the adjective he had used was lost on them in the tension of the moment. Her voice was raised and harsh.

"It's not a 'bloody excuse'. It's called being a woman." He held his head in his hands in a melodramatic pose that made her smile inwardly at the all-consuming male impulse. Her voice softened. "I'm as disappointed as you, Jimmy – honestly. Look, I'll definitely be okay by tomorrow night. I absolutely promise – one hundred per cent and I can't wait. Anyway, we can still have a nice time tonight."

He moved over and sat next to her on the settee and she put her arm around him. He put his head on her shoulder and she stroked his face and hair and admonished his lust as she had done on his first attempt at the club, but this time her voice was babyish.

"My naughty little James will just have to be a good boy for one more night. And then see how naughty Zina can be. You wouldn't believe it." She took her arm away and went back in the bag, pulling out a bottle of champagne and an envelope which he opened to reveal a hand-made card saying 'welcome to your new home'.

"Sorry about the home-made card. You can't buy them here. That's something there'd be a market for with your business." Inside the card were two tickets which he looked at blankly.

"And those are entrance to some big game tomorrow afternoon. VIP tickets for the best seats. We use them for our most prestigious clients. I know you said you liked football." He felt a lump forming in his throat. He didn't deserve for life to be this good. He kissed his thanks and put the champagne in the deep freeze to cool rapidly and then fixed her drink and refreshed his own and went onto the terrace and lit a cigarette. The sun was beginning its descent and he sucked in for the umpteenth time now the joy of the sunset, with its perfect accompaniment of gin and quinine. The warm breeze ruffled the flags on the beach as the waves crashed onto the angular rocks. The sea here was not compatible with swimming but its ferocity and clean beauty filled him with a thrill every time he looked at it. It would make for an exhilarating companion and a soothing bedfellow in the years that now stretched ahead of him with such promise.

The night was one of sensory bliss, enhanced if anything by the postponement of the ultimate prize – the sadness of the post-coital mood supplanted by the delicious anticipation of tomorrow. They drained their glasses and took the champagne to the water's edge, Prior holding the bottle in one hand and two flutes in the other, Zina's arm around his waist as they felt the satisfying connection between the warm ground and their bare feet. They drank quickly, finishing the bottle as day turned to night, Prior's intoxication due more to a combination of his unconstrained mood and Zina's devastating desirability in the light of the shimmering dusk than the effect of the alcohol. He whispered his love in her ear, the scent of her hair an uncanny evocation of a barely remembered first love. What was the talcum powder whose smell remained more vivid in his memory than the girl herself? Blue Grass? Lemon Grass? He couldn't recall. She answered with a kiss and he read the reciprocation in her eyes. He would one day melt that stubborn resistance to the expression of a sentiment he knew she felt. The time came to return indoors and reluctantly they turned from the secrets of the deep, its mystery intensified by the veil of darkness; the ebb and flow, the crash and roar more ominous with the cloak of anonymity.

Back at the apartment they drank two more large gin and tonics each as Prior fiddled mysteriously in the kitchen before triumphantly setting down on the dining table plates and dishes of lobster and mayonnaise, various salads, fresh bread and French fries which they ate decadently to the accompaniment of a bottle of Muscadet. He pushed aside a fleeting image of the repast he had witnessed a day or two earlier and they took their coffees to the terrace with a bottle of cognac. His choice of music on the good quality sound system that was part of the package was to Zina's taste and they danced and touched and experienced a physical closeness in a marathon of restrained foreplay that augured well for the culmination hence. They fell asleep entwined on top of the bed at two a.m. and when he woke at five she was gone.

In spite of his throbbing head and severe dehydration he couldn't return to sleep so he drank two litres of bottled water from the fridge and went to the beach, walking until he reached a spot where it was safe to plunge into the reviving sea. Sal was cool before the dawn, and the sea bracing and he returned home feeling remarkably fresh considering the lack of sleep and prodigious consumption of alcohol. He scrambled some eggs and ate them with the last of the bread and by his third coffee all was well with the world again.

Zina had made it abundantly clear that the second ticket was not for her and he thought he would offer it to Abdulai. He climbed into the 4-by-4 and drove towards the town like a child learning to ride a bicycle – at first slowly and cautiously with the equivalent of a few wobbles at junctions and when negotiating his way past pedestrians and stray dogs – his confidence gradually building to an impressively smooth arrival on the sand outside the shop. He jumped down athletically and sauntered towards the open door but Abdulai had observed his arrival and was on him almost immediately. They turned and went back to the vehicle and after circumnavigating it in a tour of inspection, he jumped up with Prior's nod of permission and sat at the dashboard, craning his neck to look at the plethora of knobs and dials. He told him about the football and was surprised by his lack of enthusiasm. He seemed far more excited by the Range Rover. He spent the rest of the morning shopping and took his purchases home and unloaded them before collecting his friend and driving to the stadium.

As the match unfolded, the reasons for Abdulai's previous absence of excitement became clear as he castigated the players on both teams for their woeful inadequacies. He seethed in a ferment of agitation, his frustration occasionally boiling over into loud volleys of reproach before he returned to bite what was left of his nails. Prior could understand how painful it must have been for him to watch the feting of players far inferior to him who, for whatever reason, were given an opportunity denied to himself. The game ended and they headed back to town and finished the outing with Prior buying them both drinks and a meal. Zina was due at seven and he pressed a note into Abdulai's hand so he could continue the evening and hurried back to the vehicle. His watch showed six-twenty – just time for a quick shower.

He ran up the stairs and cursed as he dropped the keys, fumbling in his haste. The cleansing ritual was of particular importance tonight. He opened the door and took the few steps from the passageway to the arched entrance to the living room and then froze suddenly in shock. The first thing that registered as abnormal was the door to the terrace, unhinged and swinging slowly back and forth, energised by the wind. It took his focus away from and momentarily postponed the real sense of his disquiet. Sprawled on his cane suite, bottles of beer in hand, were Zina and Ramon.

In a split second his brain unconsciously weighed the complex ratios and relationships between feelings, thoughts and action. Their expressionless faces were both turned on his. They had made their move. The next move was his and it provided him with more thinking time. Feeling was fear and hurt. Thought was dictated by feeling almost entirely. The minute possibility of an innocent explanation to contradict the sensation in his gut dictated his action. He smiled. Such is the human capacity for self-deception.

"Glad to see you've made yourselves at home." He looked at

Zina, the smile evaporating as he turned to nod in Ramon's direction.

"What's he doing here?" She replied in a matter-of-fact way, the enjoyment of the control she held manifest in the cold eyes and derisive lips.

"He lives here. Off and on." His face contorted in bewilderment and he grabbed the back of his neck to massage some blood to his constricting brain. He walked over to the fridge and took out a bottle of beer and took the cap off with his teeth. His stomach was uncharacteristically full after the burger and chips with Abdulai and this negated the effect of the long draught he took from the bottle. Acid rose up his oesophagus and into his mouth and he went to the terrace and spat over the parapet. He heard Zina say "Charming," before he returned to the room and sat down in a chair opposite Ramon who half lay across the sofa. Zina sat to his right in the other chair. The last iota of hope he had been clinging to was disappearing. Like Don Corleone, he wanted to be given bad news right away.

"Just explain Zina. No mind games. No knife twisting. Just the facts. Please." He looked at her as she stared back at him, searching in her face for a clue, a touchstone for the Zina he thought he knew. Enigmatic, capricious, spiky, cold – yes. But with enough saving graces for him to fall in love with her. Or perhaps he fell in love *because* of those qualities, always trusting in an instinct that a compassionate humanity lurked deep beneath the barbed surface and that he was slowly finding his way down to it. With each of her words the illusion disintegrated.

"I own the flat. Everything was a lie. The papers – all phoney. Lawyers, vendor, phone calls – all made up. Non-existent. Those visits to Government offices? Sorting out other business. The bank account you transferred into? My own. Easiest eighty-eight grand I've ever made in my life." There was no hint of guilt, no trace of remorse. She might have been describing a minor misunderstanding. He felt strangely detached from what he was hearing. Somewhere from some optimistic recess of his mind a defence mechanism kicked in. She was lost to him, he accepted that, but surely there was no way she could get away with this. He would reclaim the money and he would get over her. Wouldn't he? In time? He had plenty of it. A sudden sobering thought brought him back to reality. The giant on the couch who had still said nothing, only staring at him in that gormless, mocking way; he was there for a reason and he doubted it was social. Surely she wouldn't go that far? An incipient fear that she certainly could grew gradually more intense. The keys in his shorts pocket were digging into his thigh and he took them out and threw them on the table. Despite a conscious effort his voice betrayed his nervousness.

"So everything was a fraud. Even last night? You must be some actress." He looked pointedly at Ramon, spurred on by a kind of death wish perhaps.

"No. I quite enjoyed the lovey-dovey bits. Perk of the job. I've got to admit I did quite fancy you." He glanced at Ramon, who appeared indifferent, and his brain quickly began piecing together the events of the last few weeks. With hindsight all the nagging little questions were answered. The tickets today to get him out of the flat. He had to acknowledge a grudging admiration. She was so smart.

"So how long ago was it all planned?"

"From when you first said you wanted an apartment." The hurt returned.

"But why me? Couldn't you have worked this scam on anyone? Or maybe you have. Over and over for all I know." She sat with her legs pulled up under her, completely relaxed, revelling in this dissection of the confidence trick. In spite of everything he couldn't prevent a tantalising glance at her pants – visible at the crotch with her short dress riding on her haunches. Was there no discernment in this crippling lust, he thought bitterly, no sense of a time and a place? The realisation that the prize promised to him belonged instead to this hirsute oaf rekindled his anger and restored some fight.

"You won't get away with this you know." Ramon suddenly became alert and the frost returned to Zina's eyes as a thin smile formed on her lips.

"Oh I think we will." She paused for effect before adding quietly, "Robert."

His predominant emotion was strangely one of relief. Relief that he was finally sharing his onerous burden. Relief that there was a reason for Zina singling him out other than his potential gullibility. Relief at the reduction in the likelihood of violence, terminal or otherwise, as a means of securing his silence. It was a long time before he spoke. When he did he surprised them both by going down without a fight.

"How did you know?"

"I had a boyfriend once in England – a long time ago now, shortly before I came out here. He lived near me and worked with you on your paper. Adrian Green?" He instantly recalled him as a 'bits and pieces' man – boxing, snooker, darts – who eventually, rather illogically, became the paper's racing correspondent. Prior had disliked him intensely.

"You obviously don't remember but I met you once on a works night out you were having. We get the papers here now and then from tourists or flight crews and I make a point of looking at Adrian's articles and I've seen your mug shot frequently. Obviously when the news broke about the rape I was interested and of course I could follow it on the net. Even with the moustache and the shaved head I thought it might be you. When you lost the tash and your hair started growing I became more convinced but not absolutely sure. When I teased you on the beach that day I could see you were terrified. It all added up. I'm surprised you didn't deny it though."

"What would have been the point? I'm sure the two of you had me stitched up one way or the other. Tell me this. Weren't you a bit worried about being alone in compromising situations with a supposed rapist?" She laughed scornfully.

"And madman to boot? I'm not frightened of anybody and certainly not *you.*"

"For what it's worth, although I don't suppose you're interested, I didn't do it. You were quite safe, which is more than I can say for myself." The mutual disclosures had dissipated the tension and he was getting some kind of perverse enjoyment from the new transparency. And he would never again have to experience the bitter-sweet torment she had inflicted on him. The duller his future dalliances the better. More retrospective questions came into his mind.

"Why didn't we go all the way last night if you fancied me? You'd got what you wanted, you had nothing to lose. I certainly don't believe your excuse." Ramon got up and brought two beers back for him and Zina. Prior pointedly went to the fridge to draw attention to his bad manners and the Portuguese moved towards him and gripped his wrist and prised the bottle from his hand.

He said in a deep voice, his English heavily accented, "You wait 'til you are asked my friend. Now go and sit down."

He looked to Zina for some kind of miracle of support but her smile was cruel, her face almost demonic. He imagined the beginning of one of those abhorrent stories of protracted, gratuitous persecution that one is occasionally compelled to follow in the media. He had to fight the need to void himself. This was not quite how he had envisaged the night turning out. Even Dutch courage was a closed avenue now. He walked meekly back to his chair and sat down and she reminded him of the forgotten question posed only a few seconds ago but light years away in context.

"When you'd been going with that whore? No thank you. I told you before – everyone knows everyone else's business here." He left the other questions unasked. He just wanted to get out unscathed now. He got up and the voice that came out of his head was mournful and plaintive like an echo from a hollow sphere.

"You have me cornered; the money's yours. Let me get my things together and I'll go." Ramon stood up and pushed him back into the chair with such force that his head and neck jerked involuntarily on his shoulders.

"You wait. Zina hasn't finished." He was disturbed by her sybaritic look but she then suddenly transformed into the property agent, crisp and efficient, speaking in clipped tones.

"As part of a condominium 'your' apartment will of course be subject to condominium expenses. You don't expect the gardens and sprinklers and upkeep of the communal areas to pay for themselves I'm sure. There's also IUP tax which I will pay on your behalf as your trusted agent, along with property insurance. You'll need to set up a standing order to the amount of the charges I've detailed – two hundred euros a month should cover it. Same account as for the purchase monies. Finally, there is also a fee of €15,000 which we will call a 'float'. This *may* be returnable and will provide us both with 'peace of mind' insurance against any 'loose talk' from either party. Transfer this in the same way to the same account. Now wait here while I pack your bag." He heard her thumping about in the bedroom and bathroom and she reappeared with indecent haste, pulling his case behind her. He imagined the contrast with Caroline's neat symmetry. He stood up and reached for the keys and for the second time Ramon gripped his wrist and they fell back onto the table like toothpaste being squeezed from the tube. He was ashamed at the peevish subservience in his voice.

"I know you'll keep the ones for the flat but the car keys are on the ring."

Ramon looked him in the eyes and said, "Exactly. Now fuck off." It was a good way to end the exchange but Ramon had still to deliver his closing speech. Taking Prior by the shirtfront he pulled him close and looked down at him, his and Prior's upturned face only inches apart. His breath was a cocktail of beer and nicotine and garlic and drops of saliva from his mouth fell against Prior's lips as he spoke.

"You tell anybody about the money; we'll say who you are. You don't pay the condo expenses; we'll say who you are. You don't pay the 'float'; we'll say who you are. You decide your new life here is a hell worse than what waits for you in England and give yourself in and tell them what happened?" He drew a forefinger across his throat. "You are dead my friend. Very slowly and very painfully." He pushed him away and Prior's head hit the wall. The last hour had been a better medicine for his mania than any amount of lithium but there remained a trace of impulsiveness. Better to walk away bloodied and broken than cowed and full of self-loathing. Bones and flesh would heal. The ego would not. He threw a right at the bristled chin with all the force he could gather but it was he who recoiled backwards and not Ramon who stood stock still and began to laugh. Still laughing, he hit him back, sending him sprawling onto the floor.

As he stooped to raise him up he heard the arousal in Zina's voice as she mocked, "Be careful Ramon. Remember the strength of the insane," before releasing the gravelly laugh he had come to know so well. Prior was now at the mercy of the unpredictable brute, all thought of further statements far from his mind. His jaw hung loose and blood trickled from his mouth. The man held him for a while, weighing up his next move and eventually he let go of his hold and opened the door, pushing the case through it with his foot.

"You can leave as a man. And don't forget what I told you. Adios."

He slammed the door behind him and Prior bounced the case down the stairs, pondering on the irony of the need for a violent act to finally release a vestige of humanity in a man like that. He cast a rueful glance at the Range Rover as he struggled past it towards the road and as he set the case down at its verge and lit a cigarette, waiting for someone to respond to his upraised thumb, the relief returned. He didn't have a clue as to the reason, and he suspected it would be transitory, but he hadn't felt as content since that wet evening in London, crouching in the bushes in his first hours as a fugitive.

CHAPTER 20

He waited for twenty minutes, his hopes rising and falling with each infrequent flash of approaching headlights until at last a taxi stopped some thirty metres ahead and reversed back to him at speed without deviation. He struggled to describe Dominique's compound but the man began driving anyway in the direction of Santa Maria, his face inscrutable, Prior's impotent attempts to communicate apparently falling on deaf ears. As they reached the town, his gestures and instructions, barked in a kind of pidgin English, eventually resulted in their pulling up in front of the house.

His re-emergence shortly after dawn the next day was more a regaining of consciousness than an awakening. A painful process took him from an initial mild excitement at the thought of walking to his terrace to greet the new day to a gradual appreciation of where the events of yesterday had left him. On the beach to be precise. After leaving his case with Veronique – Abdulai would have been the preferred option but his shop was closed and he didn't know where he lived – he had lost count of the bars he had frequented and the drinks he had consumed. Some sort of moral regulator that he still possessed thankfully prevented his return to the house of the young people in the condition he had reached by the time the last bar closed and he had stumbled towards the shore, cutting through the side streets until he saw the pier to his right and felt the sand beneath his feet. He sat up and looked around, slightly alarmed at the open, unconcealed spot where he had collapsed. Fishermen were preparing their boats and nets for the hunt for the tuna, garoupa, wahoo and horse mackerel that populated the outlying ocean and a few dogs mooched about in search of food. The sky above was cloudy and he felt an unaccustomed chill.

He took an inventory of his physical condition, starting with his throbbing head. His mouth was as dry as chalk and his jaw ached. The thigh where the dog had bitten him was beginning to hurt and he pulled up the leg of his shorts to see the yellow pus forming in the onset of an infection. The incongruous elation and optimism of last night's mood was gone and he sat there for half an hour paralysed by gloom and indecision, envying the concentrated purpose of the activity around him. He had no cigarettes and he longed for the coffee that would lubricate his mouth and get the heart pumping to at least suggest that he was still alive. At that arbitrary point when inaction turns to motion he placed an open palm on the sand and levered himself to his feet slowly, feeling a momentary premonition of his own immortality as he rose. He didn't know quite what he would say to Dominique and he felt ridiculous at the confusion his sordid mess of an existence was visiting on her simple, virtuous life. He would at least summon the grace to get out and leave her alone. She had managed to survive without his unsolicited euros before; he was sure she would be able to in future.

After buying cigarettes and drinking coffee at a street café he limped away and found a position opposite the Ventura Hotel from where he could observe the terrace unnoticed. When he saw Dominique appear he darted towards its parapet and ducked below its ledge. When he finally managed to gain her attention with a series of hisses, only his eyes and forehead visible, she looked embarrassed at this rather unnecessary subterfuge. None of the guests remained from the day of his ignominious departure. She gave him the key to the rotting front door with the rusting lock, defenceless against a modicum of force, and he walked the half mile to her house, unsuccessfully struggling to resist the insidious dawning of the wretchedness of his changed situation. The clouds of earlier had cleared and the brightness of the day and the rising temperature unexpectedly added to his gathering discontent and he felt a nostalgic yearning for a dull and damp November day in England. A feeling of not being connected to the rest of the world was reinforced by the seemingly deliberate avoidance of eye contact from those whose paths he crossed. As he might have done on the tube, he searched in vain for a glimpse of human empathy. And all of life played out in the presence of the infernal, irrelevant, unproductive canines littering the sides of the road.

He wrenched open the door, the rough contact of its bottom with the concrete step loosening more of the rotting wood which fell like sawdust to the ground. The dog eyed him malevolently from a vantage point in the shade of a wall opposite but surprisingly left him unmolested as he dragged out his case and set off again. The previous weeks had passed in a blur of mainly purposeful activity and escalating excitement and he had paid little heed to objective appreciation of himself other than an assured assumption of his charismatic allure. As he staggered along, his jaw and leg throbbing in protest, he imagined this labouring European with its weighty burden was becoming quite a feature of the local landscape. He had previously resisted taxis out of reasons of their scarcity and the therapy of building fitness and strength via his boundless levels of energy, but now he toiled under the constraints of his newfound impoverishment.

At last he reached Abdulai's shop and he sat down heavily on its unaccommodating stoop and transferred the sweat from his brow to his hand and thence to his dirty shorts. His hands returned to his eyes and the bottoms of his palms pressed firmly into his eye sockets, seeking a transitory balm for the unease of his brain. Abdulai's unconscious radar saw him appear from the shop of a friend and he approached Prior with his customary feline athleticism, a hand rising and then falling onto Prior's sweaty offering. He sensed the contrast in demeanour from when they parted seventeen hours earlier.

"What's wrong man?"

Prior's eyes stared directly ahead at the entrance to the café on the opposite corner of the square at the beginning of a road of houses between the town and the shore. He spoke without turning to look at him.

"Hard times. I've fallen on hard times."

The young man's face registered incomprehension but this was not due to the slightly archaic terminology. As a national of a former British colony, the mode of speech of yesteryear was still quaintly alive and kicking. It wasn't the brevity of the period of transformation in Prior's mood either. It was just that hard times were not something he had the capacity to associate with a European.

He assumed Prior was talking in relative terms. Perhaps he had incurred a bad debt or the plummeting euro was shaving a little off his profits. He offered the obligatory but unfelt condolence. Prior turned to look at him and Abdulai was unnerved by the intensity of a look that was undiluted by the tears that had welled in his eyes.

"No – really bad times. I need you to help me."

Abdulai kicked away a stone by his foot. "Why? What's happened?"

Prior sighed. An instinct told him not to go into too much detail.

"I've been ripped off very badly. I have very little money left and I can't go home. And I'm getting sick man. My jaw is broken, my leg's going septic and I think I've got an STD." He translated by use of gestures more than words and Abdulai understood.

"I can't tell you everything – it's too complicated. I just need somewhere to stay for a short time until I find somewhere cheap to rent. I also need help to get medical treatment. You are the only person I can turn to. Be sure Abdulai, that one day, when I reach calmer waters… better times… I will make it up to you." He recalled saying something similar to Caroline. Would life be long enough to repay the mounting inventory of indebtedness? Right now he hoped not.

With the shift in relative circumstances, a different man to the one Prior knew spoke after a minimum of thought.

"Of course, Jimmy. Anything. What's mine is yours." Prior put his hand on his arm and muttered his thanks, genuinely moved and flattered at finding the person behind the sales patter.

"You can stay in my house. No problem. I have bed. You can share my food. My friend works in the pharmacy – you can meet her and she will get you good medicine. Don't worry my friend, we will take good care of you. We can go now and I'll show you my compound."

"Give me half an hour. I just need to return some keys to my friend Dominique." An uneasy look crossed Abdulai's face at the mention of the name.

"Dominique who cleans for the property business?"

"Yes. Do you know her?" He surprised Prior by looking shy. His predicament was adding layers to superficial judgements.

"A little. How do you know her?" He was startled by the sharp edge of admonishment in the question and he hoped that the turnaround in the relationship had not unleashed a retributive force to exploit the vulnerability of his post traumatic condition.

"She works in the first hotel I stayed in. She's been doing my washing. Nice girl."

He changed the subject and went back to the hotel where luckily Dominique was on the terrace sweeping and mopping away the evidence of breakfast. He pressed the keys into her palm and averted his eyes from her unspoken enquiry. As he turned he said, "I'll be in touch, Dom. Look after yourself."

She called after him, "Is everything okay Jimmy?" and he swivelled to face her, raising a hand to both suppress the question and bid farewell.

***

Abdulai's share of the compound, as a West African describes his property, comprised a single room in a small complex of ramshackle buildings contained behind a concrete wall. Prior followed him as he hauled the trunk across the yard of dried earth to the meagre building. The younger man covered his embarrassment with a show of stubborn pride which seemed to dare Prior to find fault, which of course could not have been further from his mind. He in turn feigned indifference to the paucity of the dwelling and restated his gratitude. Abdulai left him to return to the shop and he took out a notebook and pen and sat down at a table with the door open to let some light into the bare, windowless room.

He sat for some time regurgitating the momentous recent events, perversely comforted by the dimness and relative cool of the room, and with some reluctance turned to the notebook and began jotting down figures in a wooden hand, unused to writing. The stark reality of his situation explained his reluctance:

Credit on arrival: €120,000

Scam: €88,000

Hush Money: €15,000

Hotels: €2,400

Sundries: €6,000

Shopping: €1,000

Total Debit: €112,400

Credit Balance: €7,600

The numbers had come slowly, prised painfully from muddled memory of days of wine and roses, and he sat motionless, staring at the final figure with a mixture of wry mirth at its puniness and mounting panic at the implications for his life ahead.

He couldn't escape a feeling that Zina must have accessed his account in some way and worked out how much she could realistically demand.

Out of his musing he eventually settled on a twelve-month survival plan and picked up his pen again and wrote:

Monthly income: €633

Zina: €200

Rent, Utilities: €300

Total: €500

Balance to live: €133

Beyond the twelve months he dared not contemplate but the way he felt at the moment, the idea of giving himself up was starting to appear relatively attractive.

The clarification of his financial situation made him feel marginally better and he augmented the fleeting upturn with a trip into town. He negotiated the tricky and embarrassing visit to the car rental firm who advised him to report the theft to the police for their insurance purposes. He made up a story about leaving the keys in the vehicle for two minutes while he nipped into a shop and finding it gone when he returned to where he had parked. He felt a creeping unease to be back in the police station again so soon, and he was aware that he had now been in the country for over a month and the nebulous visa arrangements might become an issue. The less he had to do with officialdom the better. He lost his deposit and had to pay the insurance excess which in comparison with the wider picture seemed neither here nor there. He then went to the bank and arranged the transfer of the additional blackmail money and the standing order to Zina's account and obtained a statement which confirmed his do-it-yourself accounting.

He spent the afternoon in fitful sleep on a bed close to the floor with the door ajar in an unsatisfactory compromise between the intrusive light and the lack of fresh air and woke, blinking and sweating, to see Abdulai and a skeletal black woman standing by the bed. He pulled himself up to the sitting position and swung his legs onto the floor, standing up quickly and gingerly with a sense of being caught in an act of trespass. Abdulai took his arm and eased him back onto the bed as if he was dealing with a recalcitrant invalid.

"This is Beatrice. She works in the pharmacy. You remember I told you." She held out a limp hand and smiled shyly.

"She is from my country. She is very interested in medicine."

For the next ten minutes he was her guinea pig as she examined the sites of his distress, darting questions at him in good English and talking in a mixture of pidgin and Wolof to an apparently fascinated Abdulai who punctuated his conversation with loud 'ah ha's' of enlightenment. Prior cringed with embarrassment when he had to slip his underpants down to his thighs and felt an irritation at Abdulai's continued observation of the process. He might have had the propriety to look away. He pulled up his shorts with a sense of relief and waited for the verdict.

"The jaw is broken, but I think only a minor hairline fracture and it is not dislocated. Of course you would need an x-ray to confirm but no point of that. I will bring you pain relief and you must eat a soft diet and be careful not to open the mouth wide. It will heal itself in a few weeks. The leg is infected of course. I will bring strong antibiotics and also clean and dress the wound. In answer to your question Mr. Hudson," she had deferred response to his earlier enquiries in the intensity of her concentration, "rabies is not known here thankfully and anyway, you would be getting symptoms by now.

I will also bring tetanus injection although you say you think you may be up to date. From the symptoms you describe I think you have a non-specific urethritis which we can treat with the same antibiotics you are taking for the leg.

"There are no genital sores or heavy discharge. The only worry is HIV as this is a growing problem in Cape Verde. When I come back I will take bloods and arrange for testing although I will have to send it away for this."

She had taken on an entirely different demeanour as she spoke, the words flowing effortlessly from a command of her subject, but as she said her goodbyes and edged towards the door she became again the diffident toothy girl who had entered the room. Prior again proffered the empty words of gratitude and had his enquiries as to the cost waved away as an unimportant topic for future discussion. Her obvious passion for medicine was plainly not driven by a pecuniary motive.

Over the course of the following week, Prior maintained an existence more akin to survival than living but, supported by the touchingly attentive Beatrice, his physical decline was halted and slowly reversed. He heeded her strong entreaties against mixing alcohol with the antibiotics with a Herculean display of willpower which had an associated effect on his mental health as he benefited grudgingly from a detoxification programme enhanced by a little tablet she brought him with an inordinately long generic name. She had supplied the tablet, whose proprietary name was Librium, without prior discussion and divined solely from her own observations of his condition with perhaps a little supporting corroboration from the observant Abdulai. He spent the long days walking prodigious distances around the town and along the beach, relishing the life-giving properties of the beloved ocean, removing his dressings and allowing the salt to aid the regeneration before replacing them from Beatrice's copious supplies when dry again. A mischievous urge saw him swimming ever further into the Atlantic depths in the direction of mainland Africa until the shock one day of a potent current that found him needing to muster all his strength to stay where he was, frantically kicking his legs and throwing out his arms until the onset of a barely perceptible progression towards the shore. As with another of his passions, alcohol, he had come dangerously close to exceeding his limitations and falling victim to the power of its treacherous wrath.

He scoured the many property agencies, taking viewings of apartments tantalisingly beyond the reach of his limited resources before accepting reality and weighing up the relative demerits of functional flats and studios in depressingly alien urban locations. He deliberately rose early and exhausted himself during the day as a means of being able to retire early at night and avoid the interminable, mundane, sensory-deprived evenings in the compound. Abdulai insisted he join him and his friends and plunge his hands into the large, communal bowl of rice and bony, poor quality meat or fish streaked with the dubious stain of an astringent sauce, He was at pains to enter the disagreeable ritual so as not to offend his host or draw attention to their cultural differences and as with all things he got used to it, triumph and relief on completion of the repast gradually giving gave way to a tolerance which he supposed might eventually lead to enjoyment, although he didn't stay long enough to test that theory. His daily treat was a visit to the bakery where he bought two fresh rolls which he filled with cheese or ham and washed down with a bottle of Coke at lunchtime. The caffeine and sugar rush was a poor substitute for the effects of the alcohol but it provided a little spur to his spirits when accompanied by the postprandial cigarettes which he was also cutting down on out of financial necessity.

He thought a lot about his mental health and convinced himself that he could control his moods better than any medication. He grudgingly allowed the harsh voice of Marie Connolly to invade his conscious thought with its dictums of mood diaries and prodromal signs and CBT strategies, and he began rating his mood on some revised scale she had introduced him to, an alternative to the one to ten, whereby the span stretched from minus two to plus two with nought being the equilibrium. He put himself at minus one on most days with an occasional nought which he felt was quite appropriate given his situation. The initial craving for a drink had turned to a dull pining now, ever constant but manageable. The leg and waterworks had responded well, and into his second course of antibiotics, all symptoms were nearly gone. He promised himself his next alcoholic drink when he had found his new apartment. He deliberately tried not to think about Zina but when he could not resist the engulfing emotions, anger fought with sadness and unfulfilled lust before settling on a sense of betrayal and foolishness that no amount of self-deception could shift. He caught a glimpse of her once in her usual spot on the beach. He had studiously avoided her known haunts but on this occasion he had inadvertently walked on past his normal turning point, lost in thought, before pulling up suddenly and seeing her prone figure with the knees up, the thong leaving little to the imagination. She lay with her head to one side looking in his direction but he couldn't know whether her eyes were open or closed behind the dark wrap-around glasses. He stood for too long, unable to drag himself away from the prize that had slipped so agonisingly through his fingers. He missed her so much. He also missed Dominique, and not only at the times when he rinsed the sweat and the dirt from his clothes in the tepid communal tub of the compound. He held an unbridled affection for the artless Abdulai and Beatrice and bemoaned a world which failed to provide true recompense for their talents. He admired their easy rapport with one another, unaffected by their difference in gender and religious belief. They came from a country where, at least up to now, a Sunni Muslim like Abdulai and a Christian like Beatrice could live peacefully, respecting – barely acknowledging their diversity. But his heart lay romantically with Gina and spiritually with Dominique and he yearned for them above and beyond the simple, unconditional kindness shown by his two friends and their compatriots.

The day before the completion of his course of antibiotics he took the plunge on an apartment. It was on the first floor of a three-storey block of six apartments in an area of partial development and Prior decided it was the best he had seen for his limited budget of €200 per month. It lay about two kilometres from the southern coast of the island on the back edge of the development. The scrubland and dunes between the sea and his potential new home might one day play host to further rampant building but tourist development would be deterred by the ferocious combination of rocks and waves on the corresponding shoreline. The property was owned by an Englishman who had bought impulsively whilst on holiday and was now desperate to recoup some of his loss by letting it. He had been promised rents of at least €450 by the agents but was now faced with the cold reality of a plunging market. He returned to the office with the agent and filled in the necessary forms and wrote out a cheque to the value of the deposit and one month's rent. He was given the keys and the apartment was his.

That afternoon, Abdulai helped him move in and Prior felt again the vicarious guilt as he moved from room to room making approving noises as Prior surveyed the same images with distaste and disappointment. The living room, dining area, and kitchen were open plan and led on to a single bedroom and shower room. The rooms were sparsely furnished with the basic requirements of single bed, wardrobe, dining suite, fridge and sofa bed. The curtainless French windows of the bedroom and lounge areas led on to narrow, dusty verandas with views of scaffolding fronting half-finished buildings, the distant sea, just visible on the horizon, a tormenting reminder of what he had lost.

But he didn't care. After the austerity of the previous week and the guilt of the creeping suspicion that his friend was sleeping on the stone floor of another room, the relative luxuries of his own bed, running water, and electricity at the flick of a switch were very attractive. He hugged Abdulai and promised an invitation to a flat warming party as soon as he was organised, and as the door closed and his rapid footsteps on the stairs grew fainter, he sat on the sofa bed and took stock. The sun streamed in to the room in spite of the encrusted windows, thick with the grime of salt and sand and brick dust blown by the incessant westerly wind. He surveyed the frugal room and began making a mental list of what he needed, leaping up suddenly and going to the bedroom, bringing back his notebook and a biro to transfer his thoughts to an indelible list.

He drew a firm, straight line across the page and above it began jotting down figures which told him the picture was marginally rosier than before. By getting the apartment for two hundred he was €50 per month in credit, having previously allowed €300 for rent and utilities. He had been reliably informed that water and electricity should not exceed €50 per month if he was careful. Beneath the line he listed what he needed to make the place a little more homely – bed linen, towels, curtains and rails, lamps, and pictures for the walls. He moved on to functional items – brushes, mop and bucket, cleaning chemicals, iron and ironing board, maiden, and then to disposables – food, drink and cosmetics. By the time he was finished his list covered most of the allotted space and he began jotting rough prices next to each item, arriving at an estimated total of €520. He returned to his accounting at the top of the page and drew a line through the figures and started again. The €7,600 credit balance became €7,000 and beneath that he wrote:

Monthly Income: €583

Zina: €200

Rent, Utilities: €250

Total: €450

Balance to live: €133

He felt a rush of excitement at being able to accommodate his purchases and indulge his western addiction to retail therapy without any net loss, but then remembered the €300 he had paid the car rental firm and the €200 deposit on the apartment. He crossed out the numbers again and wrote:

Credit Balance: €6,600 (he had reduced his shopping budget from 600 to 500 out of desperate necessity).

Monthly Income: €550

Zina: €200

Rent, Utilities: €250

Total: €450

Balance to live: €100

His eyes fixed on the concise bottom figure and his thoughts meandered gloomily as he cursed the €200 hush money and lamented the stupidity of his previous profligacy, cringing in recollection of some of the more spectacular examples of extravagance. He thought about yet another line through the most recent figures and a reassessment based on a ten-month period but decided against it. €100 might be quite sufficient. He just didn't know until he tried it. At least he'd proved to himself that he could control his drinking and smoking if he had to. He could always reappraise after a month or two.

His watch showed three-thirty p.m. and he got to his feet and prepared to go out. The bank and shops would be reopening and he couldn't wait to start. He drew out €500 cash and scoured the few Chinese-owned shops with their narrow aisles and shelves piled high with stock – Aladdin's Caves of variety. Exhilarated by the range of items and the lack of need for choice and decision making over individual brands, he worked quickly and energetically, tip-toeing sideways past fellow shoppers to add to his rapidly growing pile of merchandise near the till. He bought from all the shops he could find and in each one he encountered the same impersonal lack of warmth as he handed over the money and explained that he would return later to collect the goods. On this occasion he put aside his aversion to paying for taxis – he had gone a little under budget – and they went from shop to shop, piling as much as they could into the boot and back seat of the car. He sat contentedly in the front seat with the end of a broom and mop nestling against his face and the driver helped him load the goods into the hallway of the apartment block before they returned to the town to pick up the remainder. He remembered that he would need a drill to put up the curtain poles and found himself frustrated at the last. He had managed to find everything on his list but the drill proved elusive. The driver, following a display of mime and motor noises from Prior, was not optimistic, saying only "Espargos," to denote the larger town he would need to visit.

It was too late to go now and he would have to take a minibus tomorrow. As a last resort, however, he tried the first store he had been in and he shouted his delight as he found one amongst an array of small electrical items, right next to the iron he had bought earlier. It took him to the limit of his budget and he could quite conceivably have borrowed one from one of the many workmen near his flat but he didn't care. It would be useful to have anyway. With all his new belongings safely ensconced in the living room he easily resisted an urge to begin unpacking immediately. The goods were virtually all in their virgin state anyway without the proliferation of the packaging of the 'civilised' world. He made a favourable comparison with his frenetic impatience of last March and considered his mood. It would be about eight out of ten on the old scale – Charlie's scale. Well under control.

It was now early evening and the sun was setting over the horizon to the west. An intense craving for a drink hit him suddenly and an internal struggle commenced, the arguments for and against rising independently as if he had no part in the discussion.

Somehow he clung on to discretion and he made a pledge to himself to defer gratification until tomorrow evening. He still had two tablets to take – tonight and in the morning – and besides, there were still the disposables to buy. He would enjoy doing that in the morning with a clear head. He found that the best antidote to his craving was to fill his stomach with food and he went to the little corner shop on the end of his block and bought tins of sardines, tomatoes, and macaroni cheese, trying not to look at the cold beer stacked high in the fridge. He hurried back to find there was no can opener in the apartment. Crockery, cutlery, and pots and pans were provided but not it seemed the one thing he needed. He hacked at their rusting lids with a large pointed knife, plunging it in and working it round, cutting himself painfully in the process between the bottom of his thumb and forefinger. He wolfed the food down, lamenting his forgetfulness in not buying bread that morning to go with it, and then made a coffee from the jar that had been left goodness knows how long ago and went to the veranda where he sat in one of the dining chairs. He made a mental note to buy some fold-up chairs and sat there for an hour, the edge gone from his yearning for a long drink although a few Remy Martins would have gone down very nicely with the coffee.

He tested out the shower and it worked adequately. There was no hot water but that was superfluous anyway in the heat. The jet from the head was impossible to dodge so he turned it off and lathered himself all over before turning it on again, yelling in pain and surprise as he was hit by a stream of scalding hot water. He pressed himself against the wall and then felt the sudden change to ice cold water splashing against his back. It finally settled back to somewhere in between and he quickly rinsed off the soap before it changed its mind and got out and dried himself.

A satisfying tiredness crept up on him with its promise of escape and replenishment and he resisted again the urge to start unpacking the shopping, stooping only to locate the pillows and sheets which he put onto the mattress. He took the penultimate tablet and at nearly ten p.m. fell into a sleep he hoped would quickly erase the tedious hours of darkness before the dawning of a different, more providential chapter in his journey.

He woke at three a.m. to a cacophony of noise, soaked in sweat. The French windows were open to let some air in and they creaked on their rusting hinges, blown by the never abating wind, letting in the convoluted sound of barking dogs, thumping music and raised voices. The room was lit by what appeared to be a searchlight trained on his bedroom from the building opposite. He lay in perplexed discomfort for some time, closing his eyes and silently cursing the perpetrators, but eventually conceded defeat and got up and dressed quickly. He felt wide awake and curiously rested as he followed what had rapidly become the habitual lure of the veranda with cigarette and coffee in hand. All around, the houses were lit up and laughter and music seemed to emanate from every room. Prior laughed out loud and did a little jig before going back inside and rooting through yesterday's purchases, grabbing a pen and writing 'patio chairs' and 'fan' and 'occasional tables' on a newly opened running inventory before returning to the task at hand. He set up lamps, hammered in nails and put up pictures, laid down rugs, and organised his cleaning fluids and utensils into a corner of the room, leaving the biggest job 'til last. He unpacked the drill and set it up with the chuck key and 5mm drill bit, laughing as he turned it on at four-thirty a.m. to make his first hole. What would they say back home? He doubted if anyone would hear it above the rest of the noise here. The poles came complete with screws and Rawlplugs and he worked accurately and efficiently, hooking the curtains onto the rings and stepping back appreciatively to admire his excellent measurements. The poles were the right length and symmetrical to the windows with the same extension at either end and the curtains just touched the floor, billowing slightly in the warm breeze. He did the same in the bedroom and dulled the searchlight, and then he finished by putting up two small sets to cover the windows in the kitchen and behind the sofa bed.

At 8:30 a.m., having negotiated the animated, impatient hours of gathering elation, he stepped out and walked at speed towards the town, his elbows pumping as he bade a mostly unreciprocated 'good morning' to those he passed. It was the usual mix of schoolchildren in their deep blue uniforms, labourers trundling their barrows, and the incongruous office workers in their smart clothes stepping gingerly through the dust and the dirt and the dog mess. He found Abdulai sitting on his shop front stoop scraping at his teeth with a short bristled stick and invited him to the house-warming party he had decided to schedule for tonight. He asked him to pass on the invitation to Dominique, Beatrice, and anyone from the compound who wanted to come and then sought out the taxi driver from yesterday and booked his services again from midday when he expected to have completed the remaining shopping. He had €150 left and withdrew some more from the bank to cover the extra cost of the party and save him the bother of further withdrawals for some time to come. Just after twelve he was finished and he walked back to the taxi rank where his chauffeur was waiting and they drove from store to store piling crates and bags and boxes into the vehicle until the driver began to fear for the wheel bearings. There was beer, Coca-Cola, Fanta, Sprite, spirits, tonics, wines, an ocean of the local grogue, bottled water, a bin bag full of bread from the bakery – chickens, rice, beans, vegetables, fruit, salad, sauces, spices, ham, cheese, butter, milk. Nothing had been left to chance. They deposited the food and drink at his flat and returned for the tables, fold-up chairs, fans, and two massive cooking pots. As with his previous flat refurbishment, he iced the cake with a music system he found in a wholesale warehouse near his first hotel. It was nowhere near as impressive obviously but everything is relative and he sat with it on his lap as they made their way home, lovingly nursing it like a baby.

The afternoon was spent in fevered activity and mounting panic as he raced against the clock to have everything ready in time for his guests who were due at seven. With an hour to spare however, he was in the shower washing away the sweat and anxiety of his labour followed by the luxury of half an hour sitting in his best clothes surveying his work with a satisfaction enriched by the effects of the cold beer he had so commendably postponed.

On the gas stove in the corner stood one of the gargantuan pots containing five portioned chickens simmering in a juice flavoured by peppers, tomatoes, okras, aubergines, and onions, the water laced with the fiery spices he knew would appeal to his guests. The other pot was full of the rice that would be combined with the stew. On the dining table the cloth was barely visible beneath the food and plates laid on top of it. Trays of bread, ham and cheese, bowls of salad and fruit, plates of sweets and cakes and biscuits. In the other corner, opposite the kitchen area, was his new hi-fi system playing a Jimmy Cliff CD, and placed around the room on a small nest of tables were bowls of nuts and crisps and his three new lamps with their discrete fire glow bulbs lending a warm feel and illuminating the paintings of boats and sunsets and market scenes he had bought from Abdulai. The new television was still unpacked in the bedroom where a fan whirred, cooling the room for later. He drained his first bottle in two gulps and padded euphorically across the soft red and white rug towards the bulging fridge and took out another.

At just after seven, with the empty bottles steadily filling the waste bin, he leant over the parapet of the living room veranda and spotted a group of five figures in the distance moving slowly towards him. When they were close enough for recognition his eyes searched first for Dominique and he felt a rush of excitement as he made her out in a short pink dress. She walked alongside Beatrice in a green and white tie-dye dress behind Abdulai and two of his friends, who didn't appear to have deviated from their habitual apparel for the occasion. He called out to them and waved and went down to open the front door and welcome them in.

The two girls sat demurely at either end of the sofa, clutching the soft drinks they had ultimately procured from a disappointed Prior, who had tried to force an alcoholic drink on them. The men sat at three of the dining chairs around the table talking in low voices, sipping desultorily from their bottles of beer, indifferent to the effect that so fired their energised host. He mixed himself a large gin and tonic and returned to the patio chair he had positioned on an angle to the sofa and delved into a carrier bag Dominique had given him on her arrival. He pulled out a piece of cloth rolled into a bundle and held it aloft by two corners as it unfurled to reveal an African tunic shirt in kaleidoscope colours of pale blues and greens and pinks. He smiled in genuine pleasure and by way of forestalling any hint of an unfelt disappointment he pulled the shirt he was wearing over his head and put on the gift immediately. He searched the faces for a clue as to the donor and Dominique looked down and smiled. He glowed at the intimacy of a personal present and kissed her full on the lips before she had time to turn her head. Beatrice had bought him a set of tea towels and forewarned by his assault on Dominique, she managed to avert and lower her head so that his eager lips met only the hairline just above the temple. A ponderous elephant wood carving from Abdulai's antediluvian stock completed the presentation and Prior threw an arm around the neck of his seated friend and put his head close to his in a pose of masculine affection. One of his companions spoke.

"From all we three," and Prior high-fived the two men and changed the CD to one of his compilations, recharging his glass before launching into an emotional speech of welcome.

"I am honoured that you have all accepted my invitation to join me in this house-warming party and I thank you for the generosity of your gifts. Since I have been in this country you have all shown me nothing but kindness and I will always be in your debt. You have shamed my own countrymen but that is another story that I won't go into at the moment. There is much I would like to tell you my friends, but I can't. Maybe there will come a day in the future when I can. Believe me when I tell you I am a very well-known and successful man in my own country." He glanced at the females to see if they looked impressed but they retained the same slightly embarrassed expressions. Prior paused his speech and spoke directly to them, saying, "C'mon girls, lighten up. This is a party," before returning to his main text.

"And so comrades, I beseech you to see my home as your own. Not just tonight but at any time. As one of you so movingly said to me once, 'What's mine is yours.'" He paused for effect and looked round the room, looking into each of their eyes. "I mean that. I really do." He lit another cigarette and drained his drink.

"So enough of that. I can see empty glasses and empty stomachs. I will get you all another drink, we will have a toast, and then you can help yourselves to the food whenever you are ready. It is a self-service buffet comprising a collation of cold cuts," he smiled ironically at his deliberately irritating description as his arm swept away from the dining table in the direction of the stove, "and a hot ragout à la mode de Prior which would blow the heads off lesser mortals than your good selves. Please eat as much as you want." He went to a cupboard and brought out six glasses and poured large shots of the local grogue for the men and an amber-coloured ponche for the women, a grogue sweetened with honey. He handed out the drinks, accepting no rejection from the giggling, resistant Beatrice and Dominique, who reluctantly took the offering out of a wish not to offend. Prior mused on the irony of the abstemiousness of the two Christians on the sofa whilst the three Muslims at the table drank without reservation.

The toast completed, the men needed no second invitation to fall on the food, heaping mountains of rice onto their plates and topping it with the warm stew. The women were more reticent and watched the men, cradling their untouched drinks as Prior drew his chair closer and asked Beatrice, "So what brought you to Sal?" She seemed relieved by the normality of the question. Something about Prior's changed demeanour had made her uneasy.

"I come to look for opportunity. My country is very poor. Very few jobs, very few possibilities." He felt sad. This is just what he would have said about Cape Verde. As with the sound system, everything is relative.

Dominique went to help herself to food and came back with two plates, one of which she put on the table in front of Beatrice. They started to eat and Beatrice made an approving noise when her mouth was empty.

"Mm. This is very good. What is à la mode de Prior?" He looked bemused.

"À la mode de Prior?"

"Yes. You said the stew was called à la mode de Prior." His elation took a sudden dip but a quick consideration of the facts appeased his angst. Their worlds were so far apart. It was his first slip in two months and that, he told himself, was something to be proud of.

"Oh… À la mode de Creole, I said. You misheard me. Creole." He laughed and returned to the conversation. "So you just came alone, not knowing anyone?" She was happy to be talking to him of something other than his own health.

"No. Abdulai was here. He is my brother's best friend. He write me to say he has found a job for me at the pharmacy. He knows I am very interested in medicine." He noticed the men's plates were empty and called over to tell them to help themselves to more and replenish their drinks from the fridge.

"So where did you learn about it?"

"Medicine?" Prior nodded. "Well in sixth form I achieve grade A's in Biology and Chemistry advanced level and grade B in Mathematics. I also do much reading. My dream is to go to medical school to train to become a doctor but it will never be possible. My parents are very poor. I am just lucky to have the job I have. The pay is five times greater than back home and I can support myself and send money home to my family." Prior leant over and squeezed her ebony thigh just below the hem of her dress.

"The world is not fair, my love. If I could help you I would. One day I will." He took her glass and refilled it. Dominique's drink was virtually untouched and she was standing at the table, spooning her food and talking to Abdulai in the pose that so enchanted Prior with one foot behind the other, the back leg bent at the knee. He shouted over, his voice loud and raucous, "Oi, N'Jie. Too much talking and not enough action. This is supposed to be a party. Take Dom for a dance please." Abdulai turned round.

"I can't dance to this. Let me choose something."

"Be my guest."

Abdulai rummaged through Prior's CDs and turned off a slow Tracy Chapman record and found something faster. They found a space in the cramped room and began gyrating and Prior took Beatrice's hand and pulled her roughly to her feet. He launched into a frenzied rock and roll routine and lost his balance, falling into the music system and knocking the contents of the drink Abdulai had placed on the top over his shirt. Barely without a pause he pulled it off and continued dancing bare-chested, kicking the empty glass into the corner of the room, his hands all over her. As the song finished she prised herself from his grip and sat down quickly before he could inveigle her into another dance. The other two were now dancing close together, their hips bouncing lightly off each other in time to the music as they spoke softly, their faces close. Abdulai's friends were leaning over the veranda having a shouted conversation with people on the street below interlaced with much mirth as they spun round, bent at the waist in laughter.

Prior called to them, "Invite them up for goodness' sake. Let's get this joint jumping." He turned up the volume and sat down heavily next to Beatrice so their thighs were touching and took her glass from the table and put it in her hand.

"Drink up Bea. The night is yet young." She shrank from him and tried to shift her position but she had nowhere to go.

"No more for me, Jimmy. I have work in the morning. I must go soon." She looked anxiously towards Dominique who had her back to her. He put his hand on her thigh and his face close to hers.

"You know Beatrice; really, I can't thank you enough for how you have helped me." He moved his lips towards hers and this time followed them as she turned her head, enabling a momentary conjunction. She stood up and looked down at him, incensed.

"Please you stop now. You think all African girls are like the one who give you disease? I am not that kind of girl. I want to go home now." Her companions were aware of a vague commotion and after a brief exchange out of Prior's earshot, Beatrice moved to the door and waited while Abdulai spoke.

"We must go now, Jimmy. The girls have work in the morning and I will walk them home. Thank you for the party." Two men and four women suddenly appeared at the door and looked enquiringly at Prior who waved them in and told them to help themselves to food and drink. He looked at Beatrice and then at the other two, holding out his arms in a gesture more of appeasement than contrition.

"Oh come on. I just wanted to show my gratitude. That's all." He said to Beatrice, "I don't even fancy you, honestly. Now please stay and let's forget it. I won't touch you if you don't like it. I'm just an affectionate guy and I've been through a lot. With the drink and everything…" The words tailed away and his smile was lopsided from the still recovering jaw. "Now like I said, the night is still young." He shouted, "Let's party!" and went to fill his glass with more grogue. When he turned round again they were gone.

For the rest of the evening he felt like a stranger in his own house. The four couples spoke in their own languages and answered his attempts at English conversation perfunctorily and with an air of impatience. They danced with each other intermittently and Prior danced on his own – ever more outlandishly in an attempt to gain some attention but he was largely ignored. He gave up eventually and sat brooding on the sofa drinking grogue from the bottle and chain smoking. The only satisfaction he gleaned was from watching the food and drink steadily disappear until there was hardly anything left

– the traditional sign to the host that at least the guests had enjoyed themselves on one level. Aside from this meagre consolation however, his rancour grew steadily in direct proportion to his blood alcohol level and he finally exploded, standing up and shouting, "Right! Enough. Get out. The lot of you. Out. Now." He lost balance with the force of his vitriol and swayed, grabbing onto the corner of the kitchen unit to prevent his falling, his half-closed eyes trained malevolently on his unwanted guests. There was a moment of surprised silence followed by isolated pockets of incredulous laughter which grew to a unison of unrestrained hilarity.

Prior walked to the door and opened it, standing there as they filed out – the men all well over six feet, dwarfing the indignant, dishevelled, bare-chested man who could still manage a lecherous glance at the retreating posteriors of the departing women. He slammed the door behind the last of them and went straight to the pile of CDs, searching for the succour of his favourite compilation, before returning to the couch and sitting in bemused contemplation of the vagaries of fate before the blanket of oblivion arrived to cover the wretchedness of his self-destruction.

CHAPTER 21

At a collection point at an arrivals terminal at Heathrow airport, a large man in a green anorak left his minibus with its engine running and paced up and down in front of its glass façade. He peered anxiously in all directions, the mobile enveloped in his large hand clamped to his ear. His normally deep voice was strangulated by the mild tension he felt.

"Mr. Wainwright, it's Charlie. Where are you? I'm outside the terminal waiting." He stopped and listened, his apprehension mollified slightly by the connection. "Okay. Five minutes then – I'll be alright to wait that long."

A few minutes later, with Mr. Wainwright and his family and luggage ensconced in the vehicle, Charlie drove quickly away through the maze he had come to know so well and out onto the roads taking them south. He absently considered the familiar change in atmosphere from two weeks ago – the animation and anticipation replaced by a reserved reflection as they gazed out of the windows in melancholy contemplation, the relentless teeming traffic under dark March skies providing an apt backdrop to their thoughts of the return to the daily grind. He had been up all night and longed for the large breakfast and comfortable bed that awaited him on completion of this job as he negotiated the tail end of the morning rush hour.

He had been doing his new job for nearly five months now and he was exhausted. The initial relief at escaping the hold of his NHS paymasters and the novelty of an uncommonly large sum of money at his disposal had now worn off. Most of the lump sum had gone in handouts to his children, the minibus, a holiday, and the clearing of his accrued debts. In his work he had replaced one kind of stress with another but on balance he was happier now. The hours were long and the driving arduous and repetitive but at least he was his own man, unbeholden to managers, colleagues or patients and it had done wonders for his self-respect. He forced himself to work long hours for less money than his NHS salary but the pension took him above his previous income. His marriage was over in all but name with both of them bound together only by a cloying bond of habit and trepidation at a leap back to a forgotten world of independence and solitude.

The mutual promises he and Robert Prior had made to stay in touch had not materialised and it was with genuine upset and apprehension that he read the stories of the rape in the press just before last Christmas. The apprehension stemmed from a customary unease following an incident relating to a patient he was, or had been, involved with, and many of his thoughts around the time were along the lines of whether he should have foreseen the event. He was asked to contribute to an internal enquiry ordered by the Trust – a knee-jerk response to deflect any possible criticism which achieved little in terms of constructive outcomes. Any external enquiry would be contingent on Prior being found guilty. When reading Prior's case notes to refresh his memory before his appearance at the enquiry he took the opportunity to jot down Caroline's phone number, and that evening before going back to work he called her. A man answered and went to get her.

"Forgive me for phoning out of the blue, Mrs. Ross. My name is Charlie Vaughan. I was Robert's community psychiatric nurse for a short time after he was discharged from hospital." She remembered Robert talking about him and how he had preferred him to his replacement but she was instinctively guarded.

"Yes?"

Charlie felt rather nervous, being thankfully out of practice at phone calls to patient's relatives. They were rarely the easiest of exchanges.

"I'll get to the point. I'm calling in relation to the alleged rape. I've got to be honest, I've been rather troubled by it, can't stop thinking about it. I've left the NHS now and I'm working for myself so I'm out of the loop. Tell me to get lost by all means if you think this is a bit irregular but I just wondered if you had a view." There was a pause on the other end of the line.

"A view on what exactly?" He began regretting his decision and his voice became halting, uncertain.

"Well… listen, I'm sorry to resurrect this – I'm sure it's been very upsetting for you and your family. Basically, well… do you think he would be capable of this?" There was another long silence. Vaughan held his breath.

"Capable? Yes. I suppose all men would be capable. Do I think he did it? No." Charlie sighed with relief.

"Well it's reassuring to hear you say that. I suppose that was why I phoned. I liked Robert and we got on well. He would have had to have acted very out of character to the man I knew. I've got to be honest." This phrase, delivered in a slight Welsh lilt, seemed to be a regular part of his speech, thought Caroline.

"He used to have a moan about women and I suppose I joined in a bit. Two grumpy old men together."

Caroline interrupted. "Ah – so you're phoning to try to assuage your guilt – I see."

"No, not at all. I…"

"That was a joke, Charlie. Can I call you Charlie?"

"Of course."

"Look. I really don't know for sure. I hadn't seen him for years until the hospital. And he didn't have a diagnosed mental illness when we were married. I stress 'diagnosed'. He could have changed. I know nothing of his present life. I'm just saying that based on the man I know, the father of my children; my gut feeling is that this wasn't him."

"Right. Thanks. Terrible business anyway. I just hope they catch whoever did it – Robert or not."

"Umm. If they do find him and he goes to court, what would you expect to happen? If he was found guilty, I mean."

"Almost certainly a transfer to a secure hospital where he'd stay until a Mental Health Tribunal deemed him ready to come off the section. Then he'd either be discharged or transferred to a prison to complete his sentence. If it *was* him I'm sure his defence would be able to show he was mentally ill at the time."

"But what if he pleaded not guilty and they convicted him?"

"You mean if they hadn't used the mental health card prior to the verdict?"

"Er… yes. I suppose that's what I meant. I mean they wouldn't would they unless they were using it in mitigation. And if they're pleading not guilty there's nothing to mitigate."

Charlie combed the depths of a knowledge that was rapidly becoming hazy with the heartening distance he was placing between his past and present lives. "I think the defence would then ask the judge to adjourn for pre-sentencing psychiatric reports. His mental state at time of sentencing would have relevance as to an appropriate custodial placement. The outcome would probably be the same as I have just outlined."

"But by belatedly acknowledging his illness, wouldn't that be suggestive of an admission of guilt which might prejudice any appeal?" Charlie sighed. He was beginning to yearn for the comparative simplicity of the M25.

"Well not necessarily. The prosecution would have honed in on his mental health. His defence team would say it had no bearing on his alleged involvement in the incident but that his current mental state has relevance in terms of where the judge sends him."

There was a pause while Caroline thought. Eventually she said, "I suppose so. As you say it's not as if his illness has come as a surprise to the jury. I was mistakenly thinking confidentiality would apply."

"No. Not in a court of law." He was relieved that she either sensed or shared his fatigue with the topic as she changed the subject.

"Right. Goodness knows where he is. How do you think he'd stand up to not taking medication? I'd imagine that as a fugitive he wouldn't want to draw attention by registering with a GP." He glanced at the antique clock on the wall of the entrance hall to his Victorian house, noticing again the dinginess of the olive green wallpaper and threadbare orange-patterned carpet. He longed for a domestic renewal to augment the one in his professional life.

"Er. How can I explain this? Let's say that a hundred – a thousand people suffering with bipolar disorder would present with a thousand different combinations of symptoms, behaviours, levels of severity.

It's hard therefore to predict how it would affect one individual. I would say though that almost certainly he will experience extremes of mood that are likely to be at least as severe as his first episode in hospital last year, especially given his rather desperate circumstances. He obviously won't have the balancing effect of the lithium or the cosh of the anti-psychotic. In a way it's perhaps relatively preferable to have bipolar rather than another psychosis such as schizophrenia in that what goes up must come down. I obviously wouldn't want to worry you but you probably expect me to be honest. He could get into some quite serious scrapes when he's high and the lows would be pretty horrendous given that he's probably quite isolated, skint and being hunted. I mean you don't need me to tell you that – it's common sense. Also, during the manic phase, he'll find it hard to keep his identity secret I would imagine, with the chaotic, disinhibited behaviour. He obviously has up to now though."

"Right. Thanks. You said he used to moan about women. Was that me mostly?"

"Oh no. He never mentioned you. Just in general terms. He always stressed how much he liked women. I think it was the more strident breed of feminist he had a bee in his bonnet about. There were a lot on his paper obviously. He used to say they turned everything into a gender issue. That's why he liked sport, with its rules and measures of performance. I think he was trying to say he liked the unambiguous nature of a sporting result, a measurable outcome as opposed to the rather vague, nit-picking criticism of men by the feminists. He said they were the new sexists – the equivalent of the male chauvinist pig. He hated racism as well – the way it's now cloaked in negative assessments of black players in team sports where there's no real measurable statistics like there are in cricket or golf or athletics, say."

"Robert was rather old-school male. His mother used to do everything for him and his brother and their father. He grew up in a time when the gender balance was unfairly tilted and it was a bit of a shock when we said enough is enough. He fell out with his mother soon after he went to London and they haven't spoken since. All very sad really."

"Do you mind my asking what they fell out over?"

It was Caroline's turn to sound hesitant. "I think you'd better ask him that if you ever see him again. He'd say we'd been gossiping and be warned – he's very touchy on the subject of his mother."

"Of course. No. Sorry I asked. Well listen, Caroline; I've got to get back to work. It's been great talking to you and let's just hope our gut feelings are accurate and they can catch the man who's done this."

"Yes. I'm glad you phoned, Charlie. I obviously think about it a lot too. The papers have all gone very quiet on it. I presume the police are still looking for him."

"Well not actively now I don't suppose. Just keeping an eye open and hoping he'll make a mistake or that someone will recognise him. The problem is I don't suppose they're looking for anyone else as their minds are made up. Oh, one thing I forgot to mention; apparently they could go ahead with a trial in his absence if he's not caught after a certain length of time." Caroline stretched and blinked at the late afternoon sun coming through the conservatory window. Spring had truly arrived.

"I hadn't thought of that. Let's hope not. Anyway, let me have your number and I'll call you if I hear anything and vice versa. But call me anytime, even if you just want another chat." They said their goodbyes and both felt a little cheered by the exchange; the small comfort of a shared perception to allay respective guilt and create an illusion of action where in reality there was only impotence and riddle.

CHAPTER 22

Prior regained a form of consciousness at an hour only vaguely defined by the sun that penetrated the new curtains and illuminated and emphasised the carnage of the previous night. He lay in a semi-stupor of disgust and despair with obsessive thoughts of leaden, unclimactic sex overlaying a deep portent of gloom, unable even to answer a pressing call of nature, and he felt the warm liquid envelop his crotch and thighs with a detached indifference. He spat the phlegm produced by his aching chest onto the floor beside the couch and it was only when the faint sensations of nausea grew to something more imminent that he staggered to the lavatory and retched up the acid and bile from an empty ulcerous stomach, the blood vessels turning his face a venomous crimson, the bloodshot eyes awash with the autonomic tears that floated the darting flecks. He undid his sodden trousers and dropped them to the floor with the stained underpants, stepping out of them and wrapping a towel round his waist before going to the bedroom. He flopped heavily onto the bed and spent the remainder of the daylight hours, however many were left, in and out of something akin to sleep.

It was dark when he woke again from what felt like a relatively long spell of unconsciousness and he fumbled for the bedside lamp and looked at the clock which told him that it was nine p.m. He got up and stood at the door to the living room, barely able to look at the shambles discernible in the light cast from the bedroom. He turned on the overhead light and sat on one of the dining chairs, remembering the state of the settee. At his feet lay the shirt Dominique had given him, crumpled and dirty, ingrained with a grogue-stained shoeprint. He picked it up and buried his face in its cleaner side seeking a vicarious refuge in its tenuous association with her simple goodness. He experienced the uncomfortable feeling of knowing what he needed but not what he wanted and of not possessing the motivation to satisfy either anyway.

Eventually the habits of his adult lifetime infiltrated the grey thoughts and he turned to the crutch of the pack of cigarettes on the table, finding it empty. Cursing softly, he dressed in the first clothes that came to hand and rummaged for some money before going out. His head throbbed and his heart pounded as he stepped over one of the infernal dogs lying across his doorstep. He was not a dog lover but he could feel no affection for these ones in the way he might grudgingly have done for the family pet of an acquaintance back home. These filled him only with unease as he ran the gauntlet of a landscape framed and littered with their seemingly uncontrolled, autonomous presence. It was only a matter of time before their suspicion and soft growls would turn to the outright savagery of the pack as they smelt his apprehension turning to fear.

To his chagrin the shop a few yards from his apartment was inexplicably closed and he had a half-mile walk to the nearest alternative. With each step he took away from the comparative safety of home he felt an increasing anxiety. His heart palpitated alarmingly and his neck jerked involuntarily at each bark of a dog or shout of a human and as he left the residential area to cross the vast plain of scrub and rubble and litter to the shop on the edge of the next conurbation, he felt exposed and vulnerable and took to running and ducking down by rusting oil drums and piles of rocks at periodic intervals to make himself less of a target. With an incommensurate sense of relief he could see the shop was open and he presented the money with a shaking hand and took the cigarettes from the shopkeeper in a depressingly cold and impersonal exchange. He circuited the patch of waste ground on his return, staying closer to the large houses on its perimeter with their façades in garish yellows, deep pinks and blues. They appeared massive to his frightened eyes, reaching with their sequestered secrets to touch the blue slate skies elucidated by a nearly full moon. A woman in African costume called out to him from a stoop, sitting beneath a dim uncovered light bulb, “My friend – you like short time?” and he hurried on from the invitation of her gold-toothed smile without reply.

A cat lay dead at the side of the road, killed no doubt by one of the dogs, the flies buzzing around the carcase, no-one in this godforsaken place having taken the trouble to move it to some pointless but symbolic resting place. The relief on closing his front door against the tangibility of his alienation was immense and his pulse began slowing immediately as he hungrily opened the pack of cigarettes and drew deeply, inducing the inevitable cough which was severe enough to bend him double and produce another bout of retching. He tried another puff with the same result and reluctantly stubbed it out and began a desultory search for something edible. He found a tomato in the barren wastes of the fridge and pressed it onto a piece of stale bread left on one of the plates, crushing it onto the bread with his thumb so pips and juice squirted onto the floor. He forced it down with no pleasure whatsoever, an automatic sop to a tenuous instinct for survival. From amongst a sea of empty bottles he found one that was half filled with honey-sweetened grogue and he swigged from it painfully, his gullet inflamed with the caustic acid, his stomach sparsely protected by the pitiful meal. His brain drew little comfort from the alcohol; if anything it heightened his discomfort. It was satisfying a purely physical need and he drained the bottle and found another containing gin. He mixed a large slug with the last of a bottle of warm, flat tonic water, threw back his neck and laid down his head in continuation of the search for that elusive place where there is no pain.

***

Even in his eventual return to an unearned sleep he couldn't find anything resembling this place. In his dream he walked hand in hand with Zina through an enchanting, verdant forest of dense vegetation eclipsed by vast oaks and chestnuts lining the leafy path. They were young – children of indeterminate age – and he felt a warm sense of mutual love and togetherness. They seemingly walked without purpose alongside a running stream dappled by the sunlight that infiltrated the branches above and there was an unspoken promise of an imminent consummation beyond the innocent holding of hands. It was with a creeping sense of disquiet and disappointment that they arrived at the edge of the forest and looked ahead at fields of wheat and barley, exposed to the glare of an undiluted sun. Instead of turning back to the sanctuary of the wood, Zina led him on towards a lone combine harvester in a field beyond, her step quickening.

Something made him look back over his shoulder and he was aware of malign, shadowy figures fringing the forest, dissuading a return. They were of indeterminate species, their eyes luminous and staring. Zina turned to him and laughed, her discrepant gaiety emphasising his increasing discomfort. She released their hand-hold and mounted a fence separating the fields and ran on ahead towards the vehicle. By the time he caught up with her she sat on the knee of its driver, a smirking adult Ramon, looking down on his forlorn, pre-pubescent confusion. Behind him, the figures had encroached from the woods and their heads were visible above the fence, their translucent eyes staring in bovine menace. Some foreboding caused him to turn and begin running and just before the pursuing harvester shredded him along with the ears of wheat he awoke with a cry of terror and lay motionless as dream was gradually replaced by a reality no less horrifying – only different.

***

For the next week he didn't leave the flat. He spoke to no-one apart from the boy in the house opposite who he hissed at from the veranda to gain his attention before going down the stairs to meet him at the front door, staying close to the wall with his heart pumping at the risk he was taking. He cursed his forgetfulness and told the bemused lad to wait while he returned to the apartment for some money. The boy came back half an hour later with the 200 cigarettes, bottles of grogue and tinned food Prior had requisitioned, excited by his financial reward and the anticipation of future remuneration which materialised twice subsequently with instructions to buy more grogue. He needed it to stop shaking and sweating and chose the cheap option because of the almost fatal damage to his budget incurred by his pre-party spending spree. For twelve months now read nine months.

He kept his door locked and curtains drawn, opening them at the bottom corner occasionally to scrutinise potential sources of danger or look out for the boy when his stocks were running low. The endless cigarettes took the edge from an already almost non-existent appetite which he only appeased with a tin of cold beans or rice pudding when the cramps became too oppressive, and he drank the insanitary water from the tap which further damaged his creaking digestive system. The time passed without a diurnal or nocturnal pattern of sleep or activity. He kept the lights off and whether it was dim or dark – it made no difference – he slept if and when he could, usually awakening in panic with fevered eyes, his brain unable to differentiate between dream and delusion. The dreams were vivid, laced with fear and dread, a recurrent one being the ascent up the sinister labyrinth of stairs and rooms of a tower that led to the chambers of the ogre Ramon. When awake he lay for hours staring vacantly at the ceiling, compulsively compiling his obsessive lists with the panic spreading from head to groin at his diminishing powers of recall, the threshing of his neck on the pillow providing scant solace. When his unconscious mind disagreeably encroached, he grimaced with guilt at the previously unacknowledged mindless cruelty and thoughtlessness of so many of his past actions and behaviours. The flaccidity of his self-determination was matched by that of his manhood and if he had possessed the energy, or was it courage, to match his motivation he would have ended his sordid existence without a second thought. He saw no hope; no meaningful future. He watched the flies on the wall taking a break from their gorge in the adjoining room and asked himself why his life was, or ever had been, any less pointless than theirs.

They were out to get him, that was for sure. So if his life was so worthless, if he had no fear of dying – then what was he frightened of? Perplexity over the uncertainty of what lay beyond was a common concern shared by most of mankind and its postponement was only prolonging the agony; and no conception of hell could be worse than his current situation. No. It must be simple physical cowardice in anticipation of the pain they would inflict – they would not be beyond torture. The same cowardice that prevented his taking matters into his own hands he supposed.

Incapable of rational thought or decision, he lay wrestling with the issues until the clue to the answer was presented by the very impotence that handicapped him. Inaction was also a form of action and would lead him eventually to where he knew he wanted to be.

He stopped eating altogether and when the last of his cigarettes were smoked and grogue drunk he fell back on the grey corrugated sheet without further will to search out his runner and then closed his eyes in silent entreaty to the higher being he so wished existed.

He half woke – he couldn't guess how many hours, days, weeks, later – to the sound of voices in the street and then a vague rustling sound from close by. Too close. With a massive effort he rolled to the edge of the bed away from the French window and dropped onto the floor and rolled back in the other direction so he was wedged under the bed. The noise was getting louder and he located it about three metres away from where he lay. Someone was on the veranda trying to pick the lock.

His eyes searched frantically for something he could use as a weapon and to his relief he saw the empty grogue bottle which he could just reach by shunting his skin and bone across the dusty floor. He got back out of view just before the doors thrust forward, ballooning the drapes upwards, and Prior saw the shadow of one person thrown onto the floor by the sunlight behind him. He could tell from the frayed cuffs of the jeans and the heavy training shoes that his unwelcome visitor was male. The man stood still, obviously surveying the room, and then his ankles moved out of Prior's eyeshot. He stopped at the doorway to the living room and he heard him say, "Hot damn!" to himself. In his enfeebled and disorientated state he couldn't place the voice, although he knew it sounded familiar. If he was going to use the bottle he realised it was now or never. It wouldn't be of much use if he was discovered under the bed, trapped and unable to swing. But he possessed neither the strength nor the volition to move and he just lay in wait for the vagary of fate. He heard the steps getting closer and then saw again the shoes, this time on his side of the bed. He held his breath, his eyes fixed on them, and suddenly one shoe jerked forward and a knee dropped behind it followed by the inclined face of Abdulai. They looked at each other, one in surprise, the other distrust.

"Who sent you?"

Abdulai looked baffled.

"Nobody sent me, man. We were worried about you. Anyway, aren't you coming out? I'll just go and let Dom in – she's waiting outside." Prior heard the latch click open and he moved as rapidly as he could to get to the front door to lock them out. He wasn't quick enough though, and Abdulai returned with Dominique just as he reached the door. He eyed them suspiciously, still holding the empty bottle as Dominique put her hands to her face and let out a cry as she looked first at him and then the room.

"Oh Jimmy. You are so sick. You need the hospital. And the room!" She put her hand to her mouth and could only say, "Ooh la la!"

Prior's legs ached even under the puny weight they were sustaining and he almost fell into the seat of one of the dining chairs and rested his head on his left bicep, staring hollowly into space. His right arm dangled at his side and Abdulai gently removed the bottle from his limp grasp. When he spoke it was to the wall opposite, the effort of eye contact too great.

"What do you mean by breaking into my house? I thought you were my friends." His voice was hoarse and barely audible and he looked smaller, older.

The other two looked at each other and Abdulai answered, "Of course we are your friends. That is why we come. No-one has seen you for more than one week. Someone let me in to the outside door and I was knocking your door for ten minutes. No answer."

Dominique carried on, "We were greatly feared for you. Now I am happy we do this. Now we can help you."

Prior's face remained expressionless. He was not the person they remembered; physically or cerebrally.

"How do I know I can trust you? How do I know they haven't sent you?"

"Who?"

"Zina and Ramon." Happily they lacked the experience or capacity to understand the convoluted, deranged thinking of a mind unbalanced by the poison of 'civilisation'. As Prior had predicted to Caroline, they were too concerned with survival to allow themselves that dubious luxury. Abdulai's confusion was total as he knew neither.

Dominique said, "Why would Zina send me? I never speak to her of you. Never." He said nothing and Dominique got up to open the door onto the patio to allow in some fresh air to attenuate the putrid smell of the room. When she sat down again he lifted his head and looked them both in the eye for the first time.

"Whether you were sent or not, I don't know. All I know is I don't want you here. I don't want your help. I don't want your concern. I just want to die." He saw the alarm in their faces and once again they appeared unable to relate to his state of mind. Dominique stood up and led Abdulai by the hand into the bedroom. Prior heard them speaking in low voices as they busied themselves with something and then they came back and lifted him with an arm under each of his armpits and walked him through to the bedroom which had miraculously been transformed into a place of some tranquillity and order, the sheets and pillow cases changed, the floor swept and mopped, the surfaces wiped and the bottles and ash trays removed. He lay in blessed nullity after his relative exertion, the thumps and scrapes and soft laughter from the next room a comforting backdrop to the suspension of his thought and emotion.

It was dark outside when he woke and his bedside lamp was on. Beatrice sat on the bed with her fingers on his wrist, glancing at her watch before taking the thermometer from under his armpit. The other two stood on the other side of the bed watching like anxious relatives as she wrapped a pad around his bicep and began inflating it with an oval rubber ball, staring at the numbers on the attached gauge. A sob from who knew where convulsed his chest as he looked at the stethoscope in her small ears and the tight ebony curls on her graceful head. Her concentration was total, her dedication to her thwarted vocation complete. He accepted the manipulations without opposition, all resistance spent, all fight dissolved. He meekly opened his mouth and she popped the small tablet on his tongue with one hand and he gulped from the glass of water she offered with the other. Her tone was brusque but without the harshness that he knew would be justified under the circumstances.

"This is the same tablet you took before. For withdrawal symptoms. It is another week's course starting with a high dose and reducing day by day. I have written down what you must take." She pointed to a piece of paper on the bedside table. "As I told you before, you absolutely must not drink alcohol when taking them – it could be dangerous. I have checked you over and you will be okay. Just dehydrated and malnourished. Your liver is damaged but you are still young enough for it to repair. You have to stop drinking though, Jimmy – really you must. You know that."

He looked at her sweet, concerned face and nodded, restraining his real thoughts.

"I won't be back now but Dom and Abu are going to look after you. I've told them what to give you to eat and drink and you must do what they tell you. Abdulai is going to stay here tonight – you will be safe. Please believe me." She stood up and offered him her hand, into which he placed his own before enclosing it with the other. His weak smile carried the acknowledgement that it is better to have tried and lost than not to have tried at all.

***

The following morning he sat up and scratched his week's beard growth and looked at the scrambled eggs Abdulai had brought him with distaste. He pulled himself up, however, onto the pillows behind his head and ate the insipid offering without pleasure in deference to the efforts of the chef who leant against the wall opposite with his hands joined behind his back. He felt weak and defenceless, his brain raw and vulnerable as if it had no skull for protection and it throbbed with a dull ache from excessive sleep and the unresolved conflicts that fought somewhere deep below the conscious mind. Abdulai's caged vitality and impatience to be gone in search of his precarious living emphasised the chasm between their positions and he forced down the last of the eggs and threw his head back on the pillow in relief as the young man took the plate and fork from his hand.

"Very good, Jimmy. Is nice yes?"

Prior made an attempt to move his head in his direction but his neck was stiff and unbiddable and his eyes remained focussed on the curtained French window alongside the bed.

"Very good. Thank you."

"You are welcome. I am going now. Dominique has prepared some food for you in the fridge for your lunch and she said for you not to forget your tablets. She will be coming tonight after she finishes her work."

He lay for long after he heard the door close and Abdulai's raucous shout to an acquaintance and his quick step in response to the freeing of the chains. He felt again the detachment of the invalid from the noises that indicated a world going on outside, the conflicting relief to be away from it and uneasiness at what it may be plotting to visit upon him in his defenceless state. The soft ringing in his ears provided a monotonous, relentless score to accentuate the knowledge that there is no escape from what is without or within. That can only be found in the oblivion he craved, but even then, who could be certain that it would be the end? His anxiety rose as he contemplated the hell of eternity. He then tried to imagine what oblivion would be like and reached that dead end common to million upon million before him.

It was only the swelling need to empty his bladder that finally dragged him from his bed. He felt dizzy and had to stand for a few moments before gaining the equilibrium to move unsteadily to the bathroom. He moved onto the living room and the vertiginous sensation returned, causing him to sit down heavily on the bed which Abdulai had restored to its usual sofa status. His friend's body odour clung to the fabric – a strong but not unpleasant smell of honest sweat and endeavour and he felt strangely comforted by its company as he sat and admired the cleaning and tidying they must have done yesterday. He had a sudden urge for a smoke that he knew he wouldn't have been able to resist if he had any and instead took a tablet from the small box on top of the fridge, washing it down with a glass of water dispensed from a quivering hand. He was reminded of a story his seafaring uncle told him of pathetic pink-faced men with their improvised pulley systems involving a necktie fastened to a wrist so they could use the other hand to haul their first drink of the day towards their clamouring mouths. He returned to his seat and waited for the chemicals to work their calming magic, and when the brain was sedated and the body compliant he opened the refrigerator door and took out a plate containing two rolls filled with cheese adorned with a small garnish of lettuce and tomatoes. He felt the constriction in his throat as he thought of Dominique remembering him when she went to the bakery that morning and then seeking out the cheese he knew was alien to her palate and going out of her way to come to his apartment, letting herself in with the spare key he had given them to prepare the meal. He wondered how she was fitting his latest aberrations into her unrelenting schedule.

Again he had no enthusiasm for the food but he forced it down, chewing methodically as he stared blankly ahead until the plate was empty. With the full stomach came a return of fatigue and he took another tablet and returned to his bed where he spent the rest of the day in various shades of unconsciousness.

He came out of a vivid dream to an insistent knocking. As he slowly translated fiction to fact he stumbled towards the door, wishing he was still in his reverie. Caroline had sat alone in the second open carriage of a train in the amusement park of a seaside resort in England. The birdsong seemed to celebrate the perfection of the balmy day and the vividness of the colours of the trees and grass and flowers. As he began to climb into the foremost carriage, just behind the engine, she beckoned him to take one further back and he meekly complied and got into another behind a girl who knelt up on the seat and looked back at him, his eyes fixed on the fleshy thighs beneath a skirt that barely covered her underwear. She made it plain that she was available to him and his initial incredulity had turned to an aching longing before being cut agonisingly short by his rude awakening. He stubbed his bare toe on the metal leg of one of the dining chairs and winced, waiting for the pain to subside, before saying suspiciously, "Who is it?"

"It's me, Dominique. I have more food for you, Jimmy." He thought he had heard another voice – a male one.

"Who is with you?"

"I have brought a friend to meet you. He can help you, I promise. Please to let us in." He felt confused. He thought he could trust her but he didn't like the 'us'. It made him feel excluded and he remained wary. He bought some more time.

"Who is he?"

"Just a friend from my village – he wants to speak with you. You know you can trust me."

Prior said, "Wait one minute," and went over to the kitchen area before returning to the door, his hand clutching a bottle. He opened the door and moved back quickly so he was facing the intruders from a few metres away. Dominique entered first and behind her was a short swarthy man in a black cassock that reached to his ankles, the austerity of his garment broken only by a semicircle of white at the collar. Prior recoiled in shock and edged backwards past the dining table towards the bathroom. He began to shake his head in slow, emphatic movements.

"Oh no. No. No." He moved to the wall so the table was between them and increased the pressure on the neck of the bottle.

"You've tricked me, Dominique. I don't do religion." He saw the embarrassment and disappointment on her face and tried to curb his rising anger.

"You sir, are not welcome. Please just leave." The man said nothing and stood at the open door looking at Prior with an expression that he found oppressive in its inscrutability and he looked away to the floor. Dominique put the carrier bag she was holding on a chair and spoke in a voice that was barely audible. She was struggling to fight back tears.

"This is some food I bring for your dinner. Father de Freitas and I will go now." Prior reached out and grabbed her wrist, speaking with an urgency he had not experienced in days.

"No, not you. Please stay." His eyes were watery and his jaw slack and there was a whining supplication in his voice. A look of mild disdain and exasperation crossed the priest's face to finally betray a hint of emotion and Prior released her wrist.

There was an awkward silence before she said, "I have to go home to my sister and brothers and prepare for the next day."

Prior looked down at the table.

"I know how busy you are, Dom. Anyway, why did you bring him?"

"Because I know you are troubled in your mind." Prior glanced at the priest and then looked at her again.

"So what could he do even if I was? Is he a psychiatrist, a counsellor?"

He could see her trying to translate the unfamiliar words before she replied, "We have little necessary for those people here." She searched for the means of conveying her message in a language he noticed she was mastering very quickly. He would love to iron out the increasingly few mistakes and bring her to fluency. The girl in the dream would not leave his thoughts and he felt an agreeable stirring of the repressed libido as he looked at her.

"We look after each other. When it becomes difficult we have our church and our faith. 'Come to me and you will never go hungry or thirsty.'"

The priest's silence was starting to intimidate him and Prior gave him a furtive look before discourteously returning his gaze to Dominique and saying, "Doesn't he ever say anything?"

Her face was clouded in bewilderment and she suddenly felt out of her depth. Prior's rudeness was betraying a loyalty that was now appearing misguided and her tears turned to anger.

"Please you speak to the Father." The curtness of her tone deflated him and he sunk into a chair and covered his face with his hands. He slowly raised his head and addressed the priest, putting aside the irritation he felt.

"Thank you for coming but you are wasting your time. I have no belief. You can do nothing for me."

The man stood in the open doorway and he remained there, behind the threshold, as he said, "It is true; I can do nothing for you." He spoke with the suggestion of a wry smile on his lips under the still inscrutable brown eyes. His accent was Portuguese, the voice of a higher pitch than would be expected from the rugged face. Prior was surprised.

"So, I'm sorry. I ask again, why are you here?"

"Only God can help you. I am merely his channel." He was again surprised and faintly diminished by the command of a foreign language. Prior stood up gingerly, feeling tired now, his hands on the table to give him leverage. The coldness of his eyes belied the mock civility of the words.

"Well thank you again, vicar. I'm sure you are a well-meaning man. But as you imply, only a man with all the usual imperfections. You just have a delusion you cling onto to try to make some sense of the pointlessness of it all. You probably need more help than I do." He spoke with a smug complacency, given licence by the dog collar; the cowardly assurance of insult without reprisal. He moved towards him and offered his hand.

"Now if you'll excuse me, I have things to do."

The priest took the hand and held it in his whilst replying. Prior was nearly a head taller and looked down on him with an air of long-sufferance. Without raising his voice the shorter man said, "You are a fool. You feed and nurture the cravings of your body but you neglect your soul. Whether you believe or not, your mistaken values have brought you to a bad place. And I am not meaning Cape Verde. You should feel lucky that its people here…" he put out an arm towards Dominique, "have taken pity on a stranger and given you so much when they have so little." His eyes never left those of a disconcerted Prior who was stunned into silence. He stared back at the priest and spoke more in exasperation than anger.

"Your God must have a wonderful sense of humour. He gives us these powerful drives, he furnishes the earth with these euphoric substances and then sits back and watches them destroy us." A quizzical look came over his face. "Anyway, why do you make these judgements on me – what have people been telling you?" He gave Dominique an accusatory stare.

"I have been told nothing that it was not in your own interest for me to know or that I could not divine from just being in your presence. I am here because people were concerned about you. Yes – He has given us the procreative urge. Yes – He has provided plants for pharmacological benefit. It is us who distort and abuse these things." Prior could think of no retort. The priest's unexpected animosity and refusal to be shouted down had evoked a grudging desire to continue the discourse even though his brain was numbed and slow to respond.

"I am told I suffer from a mental illness. Why would your God wish that on one of his children?" He knew Dominique was late but she stood impassively, fascinated by what she could understand of the two men's conversation. "Or indeed any of the suffering in the world." The priest smiled.

"Those questions again. I am sure you have heard the answer of the church before. He gives us free will to decide our course. Most of the suffering is caused to one another by one another." He said quickly before Prior could contradict him, "Yes, I know you will say what of the stillborn child, the genetically deformed, the organic and functional mental illness you refer to. The tsunamis, the earthquakes. I don't know, none of us know. We just have faith that all will be revealed."

"Wouldn't it be easier to accept the weight of evidence that there is no God that would allow all this?" Still the man stood at the threshold, unsure as to whether no invitation to enter was deliberate or inadvertent.

"For all their huffing and puffing your scientists have not come up with a better explanation. For every case of sorrow I can find one thousand examples of goodness and His works of wonder in our small everyday lives. My friend I am not an evangelist. There is no need of that in this society. You have my offer of help – it is yours to accept or reject. I will pray only that you find a way out of your suffering. It is not for me to say how that will happen." He enigmatically quoted Proverbs. "A man of understanding sets his face towards wisdom but the eyes of a fool are on the ends of the earth," and Prior experienced a momentary perturbation as he remembered his earlier rumination before his irritation returned. What on earth was he doing having this irrelevant conversation with this uninvited character whose only credential was his antiquarian garb? He could have been anyone. He didn't like the deference shown to him by Dominique either. He pulled himself together.

"Leave me out of your prayers please. They won't make the slightest difference. Go now and leave me alone – both of you." They turned and shuffled away without further reply and he was regretting the last three words even before he heard the decisive closure of the communal door at the foot of the stairs.

***

One night a few days later Prior stood at a British-owned bar in the main street of Santa Maria. He had taken the last Librium tablet the day before and fought what rather too quickly became a losing battle against the desire for an alcoholic drink. He had not left the flat for over two weeks and his brain felt befuddled and his nerves raw as he traversed the depressing terrain between his home and the town. He had been standing there for a good five minutes without being served despite it being only six p.m. and virtually empty. The barmaid, a local girl, flitted around putting ashtrays on the tables and busying herself with small jobs behind the counter. She appeared rather full of herself and bantered coquettishly with two British men and a woman who he assumed to be the owners. He stood with increasing discomfort, feeling painfully self-conscious, his ire rising but unable to speak or attract her attention because of his awkwardness. Just before he was about to turn and walk out she finally seemed to notice him and without a smile or an apology she said, "You want a drink?"

He thought of the smart, facetious replies a confident Prior might have used before saying meekly, with the hint of a stammer, "Two superboks please."

She turned and went to the fridge and took off the tops and placed the beers in front of him, taking the note and going to the till. The change fell onto the bar before it reached his slightly trembling hand, such was her obvious disregard for him. He glimpsed his reflection in a long mirror behind the bottles and was dismayed by how pale and insipid he looked as he gathered the coins. He saw the tariff on the counter and a quick mental arithmetic told him he had been short-changed by a euro. She was now at the other end of the bar talking archly with one of the owners, a tanned, balding, middle-aged man with excessive gold jewellery, slit eyes and a sneer for a mouth. He felt incapable of causing even a minor scene and said nothing, the long draught of the strong beer almost immediately producing the longed-for antidote to the bleakness of his reality.

He finished both bottles quickly, impatient to be somewhere else, and stepped with relief onto the pavement, an unconscious radar making him turn left and cross the street. He cut through the small square by the Cultural Café and came to rest at a fish beach bar/restaurant where he bought two more bottles from a more approachable barmaid and took them out to a bench on the edge of the beach. Tourists at tables on the terrace, mostly couples, eyed him with surreptitious glances as they ate their meals, a rogue male brooding rather unsettlingly on the fringes of conventional life. The alcohol had calmed his nerves but he retained the self-consciousness of the person on their own – the need to appear normal and to convey the message that his solitude was a freak of circumstance rather than as a result of any congenital undesirability. He tried to meet their fleeting eye contact with a bluff, manly, half-smile and nod of a man of the world but they looked away quickly before he could impart his message.

What the hell? he thought vengefully, as the third beer released more endorphins. *Who needs them and their safety-first, unimaginative lives-by-numbers anyway? They're probably a little apprehensive to be so far from the womb of the hotel, poor things.*

A man appeared on the terrace of a white villa directly to his right and leant on the parapet looking out at the sea, now black beneath the departing sun. Ribbons of white foam ran capriciously at intervals all the way back to the pink horizon where he focussed his eyes with a wistful, unidentified yearning. Solar lights along the wall of the villa flicked on at random, throwing illumination on small flowers in pink and red and white. He noticed with a warm nostalgia that they were the pelargonium he associated with home. As the edge of the tide lapped at posts supporting the short pier he felt a burning envy for the man, fresh from the power shower in his shorts and starched white shirt, probably indulged and nurtured by a loving woman and seemingly at peace in his idyllic dwelling. The alcohol could divert but not erase the thought of the intoxicated stumble through a minefield of dogs and decay to the insalubrious hired quarters that awaited him later.

A faint nausea and growing light-headedness told him to order some food and he ate omelette, fries and salad, washed down with a bottle of red wine from which the giggling waitress adamantly refused his offer of a glass or two. He sauntered back to the centre of town with an aimless purpose and on a whim ordered a large brandy with ice and took it out to one of the bar's kerbside tables where he watched the meanderings of the revellers. An increasing air of melancholia engulfed him as he sat in the midst of it all; anonymous, unconnected, immaterial. The alcohol was in one of its perverse moods, shying away from the brink of ecstasy and obdurately returning him to the abject person of a few hours ago. As his second brandy saw his mood branch towards self-pity and bitterness, a man dressed in leather jacket, white vest, and jeans sat down at his table uninvited and spoke immediately in conspiratorial tones. The head that tipped towards his own was shaved and the face skeletal with sunken cheeks and cruel eyes. He went straight to the point, Prior surreptitiously covering his nose against the staleness of his breath.

"You want a woman? I can find you nice girl. Small price." Prior leant back and looked upwards. He felt dead from the waist down.

"No thank you." The man looked suddenly spiteful.

"Why? You don't like woman?" Prior sighed in bored irritation.

"Yes, I like women. I'm married."

"So? Your wife is not here. What's the problem?" He wondered idly at what point he would have to become more assertive like with those awful telephone cold callers that were on the increase back home.

"She's in the hotel. I'm going there now." The man wouldn't give up.

"So why she no come with you?" The point had been reached. He turned to face him.

"Okay, enough my friend. The answer is no. Try someone else."

The man didn't move from his chair. His hand went to Prior's cigarette packet on the table and he took one out, adding as an afterthought, "I can take one?"

Prior waved a dismissive hand.

"Yes – take one and go." The absence of any trace of humanity in the wolf-like face was disturbing and Prior sensed instinctively that in his misery he carried the look of the hunted which fed the man's persistence as it had the barmaid's callousness. He was saying the right things, feeling the appropriate anger, giving his fiercest looks, but on a subliminal level the man could smell his vulnerability.

"Please my friend, lend me €20." Prior felt like a fighter on the ropes. He wished there was a referee to step in and end it. He cast his eyes around him and everywhere were smiling faces, engrossed in each other. He stood up and drained his glass and then jumped from the patio step and walked away rapidly. He glanced over his shoulder and the man was about ten metres behind. Prior cursed his stupidity at turning left from the bar in the direction of the quiet end of the street and his fears were soon confirmed at the next corner as he felt a sharp object pressed against his back and heard a voice telling him to keep walking down the side road until he told him to stop. In an entry he was relieved at knifepoint of his watch, gold signet ring, cigarettes, lighter, and €100 in cash. He was left unharmed but in no doubt as to what would happen if he told anyone, particularly the police. He felt again the strange detachment akin to relief, the sense of being carried along by an irresistible wind which he had experienced when he escaped the clutches of Ramon. He went back to the high street and found his legs taking him across the road and a few metres down and then his hands lifting the latch and swinging open the large wooden gate to the church. The doors were locked but he noted the information contained on the glass enclosed notice board lit by a lamp above it.

He fell into bed remembering nothing of the walk home and wondering why he was still alive. That was the pimp's most grievous affront – that he had not brought an end to all this and put him out of his misery.

CHAPTER 23

Prior sat in a small airless room annexing the main body of the church awaiting his turn. The two women ahead of him were dressed in sombre outfits and studiously avoided eye contact as they looked straight ahead. His beard had grown thick and was matted and stained. The nose and upper cheeks were red and below his eyes the charcoal skin was mottled with tiny pimples. The eyes themselves were full of terror – whether that of ruinous understanding or petrified ignorance it was impossible to tell. The nails of the toes protruding from his sandals were submersed with grime and his dirty clothes hung from a body malodorous from the sweat of many days. The door opened and the second of the two women before him came through as a green light indicated that it was his turn. He sat down heavily on the hard chair in a small booth and stared ahead at the concrete wall only a few centimetres away. To his right was a black curtain drawn across the extent of the room. The voice that came from his throat was small and hoarse and barely audible.

"Bless me Father for I have sinned." He was surprised by the terseness of the reply.

"Speak up please." He made a conscious attempt to raise his voice.

"Forgive me Father for I have sinned." There was a long pause.

"In what way?" Prior began to sob softly.

"I have committed rape, Father. A long time ago in another country." There was another long delay before the priest replied.

"And were you punished for this in criminal law?"

"No, Father. I escaped before I was tried."

"I see. You know then what you must do. You must show genuine remorse; you must ensure you take all steps to avoid the possibility of this recurring in the future; and you must amend your behaviour, seeking professional help if necessary. I cannot betray the confession of a penitent unless in exceptional circumstances and only with the permission of the penitent. Even then I refer the case to my superiors and not the civil authorities. However, I would encourage you to accept the punishment of the state and give yourself up to protect both you and any potential victims. You have taken the right step today but it is only the beginning. I say again – you know what you must do. You also know that it is not in my power to dictate the recital of the rosary in your case. Go and continue on the path to redemption." He added a postscript. "Please do not use the sacrament of the confessional again. If you wish to speak with me I am available after Mass."

In subsequent days a form of calm descended on him and his depression began to lift imperceptibly. He surprised himself by buying a bible and he started to read it – at first with the requirement of monumental effort and minimal understanding – but he gradually found it becoming easier and after a while his reading became avid. He stopped drinking in the week and allowed himself a modest amount at weekends to unwind and reflect – always alone and at home. He began eating properly and taking care of his appearance again – shaving off the beard, swimming, and strolling for miles along the beach, luxuriating afterwards in the shower and enjoying the sleep of the chaste.

He spoke to hardly anyone apart from shopkeepers and carefully avoided crossing paths with anyone he knew. His visits to the town forsook his old drinking haunts and he took to visiting the church where he would sit in quiet reflection on one of the rear pews, usually alone, enjoying the stillness and contemplation in the cool, musty atmosphere and one Sunday, a few weeks later, he attended morning Mass, clear eyed and clear headed, having postponed his weekly drink from Saturday to Sunday. He understood none of the service, it being conducted in Portuguese, but he drew some comfort from the rhythm contained in the passages recited by Father De Freitas and the braying incantation of the communal prayers. He joined the procession for the Eucharist, and clasping his service sheet, he felt the priest's soft palms on his bowed head as he muttered some words of blessing.

After the service, when the communicants had all left the church, he walked hesitantly towards the altar where a bespectacled middle-aged woman was busying herself in some time-honoured post-Mass rituals. His voice was low and reverent in deference to her territorial, and doubtless moral, supremacy.

"Excuse me madame – do you speak English?" She looked up from the papers she was sorting, the sun from the open door glinting on her glasses.

"A little." She carried a tranquillity unfazed by an approach from a strange male.

"I was hoping to speak briefly with Father de Freitas. He said to try after Mass."

"Ah. I know he is in a hurry. He has to go to Espargos for a christening. Wait here, I will see. Your name is?"

"Hudson. James Hudson." She returned after a few minutes.

"Please come with me. Father will see you."

He followed her through an exit behind the choir stalls to a small annexe of four rooms, their doors all closed. She knocked on one of them and the door was opened by the priest in a cotton vest and boxer shorts, thick dark chest hair flecked with grey stretching from the top of the vest to the bullish neck. He ushered him in to a small chamber where a cassock and dog collar was laid across a stout table. He had been washing at a basin on the wall below a small mirror. He gave Prior that familiar unfathomable look and said, "Please excuse my haste – I should have left five minutes ago. What did you wish to say?"

"I need to talk to you. When you have more time. When would you be free?"

He moved to the mirror and ran a comb through his abundant hair whilst answering, "Tonight is a good night. After three masses and a christening this is the one evening I devote to myself." Prior felt a twinge of guilt.

"Oh, well no… I wouldn't wish to intrude on your well-earned rest. Is there…?"

Father de Freitas interrupted, "It would not be an intrusion. Anyway, my week beyond today is already fully obligated."

Prior hoped that he had managed to convey an altered attitude from the last time they had met openly and that the poor man realised he would not be giving up his pathetically inadequate free time to endure another impudent harangue. His humility was genuine as he said, "Father, I would be most honoured if you would take dinner with me. At my house." For the first time he noticed a vacillation. He sensed a reluctance to make any alteration to what he assumed was a reassuringly repetitive weekly routine. There was also the matter of collusion with a self-confessed rapist. The priest bought some thinking time.

"May I have some brief clue as to the purpose?" His equilibrium had been restored and he looked unflinchingly into Prior's eyes. It was the Englishman's turn to be slightly thrown.

"I… I do need to speak to you on an urgent matter and alter the impression you have gained of me. I also feel a need to pay recompense for my ignorant incivility on the last occasion you visited my house." Something about the atmosphere of the place was causing an unconscious adoption of a rather obsolete form of English. "You can of course stay for as long or as little as you wish. I can arrange transport if that is a problem."

"Well yes. Alright. Please don't go to any trouble and I have my own transport. What time shall I come?"

"Say about six?"

"Fine. I will see you then. And now if you'll excuse me…"

"Of course, of course. My thanks for your time."

Prior stepped from the cool of the church into the midday sun of the street. The property and commercial offices were closed, their expatriate workers sleeping off their hangovers or lounging on the beach, but the West African women with their wooden boxes of cigarettes and chewing gum dotted the wire fence opposite the bars and the craft shops, ever open in anticipation of some business that would put some food in their stomachs for another day.

His pleasure at the priest's acceptance of his invitation turned quickly to something approaching panic as he suddenly remembered that the banks were closed and he had no money. Cash machines had not arrived in Sal as yet. As he walked home he carried out a mental inventory of what he had in and whether there was any cash lying around. The fridge was well stocked with beer but little else. He knew nothing of Father de Freitas's tastes but he was sure that a tin of sardines with stale bread washed down with lager would only reinforce the impression of his previous antagonism. His fears were confirmed as he threw open the fridge and cupboards and searched every centimetre of the apartment for some overlooked cache of money but his entire liquid wealth totalled 275 CV escudos in coins – about £2.50. He sat for half an hour considering his options with a progressively dawning sense of the hopelessness of his situation. There was no-one he could ask. He had nothing of value he could offer as security to induce one of the general stores to release goods to him – his watch and ring had gone. He had nothing to sell, no service to render. He had no cheques, no friends who could offer anything beyond their good will. He realised he was stuck and his response was to pace the flat in the hope that the activity might spark a eureka moment. Despite the upturn of the previous days his recovery was fragile and based on a tenuous enlightenment, and an agitated depression was only a stumbling block away. He stood facing the wall of his living room, rhythmically tapping his forehead against the concrete, close to tears of frustration. With his eyes tightly closed, the germ of a last idea came to him from the black void, an almost impossible long shot, but nonetheless a faint thread of hope.

He did know someone who was detached from the irksome complexities of his disastrous fiasco of an existence thus far in Cape Verde who had provided a comforting touchstone to the conventions of culture and roots so overtly despised but covertly yearned for. Introduced by Zina, he was on nodding terms with Trevor Baker, a horticulturist from somewhere in the midlands of England, an uncomplicated individual who made a precarious living from cultivating plants and selling them to the hotels and expatriates for their gardens. He was an agreeably approachable man who Prior had noticed appeared either unmoved by, or more probably unaware of, Zina's thinly disguised mockery. He cringed at the recollection of his own sniggering connivance in her derision.

He knew that he made a habit of taking his wife and young children for Sunday lunch at the restaurant on a small pier where he had gone with Zina that evening. He might still be there, or if not, he knew that after lunch they went to the same spot on the beach close to the restaurant. He walked with an urgent impatience, peevishly annoyed at the necessity for travel. In his haste the thigh where the dog had bitten him started to ache, the damaged muscle protesting at the unaccustomed strain being placed on it. As he reached the restaurant and scanned the tables ahead, an immense relief engulfed him at the sight of the back of Trevor's head, the curly pale red hair flanked by slightly protruding ears. To his right sat his rotund wife, and opposite them their children, a boy and girl of about eight and nine. He went to the bar and bought a Coke out of his meagre change and stood hoping for an opportunity to speak to Trevor on his own, an intuition cautioning him against the predictable response of his wife to the scrounging of a virtual stranger when, by all accounts, her own position was so penurious. His moment came when Trevor went to the gents and Prior followed him in. Trevor greeted him in his usual enthusiastic manner, the midland vowels contributing to a sense of unaffected good humour.

"Hello Jim. Didn't notice you in there. How's things?"

"Hi Trev. Not brilliant to be honest. In fact I came with the specific intention of looking for you." Trevor gave him a puzzled look.

"Oh?"

"I need to ask a favour of you. I know we hardly know each other and this is very cheeky but I'm a bit desperate to be truthful." He explained his predicament, moving the mugging incident forward to having occurred the previous night, and assured him that the money would be returned first thing the following morning after the banks opened. Trevor's pink face, out of its element in this climate, creased in concentration.

"Gwen should have some in her purse, Jim. I don't know how much – not a lot I wouldn't imagine. How much do you need?" Prior felt awful.

"Well anything really – the more the better up to say €50."

"Let's go through and I'll ask her." Trevor went back to the table while Prior hovered uncomfortably at the bar, not knowing quite where to look. Trevor looked up and beckoned him over and he approached diffidently, sheepishly acknowledging the woman and smiling at the children. He felt somehow dirty and shady and not a little ridiculous. Her voice was kind, the accent the same as her husband's.

"Sorry to hear about your troubles, Jim – so unusual in Cape Verde. Very bad luck. I can pay for our meal with a cheque (the restaurant didn't accept cards), and let you have the €40 I've got. I'm afraid that's the best I can do." The relief overwhelmed him again and the words were a frustratingly inadequate means of expressing his gratitude. He took directions to Trevor's small market garden where he would go tomorrow and headed for the town, all pain gone from his leg, the insidious depression nipped in the bud until the next time.

By five o'clock he was ready and he sat on his veranda with a cup of coffee and a cigarette, basking in the warm glow of meeting his deadline with the additional advantage of insufficient time to spare to protract the restless anticipation common to the host. Freshly showered and shampooed, he had put on the black trousers and white short-sleeved shirt he had not worn since the flight here that seemed so long ago. With the money he had bought a whole cooked chicken from the only fast food outfit he was aware of in Santa Maria. Situated on one of the side roads off the main drag, it was a vibrant, scurrilous stretch seeming to crystallise all the excesses of a Harlem or a Kingston into one small road no more than about fifty metres in length. He had bought lettuce, tomatoes, and onions from one of the street-side women and made a tossed salad dressed with a little olive oil, garlic and lemon juice. He had parboiled and then fried some potatoes which now sat in a dish on the unit ready to be reheated later. He had bought some cakes and bread and then olives and peanuts to accompany the brandy or red wine he hoped the priest might accept. He knew from the lingering aroma of his cassock that he liked a cigar and he had completed his purchases with a small packet of coronas.

At ten minutes past six he heard the approach of a vehicle, its revs high and exhaust clamorous, and he looked over the parapet to see a small white Citroën pulling up outside. The priest got out on the passenger side and extricated himself slowly from a gaggle of children and dogs, talking to them in tones both firm and jocular as he edged towards Prior's entrance and rang the buzzer.

Once the door was closed and the priest stood in the room, Prior felt suddenly shy and awkward. It was as if he had stumbled unwittingly onto a treadmill that had carried him unthinking to this place he had now arrived at and he felt uncomfortable and at odds with the destination.

"What can I get you? Wine, beer, brandy, coffee; a soft drink?" He suddenly hoped he didn't opt for the latter – he had none.

"A glass of red wine would be very nice. Thank you." His choice relaxed Prior a little and he uncorked the bottle and got himself a beer. He then ushered the priest onto the veranda and put the drinks on the small white plastic table between the two patio chairs before returning to the kitchen for the nuts and olives. The man took a sip from his drink.

"I'm afraid I wasn't presumptuous enough to allow it to breathe, Father. I hope it is palatable." The priest waved a dismissive hand.

"It is very good." He picked up the bottle.

"Ah, Spanish. Very underrated wines. Even though it pains me to say so as a man from Portugal." Prior laughed.

"Yes. Like the English and the Scottish. Do you think of yourself as foremost a Latin or a European?"

"I don't deal in race, I deal in humanity." Prior felt a momentary deflation. The sooner he cleared the air the better. He offered the priest a cigarette which he declined and then a cigar which was accepted. Prior lit up himself and drained his glass to within an inch of its base.

"I assume you knew that it was me in the confessional. My apologies for that as a non-Catholic."

"After your second sentence I suspected it was you. I confess I allowed my curiosity to get the better of me."

"I see. The main thing I need to tell you is that I revoke my confession, Father. If I were a rapist I hope I would not ask you to taint yourself with a semi-social connection of this kind. I would not be that low. I was very sick when I confessed – my depression had become psychotic. I imagined things that I can now see in my miraculous clarity to have been delusional." The priest's glass was empty and Prior took the bottle and held it at a forty-five degree angle with an enquiring look. He nodded and Prior refilled the glass and continued, "You will be confused by my change of heart from when you were last here. So too am I. Please excuse me for one minute." He went to the fridge to get another beer.

"A few days after I saw you and Dominique I went into the town. Everywhere I saw the folly and evil of my existence. The drunkenness, the lust, the superficiality, the insanity driven by ego. It was as if I had stepped outside my body and was observing myself and my life as a bystander. The empty carcase I saw was being picked clean by predators caught up in this nefarious world – I was insulted, scorned, and ultimately stripped of all my possessions. I mean that literally, Father, not metaphorically – I was mugged at knifepoint."

For some reason he laughed but the priest remained impassive, drawing on his cigar and looking out above the top of the tall building opposite at the transmuting sky. His expression was almost trancelike.

"Before I went home something drew me towards the church and I made a mental note of the confession and service times. I can't tell you why. I was operating on autopilot. For the next week or so I returned to the lifestyle that I had slipped into before I was rescued by my three friends – not drinking, eating, or washing – my mind a tornado of pain far worse than anything physical could be. I was waiting to die and the sooner the better. But one morning some force took me out of the bed and out of the door, still dressed in the clothes I had worn all that time in bed, and propelled me towards the church. I don't ever remember checking the time but you were there waiting. It was some kind of miracle because from that moment on my life has begun to improve." The priest turned to look at him briefly and then returned his gaze to the sky. The sun had now retreated behind the building, its declining rays emerging between the one opposite and the one next to it.

"Did you have treatment for your illness at home?" Prior paraphrased his psychiatric history up to the point of his escape.

"And the accusation of rape. Why did this happen?"

"I was with the woman earlier in the evening." He felt uncomfortable talking to a religious man of such things.

"We became… friendly, outside, if you know what I mean. This in itself was a sin, I know, because she was married. However, she wished to stop when we reached a certain point and I respected her wishes and left and went home. It was some time after that when she was raped. Of course because only my DNA was found on her I was a strong suspect; the only suspect. But I swear to you Father that it was not me. I would never be capable of that."

Father de Freitas stubbed out his cigar in the glass ashtray and brushed ash from his grey trousers and then looked Prior full in the eyes. "Even when your mind is sick, your resolve and standards enfeebled by alcohol?"

He realised the understandable doubts over the reliability of his testimony given his previous explanation for his confession.

"Let me explain my understanding of this illness they say I have. During this incident I was in the manic phase. I accept my judgement is impaired; my behaviours can be wild, irrational, self-indulgent. Some people become psychotic in this phase. That is to say they can be thought disordered, their concepts of reality distorted. This doesn't happen with me, apart perhaps from some delusions of grandeur. But even then the grandeur is based on realistic vanity. I don't wish to sound boastful but I am a successful man with a minor public profile, believe it or not. Let us just say I don't think I am the King of England or the heavyweight champion of the world. I have clear recollection of everything when my mood comes down. When I am high I know what is happening but I don't want it to stop – it feels so good. When I was in hospital I spoke to a man who had bipolar disorder and who had also taken amphetamines. He said that the feeling when manic is better even than the effects of the drug.

It is in my depressed phase that, increasingly, I seem to be subject to psychosis. I have delusions of persecution, maybe even paranoia, indescribable feelings of guilt and worthlessness that on this occasion tipped over into the delusion that I had done something which I now know I didn't." He poured another glass of wine and got himself another beer and waited for a reply.

"I am sitting in your house, drinking your wine, shortly to be eating your food. I am not here to judge, only to understand and share my understanding. My advice remains the same and you can take it or leave it. Go back to face the process of man's law. You have nothing to be frightened of. If there is a miscarriage of justice then be sure you will have your reward in heaven. Are you not in prison now anyway?"

They talked for a while, the priest interested to hear the details of his escape and refuge and life thus far in Cape Verde which Prior truncated and anonymised to protect Caroline and Zina. When he had finished Father de Freitas felt in his trouser pocket and pulled out a small bible. Prior glanced at the text which was in Portuguese.

"For some reason I am drawn to the second letter of Paul to the Corinthians." He began to read a passage, translating expertly for Prior's ears.

"'I have met dangers from rivers, dangers from robbers, dangers from my fellow countrymen, dangers from foreigners, dangers in towns, dangers in the country, dangers at sea, dangers from false friends. I have toiled and drudged, I have often gone without sleep, hungry and thirsty, I have often gone fasting, and I have suffered from cold and exposure.'"

He flicked through the pages, quoting short passages at random. 'If a man must boast, let him boast of the Lord', 'we want you to do what is right even if we should be seen to be discredited for we have no power to act against the truth, but only for it', 'so many people brag of their earthly distinctions that I shall do so too. How gladly you bear with fools, being yourselves so wise'. He turned the page and read a longer passage.

"'I am obliged to boast. It does no good; but I shall go on to tell of visions and revelations granted by the Lord. I know a Christian man who fourteen years ago (whether in the body or out of it, I do not know – God knows) was caught up as far as the third heaven. And I know that this same man (whether in the body or out of it, I do not know – God knows) was caught up into paradise, and heard words so secret that human lips may not repeat them. About such a man as that I am ready to boast; but I will not boast on my own account, except of my weaknesses. If I should choose to boast, it would not be the boast of a fool, for I should be speaking the truth. But I refrain, because I should not like anyone to form an estimate of me which goes beyond the evidence of his own eyes and ears. And so, to keep me from being unduly elated by the magnificence of such revelations, I was given a sharp pain in my body which came as Satan's messenger to bruise me; this was to save me from being unduly elated. Three times I begged the Lord to rid me of it but his answer was, "My grace is all you need: power comes to its full strength in weakness." I shall therefore prefer to find my joy and pride in the very things that are my weakness; and then the power of Christ will come and rest upon me. Hence I am well content, for Christ's sake, with weakness, contempt, persecution, hardship, and frustration; for when I am weak, then I am strong.'" He closed the book and took a long drink from his glass. Prior lifted the bottle again and the priest looked at his watch. It was seven thirty.

"Perhaps another glass with dinner. I cannot stay too late." He took the hint and excused himself and turned on the oven to full heat and put the potatoes and chicken inside while he laid the table. When everything was ready he called him through and they sat facing each other. It was dark now and the breeze carried the cooking smells from other houses into the flat to mingle with their own. Outside, there was a rare moment of quiet as presumably people ate, children prepared for bed, and dogs skulked in search of food, their mouths dripping, their taste buds enlivened by the maddeningly alluring aromas.

"That was a very interesting passage. I have started to read the bible. I read first the four Gospels and am now working through the Old Testament."

"Please do not take it too literally. I would not want you to be put off by what can sound a very wrathful God." Prior experienced some discomfort. There were questions he wanted to ask arising from his reading but he didn't want to spoil the atmosphere or the meal. The priest's last remark was too good a cue to miss, however.

"I wanted to ask about a passage in Matthew. Only for clarification you understand, I'm not trying to pick a fight. You called me a fool that time and were fully justified. But Matthew says anyone who calls his brother a fool will burn in the fires of hell.

"You see I have trouble with the literality of even the Gospel sometimes. In the same chapter he says that any man looking on a woman with a lustful eye has already committed adultery in his heart.

Now that I am pretty sure excludes about ninety-nine point nine per cent of the heterosexual male population from the gates of salvation."

The priest wiped his mouth with his paper napkin and thought.

"You are right with your first question. I used the wrong word and I apologise. I should have said you are misguided. I wanted to shock you. A kind of spiritual electroconvulsive therapy perhaps. The second quotation is allegorical I am sure – an encouragement towards a striving for purity. Maybe we can learn from the Muslims with their yashmaks and long robes." Prior felt better for having got it off his chest and didn't pursue the issue, instead watching as the other man ate voraciously, helping himself to more salad and bread. He must have discerned something from his faintly amused look.

"Please excuse my gluttony. I eat very frugally normally. This is a real treat. It is delicious."

"No, no – I was enjoying your enjoyment. Please have as much as you want." There was silence as they both ate before Prior said, "Can you explain a little of the passages you read. Of course a lot of it is self-evident."

Father de Freitas finished his mouthful and said, "I cry for the West sometimes. So many aspire to be an expert or a celebrity or a millionaire. 'So many people boast of their earthly distinctions'. 'I will destroy the wisdom of the wise and bring to nothing the cleverness of the clever'. There is little humility any more. I say again, I do not judge. I understand the pressures people are under – the media, advertising, the capitalist ethos, easy credit, the plague of communication. Temptation is very accessible."

"But surely it is human nature to acquire more, to follow one's ego, to advance technologically. Don't tell me there is one Cape Verdean who doesn't desire the same things."

"Cape Verde is perhaps the most striking example of the evils of the developed world – its striving for acquisition. Your country and mine are more culpable than most. I cannot look at a local person without seeing the greed and cruelty of the 'civilised' world etched in their coffee skin. They didn't ask to be created out of violation and left marooned on these barren islands to scrape a living or travel the world in search of a dubious inheritance, leaving loved ones behind, perhaps forever. It is a testimony to the people's resilience and ingenuity that they have made such a relative success of things. On the UN quality of life index they are top in West Africa." Prior continued to play devil's advocate.

"Ah. A capitalist barometer. Yes, I heard that. Also the highest GDP. I had a girlfriend here who told me. She was in the property and finance business. She cheated me out of everything I have almost." For the first time the priest used his assumed forename.

"James. You seem an intelligent man. Can you not see a pattern in your life? You are accused of rape. You are the victim of a confidence trick. You are mugged. These people or situations did not come to you. You sought them out, invited them in, by choosing a path of evil. The first thing I noticed about you was your anger. You should know that anger is often the expression of a search for love. I quote – it was not my original idea. You are looking for love. I hope you know that you have found it." Prior poured the last of the wine into the priest's glass. He thought of opening the second bottle but decided against it. He felt embarrassed and couldn't think of anything to say.

"To return to your original question. It seems to me you have been looking for the third heaven here on earth. You will not find it. The West will not find it. It grieves me to see the demented search that takes people ever further away from that which they are looking for. Accept that paradise is not attainable on earth. Accept that life is only a transitory journey filled with pain. Bear that pain with dignity and courage like the slaves. Accept also that you have been given a cross to bear; that is to say, your mental illness. Don't dispute its existence and be glad that God has provided, through nature's balance, the drugs to correct it. Accept therefore the help and treatment offered. And remember; God will never let things get too bad for anyone. Too intolerable." Prior took the plates away to the sink and retuned with a plate of cakes. Father de Freitas took one and washed it down with the rest of his wine.

"More wine, Father?"

"Oh no. I've had more than enough thank you."

"Coffee?"

"Yes – that would be nice and then I really should go." He

returned to the veranda while his host cleared the table and waited for the kettle to boil. He took out a tray and put it on the small table. Father de Freitas added milk and sugar while Prior took his black and unsweetened.

"A small cognac to go with it?" He could see him wrestling with his conscience.

"Well perhaps a very small one." Prior came back with the bottle and two tumblers, apologising for the lack of proper brandy glasses. They both lit up and sat back in soporific appreciation of the faint breeze and the blackness of the night sky lit by the thin sliver of a new moon. In the dim light coming through from the sitting room the priest's face was pink from the wine, his dark eyes fluid and Prior voiced the question his mind had framed while he had busied himself with the small domestic chores.

"If He will never let anything become too intolerable then how can you explain some things one reads about? For instance, the little girl – alone and isolated in her innocence and lack of understanding; subjected to month after month of sustained, systematic cruelty at the hands of her own flesh and blood, those people who, God knows, she should be able to trust; and then her miserable, pathetic demise." His voice began to break and he could barely say the next sentence, "How could you look at that crumpled little body and say that was God's will?" The man's response was immediate and impassioned and Prior wondered if the drink was finally getting to him.

He said in what was almost a shout, "How could you say that it was not! He took her and brought her to Him before it became too much to bear. As I told you before, man has free will. Satan exists. Evil is everywhere and that is the choice some take. So how can this be the end? Yes – if that was the end for her, and sadly many more like her, there would be no God." He raised his voice again. "How can you *not* believe there is a reckoning? How can anyone live for another minute with the thought that those few years of misery and pain would be the sum total of her existence? And what would be the point? There has to be a point and that is why I believe."

The brief wave of fervour abated and both men sat in pensive silence, sipping occasionally at their drinks. It was Prior who spoke first.

"I have enjoyed talking to you very much. Please understand that I question not to take a set opposing position – only to look for clarification, explanation. I feel the germination of a faith but it is callow and precarious like the life of a new born baby. I am reassured however by your answers. I will continue with my reading and hopefully speak more with you."

Prior was struck with a realisation that his words sounded like an invitation to bring the evening to a close and this was the last thing on his mind. He understood the colossal demands on the man's time and he wanted to make the most of this propitious opportunity which he knew was unlikely to be repeated. He said quickly, "One problem I have had with religion – something that has fed my scepticism – is that I have seen many selfless, generous, good people with no faith and some mean-spirited, spiteful people who go to church every week." The statement hung in the air like a vague indictment. Prior felt sorry that the hasty attempt to prolong the priest's stay had necessitated further work on his part. This was supposed to be his night off. In the dim light of the veranda his dark face betrayed no suggestion of tedium. Prior surmised that he probably considered himself to always be working and that he would have fielded this question many times.

"If you have read these people correctly I would have to say that the former are blessed with the grace of God whether they know it or not. The latter could be dismissed as hypocrites but I would prefer to be more charitable. Perhaps they are unhappy people for whatever reason. I'm sure you are mistaking their unhappiness for badness. They are trying to assuage their discontent through their faith. Have you ever seen a happy person who is unpopular? Or a miserable one who is sought after? And of course it is self-fulfilling. The more attention the former gains the happier he becomes. The further the isolation of the latter, the more miserable he gets. We say of them who are always smiling – he or she is nice. Or of those who scowl – they are horrible. But the approval of our peers is not something God encourages us to see as important. 'The Lord is my light and my salvation – whom shall I fear? The Lord is the stronghold of my life – of whom shall I be afraid?' Yes, you will say, 'Why doesn't God make his believers happy and the unbelievers sad?' When you read the New Testament you will have your answer over and over again – 'Blessed are the poor in spirit for they will inherit the earth.'"

Prior looked pensive and Father de Freitas anticipated his question.

"I am not saying all Christians must be unhappy on this earth. Whatever the hardships they endure – and I know how strong the temptations are to indulge in a sensual, hedonistic life – deep down there is joy when weighing the brief transience of earthly existence against the might of eternity." Prior filled their cups with more coffee from the stainless steel pot, now lukewarm and cloudy, and offered him another brandy.

"One more and very definitely the last. Then I will phone my driver." Prior poured and his guest allowed a generous measure to line the base of the tumbler and creep up the sides before holding up a halting hand.

"I know something of what you are talking about from first-hand experience. I have lived the two extremes, as you know. I have noticed that when my mood is elated people warm to me – at least in the early stages before I become irritable and insensitively opinionated and need the instant gratification of the psychopath. I seem to emit a charisma that draws them to me like a moth to a candle. It is when I plumb the depths of despair, when I really need the kindness and attention of others that I find myself alone and unloved." The priest re-lit the cheroot which had gone out.

"As I have said, as followers of Christ we don't place too high a stall on the acceptance of others. However, ask yourself if you would still be here, talking to me now without that love shown to you by Dominique and her friends. And who do you think was motivating their actions?"

Prior felt somehow sheltered in the company of this didactic man, protected from indecision, or fear, or pain by the strength of his convictions. He experienced the clarity of mind of a manic episode without the illusory elation – just an inkling of embarking on a journey to a more comfortable place with the weaponry to take on whatever life decided to fling at him with a new equanimity. Before he could respond to the rhetorical question the priest asked him about his work, surprising him with the depth of his knowledge of football.

"Ah – the beautiful game. It is very frustrating to be Portuguese. It is our national sport. Yes, I know it is yours also but you have great success in other sports. For us it is our only sport of note. Tell me of any great Portuguese tennis players or golfers or athletes. Unlike our great rivals, Spain, for instance. We have produced some wonderful individuals – Eusebio, Figo, Ronaldo, Nani from these very islands, but what have we won?" Prior felt a little disconcerted by the abrupt shift in the conversation.

"Well… Benfica."

"I mean at the international level." He looked at Prior with a mischievous gleam in his eyes, "But you with your functional, unimaginative artisans – you have won the World Cup! Like I said, you will not find justice in this world. Prior reeled off a few names of his own and the priest again surprised him with both his knowledge and his irreverence.

"Apart from Charlton, defenders or flawed geniuses. No-one with the body of work of a Ronaldo or a Eusebio." They both smiled.

"Of course I am only joking. It is the way of the football man to be blind to anyone but his own team."

"Yes. Seriously though, don't you think it has become too much of a religion now?"

"It has always inspired passion. It just reflects society in my opinion. Christian society grows more secular by the day. We can't blame football for that. If it wasn't football it would be something else. In some ways it has done much good."

Prior thought back to the seventies and eighties when he was a boy on the terraces at Goodison.

"Yes, with racism for instance, certainly. I remember the horrible abuse of black players at the club I supported as a boy. I stopped going when I found myself wanting the other team to win because I was so ashamed of my own supporters. It's more or less outlawed now in my country. Don't get me wrong – it's still there under the surface, but at least that's where it remains. Without oxygen, who knows, hopefully it may die. At least youngsters going to games now aren't lured into thinking that this is acceptable, even normal behaviour anymore. I wrote a piece once about how the game allows a male to express emotion in ways that would be taboo in almost any other situation. He can become apoplectic with rage; he can cry over his defeats and wear his overt grief as a badge of honour; he can profess his undying love for his team with a degree of passion I daresay his loved ones would not recognise. One wonders what we would do without it." The priest looked at his watch and sat up straight from his slumped position.

"I have played on your hospitality for much too long." He pulled a mobile from the opposite pocket to the one which held the bible and pressed some numbers with his thick, hairy fingers and put it to his ear. He began speaking in Creole and when the brief exchange was completed he pressed a button and returned it to his pocket.

"I'm sure you are thinking this is very 'servant and master'. I usually drive myself. Tonight, because I suspected I may have a drink, I engaged Pablo, one of my young parishioners. Don't worry; he is very grateful for the remuneration. He has been waiting at his house near to here.

Prior began to offer to pay for the transport and pulled up hurriedly as he remembered he had spent almost all of the forty euros. He said instead, "I didn't think people worried about drink driving here." Apart from the slight glow on his upper face and forehead and the damp tranquillity of the eyes, the priest's appearance and demeanour were no different to when he had arrived. The emotion of earlier was obviously occasioned by the depth of his compassion and he still seemed to be in total control of himself. He shrugged.

"I'm sure I could safely negotiate my return home but I would prefer to err on the side of caution. I accept my role gives me licence but I don't wish to abuse my freedoms. You are right – there are no drink driving laws here yet but this will change." He stood up and leant with his elbows on the parapet, the muscular hands clasped together. "I expect you are tired of my lecturing but I have a few thoughts to pass on before I go – ignore them if you wish. Enjoy alcohol – I do as you can see – but be its master, use it as a reward, a therapy, not a way of life or it will become all-consuming and everything will become subordinate, even your family. Don't bear a grudge against those who have ill-treated you. Vengeance is with God if it is merited. Don't give them a second thought. Move on. Don't let them ruin you twice – once in the deed and again in the remorse. Finally, go home, give yourself up and accept the treatment for your illness. Nurture your faith and you will never feel alone again."

A car drew up outside and the priest turned to face him. They shook hands and he offered his thanks for the hospitality.

"Think nothing of it. Thank you for giving me your time. Thank you for everything, Father."

"I'm afraid I won't be returning the compliment – I don't entertain but I do hope I may see you at Mass while you are here."

"Sure. I'll think about your advice but if I do go back it won't be immediately. Also, I understand what you are saying about vengeance but right now if the threat of blackmail was lifted I would go to the police." Father de Freitas smiled.

"Fine. I meant it when I said you can ignore it. I am not my brother's keeper." They went through to the front door and shook hands again. Before he turned to go down the stairs he said, "Don't forget that you too have helped me. Don't you think there are times when we too can doubt? It is stories like you tell that reaffirm our faith, confirm the power of prayer. I can assure you that you were being prayed for."

He closed the door and tidied the flat, bringing in the coffee tray and washing the cups along with the dinner plates. He felt mellow but not drunk from the three bottles of beer, glass of wine and two brandies, and pleased to have no inclination to continue drinking or go out into the night. Instead, he locked the veranda door, made himself a sandwich from the remains of the chicken and went to bed.

CHAPTER 24

Prior dropped down heavily onto the street feeling a twinge in an Achilles tendon as he headed in the direction of the town and the bank. He felt refreshed from a good night's sleep and had woken only once, at five, with a pressing need to empty his bladder. Like the Formula One driver forgoing a final pit stop however, he had resisted the call of nature. He had learnt from bitter experience that by the time he returned to bed the brief stimulation would prevent him from going back to sleep and he tolerated his discomfort and claimed the prize of an additional two hours. His mood was level but with a trace of nostalgia for an evening of innocent gratification that would not be repeated. He knew from the aridity of his mouth and the tension around his temples that he had taken a drink but he experienced no regrets. In his new circumstances, the paucity of the bank balance he checked as he withdrew the cash to repay Trevor no longer filled him with apprehension. He would be taking Father de Freitas's advice at some stage and the dwindling funds would serve him well as a final arbiter in the timing of that decision.

He had a rough idea where Trevor had his market garden and he meandered towards it along unfamiliar paths through new developments to the north of the town. Time was an immaterial commodity and he strolled at a leisurely pace, no longer driven by an inexplicable urgency, taking in his surroundings through different, more favourable eyes, not knowing if this was due to the more aesthetically pleasing environment or his new enlightenment. With his sojourn nearly over he wondered if he would ever return – if he *could* ever return. He was still struck by the apparently arbitrary nature of the project of creating a city to meet the anticipated demand but then found himself on a rare street that appeared to be close to the finished article, with rows of small white villas on either side set behind gated walls above which exotic plants opened their vivid petals to the rays of the late morning sun. Dogs were scarce here, as were people apart from the life indicated by the distant cries of construction workers in neighbouring buildings. At the end of the development there was an abrupt renewal of the rubble and litter more reminiscent of his own vicinity and away to his right, the east, he saw a collection of huts and greenhouses which he assumed to be what he was looking for.

Prior found Trevor in one of the greenhouses that seemed slightly superfluous under the almost constant year-round sun. He was engrossed in half filling pots with soil and then taking plants from smaller pots and introducing them to their new, more spacious surroundings. He looked up with sweat glistening on his pale face and smiled broadly.

"Oh hi Jimmy. Potting-on." He wore only baggy black shorts and a dirty pair of white plimsolls with black socks. His hairless upper torso was pink, his chest and arms insignificant below narrow shoulders. Zina would have had a field day.

"Hello Trev. I've brought the money. Impressive place you've got here." It wasn't but he couldn't think of anything else to say.

"Oh yes, thanks – on both counts. You didn't need to have hurried. We could have waited. Would you like me to show you round?" Prior feigned enthusiasm – he had no real knowledge or interest – and Trevor became animated with the assumption of the fanatic that everyone else must be similarly absorbed in the subject of their fanaticism.

"All of our plants are grown from seeds or cuttings. Mostly local and indigenous to Cape Verde. We get some from Santiago as well. It's very hard as you can imagine with the salt and the wind and the lack of rainfall. We have to use plants that can tolerate salt. As you know, most of the water on Sal is from the desalination plant in Palmeira and very expensive. Everything's at an early stage here but they're looking at wind-powered desalination and also encouraging developers to factor in the water provision as part of their new developments." In another greenhouse he picked up a pot and trickled the earth through his fingers. "We even have to buy in our soil from Terre boa on the outskirts of Espargos."

They toured the estate with Trevor maintaining a constant babble as he showed Prior the salt-tolerant grasses such as paspalum and Bermuda grass; aloe, cork trees, bougainvillea, oleander, hibiscus, papaya, and bananas. Prior nodded and oohed and aahed and said 'I see' at the appropriate moments, and even found the opportunity to squeeze in a question or two.

"We've done the landscaping and planting for three major complexes. A lot of the new home owners want gardens and we provide the plants and the initial layout and the on-going care if that's what is requested. We're also getting into swimming pool maintenance. We also retail plants and horticultural products." He folded his arms and looked at Prior in triumph.

"Jimmy. If it's flora – you name it… we do it." Prior smiled and handed over the money.

"Get something for the kids with the extra and thanks again Trevor, you saved my life."

"Not at all. Any time. Would you like a coffee?"

He thought for a moment and then said, "Why not? I've got nothing else to do."

Trevor led him over to one of the huts and they stepped inside. It was obviously the office. He poured two coffees from a well-used thermos flask and sat down behind a desk piled with papers, books, pots and other paraphernalia, beckoning Prior into the other chair.

"Excuse the mess. I'm always meaning to sort it out but never seem to get the time. Gwen used to do the admin but she's got a job at the kids' school now so everything's gone to rack and ruin I'm afraid." One of his workers, a bare-chested local man, appeared at the door and Trevor gave him some instructions and then said to Prior, "What exactly do you do Jim, if you don't mind my asking? I don't think you ever said."

"No, I don't mind you asking. It's no big secret. I'm looking into setting up an import/export business. I've more or less completed my research now."

"Any good? Will you be staying?"

"There's a market, yes. I'll be going home soon to tie up some contacts at the other end. Then I daresay I'll be back."

"I could probably put some business your way now I think about it." Prior tried to change the subject.

"Well we can talk about that some time, Trev. When did you last go home?"

"Friday night." He let out a laugh.

"No, I know what you mean. We do think of here as home now though. Haven't been back to England for two years but we're saving up to go next Christmas. Gwen's mum's not been well." Prior's eyes surveyed the room, noticing the lack of any evidence of an electricity supply as Trevor looked at him with a slight air of discomfort and said, "Do you still see that Zina?" before lowering his eyes from Prior's gaze.

"Er… no. That didn't work out. We weren't an item for very long actually." Prior sensed that the other man continued to feel uncomfortable as if he wanted to say something but daren't.

"Have you seen her recently?"

"Well, just bumped into each other now and then. I don't know her very well. Not socially." He hesitated before saying, "I'm not that keen on her to be honest." Prior sensed the need for his probing to be gentle or he would lose the fish.

"That makes two of us. I won't go into details but she didn't treat me very well. Complex woman." Trevor didn't reply and Prior perceived his impatience to be back in the greenhouse with his hands back in the soil. He had nothing to lose now and he took the plunge.

"I get the feeling that there's something you're not telling me Trev." The ingenuous man looked slightly startled and then his face took on a worried, thoughtful countenance.

Eventually he said, "If you'll promise to keep this to yourself I'll give you the local gossip. It's really not my style this, Jim. I just like to keep myself to myself and look after Gwen and the kids. We're just an ordinary family. You might have heard it anyway."

"I doubt it. You have my word – I won't tell a soul, I promise."

Trevor spoke with a diffidence, detaching himself from the words with a frequent 'this is only what I've heard'. He was obviously unused to and uncomfortable with the purveyance of tittle-tattle. It was as if he felt he had an unpleasant duty to warn Prior, albeit a little too late.

"She came here quite a while ago – well before me – right at the start of the building and tourism. Apparently she quickly shacked up with a guy called Julio Pereira, the owner of an international law firm with its head office in Lisbon but other offices around the world including most of the CV islands. Zina would have been about twenty-seven or twenty-eight I think and he was in his late sixties. Anyway, he had a sprawling villa built overlooking the sea in Palmeira and she moved in with him."

"Was she working herself then?"

"Oh yes. She's always been with that property company. Didn't need to I don't suppose but there's not a lot to do here if you're not working. It'd drive you mad."

Prior offered him a cigarette. "No thanks – never used them."

"Do you mind if…?"

"Oh no, go ahead. I'll get an ashtray." Trevor rummaged in a cupboard and produced a plastic pot into which he dropped a piece of cardboard to cover the hole.

"Anyway, one day they found Mr. Pereira's body washed up on the beach. There was a lot of speculation at the time but eventually the conclusion of the inquest was misadventure."

"Why? What were people saying?"

"Well, it was before my time but I've heard from people who were here then that Zina and a guy called Ramon were murder suspects. It'd be easy to suffocate someone and throw them in the sea." Prior's stomach fluttered uneasily.

"She inherited just about everything you see – the house, the business. He left some money to his children in Portugal apparently but he left Zina a very wealthy woman, believe me."

Prior thought disconsolately of the standing order depleting his meagre resources. Pin money to her no doubt. Why? He considered telling Trevor but something cautioned him to pull back. The reticence was contagious and the other man said quickly, "Like I say, Jim, it's only hearsay and it's not fair to judge."

"No, no – of course. This Ramon. Were they together?" Trevor cleared his throat.

"I think so – at the time. I don't know about now." He looked confused and stammered, "Well of course I don't suppose they are, you being with her and all – at least until recently."

"What's he like this Ramon?" He looked down again at the floor.

"Again, it's only what I've been told. Please don't say anything. It's rumoured that he's a major drug dealer. He's got a big luxury yacht they say is not just for pleasure jaunts. He's always had boats. That was one of the reasons people said it would be easy for him to take a body out to sea."

"Um. Looks like I had a narrow escape. Not the sort of people you want to be mixed up with."

"Well – if it's true. Who knows?" He stood up, his inherent docility making him reluctant to be the one to end the conversation. Prior took his cue.

"Right – I'll let you get back to work. Thanks again for everything – the money and putting me in the picture. Don't worry, this conversation never took place – you can trust me." Trevor saw him to the edge of his land and they shook hands.

"We'll have to meet up again to talk business. You can drop by any time. I could certainly give you some orders." Prior gave a half-hearted assent and turned and walked away, noticing a downturn in his mood at a sudden appreciation of the isolation and inertia that stretched before him. All avenues to a network of socialisation and activity seemed closed and with a bitter realism he saw no alternative to giving himself up sooner rather than later.

***

How solitary he had become was emphasised by the fact that he saw no-one for the remainder of the week. He continued with his new abstemiousness, delaying the gratification of alcohol until Saturday, and he began to value a routine that split his time between the beach and reading the bible. He derived an unexpected comfort from the simplicity of his life and the rationing of sensual input, and he decided to postpone the decision on when to surrender his freedom. That some of the sense of calm came from his recently discovered fatalism was not in doubt. Neither was the fact that his reduced alcohol intake was anything other than a positive influence. It was however, the age-old text that was most instrumental in providing him with that sense of proportion that led to the possibility of an inner peace. He struggled with the meaning at times and shrank from a wrathful God who opened his eyes to a lifetime of previously unacknowledged misdemeanours. He was also surprised by the number of everyday phrases that he now realised had their origin in the bible. At lunchtime on Saturday he finished reading Proverbs and closed the book and set off for the beach, mulling over its words as he squinted at the sun, shuddering with mild pleasure at the sneeze that was less fulfilling but a good deal less hazardous than its older brother.

The breeze was strong that July afternoon and the sun unusually subdued, hiding behind grey clouds spread thinly across most of the sky. The waves were larger and more powerful than normal and Prior played childishly in the water, teasing himself with fear by standing only fractionally inside the safe zone from where he could plunge through the wave just before it gathered him in its fury and crashed him against the sea bed like a garment in a washing machine. Sometimes he rode the waves, catching them at the crest and being propelled at great speed towards the shore before feeling the brake of the sand on his chest and stomach and thighs, the force strong enough to skew him sideways and then onto his back. Driven by a kind of risk compulsion he increased the stakes, moving further along the beach in an eastward direction to where the sea carried the threat of real danger of serious harm both in its increasing ferocity and its outgoing pull. His apprehension was heightened by his detachment from the rest of humanity. To his right he could see no-one and to his left the beach-dwellers were remote and alien in their immunity from the unorthodox. He dived through wave after wave in an ecstasy of panic and then relief, having to muster all his strength to haul himself back again to be in front of where they broke, the time between his return and the crash of the next precariously short.

Finally, his luck ran out. Short of breath and with his muscles drained, he turned and stood to face a twelve foot wall of water, foaming at its crest with the saliva of a thousand dogs in anticipation of their prey. Above it, the treacherous sun had broken through to radiate his split second of terror. Just too far away for the plunge to safety, the next moments passed in a vortex of helplessness, the instinctive hands that protected the precious brain his only defence against the savagery of the wave. He was tumbled and pounded at tumultuous speed before being dumped contemptuously on the shore to take an inventory of the damage as the spent brute ebbed back to re-join its forces for the next attack.

His first thought was that at least he was conscious and his first action was to roll away a few turns from the sea towards the shore. An intuitive appreciation of the absurdity to an onlooker of his lying parallel to the ocean in wet sand occasioned a reflex bow to convention and he dragged himself to the dry ground beyond and sat facing the horizon like an animal licking its wounds. His left shoulder and hip ached and the whole of that side of his body was grazed and bleeding from the friction contact with the sand. The salt water was stinging and increasing the pain. He felt liquid running down the right side of his face and the blood on the hand he raised to touch it confirmed a gash to his upper cheek. Other than that he seemed to be okay and with a predominant emotion of relief he stood up and walked slowly back to his towel. He dried gingerly, patting at the traumatised skin before pulling on his shirt and shorts. Feeling rather ridiculous, he left immediately to forestall any potential concern from a passing tourist. He doubted the need to worry about that, having grown used to the studied disregard for a male on their own, but he knew from ironic experience that attention was rarely offered when sought, only when unwelcome. He took a detour past the pharmacy on the way home to buy some antiseptic cream and powders and some dressings and fell through the door to his apartment in late afternoon, not knowing that trial and adversity were about to develop into a night that he would ultimately look back on as perhaps the happiest and most rewarding of his life.

***

He took a long luxurious shower, the grey skies and self-nurturing instinct causing him to take the unprecedented step of turning the dial towards the red mark and feeling for the first time in six months the hot water splashing over his skin. When he finally dragged himself away, the clean sweat stung him again and he dried and sprinkled on the pleasantly scented antiseptic powder. The gash below his right eye which must have been caused by contact with a small rock was deep and about five centimetres long and he smeared it with antiseptic cream and applied gauze dressing, which he fixed on both sides with tape. The fact that it was Saturday night added to the authenticity of an empathic commune with the countless gladiators of contact sports around the world parading their injuries like trophies of war, and he glanced in the mirror at his bruised shoulder and hip with a coy pride. The fact that he was not in any great pain and had a gut feeling that he would heal naturally further induced a satisfying sense of bloodied exhaustion. He bought some cold beer and a bottle of grogue from the corner store and then put on one of the compilation CDs that he never tired of and made up a plate of cold fish mayonnaise and salad for later. He took a bottle of beer to the veranda and enjoyed his first sip of alcohol since he had entertained Father de Freitas six days ago. It was only 5:45 but he would drink slowly and retire early to ensure he would be in a fit state to attend Mass at eleven the next morning. He had deliberately designated Saturday as his drinking night because of this intrinsic curb to excess.

As he sat enjoying the sensory osmosis of nicotine, alcohol and melody he reappraised his situation. There was a newfound confidence in his insight. He had somehow won some unconscious battle within and had gained a self-awareness that acknowledged the existence of an illness. He looked ruefully at the bottle in his hand and knew he needed to keep his friends close but his enemies even closer. His judgement was chronically fragile – today had shown that. His capacity for euphoria went beyond normal bounds – the feeling that was developing now told him that – and he knew he would need medication at times in the future to balance and restrain the recalcitrant brain chemicals. He considered again the conundrum of whether to stay or go. As in the way of hypothetical budgets, his endless jottings and calculations and projections had proved depressingly over-optimistic and the reality was that he could probably survive for about six more months without the unpredictable expenses that he had to accept were more or less inevitable. He had hopefully diminished the loose cannons of mania and alcoholism but nevertheless, the only certainty was uncertainty. His heart urged him to remain, to take his reward before he took his punishment. To savour and build on his changed values and pleasures. His head warned him that to postpone the surrender would only heighten the intensity of its anguish. It wasn't like old age where perhaps God increases the discomfort to soften the departure. He got another beer and was reminded to take out two bread rolls from the freezer compartment of the fridge to go with the meal. They would thaw in an hour. He wouldn't allow indecision to spoil his contented mood and he procrastinated, telling himself that there was no hurry. He changed the CD and put his lamps on as the lengthening shadows outside prefaced the onset of dusk, and then leant over the veranda wall to take in a little of the ambience of the neighbourhood while there was some daylight left.

He had to confess that the people remained an enigma to him, even after six months. Very few spoke any English and his own Creole had stuck in first gear. He was surprised at how unfazed they appeared to be by the presence of a lone, unexplained Caucasian male in their midst. Even in the shop he frequented almost daily he was treated with a cool indifference, the transactions cursory and mercenary, and he divined no hint of a sense of good fortune at the existence of a very profitable source of regular business on their doorstep. He had to accept most of the blame for this. He had a phobia of small talk and without any obligation whatsoever in this direction given the limitations of language, he knew he must appear dour and unapproachable. He allowed that the kindness and generosity of spirit so apparent in Dominique were traits that sprung from this nurturing environment where he had so incongruously come to rest. Continuing with this theme of benignity, not fuelled for once entirely by alcohol, he saw not the half-finished, seemingly abandoned buildings, or the copulating dogs, or the dead cats, or unfathomable countenances of a previous sensibility. Instead he noticed the universal inflection of innocence in the voices of the children, the mutual trust and affection between them and the dogs, the sense that despite the poverty and shabbiness, the children were loved and valued, and above all, safe in a world where happiness was more a preferred option than a right.

He was about to fetch another beer but in turning he saw something in the distance out of the corner of his eye. Walking in his direction along the main road were two figures that inexplicably drew his gaze. As they came closer he saw that they were both female, one tall, dark, and slender, the other a little shorter – white and of early middle age. He stood transfixed, his heart rate rising – at first slowly, and then starting to race and pound the nearer they got. The taller woman was undoubtedly Dominique, the languid, effortless grace of her movement now so well known to him. The gait of the other was also strangely familiar but it was only when they were about twenty-five metres away that he gave out an involuntary cry of disbelief and incomprehension as he saw that it was Caroline.

They both looked up at his exclamation and he watched Dominique touch her arm and hasten away, her job done and not wishing in her innate diplomacy to intrude on a potential scene of such intimacy. Caroline held out an arm in impotent protest at her haste and then turned her eyes back to the veranda, now empty. In an instant the front door was open but they stood apart for a moment, separated by the three steps, both paralysed by shock of different hues. The clinch when it came was synchronous and they clung to each other under the harsh porch light, the tears rolling down their cheeks and soaking the dressing on Prior's incredulous, ecstatic face.

***

They sat alongside each other on the sofa bed with Caroline's glass of grogue on the table in front of her. She hated beer and Prior had nothing else. This was one occasion when she felt the need to fortify herself against the unknown. Perhaps because they knew there was so much to say they said nothing for a while, delaying the sumptuous moment of enlightenment, filling the chasm with smiles and platonic touch while she cast an investigative eye over his surroundings and he savoured the delicious moments of uncertainty like a child on Christmas day, reluctant to finally unclothe the long awaited gift for fear of disappointment. At last she said, "Oh Robert. I suppose it wouldn't be you if there wasn't something unusual. What on earth have you done to your face?" The eye above the cut had now turned almost black; he had forgotten all about it.

"Swimming accident this afternoon. Nothing serious. How did you find me?"

She raised her eyes to the ceiling. "With great difficulty. I've been here since yesterday."

"Where are you staying?"

She looked round the flat again and said a little guiltily, "The Rui.

My flight arrived in the afternoon and I was tired so I didn't do much. Just settled in. Today I must have walked about ten miles. I've been to all the hotels, property agents, bars. I showed them your photograph but no-one had seen or heard of you. As a last resort I went to the police station this afternoon and apparently you had a night in custody there, surprise, surprise. They said you were of no fixed abode but remembered that a girl called Dominique had visited you and one of the policemen took me to her home. She wasn't there but her sister took me to the little hotel where she works – must have been the only one I missed – and of course she recognised your picture. She was very protective, I must say. I had to almost plead with her to let me know where you live. I met her when she finished work and she brought me here. Isn't she a bit young, Robert?" He thought he detected a hint of churlishness beneath her habitual irony.

"Oh for goodness' sake Caroline – nothing like that. That's the first place I stayed in after I arrived. She's just been doing my washing that's all." Caroline was defensive.

"I wasn't suggesting... anyway – forget it. I've more important things to talk about." She looked intently at him and allowed a slow smile to spread across her face. As donor of the gift she had longed for this moment even more than the recipient and she was now somehow loath to relinquish its custodianship. In a deliberately quiet voice she said, "They've caught the man who raped Naomi."

Prior said nothing at first. He had often shared the fantasies of those who did the lottery although he didn't do it himself. He supposed the opportunity for idle reverie was a fair return for the stake but that was all it bought. This was immeasurably better but all he felt initially was the stupefaction of shock. Gradually the thoughts seeped in and then they came in a rush, crowding in on a brain not equipped to cope with the glut of implications for his life ahead all at once. Action being so much more eloquent than words on these rare human occasions, they held each other tightly again and wept with the relief of validation and vindication. When curiosity caught up with and overtook emotion he said, also quietly, "What happened, Caroline?" She took a deep breath.

"They arrested someone for another rape two weeks ago. The victim was a woman from the same area. He was actually caught running from the scene by some passers-by. If that wasn't enough they got DNA as well. He was wearing a condom but they got it through his skin under her nails, and blood – she'd managed to scratch him. It was open and shut. He had to admit it and then he confessed to two other rapes, including Naomi. Didn't you hear anything?"

"I've not heard the news or seen a paper or been near a computer since I got here."

"It put us in the quandary of how to tell you. We thought you might hear and contact us but when we heard nothing Doug suggested we come to you. The trouble was you were so well hidden." They talked some more about the case – the man was on remand and would be pleading guilty to three rapes and the police had closed their enquiries again. They had been planning to proceed to his trial in his absence but obviously wouldn't be now. Doug had done some research and it appeared that Prior's section 35 Remand for Assessment was now immaterial and would be quashed and he was free from outside restraint. He told her in detail of his time in Cape Verde including the humiliating saga of his involvement with Zina and she interrupted him. "I think I went in that property agency. What does she look like?"

Prior tried to give an impression but how could he possibly convey in words the charismatic allure of such a woman?

"Yes, I think she came over. There were about five of them gathered round the photo. No-one said they knew you." Prior sighed.

"You don't surprise me." He refilled her glass and she laughed in that familiar way.

"It's not bad, this. I could get quite used to it." He completed the account of his stay up to the present moment and they sat in silence for a while, assimilating the narrative in their own ways from a retrospective viewpoint. Eventually she turned to him and said, "I've got something else to tell you. We are now grandparents!" He felt a sting. It emphasised his estrangement.

"Who?"

"Laura. We have a little grandson, Tommy. He's six weeks old. He looks like you, poor little mite."

Prior gazed into space with a faraway look and then said,

"Grandchildren are the crown of the aged."

"Sorry?"

"The Old Testament. A line from Proverbs. I've been reading the bible." Caroline couldn't restrain an uncertain smile. She didn't know if he was joking.

"Really?" His face remained straight.

"Yes, really. I've changed a lot, Caroline." She felt a bit uncomfortable and erased the smile.

"Well good, fine. Just be patient with me Robert – it'll take a bit of getting used to that's all; you and religion have hardly gone together in the same breath you have to admit. Anyway, what's this about 'aged'? We're only forty-four for heaven's sake."

He smiled.

"So how long are you staying?" She looked non-committal.

"I don't know. I've only got a one-way ticket. I don't know how often the flights are to the U.K. What about you?" He looked pensive.

"I don't know either. This is such a bolt from the blue. I'll give it some thought. Not tonight though." He remembered he hadn't eaten and broached the subject of food. She admitted she was hungry and they shared the meal he had prepared. They sat at his dining table and the conversation was fluid and easy as she told him about the children, what had been happening in the world, her contact with Charlie, and they took their coffees out to the veranda along with the brandy he remembered was left from the priest's visit. He filled their glasses and they sat saying nothing, allowing their respective thoughts to settle as they stared up at the sky. He turned his eyes away and looked sideways as if seeing her for the first time. She looked beautiful in the light of the waxing moon. The hair was black and glossy; dead straight and longer than he was used to seeing it. Her aquiline features with the slender, down-turned nose in profile were augmented by the brown, or was it aubergine lipstick she had just refreshed, giving her a slightly vampish look.

He took her hand in his and she didn't resist. She broke the silence and said hesitantly, "How's your mental health been?" He let out an involuntary noise somewhere between a sigh and a tut.

"Oh Caroline, do we have to?" He caught her uneasiness and wanted nothing to spoil the night so he said quickly, "No, of course you have a right to know. Sorry. Up and down, peaks and troughs. That's the nature of it. The important thing is that I've acknowledged it and I'm learning to understand it and that's half the battle. I just didn't want to talk about it now but let's get it out of the way. I know that I no longer have to fight it alone." He looked up pointedly and continued, "Considering I've had no medication for six months I think I'm very lucky. I'm still here aren't I?"

"Yes, and looking very well I must say." She immediately looked embarrassed at an emphasis she had had not consciously intended and released his hand, ostensibly to brush some non-existent fluff from the too-short skirt before saying hurriedly, "Your paper's been full of the story. I'm sure you could get your job back; they sound very sympathetic towards you." It seemed like another world she was talking about. He felt a rush of anxiety and then wondered if he could ever get seriously wound up enough to write about something as trivial as sport again.

"There's a lot of thinking to do. The money I owe you is another thing. Don't worry – that's my first priority."

"Well you know it's not ours." That plural again. He knew his resentment was unreasonable but he couldn't help it. She realised that she was getting a little drunk – the sparse meal had not been enough to dampen the effect of the grogue and the brandy to any degree and she knew it was time to go.

"I should be getting off now, Robert. It's been a long day." He felt a twinge of disappointment.

"Already? Stay a bit longer – one for the road at least." He continued, trying to keep the tone light, "Stay the night, why not?" She looked curiously shy like the girl of twenty-six years ago.

"No – I don't think so. I'd better just go and I'll see you tomorrow."

"You can have my bed – I'll sleep on the sofa bed. We won't get a taxi now at this end of town."

"Well I'll walk. It's only about four kilometres. It'd be nice in the moonlight along the beach." He looked resigned.

"Okay, but I think you're mad. I'll walk you back." She began to protest half-heartedly in deference to protocol but he stopped her abruptly. They both knew her walking alone in an unfamiliar country, late at night and tipsy, was not an option.

With the battle won she perversely began to have second thoughts, but she resisted them and they set off together past the neighbouring houses, randomly lit and mysteriously inhabited by people of whom Prior knew virtually nothing, rendering him unable to answer any of her pertinent anthropological enquiries. He realised his reticent grunts could be mistaken for ill temper, a sulk in response to a rejection, so he said to allay the suspicion, "I've just lived in isolation, Caroline, like you advised – accepting those who came to me but not reaching out to anyone. Apart from Zina, I suppose. I've not exactly been on a sight-seeing holiday."

They walked to the edge of the town and turned right at the Pirata nightclub towards the beach. They took off their shoes and Prior rolled up his trousers and took her hand again as they walked close to the sea, water washing over their feet as they squelched through the engorged sand.

They parted at the gates of the hotel – one with reluctance, the other relief. He looked enviously at the front of the hotel with its elegant swing doors and carpeted interior and imagined the soft muzak and unremarkable murals adorning the massive walls, reassuringly bland in their artistic antithesis – a comforting homage to monied ignorance. He put a hand on her shoulder and said, "Thanks for having faith in me. Without it I most definitely wouldn't be here tonight. I couldn't have handled a forensic hospital."

She looked away and then back at him, choosing her words carefully.

"Thank you for being honest. Of course I didn't think you could have done such a thing but I couldn't be one hundred per cent – no-one could. Please don't take offence Robert. That tiny doubt has put me through hell; and Doug of course."

"No offence taken – only real gratitude, Caroline – to you and him. Anyway, what about tomorrow?"

"I've got a feeling I'm going to sleep all morning. Then have some lunch and go to the beach. What about you having dinner with me here and then we could see the hotel entertainment or something? I really don't feel very adventurous."

"Sounds okay. I might join you on the beach." They arranged a rendezvous and time and agreed that if he didn't make the beach they would meet in reception at seven.

They kissed fleetingly on the lips and he loitered behind the gates watching her approach the spectacular citadel, still his lawful wedded wife in the eyes of God. He stood in a state of trance, picturing her collecting the room key from the dimly lit reception desk and then washing away the grime of the day before supplementing his paltry meal with room service and slipping between the clean, starched sheets in the air conditioned room, saving herself for the indomitable Doug. He shook himself metaphorically. He kept forgetting his cause for jubilation, locked as he was into a ritual of negative thought that was hard to break such had been its longevity. With the alcohol and exhilaration wearing off he became more aware of the injuries of the previous afternoon – it was now after midnight – and was tired and aching when he finally got in. He pulled off his clothes and shoes and changed into boxer shorts and stood again on the magnetic crow's nest of a veranda with a brandy and his last cigarette, looking out into the black of the night at nothing in particular, his horizons limitless once again.

CHAPTER 25

Prior sat in the corner of the back room of a cyber café in Santa Maria looking at the internet page in front of him. The room resembled an aquarium, with its doors tightly closed, and around him the walls and ceilings were of toughened glass. Above and below and to all four sides the room was enclosed by water, through which floated not fish, but people. He read from the text on the screen, 'The new ice age continues to take its inexorable grip on the countries of Northern Europe and North America. The sea-ice concentration of the North Atlantic is approaching seventy per cent and icebergs are presenting major obstacles to shipping. Energy stocks are dangerously low and the death rate, particularly among the elderly, is reaching epidemic levels.'

He was suddenly distracted by two of the ephemeral forms and he looked upwards to see the bodies of Zina and Ramon float by, naked and entwined like the figures in a Klimt painting, their bloodless lips poised for conjunction, their eyes stark and staring. He turned back to the screen and saw another article. 'Cape Verde, an archipelago off the West Coast of Africa, has now officially overtaken China as the country with the highest gross domestic product per capita. This is exclusively due to the huge demand for salt in the West in view of the new ice age and the regeneration of the abundant salt lakes occurring naturally on the islands. It has also attracted worldwide admiration and envy for its unprecedented harnessing of wind power which now accounts for ninety per cent of its energy source and has helped drive the massive desalination projects which have turned the barren scrubland of some of the islands into verdant pastures of horticultural wonder.'

With a sharp sadness, he saw a young woman float past clutching an infant to her breast, her matted hair draped over its tiny body, and behind them came Caroline and Doug, large and shark like, drifting towards him and pressing their doleful faces against the glass. A new page had appeared when he looked away from their plaintive, disturbing eyes.

'The twenty-first century success story that is Cape Verde has been plunged into tragedy by the effects of a volcanogenic mega-tsunami. The underwater explosion close to its shores which triggered the disaster is yet another example of the volatile and changing ecology of the world as we approach the second century of the third millennium. President Gomez, who has declared a state of emergency, said, "I ask my people for the calmness and fortitude that has so characterised our struggle over the many years of our history as we set about the rebuilding of our nation. The death toll is rising and includes a high proportion of Western tourists and affluent residents and employees of prosperous property businesses in frontline locations. It appears that loss of life in the indigenous population has been mercifully insubstantial."'

A door suddenly opened and he felt himself being sucked from the room and transported rapidly towards the surface which he broke with a splash, spinning three hundred and sixty degrees to survey the aquamarine sea around him beneath azure, cloudless skies, the white sand of the beach ahead fringing the lush green grass and spectacularly colourful flowers behind. On the horizon he discerned the outline of a ship travelling due north and he began swimming desperately towards it in vain, hopeless pursuit, the thrashing arms unable to afford even the pace of a snail and then he stopped and lay on his back in mute submission, his bewildered eyes blinded by the harsh rays of a merciless sun.

***

They met in reception and went straight through to the restaurant, sipping their drinks while they waited for the food. It wasn't Saturday but Prior had ordered a large gin and tonic and a bottle of wine with the meal. He felt he could relax his self-imposed regime in the light of the exceptional circumstances. He said, "What happened to you then?"

"I'm sorry?"

"I went to the beach. Couldn't find you anywhere."

"Oh sorry – I didn't go after all. Had a look round the shops instead." He felt drained, emotionally and physically, and surprisingly devoid of conversation. Caroline looked tired and her nose and cheeks were sunburnt.

"Everything alright?" He was reminded of the irritation he had always felt at that remark in its implicit entreaty to an unfelt bonhomie. It usually meant that *she* was not alright and had often been the precursor to a row.

"Yeah. Just feel a bit anticlimactic I suppose; and I didn't sleep well last night. Weird dreams."

"Mm. It's funny how the mind works. I don't think we possess the capacity to go from abject misery to unbridled joy just like that, whatever the changed circumstances. Give it a bit of time."

"I've been thinking a lot today. If I go back to say eighteen months ago, I was in a much better position than I am now even given what's happened. I had a great job, plenty of money, my mental health. I know I should be happy at the relative improvement but all I feel today is angry. I didn't even feel like going to church. Not in the right frame of mind." She inadvertently raised her eyebrows.

"Well just feel what you feel. It must be part of some natural healing process. I've booked my flight by the way." He looked surprised.

"Oh right. When is it?"

"Tuesday morning – day after tomorrow." He experienced an irrational sense of betrayal but said nothing. Their food arrived and he asked the waiter to bring another gin and tonic, pouring himself a glass of wine to fill the gap before its arrival.

"Why so soon?"

"I've got to go back to work for one thing – don't want to use up all my leave; and Laura needs me."

"And I don't?" She put down her knife and fork and gave him the look that told him the gloves were off.

"Oh for God's sake stop being so pathetic, Robert. You know we're history. Don't you think we've done enough?" She was close to tears.

The anger rose in him and he drained his glass of wine as the waiter set down his fresh G and T. He said nothing, squirming internally in shame at the petulant demon driving his unwarranted pique. He got up and said, "I'm going to the loo," and he walked outside to the front of the hotel and lit a cigarette. He half expected her not to be there when he returned but she was, and he felt an agonised compassion as he watched her across the room, picking demurely at her food and trying to act as if nothing had happened; drawn to this alien place by his wild indiscretion. He sat down and said simply, "I'm sorry. Very sorry." She said nothing and carried on eating, not looking at him. His appetite had gone and he pushed the food to the side of the plate and straightened the knife and fork.

"Looks like you've taken the brunt of all my built-up sense of injustice. Please just forget it Caroline – I'm not myself." She finished her mouthful and looked up at him.

"Well that's where you're wrong. You are being yourself, Robert. Self-centred. The whole world revolves around Robert Prior." He felt the ire rise again, coupled with an incomprehension at the way the conversation was going. If the world was a stage then this part of the script was badly misjudged. He found it inconceivable that he was being forced to defend himself on this of all nights. The lowered forehead and raised upper cheeks squeezed his eyes into exasperation and the open mouth reflected his incredulity. She had seen that look so many times before but its sting was long spent.

"Oh. And you're not." He leant towards her and looked around the room. "All these people here, bestowed with selfless altruism. Not a thought for themselves even though they're locked into their minds and bodies until the end, unable to escape for even a split second from who they are. Who the hell isn't self-centred?" His anguished look bore the frustration he felt at the inadequacy of the words to fully express his anger.

"Don't be sarcastic. I'm talking relatively." Her face softened and her voice was sad rather than angry.

"You take, Robert. You see other people, particularly women, as a resource for your vanity and your gratification without giving anything back. Then you wonder why your life has become so loveless, so disastrous. You can't blame everything on the illness. I don't know what you've been doing since you left us – it's not my business but I don't suppose it's involved much in the way of normal reciprocal involvement." She was employing a woman's trick of using a supposition to draw out more information from a defensive male than he might normally give in his reticence to discuss affairs of the heart. "And you put that above your own flesh and blood. I know you tried a bit at first but it didn't last long."

He was becoming inured now and resigned to the inevitability of the exchange seeing out its unhappy course. He supposed the freeing of his chains had now given her licence to give vent to her real feelings. "I'm not having that. I went through hell and you know it. In the end I just thought it was doing them more harm than good and they needed some stability. I could see how much they liked Doug."

"You didn't know how lucky you were. I could have been one of those bitter women who use the children to punish their partner but you know I would never do that – I love them too much. Whatever your twisted logic, you were wrong to stop trying. Graham in particular has never forgiven you and Laura has internalised it, but she's still heartbroken. Maybe Helen got off the lightest because she's the youngest and wasn't so aware of what was happening."

The waiter cleared the plates and they declined pudding but ordered coffee and cognac which they took onto the hotel terrace. They sat down in the comfortable armchairs, the moonlight shining on the swimming pool ahead where some laughing, shouting people swam. When they were settled he said, "You know your trouble Caroline – you're part of that army of invulnerable middle-class English smugness. The county set. You can afford to be beneficent, to cast your pearls before swine because you're untouchable. 'I was hungry and it was your world.'" He despised the unreasonable, scatter-gun spite, his only defence being that he was deliberately shifting from wronged to wrongdoer to regain some compassion for her.

She said levelly, "You really *are* pathetic – still the immature, 'angry young man'. You can't hurt me any more Robert." Others were filtering out onto the terrace; contented, relaxed holidaymakers in their apparent cocoons of healthy conventionality far removed from the unhappy little historical drama being played out in their midst.

"I don't want to – I never did. You asked me what I did after we broke up. You were close. For a long time I eschewed emotional commitment, yes. Who could blame me? But I was a relatively young man. I had my needs, I was well off so you can imagine the rest. In the few months before my arrest a kind of sea change was developing. Perhaps I was finally getting over you. I met a girl in Spain and I wanted to take it further than a one-night stand. And I saw Naomi as being more than that I think. In a funny sort of way the shift of perspective seems to have precipitated my breakdown."

They sat for ten minutes without speaking, listening to the low bass notes and drum rattles as the band warmed up in an adjacent room. Prior ordered more coffee and cognac and gradually the optimism of yesterday began to permeate the unexpected acrimony.

"I know we are as you say, 'history'. That doesn't negate what we had. We don't have to be enemies do we? Just disparate." She sighed.

"Of course we're not enemies. Disparate? You mean you went for the glamorous job and the recognition and the high-class call girls and I brought up our family and then built a career for myself from scratch and found a safe, dull man to protect it all from collapsing? Yes, I suppose that's disparate." He frowned in discomfort at the tenacity of her contempt for him. She in turn suddenly looked guilty and said hastily, "I take that back about Doug – he's a good, kind person. I didn't mean it. It's just that whatever they might say in that middle-class, right-wing, gutter tabloid that pays you all that money, even by the late nineties a single mother wasn't such a good thing to be."

He winced inwardly at her reclamation of the higher ground, a little cowed by a strength of feeling he hadn't seen before. It was particularly disquieting that in this unfamiliar land, amongst strangers, his biggest threat seemed to come from someone he had at one time felt joined to at the hip.

"I didn't have you down as one of the sisterhood; but then there's obviously a lot I don't know about you." She gave a rueful smile.

"What? Just because I said single mother you automatically assumed I'm a feminist? I'm not as extreme as some of those columnists in *your* profession who slag off fifty per cent of humanity as if they're representing the views of all women, no. But the tide had to turn. You and your sort were the tail end of untold generations of men who'd had it all their own way since time immemorial."

"My sort?" He sounded deliberately incredulous.

"I feel sorry for you and your generation in a way, Robert – carrying the can for all those years of injustice. You didn't know any better, I suppose. Your father never washed a cup or ironed a shirt in his life."

"No, but he brought in good money. Mum never had to work. One wasn't superior to the other – men and women just had different roles suited to their biological differences. Don't tell me he was the boss – she never stopped nagging him. In fact she literally nagged him to bloody death. You lot are always on about control. Controlling men. Women have always controlled men with their nagging." It was her turn to express disbelief.

"You lot?" Didn't you ever realise how unhappy your mother was? She was a very intelligent person. Do you really think that was the sum total of her ambition – waiting on three men all her life?" Their voices had become raised and others were casting surreptitious glances in their direction and they both looked slightly sheepish.

Prior said quietly, spurred by a conciliatory pressure, "Look, I accept a lot of what feminists say. It's just that I've noticed how anomalous they can be. The feminist in them wants us up to our elbows in nappies and dishwater and ironing and then the woman in them sneers at us for our emasculation. It's very confusing, I can tell you."

"Oh poor you. So we go to work and then come home and do all the housework and get the kids to bed so you can feel like a man. Listen Robert, I don't think I want to talk about this anymore. Or anything else for that matter." She gathered up her handbag and stood up, looking down at his bemused expression. With a seemingly momentous effort she managed to mutter, "Give me a ring sometime when you get home if you want," and then turned and walked quickly towards the lift, Prior's eyes following her like those of a doleful puppy being left at the kennels by its retreating owner. Or was there the bloodlust of the aroused pit bull in those same eyes? It very much depended on which side of the fence one sat.

***

She got up early the next morning and after breakfast walked into the town. A minicab drove slowly by and she raised a hand to the driver, who stopped, and she clambered aboard with a cursory greeting. She was only the second passenger and a wait began to see how quickly the transport filled up. The driver would not leave until at least eight of the ten seats were occupied. She was in no hurry and she watched with interest as an assortment of people gradually joined the bus and the driver pulled slowly away, trawling the town for two stragglers to make up a full complement and earn him one thousand escudos – one hundred for each passenger on the twelve kilometre trip to the neighbouring town of Espargos. He hooted his horn and looked enquiringly at every pedestrian he saw, filling the ninth place before cutting his losses and hastening away to join the highway which cut a swathe through the tall black mountains en route to their destination. They were flagged down just past the airport by a large woman who squeezed into the last seat, the driver's phlegmatic countenance unaffected by this minor triumph of full occupancy. She could have paid ten euros for the convenience of a taxi but was pleased to have experienced a small fragment of local life. She got out and began walking along the Rua 5 Julho, stopping at the first café she came to where she bought a coffee, taking it out to a roadside table.

She skimmed through her travel guide, learning that the town took its name from the wild yellow-flowered, red-berried asparagus bushes said to grow on sandy parts of the island. She was glad to be away from the bustle and the cloying touristy nature of Santa Maria, alone and undisturbed with her thoughts and reflections on the previous evening. She spent the rest of the morning strolling around the town with its limited shops, buying some CDs of local musicians as presents for Doug and the children to add to the duty free stuff she would get them at the airport or on the plane. She had belatedly remembered to slap some sun cream on her angry and complaining face and as it turned midday and the heat intensified she found a restaurant and ordered a fresh tuna salad before going out in search of a minicab to take her back to Santa Maria. She was soon in luck as the last passenger needed to make up a full load.

She spent the afternoon on the beach and then packing before a quiet night in the hotel, transfixed by the music on offer, the lifeblood of the island. From the mouth of a leathery old man came a mournful, soulful apogee sound augmented by the guitars and drums played with a technical proficiency behind him. She jotted down the group's name and made a mental note to look for a copy of their CD at the airport tomorrow. The man figured unsettlingly in her dream of later that night, chasing her along the beach and into the sea before stalling at the water's edge and standing motionless as she swam frantically away towards the horizon, turning anxiously to see if he was following her. He wasn't, but he continued to stand, his blue dungarees having metamorphosed into a pink, strapless frock, the mouth smiling derisively below bloodshot eyes that cautioned her against a return.

***

She sat on the coach, watching it fill up as beneath her the reassuring thumps and vibrations told her the baggage was being loaded. She dreaded the next twelve hours and longed for that moment when she could open her front door and close another onerous little chapter. At the airport she detached herself from the teeming throng, jostling and angling to steal a march on each other. What was the point? she thought. *We'll all be leaving at the same time*, and she browsed idly in the shop, her spirits lifting at the sight of two CDs by last night's band. She agonised briefly over which to buy and then laughed at her stupidity and bought them both. As she left the shop she saw Prior standing with his back to her, looking at a notice board. She felt less angry now, softened by the resignedly fatalistic mood of the long-haul traveller. After the intensity of their last exchange he now carried the faint comicality of the unknowingly observed and she couldn't restrain a slight feeling of affection. She resisted a fleeting impulse to sidle past and move through undetected and walked towards him and tapped his shoulder. He turned round and they looked at each other for a moment.

"I'm glad you saw me, Caroline. I didn't want to leave it like that." She looked down a little shyly.

"No. Thanks for coming." She looked anxiously in the direction of the departure entrance and saw that she was the last one not to have gone through.

"We'll have to be quick, Robert. I haven't been through immigration or checked in yet."

He said, "Why, what did you have in mind?" and she joined in with his smile.

"Have you decided when you're coming back – or if?"

"Definitely coming back. Soon I think; in the next month anyway." She had a thought.

"Have you got the fare?" He did a quick calculation.

"Oh yes – just about."

"Good. Listen, I'll have to go. Let me know when you're home, Robert."

"I will. I've been thinking Caroline. Do you think I could see the children again? And my new grandson?"

"That's up to them. They're adults now. We'll talk about it in England." She moved her face towards his and they kissed, Caroline averting her lips as he placed his on her cheek. They hugged and it was with mutual reluctance that they relinquished their hold and she turned and walked away, pushing the trolley, her leather-soled shoes clicking like an old football rattle on the hard floor in the near empty hall.

***

Outside, Prior raised his face to the sun and closed his eyes against its glare before engaging a taxi to take him back to Santa Maria. His mood was bittersweet. After drinking on both Saturday and Sunday he had nipped in the bud the strong temptation of last night to nurture another habit and he felt the benefit in his clarity of mind and levels of energy. As he looked away to the east which held the saltpans of Pedra de Lume and Santa Maria further to the south, he experienced a conflicting pull as he imagined the aircraft behind him preparing to leave for an entirely different world of unlimited opportunity for both triumph and disaster. As he got into the car something told him that he was learning to set the boundaries; the tramlines within the chasm that could see him safely home.

CHAPTER 26

For the third day running he walked along the beach at the time she should be there. He knew he could be playing with fire but he had to see her one last time. Something made him reluctant to go to her workplace. Better, he thought, the impression of an impromptu meeting. His heartbeat quickened as he neared her usual haunt and he recognised almost instinctively the narrow silhouette lying on its back with one knee pointing to the sky. She didn't notice him until he was standing over her in his white swimming shorts, a towel around his neck and sunglasses pushed up onto his head, his left hand holding a pair of flip-flops. She shielded her eyes from the sun and stared at him blankly looking like she had just awoken from a deep sleep – her ivory cheek was scored with indentation marks from something she'd been lying on and her eyes were heavy and unresponsive. He gestured to the sand beside her.

"May I?" She turned her eyes away from him and gazed upwards.

"If you want." He sat down clumsily and looked out to sea saying nothing, absently observing the laboured attempts of a novice windsurfer to master the craft. Eventually he spoke.

"I'm going home soon. I'm off the hook. They've charged someone else with the rape."

She appeared indifferent, continuing to look at the sky as she said apathetically, "Congratulations."

"I just wanted to see you once more to ask you why. I know you don't need the money."

"How do you know that?"

Prior had wrestled with his conscience but curiosity had got the better of him. Nevertheless, he saw no way of her tracing the source of the information to Trevor. "I just know – it doesn't matter how. Like you've told me more than once, gossip travels quickly here."

She sat up slowly and he looked at her properly for the first time. She had a cold sore on her lip and her nose looked somehow different.

"What are they saying then?"

"That you own a big legal firm, live in a luxurious villa. Your job is just a pastime."

"Yeah, well I suppose that's common knowledge amongst my friends. Anything else?"

"No, just that." She looked fully awake now and her eyes bore into him.

"You sure?"

"Of course I'm sure. That's enough isn't it? You've bankrupted me just for the fun of it." She brushed some sand from the top of her thigh and he noticed the beginning of some cellulite.

"You remind me of someone."

"I'm sorry?"

"A long time ago." She rested back on her elbows and stared ahead with eyes that looked suddenly troubled and intense.

"I was brought up in a children's home. I never knew my dad and my mother was on heroin and on the game. Not the best role model. I was used almost nightly from the age of eight to fifteen. One of them looked like you. He was the best looking and he knew it. I was his favourite." Her voice was flat and emotionless, the starkness of the delivery making the words even more shocking.

"Oh God, Zina, I'm so sorry." She looked at him and smiled disdainfully.

"What are you sorry for? It wasn't you was it?"

"Of course it wasn't me. I'm just sorry it happened. I'm being sympathetic." She threw back her head and laughed.

"You're such an idiot." He waited for her to qualify the judgement but it seemed that was it. He squirmed in discomfort.

"Were you having me on? Is that what you mean?" She looked serious again.

"No I wasn't. It happened. You're an idiot because I've ripped you off and you go all bleeding heart over me." Despite the heat her nose was dripping and she wiped it with a tissue.

"I can separate two things. Well actually, I don't suppose you can separate them. I'm not surprised you wanted to hit back. But why me? Why not the ones who did it? They could still be prosecuted."

"I told people at the time it was happening. That just got you in more trouble. The establishment closes ranks, I can assure you. I don't want all the hassle of opening it up again now. Anyway, all men are the same, women are just meat. It sticks out like a sore thumb with you." He hung his head. He was not finding much rapport with the opposite sex at the moment. He didn't try to defend himself.

"But we're talking about children."

She appeared to be tiring of the subject and yawned and said, "I didn't get mad; I got even – in my own way. What about you – are you going to the police?" The contemptuous smile carried the threat of a dare he wouldn't win. It wasn't that though which swayed him. The sight of the damaged, personality-disordered woman in front of him was eclipsed by the image of the little girl, unloved and alone, sobbing herself to sleep with her childhood stolen.

"No. I've just cancelled the standing order." He smiled. "You could always give me the money back if it was playing on your conscience." She didn't reply or express any reaction and he changed the subject. He had the feeling that their game with him was passé. Perhaps they had their claws into fresh prey.

"How's my dear friend Ramon?"

"He's gone."

"For good?"

She shrugged disinterestedly. "Maybe. I don't really care."

"Where's he gone?"

She turned to him, finally irritated enough by his questioning to swat him away. She said, "Mind your own business," and lay down again, turning onto her side with her back to him.

He took his cue and stood up and said, "I'm going then, Zina," and he was surprised that she responded by sitting up again and looking at him. As she did so he noticed the development of a small paunch on the otherwise slender body. On the left side of her face sand had adhered to the factor 50 sun cream, giving her an uncharacteristically flawed look.

"You could always come and see my 'luxurious villa' if you wanted." He felt the instant stirring in his loins. She was the only woman he had known who could bring him to immediate arousal with just a look or a sentence. The gathering imperfections, the harbingers of a too-rapidly approaching middle age made her, if anything, more attractive in their underlining of a tangible humanity.

He thought for a long time, looking out at the inscrutable sea as an internal battle raged within him. At last he turned and said, "I don't think that would be such a good idea," and he began trudging slowly towards the pier, feeling already the beginning of the frustrated torment he knew awaited him and not trusting himself enough to look back at either her or the spiritual home he was saying goodbye to.

***

Twenty-four hours later he looked out of the window at the naked sun unadulterated by the clouds below. The aeroplane had just left Sal for the six-hour flight to Gatwick. He had arranged by email from a cyber café for Charlie to meet him and he felt a small thrill of excitement at the prospect of seeing his old friend again. As with the reverse journey of now distant memory, the only blot on the horizon of contentment was the incipient, escalating craving for nicotine.

He sipped from a plastic glass of Coke and mentally perused his last week on the island with a philosophical sadness at the inevitable conclusion, if not resolution, of unfinished chapters. He had closed his bank account, and after taking enough for his ticket and immediate expenses, had given the balance of about €4,000 to be shared between Dominique, Abdulai, and Beatrice. True to form, Dominique put up resistance, the grain of her work ethic or perhaps the comfort derived from the habit of obligation unsettled by such a relatively large sum. Abdulai's joy was heart-warming as was the reaction of the reserved Beatrice whose peck of gratitude on his cheek repaired a thousand wrongs. He wished there was more he could do to express his thanks and love, something more lasting, but he knew he only had recourse to the fleeting vehicle of money. At least his gift expressed the goodwill behind his impotence in righting the wrongs of hundreds of years.

He had sought out Father de Freitas on his last Sunday there. His faith had continued to grow as he read through the Gospels and beyond to the Acts and the Letters and he had attended Mass on each of the three Sundays since Caroline's departure. He was shown again into the room at the back of the church and as they clasped hands, Prior recalled the small thrill he had felt at the absence of discomfort during the prolonged eye contact. He told him the news with barely suppressed excitement, like a little boy telling his parents he had come top of the class. The priest had given an almost indiscernible shrug at the proof of his innocence and as Prior reflected on his initial disappointment, the small island becoming ever more remote behind him, he drew solace from knowing that the man would have still been there for him and others in the future, however the impostor decided to cast the dice. Father de Freitas made no allusion to it but Prior was aware that time was no less pressing than on the last occasion they had met here. He had thought long and hard about what he wished to say in his closing remarks but felt overcome with emotion as he looked down at this short stranger and he didn't trust his voice to chance. Instead he threw his arms around his neck and murmured, "Thanks for everything," before releasing himself in embarrassment at the unexpected intimacy.

The priest had put his hand on his shoulder and said, "Don't thank me," before reverting to his habit of using quotation to supplant pious platitude and substantiate his message. "'Father of all, we give you thanks and praise that when we were still far off you met us in your son and brought us home.'" The priest turned to pick up his holdall and said, "One thing to guard against now your circumstances have changed for the better – don't allow a creeping idea that you no longer have a need for Christ to develop. 'In future let no-one make trouble for me for I bear the marks of Jesus branded on my body.' God bless you, James."

Prior had started to correct him and give his real name but

stopped himself, not wishing to end on something so commonplace, and he left him and stood for a while in the now empty church, basking for the last time in its comforting aura of immunity, reluctant somehow to acknowledge the passing of the ardour of a new love and its shift to a more familial level.

PART 3

PASSION

CHAPTER 27

Charlie bore the brunt of Prior's relief and excitement but he was not complaining. It was good to see him again at last. He couldn't help turning a professional eye on his erstwhile patient as he kept up a non-stop, selective account of the last seven months, but he concluded the elation was a pretty understandable reaction in view of the content of his story and not indicative of an incongruous mood swing. Prior's senses and awareness were alive and he effortlessly took in the relative lushness of the August landscape and Charlie's much-improved appearance whilst he conjured up his recent memories. He had lost weight and the leaner face was happier. Prior surmised that the new job was long and arduous but the previous evidence of the battle with inconsistent managers and incompatible colleagues was no longer etched on his features.

He finished his narrative as they left the M25 and approached the Dartford crossing, and Charlie's face took on an increased concentration as vehicles funnelled towards the entrance. As they left the bridge and vehicles now veered and jockeyed for position in the required lane, Prior felt butterflies in the pit of his stomach. The suspended reality of the preceding months was brought into sudden focus as they joined the A13 and drove west on the final leg of the journey. He was faced with choices again and thoughts of work, money, mental health services, family issues crowded in. He looked out of the window and the traffic was heavy. It was always heavy. It was raining; but then it always seemed to be raining. The faces were worried; preoccupied with concerns other than the present. He was going 'home' but it wasn't home. It was just a place where he happened to reside. Charlie came off the roundabout and turned onto the road leading to the suburb where Prior lived and said cheerfully, "Yes, I know what you're thinking – he's ripping me off this driver – would have been shorter to take the A20 and cross the river at Woolwich. Shorter but longer, believe me Rob." He glanced at Prior and was disconcerted by his blank stare ahead.

"You okay mate?"

Prior stirred, "Oh yeah, fine. I was miles away. Just can't believe I'm here. It's so different, Charlie. I mean everything's the exact opposite to where I've come from. No traffic, no rain, no vegetation, no money, no future – only the present and how to survive day to day. I got used to it though. The simplicity of everything. The beautiful beach. The lack of expectation. The blessed lack of communication. I think I'm going to miss it."

"Just take your time. You've been through a lot. You don't have to make any decisions straight away."

Prior looked thoughtful again and then said quietly, "No."

They left the A-road and meandered through the built-up housing estates before finally arriving at Prior's block of flats. Charlie turned off the engine and got out and lifted the suitcase from the boot and they stood in the light drizzle looking at each other.

"What's the damage driver?"

"On the house, Rob." They entered the familiar reverse barter which Charlie eventually won and he said, "Are you okay for money Robert?"

"Absolutely. I'll have to get in touch with the paper soon though. It won't last too long. Anyway, I'd ask you up for a coffee but it's probably solidified by now."

Charlie glanced at his watch. "No, I've got to be off anyway – another pick up in an hour. Can't afford to be late in *this* job."

He smiled and handed Prior his card. "We'll have to have a pint sometime. Just give me a ring. I try to take Sunday afternoon and Monday morning off." They shook hands and Charlie leapt up athletically into the driver's seat, watched admiringly by an impressed Prior. As he drove away he felt a return of the slight dejection he had experienced on their previous parting. He realised with a sudden twinge of guilt that he hadn't asked Charlie a single question about himself. Perhaps Caroline had been right after all.

***

He opened the front door with an air of trepidation but the first thing that struck him was how little had changed. While the mutable world raged around it and his own life plunged from one disaster to another, the flat remained inert. Apart from a faint gathering of dust and an unpleasant rotting smell from the kitchen, it was just as he had left it and, given his relative stability leading up to the shock of the arrest, it didn't look too bad. Certainly a big improvement on how he had found it after being discharged from hospital following the first manic episode. He felt reassured and his first act was to pull apart the curtains which had remained closed against that early morning in late December and let in the golden light of a late summer evening and then to open the windows to the sound of birds and children playing in the park. He went through to the kitchen and pulled the black refuse bag from the metallic pedal bin, averting his nose from the stench as he tied it, and then he found a clean one and filled it with the contents of a fridge that had hummed on for seven months in blissful ignorance of his trials and tribulations. He pruned the tins and bottles in the cupboards with an unexpected nostalgia at the memories revived by the expiry dates, before skipping down the stairs two at a time to put the bags in the wheelie bin in the yard outside. He made a slight detour to observe his car waiting obediently for its next assignment, undamaged and unchanged other than a slight bulging of the tyres from a lowering of the pressure.

He bounded back up the stairs feeling the benefit of the marathon walks and swims that had been so much a part of his recent life, and then converted his unlimited energy into a succession of tasks – unpacking, changing his bed, and cleaning through the flat before tackling the mountain of mail. He finished as dusk gathered and took a shower, admiring himself in the full length mirror as he dried, salivating at the prospect of the drinks awaiting him that he had cooled in the freezer. Tomorrow and beyond held a thousand daunting unknowns. There was however, nothing to do in what remained of this night other than to celebrate, give thanks, and take his reward.

***

Prior experienced the conditioned flutter of both excitement and slight apprehension as he passed the blue and white sign informing him that there were sixty-four miles to Manchester. It didn't seem long since he had left the toll road and now the North West was in touching distance. He had smiled to himself at the glamorised Americanised terms as he bypassed the Birmingham of Doodlie and Sooten Cauldfield – The Midland Expressway, The Toll Plaza. He kept at a steady eighty, staying mostly in the centre lane, occasionally venturing into the outside lane to overtake before returning to the middle ground. He felt calm and in control, his recent relapse behind him. He supposed it had been more or less inevitable.

His work situation had been impossibly complicated and had contributed to the triggers that had seen his mood fluctuate on an almost day-to-day basis before taking off into orbit at the conclusion of a satisfactory resolution. His contract had been terminated from the time of his absconding and an amount to the value of his notice period and outstanding leave pay deposited in his bank. The money had allowed him to support himself as he engaged Blake to fight for his legal reinstatement which was the eventual outcome, and he was awaiting a decision on his claim for loss of earnings for the period between the end of his notice and now. In the event, he had not returned to work yet and was currently on sick leave. As the north western towns and cities – Chester, Liverpool, Preston – became ever more evident on the signs, he blessed with hindsight the decision he had taken that day to phone Charlie.

It was a Sunday morning and he had not slept at all the previous night. They had arranged to meet for lunch at an equidistant hotel and Prior was on his third pint of lager by the time his friend arrived. Their interaction was lopsided – the one loud and indiscreet, the other embarrassed and preoccupied – and the next day Prior opened his door to two doctors and a social worker who was also an approved mental health practitioner as a police car sat ominously in the car park, its two officers awaiting a call to arms. They were not needed as some merciful spark of rationality had cautioned him to accept a voluntary admission. He knew he would end up in hospital one way or another and the alternative of a section 3 admission for treatment (they were going to use that in preference to a section 2 due to their previous knowledge of him) with its potential for the addition of the horrendous sounding Section 117 Aftercare and Community Treatment Order, dictated his decision. He had only spent two weeks in hospital and then been discharged on his previous prescription of lithium and aripiprazole. A home treatment team had monitored him for a further two weeks, supervising his compliance with the medication, and he was now back to where he was before the incident, thankfully without a community practitioner and the only obligation being three-monthly blood tests and annual appointments with the Consultant Psychiatrist. His antagonism towards Charlie in the immediate aftermath of his perceived treachery and betrayal quickly turned to gratitude as insight was restored, and they repaired the damage of the previous outing with another lunch. Prior seemed to finally accept Charlie's oft-repeated dictum to view his medication as liberator and not oppressor and he never missed a dose of the mood stabiliser, although he was selective in his use of the anti-psychotic. His greatest source of comfort was that on coming down from the recent manic episode, the rebound depressive episode was mild and short-lived.

He felt buoyed by a new optimism as he went through the gate of the small semi-detached house in a Cheshire suburb of Manchester, although his heart thumped and his hand trembled as he pressed the bell. The door opened and she stood there, cradling a baby in her left arm, her hip pushed out to support his tiny frame. It was ten years since he had last seen her. However they had each rehearsed this moment after the rather antiseptic email arrangements, the reality of the aching chasm induced a state of paralysis and they continued to stare, the infant Tommy's mouth pursed in a hoop of incomprehension, his eyes inquisitive, before a quiet belch and a dribble of milk broke his concentration.

"Hi Dad. Come in." Prior stepped into the house and put his arm on hers and moved his lips towards her face. She offered a fleeting cheek and moved quickly away from his touch and he followed her into the sitting room where they both sat down. He let out a sigh of anxiety, feeling excruciatingly awkward as she fussed over the baby and muttered nonsense to deflect her own disarray. As the parent he knew he should take the lead and be the one to shape the conversation, but he felt momentarily helpless and he looked around the room, taking in its ordered homeliness, as he tried to think of the right thing to say.

Before she felt compelled to take the initiative he said, "It's wonderful to see you again Laura. And little Tommy. I don't expect you to welcome me with open arms. I'm just so pleased you let me come." She chewed on her lower lip in a way that reminded him of her mother and was reluctant to make any eye contact, only glancing at him in a stiff-necked, birdlike fashion when he wasn't looking at her.

She stood up suddenly and said, "I'm just going to feed him in the dining room. I'll be back in a minute," and she left hurriedly, leaving Prior agonising over her gauche discomfort, his heart bleeding for his little girl clutching the all too tangible evidence of the irreversibility of time.

After a while she came back and he spoke brightly, feigning a naturalness he could not feel, "So you're breast feeding I take it?" She smiled and nodded. He could tell she had been crying.

"Mum breast fed all of you. Only seems like yesterday." Tommy sat on her knee with a hand clamped under his chin as she leant him forward and patted his back with her other hand. His closing eyes were focussed on his grandfather and Prior felt a small thrill of acceptance as the corners of his little mouth turned upwards in a smile. It didn't matter that it was only wind. Now he had broken the ice he had opened the possibility to genuine smiles of affection in the years to come. He just had to get it right today.

"Three months is he now?"

"And a bit. He was born on the second of May."

"Your mum thinks he looks like me. Can't say I can see it myself. I hope not for his sake." She smiled again.

"And his dad… I don't remember his…"

"Carl."

"Yes, Carl. You two okay?"

"Uh-huh." There was another silence. *This is hard work*, he thought to himself. They had been so close when she was small. How on earth did he know who she was now?

The arbitrary combination of her parents' genes had resulted in her not looking like either of them, although she had inherited his blue eyes and chestnut hair colour as well as his dark complexion. She was not beautiful but Prior could see a boy would find her attractive, with her curvaceous figure and full-lipped mouth. Tommy had slipped into a state of soporific bliss.

"It's time for his sleep now." Prior had wanted to hold him but didn't wish to disturb his contentment. He panicked slightly at the thought of conversation without the little focal point to dilute the tension and then found a solution.

"Why don't you put him in the pram and we can go for a walk?" That would remove the need for eye contact. She sounded relieved.

"Mm. Good idea. I'll get him ready." She said with a sudden afterthought, "Oh – I never offered you anything, a cup of tea or something. Did you…?"

"No, I'm fine – I had lunch on the way up. I don't drink tea much but perhaps a coffee when we get back." With the baby loaded into the pram they set off to the end of the road and turned left towards the limits of the small town and the countryside beyond. The first signs of the autumn that lay around the corner were there in the blackberries that dotted the hedgerows and the hint of a chill when the sun went behind a cloud, and Laura pulled the blanket up to the neck of the sleeping infant.

"How are Graham and Helen?" As expected, Laura was more confident and voluble alongside rather than opposite her father.

"They don't know I'm seeing you. Graham would go mad. Mum said not to tell Helen or she'd be bound to tell him. They're okay. Helen's sweating on her A Level results. They're due any day now. Graham starts his second year in uni next month."

"And you. Are you happy?"

"Oh yes. Definitely. I love being a mum. I haven't had any of that postnatal depression. Carl's got a good job so I don't have to rush back to work."

"Mum said you packed in your job when you went on maternity leave." She had been a supervisor in a ladies' clothes shop.

"Yeah – I didn't like it anyway. I can always get something else when I'm ready. How about you?"

"My job do you mean?" He didn't want to get into anything deeper so he said quickly, "Er – it's okay. Football season's just started. Here we go again." He raised his eyes. He assumed his three children had been following his situation in the papers but it was not the time to discuss the rape charge or his mental health problems.

He was relieved when she replied, "Carl watches City. He had trials with Stockport. I really meant are you happy?" A lump came to his throat. What on earth gave him the right to any concern from his daughter about his happiness? He took his time to answer.

"Happiness is a way of travelling, not a final destination, as somebody once said. Up and down I suppose, as I said to your mother. I feel terrible about what happened with us and today has brought it home. I'll be happy if we can build on this – and with Graham and Helen in time. That's the only thing that would make me happy but I'm not pressuring you or rushing you. It's up to you – you call the shots." They walked on some way in silence and she suddenly let out a small cry,

"Oh – I didn't realise we'd walked so far. We'd better turn back. Carl will be home soon." She swung the pram round abruptly and quickened her step and Prior was dismayed to be reminded of her diminutive hand in his and the ponderous progress of yesteryear as he struggled to keep up with her. It reinforced again the extent of the schism, emphasised the mystery of the lost years, and they hastened in mute lament to the homecoming of the stranger who knew her better than he did.

***

He spent that night in a hotel and saw her again the next morning before returning home in the early afternoon. He finally got to hold his grandson, handling him like a piece of priceless china, terrified of dropping him or contaminating him with his putrid worthlessness. Encouraged by his daughter's benevolent interest, he grew gradually more confident and offered a nicotine-stained finger which the boy gripped in his hand, the tiny fingers clasped around it like the coils of a spring. He lifted him in the air and kissed his forehead and cheek and held him tightly to his chest, a malleable surrogate to assuage in some small way the terrible heart-rending guilt he felt.

She put him down to sleep at eleven and he found her outside the kitchen smoking a cigarette on the small patio that Carl, a builder, had laid with an expert touch. Prior had been relieved not to have met him the previous evening; happy to have stolen away before his return. The day's events had been momentous enough without the addition of a further dimension. He pulled out a cigarette from his own packet and said, "Not for me to talk but I'm sorry to see you smoke." He wasn't being entirely truthful. It made him warm to her even more if he was honest.

"Don't tell Mum or Doug. Please. I didn't smoke when I was pregnant – or drink."

"Shame you started again if you'd stopped for nine months." He felt it was the right thing to say. Of course he cared for her health, but in moderation he wondered if the peace of mind and check on appetite it gave balanced the physical harm.

"I'll give up for good after the next baby."

"Yes, I'm sure." He hoped she didn't think he was being sarcastic. He couldn't afford for anything to go wrong. He was pleased they now shared a small guilty secret. It was a start.

He spent the rest of the morning following her around as she busied about tidying, and sorting clothes, and preparing lunch. He wished he could wind the clock forward to a time when the hiatus had been filled, the bridges rebuilt, but for now he would have to endure the penance of polite conversation and self-consciousness with his own flesh and blood.

They sat down for lunch, neither of them hungry, both eager to escape the chains of the obligatory ritual. At least she had the licence to push the heavy stew and potatoes to the side of the plate and lay down her knife and fork with less than half of it eaten. Despite her permission for him to do the same and his fervent wish to do so he hadn't the heart and he ploughed on.

"No – this is lovely. You're an excellent cook. You don't get it from your mum or me. Must be Granny Prior." Tommy sat watching them from his baby bouncer next to Laura's seat, the little brain taking in who knew what for future reference. With great relief he took his last mouthful and hastened it on its way with a gulp of water. A pang of sadness came over him with the knowledge that it was time to begin the preliminaries to departure. He wanted to break the back of the drive before rush hour. She stood up and cleared their plates, mercifully vague about pudding, giving him the opportunity to decline without giving offence.

"Coffee?"

He thought ahead. "Just a very small cup. I don't want to have to stop too early." He was both upset and heartened at the same time by the trace of melancholy in her eyes as she assimilated his words. He sat laterally to her on the sofa, facing the fire, she in the armchair to his left gazing blankly at the television turned to the CBeebies channel over the head of the baby, whose bouncer was a foot or two away from the screen. The top of his forehead was visible, indicating his head was upturned to the shapes and colours flashing in front of him. He exhaled again loudly as he had shortly after his arrival yesterday and said, "Oh Laura, will you ever forgive me?" She looked down and then at him before returning her eyes to the television to escape his imploring gaze.

"I already have, Dad."

He stood up and went over to her chair and put his arms around her, resting his head on her shoulder, fighting back the tears he didn't want her to see. She placed one hand on his shoulder and another on his side and they stayed in that pose until his trembling subsided and he returned to the sofa.

"I never stopped loving you all or thinking about you. I'm not even going to start making excuses because whatever I say can't cover up the simple fact that I put myself first and some kind of process of self-deception or denial enabled me to blank out what I was doing." Tommy became a bit restless and she gave him his dummy.

"I forgive you but I can't forget. The old cliché I'm afraid."

"Well they only become clichés because they contain incontrovertible truths which stand the test of time."

"I thought they were expressions that lost their force and became a bit trite with overuse." He smiled in pleasure.

"Very good. Chip off the old block eh?" She returned his smile shyly.

"Why didn't you go to university? Mum said you got good A Level results."

"Yeah. An A in English, Bs in History and Art. I'd just had enough of education. I wanted to get in the real world and earn some money." He thought with a shudder of someone else he had known who was of the same mind.

"Besides, a degree's not what it was in your day. Doesn't guarantee you a job." Tommy's dummy had fallen onto his stomach and he began to cry. She picked him up and smiled at him. "And I wouldn't have had you because I wouldn't have met your daddy would I?" She kissed him and went back to her seat with him on her knee. The tension had dissipated and he regretted having to go.

"I always read your articles – every one. It was my way of keeping some contact. I used to imagine it was you talking directly to me. I could win Mastermind with my knowledge of sport." His eyes welled up again at the image of the little girl reading the incomprehensible drivel just because it was beneath the picture of her absent daddy. He changed the subject abruptly.

"Do you drink much then? You said you gave up drinking during your pregnancy."

This time his concern was genuine, his anxiety primeval. She gave him a confused look and then answered in a slightly defensive tone, "No. Just socially but we hardly ever go out now anyway. We have a few drinks at home at the weekends when we can share the work the next day if Carl's off. Why?" He rued his decision to ask the question. He didn't want even the hint of any discord.

"I'm sorry; it's none of my business." He paused with an anguished look. He hadn't wanted any self-disclosure yet. "It's just that I've had a few problems myself in that area. What with you smoking and being good at English, you know…" he let the words tail away. "Forget I asked. You're obviously a lot more sensible than your foolish old dad."

She took in all the information and seemed ultimately gladdened by its ulterior motive of the parental concern she had been so starved of. "It's okay, Dad. I've never touched drugs either before you ask."

He hadn't thought of that. Again his tongue wagged before his brain had engaged.

"What about Graham and Helen?" A look of exasperation crossed her face.

"Oh Dad, you'll have to ask them." She looked at him intensely, the unspoken words more eloquent than any audible reference to his belated and unwarranted meddling. He held up his hands in a submissive gesture to convey that he knew he was overstepping the mark.

"I'm sorry sweetheart, I'm sorry. I'm running before I can walk. Listen, I'll get going. Just pop to the loo if I may."

He came down the stairs and bent over the rails of Tommy's cot and kissed his forehead and murmured a few words he hoped might infiltrate the depths of sleep to a corner of remembrance. They stood at the door and muttered some stilted phrases of meaningless small talk before falling into an embrace they held for almost a minute. They finally broke and he looked down at her. He didn't have to look far – she was tall for a woman, nearly as tall as him.

"I'll be back as soon as I can. You'll have to come and stay with me as well if you'd like to." He thought suddenly of what he could offer her but there seemed to be nothing that she lacked. She was well cocooned and he was happy for her.

"If there's anything you need just let me know."

"I only wanted you back, Dad. That's enough."

He kissed her on the cheek and said, "Bye darling."

She called out as he opened the gate, "Ring me tonight to let me know you got back safely."

He turned on the ignition and drove slowly away until he was round the corner where he stopped, unable to move again for ten minutes until his shoulders had stopped heaving and the bittersweet tears had dried on his face.

***

He drove home on autopilot, replaying the last two days from every angle, imagining a hundred different future scenarios. He stopped after three hours near the end of the M1 before his bladder burst and left the service station for the last leg comprising the M25 eastbound and the M11 southbound to the A406 and on to his destination.

He felt flat when he got home, with a restlessness that wouldn't allow him to settle to anything. He tossed aside the paper as nothing would sink in and he flicked from channel to channel without finding anything remotely interesting. He knew his four hours sitting at the wheel called for a long, brisk walk but he couldn't summon the enthusiasm. With a touch of guilt and self-loathing he showered and changed, put on some music, and turned once again to the bottle. As he sat with the stew repeating on him feeling rather sad and alone he turned on an unconscious whim to the bible for the first time since his return from Cape Verde. He picked up where he had left off and read the letters of St. Paul to Timothy and Titus, revelling in the simple truth and good sense of the words, feeling the sap of his self-pity fall and evaporate into the ether. He ate before he got drunk and took himself to bed where he lay counting not his crosses but his blessings, the music of his daughter's voice calling him 'Dad' soothing him to sleep.

***

Between Tommy's awakenings and his hungry little mouth on her nipple, her sleep was restless and dream-laden. Prior figured prominently as a grotesque oversized baby sucking on the teat of a bottle filled with whisky that she fed to him. No matter how hard she thumped his back his gripes grew worse and he sobbed his discomfort until she could stand it no longer and she strapped him into her car and drove for miles at breakneck speed through the myriad lights of cars and streets and tall Victorian buildings until he finally let out a gargantuan belch and a blessed quiet descended. Her speed slowed, the towns turned to a countryside of clear blue lakes and green-topped mountains and beside her the man-child had turned back into the father who smiled at her as she drove him safely home.

***

Prior woke and leapt straight from his bed with uncharacteristic haste and vigour. He usually lay for ages procrastinating in the bliss of semi-sleep. He hummed and whistled as he waited for the kettle to boil and then felt a sudden knot of anxiety in his stomach as his dream came back to him.

He was walking alongside Laura through the wasteland of an interminable suburban development in Sal. He felt an overwhelming need to protect her from the dogs, the danger, and the capricious strangeness of an unknown land. But it was an effort to keep up with her. The faster he tried to move, the further she got away from him. He called her name in ever more plaintive cries until he could see her no more. He ran, panic-stricken, towards the horizon, tumbling through the soft sand and scrub in the direction of the beach, his recalcitrant dream legs hardly moving, until he finally reached the shore. He stood as the waves lapped at his ankles, searching left and right and ahead as far as the eye could see but she was gone, dissolved, claimed by the power of the impassive beast whose secrets were not for disclosure to the likes of a wretch like him.

With his bubble of contentment momentarily pricked by the sadness of the dream he turned to his props of nicotine and caffeine and the glow gradually displaced the disturbing fantasy again. He had spoken to her last night and she had passed the phone to Carl who had sounded so nice, so respectful, so… normal. He had seen the smiling photograph and now heard the voice and looked forward to putting the two together as soon as possible. He sat down and closed his eyes and offered up his quiet gratitude for the gift of another bridge to a better place.

CHAPTER 28

He waited nervously outside the small branch of Marks and Spencer in the neat and well-ordered town that had been her choice of rendezvous. It was a far from ideal location in his eyes, inured as he was to the dimmer venues with the relaxants at hand, but in the end he was just glad that she had agreed to meet anywhere – it had been touch and go. It was a beautiful mid-September day with the temperature in the early twenties. There was not a cloud to break the pale blue sky and a faint breeze carried the suggestion of the fragrances of the surrounding Kent countryside. She was ten minutes late. No call for panic yet but a slight uneasiness was creeping up on him. He hadn't done this for years but he couldn't remember ever being stood up. There was always a first time. Five minutes later, with his pessimism nearing the top of the scale he heard a voice beside him say, "Hello Bobby. Sorry I'm late."

He turned and she was there. He had seen her approach but hadn't recognised her. She was so different. The first thing that struck him was the hair. The wavy, light auburn was now shorter, darker, straighter. She had filled out and her make-up was a little too thick, the red lipstick a little too bright. Despite the warmth of the day she wore a flesh-coloured mackintosh, unbuttoned over a navy dress with a high white ruff collar. He still found her very attractive; she just wasn't the person he remembered. He tried to make his smile as gentle as he could to put her at ease.

"Hello Naomi. No, don't worry. Woman's prerogative."

"No, I'm usually very punctual. The family joke about it. To be honest I wasn't going to come. I only changed my mind at the last moment." She added self-consciously, "I dressed a bit hurriedly as you can probably tell."

"You look very nice."

She smiled demurely and said, "Where shall we go?" He looked at his watch which showed twenty past three.

"Um – a cup of tea, a walk. It's your town – you decide."

"We can walk down to the river and have some tea at a hotel on the bank. It's quite nice."

"Okay, lead the way."

They walked slowly through the relatively quiet streets, a large percentage of the shoppers away at the schools collecting their offspring. He wanted to talk of mundane things, cloud the vision of their last fevered contact.

"So you're not picking your children up?" The relief showed in her voice.

"I don't have to any more. James is seventeen and Nicholas fourteen. They're staying at their dad's tonight anyway."

"Oh?"

"Paul and I have separated. We're getting divorced." Despite the leap of his heart his sympathy was genuine.

"Oh, I'm sorry. Anything to do with…" He couldn't say the words.

"It was coming anyway. That business probably hastened it." They walked in silence for a while, glancing surreptitiously at each other, sorry for the need to touch on the subject so soon. Prior searched again for something neutral to say.

"It's a nice town. I've never been here before."

"It's okay. A bit quiet but I like that. There's always London if you want some excitement." He knew they were going to have to talk about it eventually. May as well inch towards it.

"Do you still use the country club?" She looked down at the pavement and shook her head.

"Never been back. Never will."

He cursed his insensitivity, "No, of course. Obviously. I'm so sorry for what happened." She looked at him quizzically and he felt ruffled. "I don't mean what happened between us, I mean what happened after. But then maybe it wouldn't if we hadn't… oh hell, I don't know."

She put her hand on his arm. "Don't talk about it yet. What about you – have you been back?"

"Oh no. I've been away since the incident. I've only been home a few weeks."

"I know. I've read it all in the papers."

"I obviously won't go back either. Reminds me – I'll have to cancel my membership."

They sat at a table under a parasol on the grassy bank watching the ducks on the river, observing the passing of an occasional craft. Birds flew in and out of the tall oaks to their right and above them a flock of swifts gathered in preparation for their flight to sunnier climes. They may even fly over Sal. They certainly wouldn't settle or they'd starve, he thought whimsically. The waitress brought out their tea and cake and Naomi poured them a cup each. Prior said philosophically, "It seems strange doesn't it that we spent what – three or four hours in each other's company. But the ramifications on our lives…"

"We're both victims Bobby… I don't even know what you like to be called. That's how little I know you."

He laughed. "Well Robert usually. Except when I turn into that horrible flash character at the country club." He looked suitably ashamed at the recollection.

"We were both off our heads. Sometimes I've wondered if it was some instantaneous divine retribution." He pondered on the observation.

"I found Christianity when I was away. It saved me. It really did; literally." He immediately experienced the absurdly immature discomfort concomitant with the admission; the laying himself open to impressions of staidness, sanctimony, of being uncool. Hardly the best chat-up line. He needn't have worried.

"I've always believed. The rape strengthened my faith. My secular friends couldn't understand it – they thought it should be the other way." He offered her a cigarette and she looked longingly at the packet before turning her head away histrionically and saying, "Get thee behind me Satan. I've given up for seventeen days. Cold turkey. I could still kill for one but I'm going to be strong." He put the packet away.

"You have one – don't let me stop you."

"No, it wouldn't be fair to tempt you." He wondered idly if it would have happened or whether they'd be sitting here now if it wasn't for the fact that they had both smoked. He knew that the whole of life was built on ifs and he took comfort again from his newfound conviction that there had to be a wider meaning beyond a random, pointless maelstrom of events leading to nothing. She cleared her throat.

"I want you to know, Robert, that I never once said to the police that it was you."

"But did you think it was me? Be honest." Her face looked anguished and he added, "Don't talk about anything you don't want to."

"No. We need to talk. I genuinely didn't know. It happened so quickly, I never saw him. It was dark and he was so strong. I've got to say…" she paused and looked down guiltily before she carried on, "I've got to say that I thought it was about ninety per cent likely that it was you." Prior looked sad.

"But we'd got on so well hadn't we? It wasn't indiscriminate lust – there was still some discernment, some chemistry surely."

"Yes, agreed, but let's face it I didn't know you from Adam and then when I heard about your problems. Put yourself in my position." He turned his head to watch a barge pass by, its captain smiling and shouting something he couldn't catch above the sound of the engine to the people on the bank.

"Yes, I suppose there was nothing else you could think."

"A couple of women I know of a more feminist persuasion said that anyway, what you'd already done was rape because I was so drunk."

He looked instantly vexed. Never in the months of self-righteous indignation or even in the moments of self-doubt had he considered this extraneous charge. He said sardonically, "And I wasn't?" She looked uncomfortable. She had no stomach for a disagreement.

"Well we know that's not the point. It's all about relative strength, primordial roles etcetera."

"I thought the feminists were into the social model rather than the biological one. They can't have it both ways." She sighed.

"I didn't say I agreed with them." He regretted the flash of defensive anger, the bitter words. They had no place in the script he had envisaged.

"I'm sorry Naomi. I'd never thought of that argument. I'd just hate to think there was any truth in it."

"Well I'm sure there sometimes is – every case is different. In our case, no. It wasn't anything approaching rape. I wanted it just as much as you and there was no force or pressure – physical or mental." He felt relieved and glad to change the subject. He couldn't escape an irrational taint of grubbiness that kept returning to permeate his veneer of justification. He was reaching for the light but the murk of that night kept encroaching.

"I never even asked what you do. I mean if you work."

"In a bank. Just on the counter. I trained as a nursery nurse but I began to feel a bit old for it. They stuck the word senior in front of my job title but it didn't alter the fact that I was doing the same as the others and getting the same money. The hours at the bank fit in well with my domestic routine – start late, finish early." He made an excuse to go to the loo and came back smelling strongly of tobacco.

"I know what you do of course, from the papers, but I didn't before."

"So not a fan of sport then I take it."

"I like tennis and athletics. Paul got me a bit interested in golf. I do scan the sports pages but we've always taken your rival paper."

They passed the time pleasantly talking of impersonal things as if there was no history between them and neither seemed inclined to terminate their meeting. Eventually however, a point was reached when a change of venue or circumstance was called for. They both seemed to sense it and went quiet. In the cold light of day with his appetites unaffected by alcohol or the avarice of mania he felt, if anything, even more attracted to her than the last time. He preferred the slightly fuller figure, padded of late no doubt by the absence of cigarettes and comfort eating. He had waited in trepidation for the irritating remark, the conflicting opinion denoting a fundamentally damaging schism, but it had not come. He banked her good points – her looks, her voice, her melancholy sang-froid, her lack of assumption, and they provided a strong insurance against the flash of disappointment that would surely come. No-one was perfect, no two people completely compatible. Above all he felt that indefinable spark of romantic interest that arises from who knows what unconscious constellation. He prayed that it was mutual.

He knew that one was usually supposed to be able to read the signs. Even allowing for the fact that he was hopelessly out of practice, she was hard to fathom. She didn't give much away in her body language and the situation was of course complicated by the demons in the closet. The disinclination was apparent in his voice.

"I suppose we'd better move on. We've had good value for our pot of tea." He wished he hadn't said 'pot of tea'. It sounded archaic somehow, framed by his enduring northern vowels. He knew it was ridiculous but it didn't fit the image he had of himself or that which he wished to portray. It wasn't exactly Heathcliff. He said it again with even more dialectical emphasis, parodying himself, embarrassed by his inward resemblance to a love-struck teenager.

The issue of 'what next' hung in the air, neither seemingly wishing to be the first to bridge the uncertainty. It was Naomi.

"Yes, I'd better be getting back. I've got some ironing to do."

"Is that negotiable?"

"I'm sorry?"

"I mean have you got to do it tonight?"

"Why?"

He wanted to stay in her company. With the potentially hazardous dissection of that night safely negotiated, he wanted to take it to another level; to show her he liked her but could behave with propriety. He couldn't bear the thought of any alternative disposal of the evening that stretched ahead. He reined in his emotions with difficulty and said as matter-of-factly as he could with a shrug of feigned indifference,

"I've enjoyed being with you, Naomi. I thought I could maybe take you to dinner. We could go back to our respective houses first to freshen up if you want and meet later." She had been gazing at him and she glanced away from his look at the end of the words. When she looked back at him he noticed the large pupils behind a film of moisture, the irises pale blue and the whites flecked with red capillaries. For the first time he saw her pain in them.

"I don't think so, Robert."

It was of a different hue but it was still frustration. Before the disappointment came pique and he felt ashamed. He gave himself time to think before he betrayed any terminally fatal reaction and said quietly, "Okay, I understand. I suppose like that place I must be a reminder of that night and what happened." A small part of him felt liberated by the rejection and he added, "Is that it or do you just not like me now you've seen me in the cold light of day?"

Her eyes focussed on the tea tray on the table, her face creased in the perplexed frown that was a recurrent feature that he remembered even from the last time. It saddened his heart in its suggestion of a resignation to a kind of self-fulfilling prophecy of desolation and ill-fate. She began to cry and Prior stood up and took her coat from the back of her chair and put it over his left arm as he guided her towards the hotel exit with his other hand. They were silent until they were on the road back to the town. She had stopped crying and said softly, "I don't know what I think these days. I can't get it out of my head. I couldn't stand even Paul touching me. I amazed myself in coming today. Going back to your question, it's the former not the latter."

His surge of elation was tempered by a little guilt.

"Have you thought of counselling?"

"I've been offered it of course. I've just never thought it does any good. You can't change what happened."

"No, true. But you don't know unless you try it. Even if it didn't help it couldn't do any more harm."

"It could bring it all back. I'm trying to forget it."

"You can't forget something like that but you can be helped to deal with the feelings. I'd give it a try." They walked on past a pub and he would have given his eye teeth to enter its doors. Instead he said, "I notice you haven't asked me about my mental health problems."

"Well, none of my business really – it's a bit of a private area isn't it?"

"I'm glad it didn't put you off meeting me. I appreciate that. A lot of people run a mile from mental illness." They walked on, the shops now visible in the distance and he said, "So?"

She looked puzzled and smiled nervously.

"So what?"

"So aren't you going to ask me?"

"No. It's none of my business as I said. I certainly wouldn't know unless I'd been told."

"So it doesn't bother you?"

"No."

He felt relief. He hadn't wanted to talk about it anyway. He just felt it was an obstacle that might need to be cleared. He hoped there would be an opportunity to revisit the subject in future in the cold light of today's reason and not the vivid witness of a hitherto unexplained phenomenon. Like homing pigeons they drew to a halt outside their original rendezvous, the shop now closed, the shoppers giving way to the early revellers. Out of time-honoured habit he felt again the pull of the cocktail hour but he held back from further entreaty to this long-suffering, tolerant woman. He smiled and said, "I don't know why we've come back here. Did you drive into town?"

"No. I haven't got a car. Paul has ours as he needs it for his job. I got the bus."

"Can I give you a lift?"

He watched her weighing it up, imagining the internal debate as to whether or not she minded him knowing where she lived, before she said, "Yes. Thanks."

They dawdled towards the car park in silence and he drove uncharacteristically slowly, having to prompt her for directions, rousing her to a 'sorry, left' or 'sorry, right' before she lapsed back into thought. They eventually stopped outside a pleasant 1930s semi about two miles from the town centre and he turned off the engine. He drummed his hands nervously on the steering wheel and looked to his left to see that she was crying again. The tears that ran down her cheek streaked the thick make-up, partially revealing the external scars she was trying to hide. He felt an overwhelming impulse to take the nape of her neck in his hand and draw her face towards his but somehow he resisted. He took a pen from his jacket and wrote something on a scrap of card that he ripped from the bottom of an old leaflet in the door compartment and said as he gave it to her.

"That's my number if you ever want to see me. I'll never bother you again unless I hear from you. I promise. I'll always be there for you Naomi. Just as a friend if that's all you want." He nearly said 'whatever' but thankfully pulled back in time. She had been staring ahead and she turned to him now, still sobbing, her face a haunting evocation of their previous parting. She tried to speak but couldn't and a lump formed in his own throat as he saw her hand go to the door handle and pull it. Out of the corner of his eye he saw her coat which he had thrown on the back seat and he reached between the two front seats and then leant over and held it out to her as she stood on the pavement. As she leaned back into the car to take it, one knee dropped onto the front passenger seat and she kissed him hurriedly before closing the door and going into her front garden as he drove away, pulling down the visor to shield his eyes from the glare of the descending sun, the red stain of her lipstick close to his mouth as he glanced at himself in the rear view mirror.

THE END

Epilogue

3rd October 2013

Dear Father de Freitas,

I thought I would take the opportunity to give this to Abdulai to bring with him – I know how unreliable the post is. As you know he has been staying with me whilst having a trial with a team in our League One (third tier) that I arranged for him through my acquaintance with their manager. Sadly they will not be offering him terms. They say the natural talent is there but at twenty-eight it is too late to hone the tactical awareness and fitness levels required. If only he could have had this chance ten years ago. He is of course very disappointed but excited at the same time at the thought of seeing Dominique and their baby daughter again.

I don't know if you heard of the death of a woman I knew on the island, a Zina Stannard? She lived in Palmeira and worked in the property business. Sadly I believe she died from an opiate overdose; whether it was deliberate or accidental is not known and the coroner recorded an open verdict. I won't go into the reasons for my connection with her out of respect for the dead but surprisingly she made a will before her death, and even more surprisingly, she left me a considerable amount of money in it. I have decided to dedicate the money to worthwhile causes and amongst other things I have given Abdulai sufficient money for him and Dominique to open a small hotel where they will also be able to live. I have also arranged for their friend Beatrice to come to London and undertake medical training. The money will provide for her tutorial fees, accommodation and keep. I would also like to make a donation to your parish funds and would be grateful if you could ask your clerk to email me the relevant bank details.

I do not make reference to this 'philanthropy' out of any wish for self-aggrandisement – those days are thankfully long gone. To borrow from your habit of quotation to emphasise your message, 'I may dole out all I possess but if I have no love I am none the better.' For Zina's sake however, I would like it to be known that from her tragic life some good has come.

I hope you will allow me the indulgence of telling you of my new life, transformed as it is for the better thanks largely to our brief but very significant communion. I am still working as a sports journalist but have made a fresh start with a broadsheet newspaper which in England tends to denote a more serious, in-depth style of presentation. I choose my words carefully, cautious not to convey any impression of feelings of superiority. I can appreciate that I am still nonetheless only a bit-part player in the gigantic escapist fantasy that is sport. I wrote a book about my experiences which was serialised in my former paper, the proceeds of which go to a charity supporting rape victims.

My mental health is stable which I put down to a number of reasons. Firstly my faith which helps me to keep a sense of proportion and strictly curtails my previous excesses in the comforting knowledge that, as you said, I will never be alone again. 'God doesn't promise there won't be darkness but he will enter the darkness with you.' I heard that on the radio the other day and it made me think of you, as do so many things. I keep a constant vigil against what I have termed the three V's of vice, vanity, and vindictiveness. Secondly, I am strict in my compliance with medication with this due in no small part to the third reason – Naomi, who is soon to be my wife.

I am sorry to introduce a note of discord, Father, as I am aware that in the view of the church my first wife will always be my wife in the eyes of God and any subsequent union is not recognised – is bigamous even. The main reason for our decision to marry illuminates another transparent sin in the eyes of the church – Naomi is expecting our child. It was not planned and most unexpected at our age (I am forty-four, she is forty) but our initial shock has turned to the joy of anticipation. Tests have revealed that everything is as it should be and we also took the decision to know the gender in advance – it is a girl. My main source of worry is the effect of the news on my three adult children who I woefully neglected during their own childhoods. I am aware that every moment I spend as the doting father I intend to be could be a stab in the heart to them. Thankfully I have re-established wonderfully satisfying relationships with my two daughters, but sadly my son has not forgiven me and is quite antagonistic towards me. At least we have opened up a communication of sorts and I will work hard at achieving an atonement that may come as he matures and the stubborn, fractious streak I confess he inherited from me mellows.

We are marrying in a civil ceremony but the vicar of the church we attend every week has agreed to subsequently bless our union. Now is not the time or the place to compare the relative attitudes of the different sects within our religion but I would be very interested to hear your views. I just remain ever grateful for the compassion shown to one of a different denomination.

Despite my newfound faith I readily admit that I am still a sinner. I am a hypocrite. I take absurd amounts of money for doing something I enjoy and at times dispose of it selfishly. Awareness of my faith occasioned a level of mockery and acrimony in my previous job that approached bullying and there were times when I outwardly denied God whilst inwardly excusing my weakness. In my new job I perpetrate the sin of omission on a permanent basis just so I have an easier life. I experience a spiteful anger inside me too often against my neighbours – usually against someone on TV sadly inveigled into our vacuous celebrity culture who would earn the pity of a more altruistic man. I still drink too much on occasions – never to the point of drunkenness now, but nevertheless to a condition where I like myself a little too much and dislike my past transgressions much too little.

The difference now is that I am aware of all this and with that awareness comes at least a striving to be a better person. I heard someone say the other day that Christians are people who know they are forgiven. I think Father, I am nearly there.

God bless you,

Robert Prior (James Hudson was my alias!)

Printed in Great Britain
by Amazon.co.uk, Ltd.,
Marston Gate.